ELMINSTER
MUST DIE

SAGE OF SHADOWDALE

Elminster, the Old Mage, the Chosen of Mystra. Across the face of
Faerûn and throughout her history, the Sage of Shadowdale, by whatever name, has always stood firm against the tide of darkness.

THE KNIGHTS OF MYTH DRANNOR

From the pastoral village of Espar to a road fraught with danger, magic,
and the dubious attentions of villains and royalty alike, the rise of the
Knights of Myth Drannor is a remarkable adventure.

ALSO BY ED GREENWOOD

FORGOTTEN REALMS

ED GREENWOOD
SAGE OF SHADOWDALE

ELMINSTER
MUST DIE

Wizards
OF THE COAST
®

ELMINSTER MUST DIE
Sage of Shadowdale
©2011 Wizards of the Coast LLC

Published by Wizards of the Coast LLC. Hasbro SA, represented by Hasbro Europe, Stockley Park, UB11 1AZ, UK.

FORGOTTEN REALMS, Wizards of the Coast, and their respective logos are trademarks of Wizards of the Coast LLC in the U.S.A. and other countries.

Cover art by Kekai Kotaki
Map by Robert Lazzaretti
Original Hardcover Edition First Printing: August 2010
First Mass Market Paperback Printing: June 2011

9 8 7 6 5 4 3 2

ISBN: 978-0-7869-5799-6
ISBN: 978-0-7869-5765-1 (ebook)
620-31683000-001-EN

The Library of Congress has catalogued the hardcover edition as follows

Greenwood, Ed.
  Elminster must die : sage of Shadowdale / Ed Greenwood.
    p. cm.
  ISBN 978-0-7869-5193-2
  1. Forgotten realms (Imaginary place)--Fiction. 2. Elminster (Fictitious character)--Fiction. 3. Wizards--Fiction. I. Title.
  PR9199.3.G759E575 2010
  813'.54--dc22

                          2010019482

For customer service, contact:

U.S., Canada, Asia Pacific, & Latin America: Wizards of the Coast LLC, P.O. Box 707, Renton, WA 98057-0707, +1-800-324-6496, www.wizards.com/customerservice

U.K., Eire, & South Africa: Wizards of the Coast LLC, c/o Hasbro UK Ltd., P.O. Box 43, Newport, NP19 4YD, UK, Tel: +08457 12 55 99, Email: wizards@hasbro.co.uk

Europe: Wizards of the Coast p/a Hasbro Belgium NV/SA, Industrialaan 1, 1702 Groot-Bijgaarden, Belgium, Tel: +32.70.233.277, Email: wizards@hasbro.be

Visit our websites at www.wizards.com
www.DungeonsandDragons.com

pereunt et imputantur
mors ianua vitae

For Brian Cortijo, because this should have been his.
And for Brian Thomsen, because he should have lived to read it.

NORTHWEST SUZAIL

1. The Royal Palace of Suzail
2. The Royal Court of Cormyr
3. Horngate
4. The Promenade
5. Darcleir's
6. The Old King's Favorite
7. The House of the Lynx
8. The Gilded Feather
9. Tathlin's Discreet Errands
10. Culder Darshoon, Cobbler
11. Rented lodgings of Amarune Whitewave
12. The Dragonriders' Club
13. Rented lodgings of Lord Barandror Murandrake
14. The Willing Smile
15. The Bold Archer
16. The Eel Revealed
17. The Lady Murmurs Yes
18. Delcastle Manor
19. Stormserpent Towers
20. Staghaven House
21. Royal Gardens
22. House with Access to Palace Cellars
23. Royal Stables
24. Haunted Wing (of the Royal Palace)

Welcome to Faerûn, a land of magic and intrigue, brutal violence and divine compassion, where gods have ascended and died, and mighty heroes have risen to fight terrifying monsters. Here, millennia of warfare and conquest have shaped dozens of unique cultures, raised and leveled shining kingdoms and tyrannical empires alike, and left long forgotten, horror-infested ruins in their wake.

A LAND OF MAGIC

When the goddess of magic was murdered, a magical plague of blue fire—the Spellplague—swept across the face of Faerûn, killing some, mutilating many, and imbuing a rare few with amazing supernatural abilities. The Spellplague forever changed the nature of magic itself, and seeded the land with hidden wonders and bloodcurdling monstrosities.

A LAND OF DARKNESS

The threats Faerûn faces are legion. Armies of undead mass in Thay under the brilliant but mad lich king Szass Tam. Treacherous dark elves plot in the Underdark in the service of their cruel and fickle goddess, Lolth. The Abolethic Sovereignty, a terrifying hive of inhuman slave masters, floats above the Sea of Fallen Stars, spreading chaos and destruction. And the Empire of Netheril, armed with magic of unimaginable power, prowls Faerûn in flying fortresses, sowing discord to their own incalculable ends.

A LAND OF HEROES

But Faerûn is not without hope. Heroes have emerged to fight the growing tide of darkness. Battle-scarred rangers bring their notched blades to bear against marauding hordes of orcs. Lowly street rats match wits with demons for the fate of cities. Inscrutable tiefling warlocks unite with fierce elf warriors to rain fire and steel upon monstrous enemies. And valiant servants of merciful gods forever struggle against the darkness.

A LAND OF
UNTOLD ADVENTURE

PROLOGUE

The Year of the Ageless One had brought early and warm spring to Shadowdale, an endless parade of short but drenching rains with muggy days between. Travel through the Dales was a matter of much sweat, slipping in abundant mud, and a profusion of enthusiastically stinging insects.

Wherefore Gaerond of the Scars was fast running out of oaths, and much of him was numb from his own slappings. Nor were the rest of the grim, veteran adventurers in the Bloodshields Band any happier than he was. If the smooth-talking Sembian hadn't paid them so much—and promised so much more if they brought back even a scrap of success—they'd have taken other roads long since.

Everyone knew the wizard Elminster was long dead and gone, naught but a long-bearded name in legend. His tower in Shadowdale had been a snake-haunted, rubble-strewn pit for longer than anyone alive could remember.

They checked when at last they came to where it had once stood; aye, a pit still, all long grass overgrowing a scum-cloaked pond.

Yet Sembian gold was . . . Sembian gold, and they'd been promised good handfuls of it, so they trudged on.

The Old Skull Inn was right where it was supposed to be, too, rising tall and proud beside the road. Newly expanded, 'twas said, two floors with porches; a soaring roof above, dark and splendid with new tiles; and from the wideswept eaves a row of large, ornate hanging metal lanterns hung on stout chains, waiting to be lit at dusk. Not all that far off.

Gaerond grunted his approval as the sharp reek of horn-grass smoke greeted him. Any bed-haven that wanted to keep stingflies at bay was a place he wanted to sleep in.

He heard the faint thud of a gong from inside. They'd been seen.

He spun around to catch Malkym's eye, then Flamdar's, ere slapping his sword hilt. Then he tied his peace-strings through it, nodded when they started doing the same, and turned back to the inn again, keeping his hands empty and away from his sides. He could snatch and hurl two longsarks in half a breath if he had to—but if the rest of the Bloodshields behaved themselves aright, hopefully he'd not have to. Which should mean a decent meal and beds—mayhap even a bath!—that night.

The tallest, widest man he'd ever seen met him at the door, smiling affably enough. Gaerond matched that smile, keeping his eyes on those of the innkeeper and pretending not to notice the two women at either end of a long serving counter who both had loaded hand crossbows lying ready on the well-worn wood in front of them.

"Rooms and a meal, for . . . six?"

"We'd like that and will pay ready coin." Gaerond tried to sound amiable, out of long habit; many folk never saw past the fearsome sword scars. "If our work goes well, that is; we've a task that won't wait. We're the Bloodshields Band and come in peace. Chartered in Arabel, came afoot from Mistledale—and we're seeking Elminster."

The host's smile held but was somehow a trifle less welcoming than before. "Six chartered adventurers, to seek a dead man? Or are you looking for treasure he might have left behind?"

Gaerond shook his head. "We've been paid well to consult with him, not offer him harm. On behalf of a patron too old in legs and back to be traveling anywhere to talk with anyone. Someone who's met with him before told us to tell all in

Shadowdale 'Old Mage still, upon the hill' if asked about our intentions."

The innkeeper's eyes flickered. Then he nodded gravely, turned, and called, deep but gently, "Thal!"

The rather dirty, barefoot young lad who burst out of the kitchens and raced to a halt just out of reach appeared so swiftly that he must have been listening. Bright eyes surveyed Gaerond for a moment ere looking a question at the hulking innkeeper.

"Guide these charter-helms to the wizard's abode and back again," came the grave instruction.

"Lanterns?" Thal chirped.

"Nay, lad," Gaerond replied quickly, "but we'll pay fair coin for guiding us. If the way's not long, nor will our business with the mage be. Our patron has ordered that no one else hear what we say or is said to us, but we'll be done soon enough and can come right back here at your heels."

Thal looked at the innkeeper for instruction, as if Gaerond hadn't said a word, but the innkeeper merely nodded approvingly.

At that, the lad smiled, nodded, and marched past Gaerond, trailing a cheerful, "This way, saers."

Malkym looked as if he wanted a tankard before walking anywhere else, but followed Gaerond in silence, Flamdar and the others trudging right behind.

The lad led them to the crossroads, which were no larger nor less muddy than Gaerond remembered, and took the road north, past some new steads already sagging into the bog they'd been built on. Beyond them the land rose, crowned by a seemingly impenetrable tangle of thornstar hedge that all manner of vine-choked wild trees had thrust up through. Storm Silverhand's farm, it had once been . . . a century back, when there still *was* a Storm Silverhand.

You'd have thought at least one or two Harpers might have survived to settle the place, to keep bellies full on its profusion of pole-fruit and all, but mayhap folk thereabouts had run them off or run them through, and—

To Gaerond's grunted surprise, the lad turned off the road down into the ditch near the north end of the wild hedge, well past where the farm gate had been—only to scale the far bank of the ditch and plunge through a dark hole in the hedge that looked like a boar run.

Huh. *Smelled* like a boar run, too; Gaerond laid one hand on his favorite longsark as he put his head down and shouldered after the lad, through crackling branches, leathery leaves, and the inevitable jabbing thorns.

Right behind him, Malkym remembered one of his curses but kept it under his breath. Mostly.

Beyond the bristling fortress of hedge was a damp, mist-shrouded forest of tall trees—thinner than the great old forest giants ahead and to their left, but already choking brambles and wild shrubs off from the light. Birds whirred away in alarm, and small, unseen beasts scuttled for cover. A few rotten, leaning poles among the soaring tree trunks were all that was left of what must once have been rows and rows of crops.

Gaerond caught sight of what might have been the roofless corner of a farmhouse, far off to the right—but no one was living or farming there anymore; they were striding through deep drifts of wet dead leaves and undisturbed, moss-girt deadfalls, with nary a trail to be seen.

And there in the trees, dusk was coming down fast.

"How far, lad?" he grunted, misliking the thought of being caught in the tangle when night fell.

Thal turned and gave a cheerful, guileless smile. "Just ahead, saer, down this path!"

Gaerond suppressed a snort. "Path" was a wild bard's fantasy if he'd ever heard one, but the lad was atop a little ridge barely three long strides ahead, and pointing down the far side of it, as if the Old Mage's abode really wasn't far.

"*There*, saers!" Thal told them happily, stopping on the ridge and waving them past, one by one, one slender arm pointing.

Blast all the gods, there *was* a path that seemed to spring out of the sloping rock falling away from the ridge, and descend, winding through a few trees, down into a dell or mayhap a cave somewhere behind too many trunks to stare through.

Gaerond peered hard at the narrow dirt track where the bare rock ended and it began, in a vain attempt to see what manner of beast had made it, then turned to snap, "Rorn!"

Rornagar Breakblade liked to walk rearguard and was good at it; he spun around without the slightest delay, knowing what Gaerond wanted.

Yet no matter how keen and suspicious Rornagar's eye, he had turned too late and beheld nothing but leaves and rocks and trees.

Gaerond's sharp gesture brought them all to a silent, hard-listening halt, but there were no rustlings to tell where Thal had gone. The forest was suddenly empty of cheerful little lads.

"Well?" Malkym asked at last, as the Bloodshields stared at each other . . . and dusk came down.

"Light the lamps," Gaerond ordered shortly. "We go on."

They did that and were well down the path among the trees, Rornagar having turned to stare suspiciously—but vainly—into the forest twice.

Gaerond's fingers were busy at his peace-strings without his eyes ever leaving the path ahead and the forest around. He could see where the way went, right into a low cavemouth ahead. A twinkle of light was escaping from the chamber, through holes in a door made of a patched and tattered hanging deer hide that had seen better days.

He stopped well outside it and waved to his fellows to join him as quietly as possible. As they gathered nigh-silently around him, each gave him the ramming-hilts-home gesture that told him they were ready for battle.

Gaerond nodded approvingly and looked to Rorn, who shook his head to silently say there'd been no sign of their young guide. Hmm, gone without coin, too; what but wager he'd been the wizard himself, in shift-shape?

With a shrug and smile, Gaerond called pleasantly, "Elminster? Elminster the wizard? Peaceful hired fellows here to confer with you!"

"Come ahead," an old man's voice quavered in reply. "Peaceful fellows are always welcome." Then it turned stern or rather pettish. "See that ye stay that way."

The Bloodshields traded smirks and came ahead.

The cave was a long, narrow hovel of damp dirt, stones, and sagging old rough-tree furniture, more a hermit's cellar than a druid den. Two small, flickering lamps hung from a crossbranch over a rude table, and somewhere behind their glows sat a stout, broad-shouldered old man, blinking at them past a fearsome beak of a nose. He had a long, shaggy white beard.

The floor was an uneven, greasy, hard-trodden litter of old bones and empty nutshells, and around the dirt walls roots thrust out here, there, and everywhere; on many of them had been hung a pathetic collection of rotting old scraps of tapestry and paintings.

"So ye've found Elminster, ye adventurers, and to earn thy hire would speak with me? Well, speak, then; I've naught to share, I fear, and if ye were expecting great magics or heaped gems, I'm afraid ye've come a century or so too late."

"Huh," Gaerond replied. "*That's* a shame. We quite like great magics and heaps of gems, we do. Can you still manage little magics?"

The old man snorted sourly and fumbled for a clay pipe with age-gnarled, shaking fingers. "If I could, d'ye think I'd be sitting here in this mud-hole, slowly starving? That'll be my price for answers, mind ye: a finger of cheese or a bite of meat, if thy pouches run to such luxuries!"

Gaerond smiled, not kindly, and shook his head. "Our shame steadily deepens, doesn't it, lads?"

The Bloodshields chuckled unpleasantly by way of reply. They had already spread themselves out and had drawn various favorite weapons—that they waved menacingly.

"You may have noticed," Gaerond told the burly old man, "that Lylar here has brought a spear. We think it'd look better adorned with your head, as a sort of wave-about trophy, when we return to Sembia. Sembians pay well for their bodyguards—and it's not every band of blades that can claim to have bested the legendary archwizard Elminster in battle!"

The burly oldbeard seemed to shrink a little in his seat. "Ye ... ye're joking, surely ...," he quavered.

Gaerond smiled his best, soft wolf smile. "No. I'm afraid not."

The air promptly erupted in a briefly deafening storm of hissing and twanging, while the old man sat as still as a stone.

As abruptly as it had come, the storm was done, all the tapestries and paintings fluttering in the wake of too many snarling quarrels to count.

Most of the Bloodshields had been driven back against the walls, so studded with those quarrels as to resemble pincushions. Gaerond hadn't been near a wall, so he was the last to fall, toppling in slow silence, disbelief plain on his dead face.

As if the thump and clatter of his landing were a cue, figures all clambered out from behind the tapestries in brisk haste, their pearl-white limbs reaching to reload crossbows or to snatch away weapons in case any of the Bloodshields might have had magical protection enough to somehow still live.

It appeared that none of them had.

The doppelganger sitting behind the table dwindled down into something long and lean that easily slid out of the wizard's robes and the suit of padded armor beneath them that had lent "Elminster" such broad shoulders, and stretched across the table to join in the work of taking up the adventurers' bodies and gear—the latter for salvage and sale, and the former to eat.

"Any trouble?" hissed a new arrival, coming into the cave still wearing Thal's face, but with a body pearl white and featureless as the others.

"None," replied one of the doppelgangers, who was busily breaking the necks of the Bloodshields, just to be sure, sounding almost bored.

"Where *is* the infamous Elminster, anyhail?" the youngest doppelganger asked. "He's still alive, yes? They say he is, you know."

Doppelgangers rarely shrug, but most of those crowded into the cave tried various versions of it, in wriggling unison.

The one who'd played Elminster answered, "He is, but he's long gone from here. No shortage of talking meat coming looking for him, though. Still some Harpers, even."

One old doppelganger grew a large mouth so he could leer, exclaiming, "I *likes* Harpers. Good eating."

Chapter
ONE

Dark Decisions

One thing's certain, in any sudden skirmish.
Before all the shouting and swords-out,
In secret, there've been some dark decisions.

Markuld Amryntur,
Twenty Summers a Dragon: One Soldier's Tale
published in the Year of the Splendors Burning

The wardrobe was a cursedly tight fit.

Even for one of the handsomest, suavest, most lithely athletic, and most debonair nobles currently inhaling the sweet air of the Forest Kingdom of Cormyr.

Even a sneering rival would have had to grant that Lord Arclath Argustagus Delcastle was all of those things in the judgment of many a lass, not just his own.

Yet, despite all of those splendid qualities, the heir of House Delcastle could *just* squeeze himself inside the massive oak wardrobe. To keep company with old mildew and older dust. Whose familiar reek reassured him that this was the palace, all right.

Left knee above his left ear and fingers braced like claws to keep his cramped body from slipping and making the slightest sound, Arclath stared into the darkness wrought by the closed door right in front of his nose and prayed fervently that Ganrahast and Vainrence would be in a hurry and keep their secret meeting brief.

So it would end, for instance, before he happened to need to sneeze.

No one ever came to this dusty, long-disused bedchamber high in the north turret—or so Arclath had once thought. He'd found the place after a feast some years ago, while wandering the palace to walk off the effects of far too much firewine before he braved the dark night streets homeward, and had employed it thereafter to enjoy the charms of a certain palace maid in private—a sleek delight since sadly gone off to Neverwinter in the employ of a wealthy merchant—and then as a retreat to sit alone and think, when that need came upon him.

It had come as a less-than-pleasant surprise, moments before, to learn that the Royal Magician of Cormyr, the widely feared Ganrahast, and his calmly ruthless second-in-command, "Foedoom" Vainrence, favored this same north turret bedchamber for private parleys.

Arclath hadn't had time to try to dodge into the little space behind the wardrobe, which stood straight and square where the bedchamber wall behind curved. He'd only just had time enough to scramble into the closet, drag its door closed, and compose himself into cramped but silent immobility before the two powerful wizards had come striding into the room, muttering grimly.

They were more than muttering now.

Arclath felt an itch starting and set his teeth in exasperation. He should have known *someone* went there to discuss confidential and sensitive matters, given the warding spells that always made his skin tingle and prickle on the stair ascending to the uppermost room.

A moment later, a glow kindled in the darkness right beside Arclath's head, startling him almost into gasping aloud.

He managed—*just*—not to do that.

Instead, he froze, chilled and helpless, as an old spell flared into life right beside him.

A radiance that slowly became a silent, floating scene of a nearby spot he recognized. That same stretch of stair where the wards tingled, looking down from the turret room.

A scene where someone stood silently, hands raised to claw at the wards that were keeping her at bay, eyes blazing in frustrated fury. It was someone who'd been dead for years, a ghost Arclath had seen once from afar.

The Princess Alusair, the ruling Steel Regent of the realm almost a century earlier; familiar and unmistakable from all the portraits and tapestries in nigh every high house of Cormyr, her long hair flowing free and face set in anger—and her eyes seemingly fixed on him.

Arclath swallowed. He could see right through her, armor and long sword at her hip and all, and by the way she peered and turned her head from time to time, it was apparent she could hear but not quite see the two wizards as they stood talking, just outside his wardrobe.

"Grave enough," the Royal Magician was saying, "but hardly a surprise. You didn't call me here just to tell me *that*. What else?"

"The Royal Gorget of Battle is missing from its case," Vainrence replied flatly, "which stands otherwise undisturbed, all its spells intact. And it was there an hour ago; I happened to walk past and saw it myself."

Arclath raised an eyebrow. The gorget was *old*. An Obarskyr treasure that had lain in its case, proudly displayed in the Warhorn Room, for as long as he'd been old enough to remember what was where in the palace.

"Elminster again." Ganrahast sighed, slamming a fist against the wardrobe doors in exasperation.

One of them shuddered a little open, freezing Arclath's heart again. However, its movement caused the spell to wink out, restoring darkness and snatching away the furiously staring ghost.

Neither of the wizards seemed to notice either the door or that momentarily visible glow. They *must* be upset.

Through the gap, the young noble saw Vainrence nod and say eagerly, "However, *this* time we've got him. I thought he'd go for the gorget—he seems to prefer the older magics—so it's one of the twoscore I've cast tracers on. We can teleport as near as we choose to wherever he's taken it, just a breath or two after you give the order; the team is ready. Right now, Elminster's in the wildest part of the Hullack, and not moving. No doubt sitting around a campfire with his bedmate, the crazed Witch-Queen, as they melt down the gorget together and feed on its power. Therlon reported in an hour ago; she blasted another steading to ashes, three nights back."

Ganrahast sighed again. "You're right. It's time we dealt with them both. Send in Kelgantor and his wolves. And may the gods be with them."

"Done, just as fast as I can muster them in the Hall of Spurs! They're more than ready for battle—and, mark you, Elminster and the Witch-Queen may once have been formidable, but they're a lot less than that now."

Ganrahast spread his hands, noting, "So others have said, down the centuries. Yet those two are still with us, and the claimants are all gone to dust."

Vainrence waved a dismissive hand. "Aye, but she's now a gibbering madwoman, and he's little more than an old dodderer, not the realm-shaking spell-lion of legend!"

Ganrahast wagged a reproving finger. "Aye, I know legend has a way of making us all greater lions than we are . . . yet its glory must cling to *something*. Be sure Kelgantor's ready for the worst spellbrawl of his life."

"He is, and I'm sending a dozen highknights with him, if blades and quarrels are needed where spells fail. This time the old lion and his mad bitch are going down. While we still have an enchanted treasure or two *left* in the palace."

A little deeper into the wild heart of Hullack Forest than they remembered it being, the gaunt, bearded old man in dark rags and the tall, striking, silver-haired woman in leather armor came at last to a certain high rock in the forest.

"This is it," Elminster murmured grimly, looking at the upthrust slab of stone. Once it had been the base of the tallest tower of Tethgard, but all other traces of the ruins were overgrown or swept away. Yet despite its innocuous appearance, he'd seen it more times than he cared to remember, in recent seasons, and knew it was the place. "Cast the spell."

Storm Silverhand nodded and stepped past him to find stable footing, as birds called and whirred around them, and the light of late day lanced low through the leaves.

Before them the rock thrust its small balcony out of the trees, spattered with bird droppings, but deserted. On its far side, a flight of stone steps descended into a tangle of wild thorns, stairs from nowhere to nowhere. Storm stared at the stony height for a long moment, like an archer studying a target, then tossed her head to send her long silver hair out of the way, and set about working her spell with slow, quiet care.

She looked as if a bare twenty summers had shaped her sleek curves and brought color to her cheeks. The Spellplague had done that, making her seem young even as it stole much of her magic, a jest as cruel as it was inexplicable. Only when looking into her eyes—and meeting the weary wisdom of some seven hundred years gazing back—did the world see something of her true age.

As she worked, an illusion of the man beside her slowly faded into view atop the rock, shifting from smokelike shadows to recognizable solidity. Not the gaunt Elminster at her elbow, but the Old Mage in his prime: burlier, sharp-eyed above a long pepper-and-salt beard, staff in hand, robes flowing, and arms flung wide in spellcasting.

Atop the rock this brighter Elminster stood, glowing vividly as it looked to the sky and spoke silent words, arms and hands moving in grand gestures of the Art . . . and nothing else happened.

A gentle breeze rose and trailed past them, rustling a few leaves, then faded again. The Realms around them was otherwise silent.

A silence that started to stretch.

"And now?" Storm asked.

"We wait," El said wearily. "What else?"

They retreated to the welcoming trunk of an old duskwood and sat together in the shade, staring up at the empty skies above for what seemed a very long time before the wizard glanced sideways at his companion—and saw tears trickling quietly down her face.

"All right, lass?" he asked gruffly, reaching out a long arm to drag her against him, knowing how paltry the measure of comfort he could lend was.

She shook her head. "These shapings are the only magic I have left." Her whisper was mournful. "What have we become? Oh, El, what have we become?"

They both knew the answer.

They were husks: Storm shapely and young-seeming, yet with her rich singing voice gone and almost all of her magic with it, and Elminster still powerful in Art but hardly daring to use his spells, because sanity fled with each casting. More times since the Year of Blue Fire than they cared to remember—perhaps more than either of them *could* remember—Storm had guided and cared for her onetime teacher after he'd seen this or that desperate need to hurl spells . . . and had ended up insane for long seasons.

They shared a hunger.

A gnawing, desperate hunger for the power and skill of their youth. Thanks to a crumbling cache that had once belonged to Azuth, they knew how to take over the bodies of the young and strong. By all the vanished gods, the spell was so *simple*!

So Elminster was endlessly tempted. To snatch a new body and build a new life . . . or to die.

It was time and past time for oblivion, and they were so *tired* of the burdens of the Chosen, but somehow just couldn't give in to the last, cold embrace. Not yet.

Not after they'd hung on for so long, working here, there, and everywhere to set things right in the Realms. An unending task, to be sure, but there was *so* much more to do.

And there was no one else they could trust to do it. No one.

Every last entity they'd met since the blue fire had cared only for his- or herself, or couldn't even see what needed doing.

So Storm and Elminster, agents of the mightiest goddess in the world no longer, went on doing what little they still could—a rumor started here, a rescue or a slaying there . . .

still at the tiller, still steering . . . the work that had kept them alive the last century.

Someone had to save the Realms.

Why? And who were they to dare such meddlings?

They were the Old Guard, the paltry handful who still saw needs and cared. More than that . . . even with Mystra and Azuth both gone, *someone* still whispered in their dreams, telling them to go on sharing their magic among the poor and powerless, and working against evil rulers and all who used magic to harm and oppress.

Yet there was no denying they were growing ever weaker and more weary. It was the fourth time they'd come to the ruins that year, and it was only—what?—the fifth of Mirtul. A warm and early spring, aye, but still—

A hawk stooped suddenly out of the sky, hurtling down at the illusory Elminster.

"Well, at least she's not a stinking vulture this time," Storm murmured, finding her feet with her usual swift and long-limbed grace, and ducking hastily away into the trees. "I'll be back when you light the fire."

She still moved as quickly as ever; El found himself turning to answer only dancing branches.

So he swallowed his words and shrugged instead. It was good of her to give him time alone with her sister—time that was in short supply these days.

The false Elminster vanished in an instant as talons tore through it.

Then the startled hawk flapped to an awkward landing and stood on the rock blinking, looking a little lost.

The real Elminster swallowed a sigh, pulled the stolen glowing dagger he'd brought with him out of its sheath in the breast of his robes, and crawled out onto the rock as he held the blade out in offering. The feel of the magic would conquer her utterly.

A little meal first, to banish her wildness. When she was herself again, there would be time enough to feed her the gorget and do her longer-lasting good.

A dreadful hunger kindled in the hawk's golden eyes, and she sprang at him, shrieking as her wings clapped the air.

As her beak closed on the blade of the dagger, the hawk melted and *flowed*, an eerie swirling of flesh that spun into a filthy, naked crone, wild-eyed and wild-haired, a bony old woman sucking on the weapon like a babe single-mindedly worrying a mother's teat.

There was a glow in her mouth as she sucked, heedless of the sharp steel—and the dagger melted away. Just as the magic he brought her always did.

She crouched on the rock like a panther, greedy mouth fighting to draw in the hilt, her body becoming larger, stronger, and more curvaceous. Her hair shone; she looked younger . . .

As she always did. For a little while.

For too many years, his Alassra—the Simbul, the once proud Witch-Queen of Aglarond and the single-handed scourge of Thay, the slave empire ruled by Red Wizards beyond counting—had been a frail husk of her former self. Dwelling alone and wild in the Dales, the Thunder Peaks, and the Hullack, shapechanging into endless guises, usually the shapes of raptors as she lapsed in and out of madness.

Magic always made her intellect and control brighten for a time, so for many seasons Elminster had been making these visits to the lady he loved. Or what was left of her.

Stealing, seizing, and digging out of ruins an endless stream of magic items, he had brought them to the rock, for her to subsume and regain fleeting control over her decaying wits.

The Spellplague had not been a kind thing.

The dagger was gone, its pommel a brief pearl on her tongue that died with the last of the glow. Then her eyes were upon him, and she was in his arms, weeping.

"El, oh, *El,*" was all she could say between her foul kisses. Her stink almost overwhelmed Elminster as she clung to him, wrapping her limbs around him, running her long fingers over all of him she could reach and clawing at his worn and patched robes to try to reach more of him.

"So lonely!" she gasped, when at last she had to free his mouth so she could breathe. "Thank you, thank you, *thank you!*"

She buried her face against his neck as the tears came, managing to gasp, "My love!" through their flood.

Elminster held her both tightly and with great care, as if cradling something very precious and fragile. As she clung to him and writhed against him and tried to bury herself *inside* him.

"My love," he murmured tenderly as she started to really sob, her body shaking. It was always thus, and he smiled in anticipation of what she'd say next, knowing she'd not disappoint him.

"Oh, my *Elminster*," she hissed fiercely when she had mastered her tears. "I've been so *lonely!*"

"So have I," he muttered, brushing the silver-haired crown of her head with his lips, "without ye."

That brought fresh sobs, but they were soon conquered; when her wits were her own, Alassra Silverhand was acutely aware of how precious every moment was. "What . . . what year is it, and what month?"

"The fifth of Mirtul, of the Ageless One," Elminster told her gently, knowing her next question before she asked it.

"What's been happening, while I've been . . . wandering?"

El murmured replies and comforting words of love as he held her in one arm, feeling among his pouches with the other. He fed her some rather squashed grapes from one, then strong and crumbling Aereld cheese from another, and finally the ruined remnants of some utterly crushed little raisin tarts.

"Ahhh, I've missed those," she said, savoring every crumb. Then a look of disgust passed over her face, and she peered around at the droppings and tiny bones strewn all over the rock. "What," she whispered, "have I been eating?"

"The usual," El told her soothingly. "Never mind that, my lady. We do what we must."

She shuddered, but that shudder became a nod. She let out a deep sigh and clung to him, arms tightening. "Oh, I've missed you, El. Don't leave me again."

"I've missed ye, too. Don't leave *me* again, Lady mine."

The slayer of hundreds of Red Wizards smiled thinly through fresh, glimmering tears. "I'm through making promises I can't keep," she hissed. Her fingers clawed at him, at his tattered clothing.

Elminster's chuckle as he drew her back from the rock into the little hollow cloaked in moss was soft and teasing. He almost managed to keep the sadness out of it.

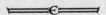

As night came down over the Hullack Forest, Storm turned back into the trees to make another stealthy circle around the stones of Tethgard, one more patrol guarding the couple abed in the moss. As she slipped between the dark trunks like a watchful shadow, she let her face go wry for just a moment.

Alassra had always been the hardest of her sisters to love, though Storm'd worked hard to keep things trusting and not too distant between them. And as long as his beloved Witch-Queen lived, Elminster would treat Storm only as a friend.

She wanted so much more, but neither El nor Alassra would learn that from her. Ever.

She held some measure of power over both of them, if she'd been the sort of worm to seek to wield it. The Simbul had been torn witless by the Spellplague, magic ravaging her mind; ever after only magic made her sane.

Magic she'd accept only from Elminster. Magic he could only give her by letting the fires within her consume the frozen fires of enchanted items he brought her—because the Spellplague had marred *him*, too. Casting spells plunged him into madness on the spot.

Unless one person—just one, in all Faerûn, for all she or he knew—healed him, with almost the only magic the Spellplague had left her. Storm Silverhand, the Bard of Shadowdale no longer. Now she was Elminster's healer, though they'd taken great care the Realms never learned that.

By touch and will she could heal his mind, pouring her vitality into him shaped by the paltry Art left to her, to bring him back to sanity almost as fast as he lost it, if she stood with him. Time and again she had done so.

So the feared Witch-Queen needed magic to regain sanity for fleeting times, magic she trusted only Elminster to give her, and Elminster needed Storm if he was to work magic at all.

The very sight of Storm sometimes enraged Alassra when she was less than lucid, and El, damn him, trusted Storm as a friend, road-companion, and fellow warrior. Not as his lady.

"I am Storm Silverhand," she told the nearest tree in a fierce but almost soundless whisper. "And I want more. So much more."

They had lain together in each other's arms and had watched the dusking sky above them . . . as one by one, the stars had come out.

She was asleep, and dreaming. Moving against him, clinging to him for comfort, murmuring, and caressing. Alassra was dreaming of making love to him again.

As still as he could keep himself, his arms going numb around her, Elminster lay awake, staring grimly up at the coldly twinkling stars.

A wolf howled, far off to the north, and there had been nearer hootings and rustlings from time to time, but El feared no foraging beasts; Storm was somewhere near, standing sentinel. She'd stolen out of the trees to stand silently looking at them both a little while earlier, tears glimmering in her eyes as she stared down at her sister—but had gone again, a softly hastening shadow, when Alassra had stirred.

Leaving Elminster alone with his brooding.

How long would she stay herself this time? He needed to find more powerful magic and have done with this business once and for all.

He was *tired* of feeding her little oddments of Art to win her a mere handful of days and nights of sanity, then doing it all again for another paltry handful a few months hence. If he could lay hands on something *truly* powerful that hadn't been twisted too wild by the Spellplague, he might be able to make the Simbul whole and sane again. There was risk, but he knew how.

The gorget he'd brought with him wasn't enough. It should buy her days, perhaps a month or more, and when she sank into deeper dreaming he'd feed it to her. When she'd have some time asleep for it to work its way through her.

Aye, he needed mightier magic. Not that he didn't need powerful enchanted items—whose wielding, unlike the casting of a spell, wouldn't plunge him into madness—for other uses. Such as destroying or at least blunting some of the more pressing dangers of the Realms.

Foes he once would have been able to blast at will or misdirect into doing good they did not intend. Back when he dared use magic, back when he still had a body that would obey him.

Back when he was still someone.

The worst of it was that he knew where so much powerful magic was . . . or had been. Yet the greater part of it was lost or buried or walled away beyond his failing strength or hidden from his fading senses. The mighty Elminster couldn't steal much more deftly than a good thief, these days; he was reduced to picking up fallen battle-spoils or plucking whatever was left unguarded. Or swooping in after someone else did the finding for him.

Someone like that young fool Marlin Stormserpent back in Cormyr, who was seeking the nine ghosts he thought would swiftly slay all the war wizards and loyal Purple Dragons and rival traitor nobles alike and deliver the Dragon Throne into his idle lap.

Lovely Laeral was gone, so there weren't nine deadly ghosts to be had. Yet there were still six, possibly seven—and if a certain Elminster commanded them, he could hurl back the shadows in Sembia and make the Forest Kingdom bright and strong again, a bastion for Harpers and those who had a talent for the Art but lacked training. A land where he could make mages trusted and respected again, and from which he could send them forth to deliver the rest of Faerûn from so much of its lawless, bloody chaos. New guardians to take up the burden of defending the Realms from all who'd cheerfully destroy it while conquering it.

Or he could let Alassra consume the ghosts, and be restored.

That much power and that many memories would be enough to make her whole again, the twisting taint burned right out of her, to stand strong at his side, his lady love once more bright in all her power and fury. Together they could tame the Realms and set it to rights.

So, the Crown . . . or the Mad Queen?

Ah, dark decisions . . .

Easily made, this time.

His Alassra.

Soft lips found his throat in the dark, just above his collarbone. She was still asleep, loving him in her dreams.

El smiled thinly. He loved the Obarskyrs and the Land of the Purple Dragon dearly, but it could all be swept away in scouring fire in an instant if that was what it would take to make his Simbul herself again.

To have his Alassra back, he would do anything.

Anything.

CHAPTER
TWO

ANOTHER BOLD NIGHT IN BRAVE CORMYR

So sing out songs and have no fear,
The wine is right with much good cheer,
Lasses laugh as jacks jest and jeer,
It's another bold night in brave Cormyr!

> from the ballad *Another Bold Night in Brave Cormyr*
> composed by Andrur Hallowstake, Bard of Wheloon
> in the Year of the Halls Unhaunted

H old! What was that?"
     The hoarse whisper came out of the night, not much
more than twice her arm's reach in front of her, where a cluster
of duskwoods stood dark and tall. Storm Silverhand froze.

"Some scuttling furry thing. What else'd be creeping
around the heart of the Hullack at *this* time of night?" The
second voice was thinner and sharper. It was also higher up,
coming from somewhere in one of the trees in front of her.

"Elminster and the Simbul?"

"*Very* funny."

Storm heard a faint scuffling as the second speaker
clambered down to the ground before adding, "Well, I can't
trace a *thing*. We're too close to the ruin. What's left of
the tower's wardings won't keep a mouse at bay, but their
decay is like a great seething hearth-cauldron in front of us,
roiling and echoing. It may be silent and unseen, but it's all
too stlarning effective at foiling my scrying magic. Trying to
find those two with spells, if they're anywhere in front of
us, is impossible." There followed a gusty sigh, then, "Heard
anything more?"

Storm stood right where she was, thankful it was dark

enough in the hollow that it was easier for the men to move by feel than by sight.

"No," said the first whisperer, a little doubtfully.

"Well, *I'm* not telling Kelgantor we heard a little rustling we can't identify, just once, and only for a moment."

Kelgantor. These were war wizards. Storm kept very still.

"What ruin?" the first whisperer hissed. "What sort of fool would build in the heart of the Hullack?"

"A long-ago fool, that's who. Your older colleagues tell me it was called Tethgard. Some fallen fortress from the bygone days of the realm, back when this Elminster—if he really *is* as old as all the legends say he is—was young. *You* know: when gods walked the earth and Anauroch was all empty desert and a dragon laired on every hilltop."

Ah. War wizards paired with highknights. Far more of them than just this pair and probably led by Kelgantor, because that was what the battle-mage Kelgantor did. All of them out in the deep forest, creeping through the night, seeking Elminster and the Simbul. *Knowing* El and Lass were here, somewhere.

There came the faintest of rustlings from the far side of the duskwoods.

"That *was* someone, to be sure," the second voice snapped. "When I—"

"Aye," a third voice growled disgustedly. " 'Twas *me*. Can't you two move through the Hullack without hissing like a pair of chambermaids hard at their gossip? Merlar, I know wizards of war can't take six steps without talking about it, but I expect better of you. I trained you."

"Sorry," the first whisperer muttered, so close to Storm that she could have reached out and slapped him without fully straightening her arm.

"Come," the third voice breathed, soft and deep, and Storm heard the faintest of footfalls on damp dead leaves underfoot. The newcomer was advancing straight toward Tethgard.

Straight toward El and Lass.

Merlar and the mage who'd been up in the tree moved to follow, and Storm moved with them, hidden amid their noise.

"Who's that?" another voice hissed out of the darkness on the other side of the three Cormyreans.

"Nordroun," the third voice replied flatly, "and who are you to be issuing challenges, Shuldroon? As I recall, you're supposed to be over on our other flank, with Kelgantor between us."

"I *am* between," came a new voice, cold and level. "The land rises to our east, and its slope seems to have brought Shuldroon and his three straying back this way, bringing us all together. So halt, everyone, before someone's blundering ends in a blade finding friendly flesh in the dark. Sir Nordroun, call your roll."

"Merlar?" came the prompt whisper.

"Here," that highknight replied from right in front of Storm. "Therlon is with me, and Starbridge our rear guard." Two nearby murmurs came out of the night as those men confirmed their presence.

"And I," Nordroun continued, "stand near enough to touch Merlar. My mage is Hondryn—"

"Here," a thin and unfriendly voice put in.

"—and Danthalus is my rear guard." Another murmur.

"Rorsorn?" Nordroun asked.

"I'm here, accompanying ranking Wizard of War Kelgantor and the mages Tethlor and Mreldrake. Jusprar's our rear guard."

Kelgantor gave his name with prompt, cold clarity, and the other three muttered theirs dutifully in his wake.

Shuldroon did not wait for Nordroun, highest ranking of all highknights in the realm notwithstanding. His tone of voice made it clear that he considered all highknights lackeys whose proper place was behind and beneath every wizard of war— and the sooner they all learned that, the better. "I am here, the knight Athlar is with me, and the knight Rondrand follows behind us." He was echoed by the two highknights confirming their presence.

"Anyone else?" Kelgantor asked, and a little silence fell.

"Good, we don't seem to have acquired any eavesdroppers," the leader of the force announced a few breaths later, his voice too flat and cold for anyone to dare to laugh. "Therlon, report."

"My spells can't detect the two we seek—or anyone else—ahead of us. The warding spells around Tethgard have decayed into an utter chaos of moving, ever-changing Art that foils all scrying magic. In both directions, I'd judge."

"I am less than surprised," Kelgantor replied. "Tethlor reported the same conditions. Enough delay. Rear guards, maintain your positions; all other knights, advance three paces, forming a front line as well as you can in this murk. We wizards will follow behind you. Rear guards, when you hear us start to move, follow on. No need for delay and little enough for caution, I'd say. Parley if it is offered, but strike back to slay without hesitation if magic is sent against us. Any queries?"

"Kelgantor," Tethlor said quietly, "Ganrahast warned us to be very careful. 'Beware Elminster,' he said. 'He's more formidable than he seems.'"

Kelgantor's voice came back a shade colder. "I've not forgotten that advice. Yet heading up the wizards of war does something regrettable but inescapable to every mage who's tried it; every Royal Magician I've known or read about has come to see lurking shadows behind every door and whispering conspirators beneath every bed in the realm. Let me remind you that no lone wizard—no matter how old, crazed, or infamous—can hope to match us in battle."

"For my part," Shuldroon put in, "I don't think this Elminster is the one in the legends at all. *I* think a series of old men, down the passing years, have used the fell name of a long-dead mage to cloak their own lesser wizardries. And this self-styled Elminster who thieves magic from us now is the least of them all, an old hedge wizard who avoids casting every spell he can, bluffing his way into getting what he wants through fear of what the mighty Elminster of old might do if roused. I've heard he dare not cast the simplest spell, because he goes mad."

"We've all heard that," Nordroun said heavily. "I hope it's true."

Storm listened as they all started to speak. Kelgantor was the calm, level-headed, coldly ruthless commander of this force, a veteran war wizard, smart and decisive. Tethlor was competent, wary, and loyal. Therlon she knew well: a good sort, along for his local knowledge, far less of a spellhurler than the others. Shuldroon was a zealous, overconfident killer, a youngling out to make his mark, with Hondryn his echo and crony. Mreldrake was a pompous, cowardly ass, a measure of how far the wizards of war had fallen these latter decades.

Aside from Eskrel Starbridge, whom she respected, the highknights she knew less well. Nordroun was head of them all, and well-regarded; Merlar was an able, amiable youngling, widely liked . . . and the rest were just names to her.

"Well, I think we'd best curl our line forward at both ends like a fork," Shuldroon was saying, "to surround the ruins, or we'll end up huffing and puffing through these trees until dawn, with the two we seek fleeing just ahead of us. Or they'll climb trees or hide amongst the trunks, and we'll blunder right past, and—"

He broke off, then, as the air around them all seemed to smite the ears with a heavy blow that was felt more than heard, a surge of flaring unseen force that came charging soundlessly out of the trees to wash over them and race on, away through the forest behind them, trees creaking here and there as if bent in a gale, though no leaves stirred.

Wizards cursed. "Strong magic!" Hondryn snarled. "Flaring as if uncontrolled, just unleashed . . ."

"I felt it," Kelgantor snapped. "The old man has unbound an enchanted item. Forward! Quick, before he destroys another!"

Storm moved with them, knowing what that flare of magic had been. Elminster had just destroyed the gorget.

Its magic was flowing into someone, either the Old Mage or the Simbul . . . but if 'twas Lass, that flood had been so smooth and quiet, with the darkness unbroken ahead, that she must be asleep or unconscious, not her raving, seething, exulting self.

"No doubt he's stealing magic for himself," the war wizard commander added as they hastened on, heedless of the din of snapping branches and rustling footfalls. "Know this secret of the realm, all of you: Elminster does indeed need magic to recover after every casting, or he goes a little mad for a while. Not mere rumor, but observed and confirmed truth. He always heals himself in the end—but each time he works a spell, he goes erratic if it's a minor magic and barking madwits if he's unleashed something mightier. So all we need do is survive his first spell, and our foe will be a staggering madman, too far gone to work a second magic on us. So when you hear my owl hoot in your minds—not with your ears; anything you hear will be a real owl—spread out and advance *very* quietly. We can't be far from him now."

"What if that was the gorget?" Merlar asked hesitantly. "Being destroyed, I mean?"

"Then their lives are forfeit," Kelgantor said flatly. "Slay them at all costs and by any means, no matter what they threaten or offer. *Move.*"

The Cormyreans hastened, crashing through leaves and branches. Someone rather tunelessly chanted, "Another bold night in brave Cormyr," a line from the old ballad popular with the soldiers of the realm. Smiling at that, Storm faded back, seeking to drop behind them all and get clear.

"Not *now*," a highknight muttered beside her ear in the impenetrable darkness, mistaking her for one of the war wizards. "You should have emptied your bladder two ridges back, when Kelgantor gave the order. If we—"

Storm knew that cautious growl and allowed herself a thin smile. Eskrel Starbridge was a grizzled old veteran . . . and one of the few highknights she'd trust to defend Cormyr. Or do much of anything, for that matter.

So she turned and struck him senseless almost gently.

Catching him in her arms before he could thud heavily to the damp leaves underfoot, she thrust the forefinger she'd dipped in her longsleep herb mix up Starbridge's nose to keep him down and slumberous. Stretching him out gently on the sodden forest floor made no more noise than the boots of his nearest oblivious fellows ahead of them . . . and passed unnoticed.

As silently as she knew how, Storm set off through the trees in a wide, swift circle. She *had* to get to Elminster and Alassra before the Cormyreans did.

The gorget flickered feebly once as Elminster whispered the last word of the incantation. Then it tingled, dark once more, and started to sink into nothingness under his fingertips, melting amid a few wisps of smoke as its ancient magics flowed into Alassra.

She stirred in her sleep, frowning, probably dreaming of someone throttling her, as the tips of El's fingers touched her throat through the fading metal . . . then smiled, her body seeming to grow more lush and strong under him as the magic fed her.

Her eyelids flickered, and she purred like a satisfied cat, stretching and arching under him, ere murmuring, "Tremble, all, for the Witch-Queen is truly back . . ."

Her eyes opened, and her arms reached up to encircle him. "Oh, my Aumar," she said delightedly, "You've—"

The spell that struck them then flung them a few feet, wreathed in snarling flames that clawed at them but could not scorch. So it tore them apart, to tumble away side by side, unharmed but furious. As if heeding a cue, the moon burst through the scudding clouds and flooded the tumbled rocks of Tethgard all around with cold, clear light.

Elminster cursed as he felt the soundless burst of sparks that meant the enspelled badge he'd recovered from a Sembian burial vault had just been destroyed, consumed in shielding Lass and himself from the attack. Which meant he had just one enchanted item left.

Without Storm's aid, he could withstand only one more hostile magic. Or hurl just one spell.

For her part, the Simbul was on her feet and glaring into the trees whence the attack had come, eyes afire. "Who dares—?"

"*We* dare, witch!" came the cold reply, as a dozen men strode just clear of the trees, some in dark war-leathers and bearing drawn swords. "You stand in Cormyr and are subject to the king's justice! In his name we call on you to surrender, working no magic and offering no defiance, and submit to our will!"

"Submit to your will? Nay, I choose my own lovers," the Simbul told them coldly. "I do *not* submit to armed men who threaten me in the forest. You strike me as brigands, not men of the Crown. Those who uphold justice call polite parley from a distance, rather than hurling spells without warning at couples they espy in the night."

"You are the mages Elminster and the Simbul, and we have orders to arrest you and obtain from you the Royal Gorget of Battle, stolen from the Crown of Cormyr. We are wizards of war and highknights of the realm, not brigands, and we call again upon you to surrender! Lay down all weapons and work no spells, and you will be dealt with accordingly."

The men were moving again, spreading out and advancing more swiftly at either end of their line, as if to encircle the couple amid the rocks.

"Where's Starbridge?" one of them muttered, looking suddenly to right and left along the line, but the man beside him—the one who'd called out to Elminster and the Simbul—waved a silencing hand, swiftly and imperiously.

"Leave us be," Elminster warned the Cormyreans, then cast a swift glance over his shoulder at a faint sound behind him. Storm was hastening up through the rocks to join them, crawling like a swift jungle cat. Heartened, he went to stand beside his lady, facing into the closing ring of men with her.

Seeing no signs of his quarry fleeing, the Cormyrean commander waved a hand, and two men strode forward from the closing ring. El recognized one almost immediately: Sir Ilvellund Nordroun, the head highknight of Cormyr. The other was a young war wizard he'd seen striding haughtily around the palace, whose name he didn't know.

"A parley, or are these two sent to wrestle us down?" Alassra mused calmly.

Elminster shrugged. "Perhaps thy reminder of proper courtesy stung them into this gesture. I've no doubt it will end in violence."

"I find myself less than surprised," the Simbul replied dryly, as the highknight and the mage came to a halt a careful four paces away.

"Yield the gorget," the young war wizard demanded. "Now."

"Youngling," Elminster said gravely, "ye stand in the presence of a queen. Can ye not manage a trifling minimum of courtesy?"

"This *is* courtesy," the mage flung back. "We could have just blasted you down."

"You could have tried," the Simbul replied almost gently, meeting his sneer with a look of disdain that made him flush and look away.

"You've heard our orders to you," he told them almost sullenly. "Obey, or face our lawful wrath—and your doom."

"Doom," Elminster murmured. "Villains always seem to love that word. I wonder why?"

"Villains? *You're* the villains here! *We* are lawkeepers of Cormyr and stand for justice and good!"

The Old Mage sighed. "Are ye still such a child as to divide all the folk ye meet into 'good' and 'bad'? Lad, lad, there are no good people and bad people—there are just *people*, doing things others deem good or bad. If ye serve most of the gods well, ye should end up doing more good than bad. I try to do good things. Do ye?"

"I'm not here to bandy words with you, old man. Give us the gorget, and surrender yourselves into our custody. I warn you, we'll have it from you peacefully—or the other way."

Elminster and his lady traded calm looks then faced the young war wizard together and said in unison, "No."

Shuldroon looked almost gleeful. "You seek to defy all of us? I remind you that you are overmatched sixfold by we wizards of war, and again by the highknights, the best warriors of the realm. See sense, man, and surrender."

Elminster scratched at his beard, looking almost bored. "So ye can slay me without a battle, is that it? Nay, loud-tongue, I've not lived so long by abandoning all my principles. Here's one ye younglings would do well to live by: if ye've done the right thing, stand thy ground."

"Sir Nordroun," the wizard commanded, "take and bind the woman. We'll see then if the old man wags his tongue quite so defiantly."

The highknight sighed. "That is less than wise, Shuldroon. I will take orders from Kelgantor, but not from you."

The young war wizard turned in swift rage. "Are my ears actually hearing—"

"They are," Storm Silverhand said in a level voice, rising up between Elminster and the Simbul with her sword in her hand. "And you should heed Sir Nordroun's wisdom, Wizard of War Shuldroon, and abandon any schemes of taking and binding anyone. A few loyal guardians of Cormyr might live longer that way."

"And just *who* are *you?*"

"Storm Silverhand is my name."

"*Another* liar using a name out of legend?" Shaking his head and sneering anew, Shuldroon put one hand behind his back and gestured.

Behind him, the ring of Cormyreans started to tighten around the three standing amid the rocks. All save one man. Wizard of War Kelgantor, it seemed, had decided to hang back and watch, wands in both of his hands, ready to unleash magic when necessary.

Storm shook her head. "So it's to be another bold night in brave Cormyr," she murmured. She laid a hand on her sister's shoulder, finding it atremble with rage, and added, "Don't blast them just yet, Lass. We should warn them once more; give them another chance."

The Simbul's answer was a low, feline growl.

"We know you're scared to use your paltry magic," Shuldroon told Elminster. "And that you have taken to not using it in favor of menacing folk and trading on your fearsome—and borrowed—reputation. Unfortunately for you, old charlatan, we don't scare."

He took a step forward and struck a defiant pose, his shoulders squared and his hands on his hips, to add, "I'm not scared."

Elminster replied dryly, "Ye should be."

CHAPTER
THREE

SPELLDOOM AND BLOOD-DRENCHED BATTLE

So the dark time beyond bitter threats comes at last?
Well, I never did think I'd grow old beside a hearthfire,
So lead me out to where the slaughter will rage,
And start the spelldoom and blood-drenched battle!

> said by Rorstal the Mage
> in Act III, Scene V of the play
> *The Harrowing of House Drauth*
> anonymously chapbook published in the Year of
> the Splendors Burning

Shuldroon's only answer was another sneer, as the ring of men closed in.

"Don't force this," Elminster warned them, looking past the young war wizard at the other Cormyreans. "There will be death. And I am more than tired of killing."

"Huh," another young mage—the one called Hondryn—replied, flexing his fingers. "We can end your weariness forever, old man."

"Aye, but should ye? If, that is, ye care for Cormyr."

"Ah, this will be the 'if ye knew the dark secrets I do, ye'd not be so foolish' proclamation," Shuldroon said mockingly. "Wherein you pose as the hidden guardian of the Forest Kingdom, its lone defender against all manner of dark creeping menaces we are too callow to know about, let alone understand."

"I see ye know the script." Elminster's smile was wry. "Do ye also dismiss how those plays usually end?"

The young war wizard shrugged. "Everyone dies, so what boots it? Perhaps I'm a harsher critic of such sad amusements than you are—you who have seen and caused so many."

"The savagery of a young cynic never rests," Storm murmured and drew her sword.

That earned her one of Shuldroon's sneers, but she had already turned to cast another swift look over her shoulder.

Tethgard's tumbled stones hindered the closing of the ring behind the three former Chosen, but the Cormyreans stood close in front of them. Kelgantor, too, was advancing, though well behind his fellows. Storm saw him glance warily over his own shoulder, seeking unseen foes in the dark forest at his back, and she smiled bitterly.

They were here for blood, these men of Cormyr. It was all too clear how this would end.

"One last chance, old man," Shuldroon said to Elminster. "Know that your own continued defiance has cost you much leniency on our part. We now have another demand: surrender to us she who was once the Witch-Queen of Aglarond. She is a danger and a peril to all Cormyr, and the king has commanded her apprehension!"

Elminster raised one eyebrow. "Ye seem to think she is my dog, rather than a person who chooses for herself. Count thyselves fortunate she's kept her temper thus far, and be warned that her patience is not eternal."

"You command here, do you not?"

"*No one* 'commands' here, lad. She's under my protection, aye, and I'll defend her freedom and her person—but she is no slave. Neither I nor anyone else owns her, wherefore no one can surrender her but the lady herself. Make such demands to her, not of me."

"You seek to duel me with words, old man. She's a drooling idiot, chained like a dog—and you hold the other end of the chain!"

Elminster looked at Nordroun and asked mildly, "Was this the most, ah, *diplomatic* wizard of war the Crown could find? A youngling so hot-tongued that he needs ye to walk at his side as his bodyguard?"

Nordroun kept stone-faced and silent, but Shuldroon went purple and snarled, "Yield to us yon woman—we'll not ask again!"

"Good," El replied. "Then we can have some peace and quiet once more? *Marvelous!*"

"Mock me not, old man! I speak with the full authority of the Crown!"

"Methinks it weighs rather too heavily upon thy brains, youngling. All this wild shouting and rude, imprudent demanding! Are ye truly rash enough to try to force me to choose between the land I love and my lady?"

"I care nothing for your loves, Elminster. I care only about your defiance, your refusal to obey. Nor is the woman our only demand; I remind you that we require the immediate surrender of the Royal Gorget of Battle that you stole from the royal palace. Yield up both of these to us, in the name of the king's justice!"

"The gorget I *retrieved* from the palace, ye mean," Elminster replied, wagging a reproving finger. "I loaned that bauble to the first Palaghard when he was but a prince, to keep him alive through a rather perilous youth. He was not then king, and it was not a gift to him—nor to the Crown of Cormyr, nor yet the Forest Kingdom. He let his Enchara wear it when needful, a generosity I approved of. However, 'twas my *loan* and mine to take back and use whenever I deemed the time right or the occasion needful."

"You lie!" Shuldroon shouted.

"I do *not* lie," Elminster replied flatly. "Thy bluster notwithstanding."

"Do you not? Sages have filled books with your falsehoods and thefts down the centuries, old man!"

"So they have, and even told truth about some of them, too. Yet I have not stolen or lied about this gorget. And as for my thefts and lies, I recall very few of them taking place in fair Cormyr. Which means they lie beyond the concerns and reach of the wizards of war."

"Not so!" several Cormyreans barked in untidy chorus.

Shuldroon added in a rush, "We follow thieves and liars wherever they go and wherever they seek to hide, even unto far and fabled lands! Just as you've always done!"

"Then it seems ye're no better than I," Elminster replied quietly. "So talk to me not of justice or being in the 'right.' Ye bring me no better argument than the menace of might: do as we command, or face our swords and spells. Well, I've a reply for that. Go and leave me and these ladies in peace, and I'll let ye live to swagger around Cormyr with thy swords and spells a while longer."

"You don't scare us, old fool." Shuldroon sneered. "Surrender the gorget, or *you* will die. Have you not noticed we have you surrounded?"

"So ye do. Well, there's yet time for ye to show good sense and draw off. This has been one of the better kingdoms, down the years; I'd not want to strike it so hard a blow without giving fair warning."

"We've heard you," Shuldroon snarled. "Deluded old fool. For far too long you've skulked like a thief and a vagabond in the halls of the Dragon Throne, while we've watched and done nothing, out of respect for the good deeds of your yesteryears. Yet you've trampled on our patience and our good nature, time and again, stealing the greatest royal treasures and magics of the Crown. Our forbearance, old man, is at an *end*. Surrender the gorget, or die."

"Ah," El said mildly, spreading his hands. "As to that, the gorget has been destroyed; it is far beyond being surrendered to anyone, by anybody. So let us have peace, and—"

"*Die*, thief!" Shuldroon thundered, flicking his fingers and crying a word that hurled his mightiest spell.

Nor was he alone. Most of the other war wizards cast swift battle magics, hands and tongues moving as swiftly as Elminster and the Simbul.

Or faster.

The night promptly exploded in great gouts of white flame as the ground shook and Tethgard erupted toward the stars.

El, Storm, and the Simbul were dashed off their feet again, the air around them shrieking and bubbling as the spells clawed at each other.

Elminster's last magic item was gone in an instant, consumed in keeping the three from being blasted to nothingness. Charging highknights were flung away in all directions—and the stones of Tethgard were hurled into the air, riven asunder.

In the rolling, shuddering aftermath of that blast, amid involuntary groans from those still alive enough to feel the pain of their ringing ears, the three former Chosen watched Tethgard crash down in a deadly cloud of ricocheting fragments that clacked and clattered off the shaking stones all around. In a trice, Wizard of War Kelgantor lost his head to one slicing shard. In the moments that followed, larger stones crushed his bouncing head and some of his limbs even before they could come to rest.

"Back!" Nordroun cried, spitting blood. "Highknights, back! Rally to me!"

"*I'll* give the orders around here!" Shuldroon screamed, staggering up from his knees with blood on his face and more of it running out of his ears. "Men of Cormyr, rally to *me*!"

"*Our* turn," the Simbul purred triumphantly. And she raised her hands like two avenging claws, Elminster at her side, and struck back.

The air shimmered, and out of that whirling chaos spun countless swords of force, sharp blades that lacked hilts and wielders but shone with purple-white, howling magic as they sliced and spun their way through screaming men.

Three wizards of war were diced in a blood-drenched instant, leaving only a drifting crimson mist where they'd stood.

Another two were hurled high into the air, ruining the spells they'd been working, and the Old Mage, who'd sent them aloft, roared a great, spell-augmented warning out over much of Hullack Forest: "Begone, or I'll not be responsible for what happens to ye! There will be more death!"

"Yours, if you don't surrender!" Shuldroon shouted back, clawing out a wand and raking the night with lightning—

—that rebounded from the heaped stones of Tethgard, ravaging a highknight caught among them.

Crouching in the lee of some of those stones, Elminster whimpered, biting through his lip and shivering violently. Storm ran to him.

"Let me," her sister hissed fiercely in her ear, one clawlike hand descending atop Storm's own, as she clutched Elminster's head.

Storm turned her head. Alassra was so close that their noses bumped. "You mustn't—"

"I *must*," the Witch-Queen of Aglarond snarled. "You think I don't know my sanity is fleeting? He needs it *now*, to be sane enough to win this fray. My head has a handful of none-too-useful Art in it—unless you want half the Hullack gone—but he knows how to foil the spells of war wizards and strike back! Take what the gorget gave me, and feed it to him!"

Elminster was chanting, words that came in a fluid rush, his mouth wet and frothy and his eyes wide and staring.

"Loross?" Storm gasped. "I've not heard that since—"

"Not *now*, Astorma! Just keep your hands wrapped around his head when he moves, and let him get up and prance around! Look, he seeks to!"

El exploded to his feet and sprinted around the rocks, flinging his arms wide and sketching strange, intricate gestures as he came out into the full moonlight. White flames sprang out of the air around his hands, trailing them as he shaped a circle in the air in front of him. Storm struggled to keep hold of his head, the Simbul clawing at them both.

Shuldroon shouted furious curses at his foe, once again visible, and sent lightning racing at the three of them.

Bright, deadly bolts that Elminster's cone of white fire gathered in, brought to his chest as a shrieking, spitting ball of blinding white conflagration—and sent howling back at their source.

The wand in Shuldroon's hand exploded, and Shuldroon with it, his last scream cut off abruptly as tiny, dark, wet pieces of ambitious young war wizard spattered the distant trees.

Highknights burst up out of the rocks and flung daggers at them desperately, racing in behind those whirling blades with swords out to—

—vanish in a great ball of flame that flared up out of Elminster's palm to blister rocks of Tethgard and then snatch itself aloft, carrying those screaming men with it, and explode up among the stars.

As blackened limbs rained down, Elminster started to sing.

Wild, off-key, and incoherent his song came, all half-words that were slurred and seemingly plucked from a dozen languages, making no sense at all.

"He's going," Storm said, her voice quavering. "Sister, have you more?"

The reply in her ear was a shriek that nearly deafened her, a scream that sounded like nothing that could—or should—come from a human throat.

Her sister tore violently away from her and was gone, flinging Storm and El down in a heap together on the stones.

Storm tried to find her footing again without letting go of El. Under her, he burst into wild, high-pitched laughter, cascades of sobbing giggles that set her teeth on edge.

She turned to see what had befallen Alassra—in time to see a lashing scaled tail rise up into the night. The Simbul had become a sleek, many-horned *thing* that looked a little like a wyvern and was flying away as fast as her batlike wings could take her, letting out another of those wild, screaming calls as she went.

Great. Alassra was insane again.

And so was Elminster. Storm looked wildly all around, wondering if she dared try to heal him—or if she'd find herself fighting for her own life in a moment or two, against a generous supply of enraged Cormyrean knights and wizards.

She put her hands on his head again, still tensely staring about.

No one moved amid the rocks. No swords came seeking her.

Out in the moonlight, she caught sight of a handful of surviving Cormyreans—a very *small* handful—fleeing back toward the trees, pelting along in frantic and terrified haste. A wizard of war waved frantic hands, and pale light flared briefly to claim them all, teleporting them elsewhere.

Somewhere safely far away, she hoped, sagging down atop Elminster with her tears starting. She'd be crying in earnest once she plunged into his ravaged mind, she knew, but in a forest this wild she dared not wait too long, for fear of something hungry coming along to feed before he was at least on his feet again . . . and they were both free of the worst of his madness.

The moon was serenely riding a nearly empty sky, highlighting a scorched and smoking battlefield strewn with pieces of dead wizard and highknight.

Tears blinded her then as she fell into real weeping.

Between her hands, the Old Mage's head quivered, and Elminster started barking.

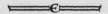

The moment she unshuttered the lantern and sat down in the little cavern facing him, Elminster frowned at her. "Ye look thin," he said reprovingly. "Scrawny. Have ye been eating properly?"

Storm gave him a dark look. "Just how do you think I heal your mind?" she hissed, angrier than she'd thought she'd be. "I draw from *myself*."

The Old Mage sighed. "Sorry, lass. I'll steal ye some healing potions when I'm back inside, for when we meet again."

He nodded in the direction of the damp old smuggling tunnel that led away from the cavern, curving into unseen distances and descending to pass under the walls of Suzail, but they both knew he meant inside the royal palace, where for some seasons they'd been posing as old Elgorn Rhauligan and his aging sister, Stornara, minor palace servants.

Storm waved a hand, dismissing healing potion thefts until some future time when they were together inside the palace. "El, are you well enough to cast those guises on us, without . . . ?"

"Turning into a drooling, yapping thing again? 'Tis to be hoped."

It was Storm's turn to sigh. "I need a little *certainty*, El," she said. "Or by the Holy Lady we both lost, I'll slip you a little more longsleep and leave you snoring for a month or more, until I'm well and truly back from Shadowdale."

Elminster chuckled. "Ye *have* grown claws, Lady of Shadowdale. A pleasure fighting battles with ye!"

Storm crooked one eyebrow. "Not against me?"

"Tease not, but tell: what word was brought back to the Crown of the fray at Tethgard?"

Storm shrugged. "I don't look like the fetchingly spotted and wrinkled old Stornara without your magic, so I haven't been able to get into the palace. The more talkative courtiers who drink at two of the taverns I've visited, however, tell lurid tales of a great spell battle against mysterious, unspecified fell wizards who slew all but a handful of the many brave, loyal, and vastly outnumbered wizards of war and loyal highknights who went up against these foes of the realm."

"Of course. And those survivors were?"

"I know Starbridge survived, because I sent him into slumber before the battle, and I've heard he's now been made commander of the highknights. And I've seen Wizard of War Rorskryn Mreldrake from afar, strolling along the promenade— as pompous and strutting as ever—so I know *he* made it back. No doubt he's been telling everyone how he bravely saved the day after the mightiest foes that ever threatened Cormyr struck down Kelgantor and the rest."

"No doubt. What of Alassra?"

"Mad again; turned herself into a monster and flew off. Right now, she could be anywhere."

"She gave her sanity right back to me, didn't she?"

Storm nodded glumly. "She always returns to the same few places. My farm, for one. Not that getting her to talk to us is going to be easy. It's going to take a lot of enchanted items to bring her mind back again."

"I'm done with dragging her back to herself for a few days or a few hours," Elminster said quietly. "It's time to cure her for good."

"That will take some *really* powerful stored Art," Storm murmured.

"I care not if I have to strip Cormyr bare of its every last item, crowns and regalia included," the Old Mage replied calmly. "If they treat me as a thief and murderer, then a thief and a murderer I shall be. I'll take what I need to make her sane again, once and for all—and send anyone who stands in my way to greet the gods. I'm done with being kind and gentle to cruel fools."

Storm frowned at him for a moment, hearing more bitter steel in his voice than she'd heard in a long time. "Be careful whom you slay, El. Cormyr may soon run out of cruel fools, if we fight many more Tethgards," she told him.

Elminster shook his head. "New ones will arise to fill the boots of those we blast down," he replied. "Every realm seems to have an endless supply of them."

CHAPTER
FOUR

TRAITORS BEHIND EVERY DOOR

Yet one thing I know full well, lord,
And will tell thee and all ears the world over;
This is a fell house, and a foul one;
There are traitors behind every door.

> said by Ryaun the Lion-Tamer
> in Act I, Scene III of the play
> *Too Many Skulls Underfoot*
> anonymously chapbook published in the Year of
> Seven Sisters.

The room was small and round. It was also dark, stale, and very dusty. Hardly surprising, being as it hadn't been used for years. Until now.

Marlin Stormserpent edged into it with shuffling care, trying hard not to bump his hot shuttered lantern into the untidy mounds of broken furniture crowding the chamber.

It had taken him some trouble to slip away from the family servants unseen, curse their diligence—but that was nothing to what trouble he'd find if just one of them followed him and overheard any of what was about to be said.

The stout old door still had a bolt, massive and old-fashioned, and he shot it firmly across before daring to open the lantern enough to see his way through the maze of yester-year's marred elegance.

Dust lay like a thick fur cloak over much of this uppermost room in the most disused turret of Stormserpent Towers. Marlin's lip curled. Of course.

His home was one of the older and grander noble family mansions in Suzail. Once there had been far more Storm-serpents clattering and prancing and sneering around the place, but, well . . . a lot of things had been grander once.

And perhaps—just perhaps—might be again.

From atop what looked like a cloak stand, Marlin took up an ordinary-looking glass orb, a milky sphere a little smaller than his head, the sort of idle ornament that had been fashionable fifty or sixty Mirtuls earlier. He went to a small round table and sat in a lopsided chair drawn up to it, setting the orb atop an empty and garishly heavy metal goblet that stood on the table.

Marlin squared his shoulders then touched the smooth, curved glass, murmured a certain word, and . . . a glowing cloud slowly appeared in the air above the orb and thickened into silvery smoke.

Smoke that twisted, swirled, and became the glowing image of a person.

Lothrae.

He had no idea who Lothrae really was, behind the mask the man always wore.

As always, Lothrae sat in front of his own orb in a chair with an upswept back like falcons' wings, in a room somewhere with walls of once-grand but now cracked and mold-stained gilt stucco adorned with a pattern of little blue griffons.

"You are late." Lothrae said those three words like cold stones leisurely dropped into an abyss.

"I—had some trouble getting free of my mother and the servants, Master," Marlin stammered, rattled in an instant and hating it. "You warned me to avoid suspicion above all else, so . . ."

"Understood. It is time."

Marlin swallowed. "Time? To begin at last?"

"To begin at last. Indubitably. I know where six of the Nine are, beyond doubt, and have strong suspicions as to the whereabouts of the seventh. Any two of them should be able to win past the paltry wards left to the Crown of Cormyr these days—and destroy any war wizard they can catch alone."

"The Nine?"

"Marlin," Lothrae said softly, "don't pretend you know nothing of this. You are certain the Flying Blade holds one of the Nine, and have long suspected the Wyverntongue Chalice holds another. You just don't know how to call forth or compel the Nine—wherefore all your stealing of old texts and drowning sages in drink seeking to pry secrets out of them. You've been so clumsy about it that some war wizards figured out what you were up to long ago."

"They—they—?" Marlin knew he was going white; he could feel the coldness rushing across his face.

"No, they'll not come bursting in on you. I took care of them as they discussed you, before they could spread word of your fumblings among all the wizards of war. Right now, among those who're left, you're suspected of being as restless and opportunistic as any other arrogant young fool of a noble, but no more than that. I was going to wait until we'd found and secured all of the Nine, but we've run out of leisure; some clever war wizards have remembered the old tales and have started their own search for the Nine, with an eye to making Cormyr unassailable. It won't be long before one of them starts wondering if the Flying Blade of the Stormserpents might just be something the Crown should confiscate—for the good of the realm, of course. So it *is* time."

"Yes, Master! Time for—?"

"You to hear and obey, Lord Stormserpent," the cold voice coming out of the orb told him dryly. "So listen well . . ."

It was getting harder and harder to force the courtier to be Lothrae; the Cormyrean's mind was actually growing stronger. Almost enough to begin fighting him.

Astonishing.

Though after all his years, he really shouldn't be astonished at what humans could—and did—do.

The strain of controlling that distant body was making this other host, a body chosen largely for its youthful agility and darkly handsome appearance, sweat profusely. He sent a mental slap through their fading link that should leave the courtier dazed and staggering for a time, and withdrew from the man's mind entirely.

Leaving himself just time to wipe his dripping face and stride to the door. If there was one redeeming quality shared by Cormyr's more ambitious nobles, it was punctuality. Only the lazy, stupidly overconfident, groundlessly self-satisfied, and hopelessly old-fashioned made a habit of being fashionably late.

Not that there weren't plenty of those among the nobility of the Forest Kingdom.

His hand was reaching for the door bolt when he heard the careful knock.

He slid the well-oiled bolt aside soundlessly, drew the door open, and murmured, "Be welcome, Lady Talane."

He felt rather than heard his guest stiffen, and added, "Yes, I know who you are. I've known for a long time, yet the wizards of war, the highknights, and the Crown behind them are still unaware of your . . . hobby. Take reassurance from that."

His guest hesitated on the threshold then sighed and stepped into the room.

It was small, dim, and richly paneled—panels that could hide any number of doors where none were visible. It held a small table with a lone chair and a sideboard. Not a picture or banner adorned any of its walls; they were bare save for a single small, round mirror. The small, plain fireplace was empty and cold. Though he was slender and darkly garbed, he dominated the room like the prow of a great gilded warship.

"You could have ruined me and chose not to," she stated, her voice just on the tight side of calm. "Meaning you have some other use for me. May I know it?"

"Informing you of that is why I asked you here. Will you sit, Lady, and take wine?"

Without taking his eyes off her for a moment, the darkly handsome man opened one of the sideboard doors, drew out a tall, dark, slender bottle of wine and a sleek wineglass, and advanced to place both on the table beside her, ere smoothly backing away again.

"I'm given to understand this Arrhenish is highly regarded at court; pray satisfy yourself that the bottle is still sealed. You'll have to pour your own, I'm afraid. In the interests of discretion, no one else is closer to us than my agents down at the doors—who I posted there primarily to make sure you reached this room alone, bringing no tiresome bodyguards or hired slayers with you. Wisely, you made no attempt to do so. Know that no wizard of war—nor anyone else, if it comes to that—can spy on us here with spells, nor approach us without my becoming aware of it. We may both speak freely."

The noblewoman nodded. "I could kill you right now," she announced calmly, hefting the bottle of Arrhenish as if to throw it, various rings on her fingers glowing into sudden life. "Give me good reason why I should not."

Her darkly handsome host smiled and held up a languid hand to count points off on his fingers. "Firstly: I am not here. You would be slaying a mere husk of meat under my control, not me. Secondly: you are not the only person in this kingdom to own and use powerful magic. Thirdly: I have plans for Cormyr. Big plans. If I want you or any other noble dead, that can be accomplished with swift ease. The kingdom would profit from many of those deaths, believe me. Yet a select few nobles can be very useful to me and to Cormyr, and if they willingly serve me in furthering my efforts, I'll reward them handsomely. If they refuse, of course . . ."

"They die," the noblewoman replied promptly, uncorking the bottle. "And you deem me—thus far, at least—one of these select few."

The darkly handsome man gave her a deep and smiling bow. She did not fail to notice that his eyes never left hers for a moment, and she had no doubt he controlled magic that could smite her before her rings could do anything at all.

Very slowly she held up one hand for him to see, spread her fingers, and made the rings on them wink out. Then she unhurriedly poured herself a glass, raised it to him in her other hand in salute, and quelled those rings, too.

Then she sipped.

After a moment, evidently finding nothing amiss with its taste, she visibly relaxed, allowing herself a small smile. "Your health, mysterious lord. How much are you now going to tell me?"

"As much as you want to know. I am familiar with both your family holdings and your personal hideaways, from the rented Sembian properties—even that squalid pleasure-girl bedchamber by the docks in Saerloon, with all of its persistent little crawling and biting inhabitants—to the fishing boats whose ownership is so carefully not linked even to you. I've even seen that little cottage in the nether wilds of Harrowdale. In short, there's nowhere you can run to that I can't find you— and if you go straight to the king of Cormyr or the Royal Magician and unburden yourself of all you learn here in hopes of gaining more by that unexpected loyalty than by working with me, let me inform you that I have planned for such duplicity. Not only would you die very promptly and painfully, Cormyr itself would be plunged into a war from which very few of its nobles would emerge. Certainly not a single member or byblow of *your* family; I would see to that."

The hand that then set down the half-empty wineglass trembled only slightly. "I understand. Speak then, Lord; tell me of the part I am to play."

"You will continue to do what you are doing as Talane. The blade in the night, the silken threat, the use of coerced or unwitting intermediaries whenever possible. Pursue your career of self-enrichment, insofar as it doesn't conflict with the tasks I give you to do. I will not explain why you'll be asked to do this or that—though you are welcome to your own speculations— but the ends I seek include a new rule for Cormyr in which more of its folk enjoy better lives. Some noble families will abruptly disappear, but others will be rewarded, even elevated. Given present company, I might mention the Truesilvers, who should, if your loyalty to me holds, rise to be the foremost family of the realm, firmly separated from the royal House and therefore unlikely to be dragged down with them by the seemingly endless would-be usurpers, but wielding more real power than anyone short of, say, the Royal Magician."

"I . . . appreciate that."

"As a measure of my unfolding trust in you, Lady, let me speak of the powerful magics that will almost certainly soon be in play in Cormyr. Listen well; familiarity with these perils may keep you alive."

His guest smilingly turned her head and cupped an elegant hand behind the ear she'd just put closest to him.

The darkly handsome man did not quite smile. "About a century ago," he told her, "certain mages began to forcibly imprison particular persons within magic items—or rather, in stasis. Their return was linked to specific actions taken upon those items."

He spread his hands in a gesture of loss. "Their reasons for doing so did not come to fruition and are now largely obsolete; all of the imprisoners have perished. Some of their imprisonments persist, but the great chaos of magic that befell back then twisted their magics awry. Some of the prisoners were lost forever when their items were destroyed; some escaped their captivity but also lost their wits; and some are still imprisoned, but . . . changed. Having powers like spells they never had before, for instance."

"They emerge uncontrolled?"

"Your own wits are as swift as always, Lady. Some are indeed self-willed and dangerous to whomever releases them. Others can't be returned to imprisonment, once out, but can be compelled by the bearer of their item. A few may yet be the perfect slaves they were intended to be. All that have thus far emerged have been wreathed in eerie blue flames, and so are known among wizards as 'blueflame ghosts,' though what rages around them are not flames any stoker of a hearthfire would recognize, and they are not ghosts."

"And some of these items are in Cormyr."

"Indeed. Notably some containing members of a once-famous band of adventurers known as 'the Nine.' Rumor has spread among certain of your fellow nobles that all of the Nine—including the lady mage who later became notorious as the bride of the Blackstaff, and one of the Chosen of

Mystra—are secretly under the command of a handful of Cormyrean nobility, who can use them to slay, harass, or seize things from rivals or . . . anyone. As is the way of rumors, these views are overblown. It's highly likely that the Lady Mage of Waterdeep never survived to be imprisoned, and it's simply untrue that nobles are striding around this fair realm right now knowing what prisoners are linked to their baubles and covertly using them."

"Yet."

The darkly handsome man smiled like a wolf. "You continue to please me. 'Yet,' indeed. In truth, a very few nobles do have custody of one of these imprisoning items, and others are kept in the royal palace in Suzail, the property of the Crown— who, so far as can be determined, have no idea what they're harboring."

"And as these blueflame ghosts may well be very dangerous, it's best they be handled through expendable dupes. Nobles and courtiers you can manipulate."

The darkly handsome man was suddenly beaming. "Your mind outleaps storm lightning."

His guest eyed him thoughtfully. "You're not telling me much," she said. "Of course."

"Of course. Prudence is not unknown to me."

The noblewoman regarded him in silence for as long as it took to enjoy another slow swallow of wine, then asked, "And so?"

"So our work together shall begin. Worry not about contacting me; I'll speak to you when I desire to—and I'll be aware when you feel the need to contact me. You should assume that I am aware of your smallest breath and your slightest facial expression, from this moment on."

That earned him another silent, cool look. "And so?"

The brief ghost of a smile did touch the man's lips at that. "Your first tasks shall be these. Legend recalls Elminster, sometimes known as the Old Mage or Elminster of Shadowdale; he is real and is somewhere in this city right now. Seek to learn what guises he uses and what he's busy doing. Learn also what magic in the royal palace and royal court buildings can easily be removed. Be aware that I have other eyes, ears, and hands in the palace; sadly, like the high houses of many a kingdom, it comes furnished with traitors behind every door. Feel free to liberate all you can without bringing Crown suspicion or pursuit down upon you—so long as you bring every last enchanted item, hiding or holding back not one of them, to me for inspection. The items I deem needful to my purposes, I shall retain; the rest you may keep for your own ends. Go now."

The lady who betimes called herself Talane set down her empty wineglass, said formally, "My lord," bowed her head, and withdrew.

The darkly handsome man regarded the door she'd closed behind her for some time before he murmured, "And if you dare turn traitor on me, Lady, I've someone who will enjoy dealing with you appropriately. Someone too dead to disobey me."

He took another glass from the sideboard, filled it with Arrhenish, sipped, then made a face at himself in the mirror.

"I *must* do something about these Cormyreans and their execrable tastes in wine," he told his reflection. "When I sit on the Dragon Throne, those who make and sell overly sweet swill like this will be swiftly drowned in it. My subjects will share in my delight in the finer things. I won't even style myself 'king.'"

Giving the mirror a smile, he tossed the wineglass casually into the fireplace. As the musical peal of its shattering died away, he sketched a herald's flourish with one languid arm and added mockingly, "All hail Emperor Manshoon."

CHAPTER
FIUE

OVERHEARD AND SPIED UPON

My Lord Bereth, if I may in one thing warn you true,
There is not a stinking jakes in all this great castle,
No proud chamber, nor yet the rudest, breakneck back stair,
Where one will not be overheard and spied upon.

> said by Arskrel the Old Guardsword
> in Act II, Scene II of the play
> *The Fall of the Proud House*
> by Darindral Haeleth, published in the Year of
> Three Heroes United

Wild terror had seized Elminster the moment he summoned his wits to begin casting the guise of Elgorn Rhauligan on himself—the madness. Come hard and early.

So he'd given up trying the spell and stood shaking and sweating in the dank deep darkness, disgusted and alone.

Storm was gone on her slow, careful, skulking way back to Shadowdale, overland by back lanes, winding creekbeds, and game trails to the familiar trees where, of late, Yelada and the elves kept busy preventing her farm from vanishing entirely back into the forest. Back to the farmhouse hearth where Alassra, too, always ended up sooner or later, seeking warmth and solace no matter how sunk in madness she was.

A kitchen Elminster wouldn't mind relaxing in, himself, to sip warm soup with his boots off and battered old feet up on the table, with Storm winking at him as she menaced his toes in mock fierceness with her carving knife. With onions sizzling in a pan and the promise of a really good meal rising to tantalize his nose, setting his mouth to watering . . .

El smiled tightly as he firmly shook his head to banish the daydream and bring himself back to the tunnel he stood in, a short stroll away from being under the grand, sprawling royal palace of Suzail. It was a narrow, low-ceilinged way, ancient and crumbling . . . but not unguarded.

Quite possibly not just by the guardians he knew, but by new perils. The soaring seat of rulership it led to was, after all, under the protection of a society of young and ambitious wizards. Mages who must all be under orders to watch for the infamous Sage of Shadowdale and to destroy or entrap him if at all possible.

And if there was one thing a long, long life in Faerûn taught even a slow-witted man, it was that *all* things are possible.

He took a step closer to the royal palace—and abruptly stopped, peering into the darkness ahead.

Something had moved, something brown and . . . bony.

Ah. An old friend, of sorts, if he wasn't mistaken.

El felt in a belt pouch, brought forth a pinch of powder, used his other hand to do the same to another pouch as far away from the first as his girth would permit, then brought his hands together and rubbed.

A faint glow kindled where the two powders met and mingled. He lifted his glowing palm like a pale, feeble lamp and stayed where he was.

As the first, familiar guardian shuffled into view.

He'd guessed right. It was a human skeleton, trudging with slow, unsteady menace. As it came, it raised a sword dark with rust.

Elminster gave it a calm stare. "Do ye really want to strike at me? Will thy shrewd strike bring crowning triumph to thy day?"

Empty eyesockets stared at him, expressionless but somehow uncertain. Then brownish bones shifted—only spell-bleached skeletons were truly white, all bards' ballads notwithstanding—and the sword wavered down again.

The old man in the ragged robe waited patiently. Three of his calm breaths later, the undead guardian of this nigh forgotten, deep passage of the palace undercellars stepped back to let him pass.

With a smile and a nod, he did so, looking back only once. The skeleton was staring after him, as still as a statue, its sword still point down.

Elminster walked on into the darkness. It was a curious thing; down the many years of his long life, he'd spent not all that much time in the Forest Kingdom. Yet now that he was back in the haunted wing of the Royal Palace of Cormyr, he felt at home.

He belonged.

Not back under the trees of Shadowdale he knew and loved so.

These cobwebbed shadows and empty, echoing rooms had somehow stolen into his heart and head and had become home.

Just when had that happened? And how?

Elminster came to a halt. Here, at the lowest spot in the passage, where the walls glistened with seepage, there was always a puddle of water. Sounds from the palace end of the tunnel always echoed here, clearly audible far from their source, and unless a foe was hard on one's heels with a blade drawn or a spell on his lips, 'twas always worth halting for a breath or two to listen for what might be waiting in one's near future.

Aye—there! The scrape of a boot, again. Someone was waiting up ahead where the passage opened out into the wider undercellar. Someone who'd already grown bored.

"My foot's asleep again, stlarn it," came a thin, waspish male voice, startlingly loud and sudden. "Taking his godsfire-damned own time about it, isn't he?"

"Huh," another, deeper male voice muttered in reply. "Probably wounded and wary—and so, slow. Thal didn't see him, remember; just Storm Silverhand heading away from the city wall right quick. Meaning the Old Mage's wits are his own again, or she'd not leave him—so back here he'll come. Back to where the magic is."

"Where he'll find us ready for him."

"I hope."

"You doubt the Royal Magician's wisdom in this?" That was a snapped, swift challenge.

The reply was wearily calm. "How many went up against him out at Tethgard—and how many came back alive?"

There was a short silence before the other man snarled, "I don't want to talk about it. I . . . Things did not go well."

"So much half the palace knows—as all of Suzail will, tomorrow. How's Tethlor?"

There was a loud sigh. "Still in a bad way, to tell true. Almost as bad as Elminster."

The Sage of Shadowdale smiled wryly in the darkness and started walking forward again. Reception foreguard or not, he wasn't getting any younger.

As he went, he felt in the breast of his jerkin beneath the scorched smith's apron and among the pouches at his belt for the things he'd probably need when he reached the far end of the passage. Handy things, Storm's Harper caches, if one didn't mind wearing gowns at the flashier end of the wardrobe . . .

Yet all gods blast this creeping madness and the magic he dared not hurl. He was going to have to waste *so* much time arguing with fools, instead . . .

Like yon two, standing with thumbs hooked through their belts, barring his way with confidence that was probably more outward seeming than truth. One was in faintly glowing black leathers: a highknight of Cormyr. The other wore the robes of a wizard—and any wizard walking around the royal palace of Suzail, even its dingiest, deepest undercellar, must be a wizard of war.

They stared back at him. The old, bearded man striding unconcernedly up the passage in the darkness, alone and swordless, didn't look like a great wizard. His clothes looked as old as he was, worn and none too clean and befitting a laborer who saw few coins and even fewer baths. Old, down-at-heel boots, stained and patched breeches, and a burn-scarred apron over a jerkin. The belt at his waist sagged onto his slim hips, loaded down with bulging pouches. He was hefting something in each hand; both somethings were small, dark, and round. And he was smiling.

Elminster gave them both a polite nod as he came to a halt and let silence fall.

It didn't last long.

"We've been waiting for you, old man," the one in robes said, his waspish voice now all smug menace.

"I had in fact figured that out, youngling," Elminster replied pleasantly. "Once, I'd've been flattered, but down my long years so many have lain in wait for me that the thrill is quite gone." He peered at them both, one after the other, tendering the same gentle smile. "I do hope ye're not disappointed."

Two faces glowered at him. One belonged to a highknight he knew, one Belsarth Hawkblade, a grim, oft-unshaven man of brutal ruthlessness but iron-hard loyalty to the Crown. The other was the man in robes and had a face unfamiliar to him—but kin to one he'd seen briefly in the fray at Tethgard; that of a war wizard busy mastering the art of the headlong, panic-ridden retreat. Scared down to his boots, he was.

"Hawkblade," he asked, nodding toward the pale, tight-faced mage, "who's thy friend? Wizard of War—?"

"Lorton Ironstone," the wizard answered curtly, not waiting for Hawkblade to speak. "And I am charged to ask you, Elminster of Shadowdale, if you will now surrender yourself peacefully into our custody to face the king's justice."

"Charged by whom?"

"Ganrahast, Royal Magician of the Realm," Ironstone snapped. "At the request of the king himself, Lord Vainrence gave us to believe."

Elminster nodded. There would be a third member of this welcoming foreguard, probably busy creeping up behind him right then . . .

"Well?" Ironstone snapped. "We require a reply, Old Sage of Shadowdale! In case it's escaped your notice, we're in Cormyr here—where *we* uphold the laws, not you. Laws that apply even to clever old archmages who customarily defy rules and do as they please. You, Elminster, stand accused of theft of Crown magic and of murder—of many sworn high-knights of the realm, including their lord commander, and of no less than four wizards of war."

"Murder? I was abed with my lady at night, out under the stars in the depths of the forest, when a dozen men set upon us, hurling spells despite my warnings that doing so would mean their deaths. We were attacked by a force that well outnumbered us, and we fought to defend ourselves. Some of our attackers fled by magic, and the rest perished in battle. Ye—who were not there—now deem their deaths 'murder'? A murderer is one who goes seeking the deaths of others and achieves them. They tried to be murderers, aye. They were also warned, all of them—and learned too late that foolish aggression has consequences."

Elminster paused then to give Ironstone a smile as thin as a ghost's. "A lesson ye, too, might well ponder at this time."

The war wizard's reply was an unlovely sneer. "Hoary old advice from a lone graybeard with a large mouth? I quake. Between, that is, gasps of disbelief at what some have the effrontery to say to try to justify their misdeeds. You admit you slew loyal Cormyreans who were on Crown business, while defying them. So you're a murderer. Don't seek to evade your fate through clever words. Nor by claiming you've led a long and high-minded life protecting and defending everyone."

The old man cast a swift look back over his shoulder, as if he could see clearly in the darkness, then faced the two Cormyreans again, still hefting the small items in his hands, and shrugged. "Yet I *am* a protector and defender. Why should that not be my justification? Ye are a wizard of war and use that to account for what ye do and the arrogance with which ye do it."

Ironstone was unimpressed. "You? Protector of what? Your own interests, most likely, that you trumpeted as those of Mystra when you were challenged. You were a meddler, a defier of authority, and a foe of kings. You never stood for any law, order, or rightful government—not like our mighty Vangerdahast."

"Thy last two sentences, I'll grant. I was not like him, though he grew to increasingly see matters as I did, as the years did to him what they did to me. He began as my apprentice—and in those days, when folk spoke of Vangey and used the word 'mighty,' the next word they always uttered was 'annoying.'"

Hawkblade hastily quelled something that sounded suspiciously like a snort of mirth.

War Wizard Ironstone shot him a look then turned his head to thrust that same glare at Elminster, who added, "Peace, fairness, and order I've sought, aye, but I'm still seeking a ruler who consistently seeks to achieve those, as opposed to finding them by accident from time to time. I may yet find one, mind; I've only been looking for twelve centuries or so."

"So you presume to sit in judgment of the Dragon Throne? To decide for yourself if you'll obey us?"

El faced him squarely. "I do. Most folk, even if they see a looming danger, do nothing. A problem for someone else to deal with, they tell themselves. They make excuses or shut it out of their minds or keep busy with the everyday things in their lives. So they do nothing. *I* don't."

"Making you, in my eyes, a rebel or at the very least an outlaw."

"Ah, another of those lawkeepers who decides on guilt without bothering with the little inconvenience of a trial or looking beyond first impressions or any of that. So tiresome, aye?"

"You mock me, old man. I say again, you stand in Cormyr and are subject to *my* authority, and I—"

"Nay. Not even the lowliest Cormyrean is subject to *thine* authority. If ye'd said 'our authority,' bothering to include the good knight who stands beside ye—"

"*Enough* bandying words. You dare not use your magic, I'm told, so you'll surrender to us now or we'll kill you."

"And how 'lawful' is that, young Ironstone?"

The war wizard smiled thinly. "You can stand where you are; you can advance, and so fall within reach of Sir Hawkblade's sword; or you can flee, giving me the right to kill a fugitive seeking to escape our custody."

"I see. Victory at all costs."

Ironstone shrugged. "Nothing matters in a fight—except winning."

Elminster's eyes were cold and steady on him, blue blazing up among the gray. "Oh? If nothing matters, lad, there's nothing worth fighting *for*."

"I tire of this," the war wizard snapped. "Hawkblade, take him!"

El promptly flung the something in his right hand into Ironstone's face. It exploded in a little burst of black powder that sent the mage sobbing to the floor in a frenzy of agonized helplessness, clawing at his face as he tried to gargle and shriek through his weeping.

"Black pepper!" the highknight snarled, snatching out and hurling a dagger at Elminster's throat. "You won't catch me with old Harper tricks!"

He sprang forward, his sword singing out of its scabbard—as Elminster plucked the thrown knife out of the air, whirled, and flung it hard into the throat of a second wizard of war, who was stealing cautiously up behind the Old Mage with a wand held ready. It struck pommel first, stunning the young newcomer into a wheezing inability to breathe. He toppled to the passage floor, clutching his throat.

Elminster kept on turning, coming round to face Hawkblade again in time to duck his left hand just under the sweep of the knight's reaching sword—and almost delicately lob the something in his left hand up into the highknight's face.

It burst with the same instantaneous ease as the pepper bomb, but its effects were very different. A sudden, blinding blaze made Hawkblade shriek and warmed Elminster's face as he ducked aside, eyes shut tight against the short but brilliant explosion. He kept on going until he fetched up against the passage wall. Then he turned and opened his eyes to survey the ruin he'd caused.

Two young fools of wizards of war writhed on the floor, fighting just to breathe, Ironstone's blinded face wet with streaming tears. Hawkblade—just as blind and in far more pain from the dazzle powder, to boot—was slashing the air with desperate, brutal savagery. He was also turning toward the sounds El had made coming up against the wall, so Elminster lost no time in ducking down to pluck Ironstone's handy dagger from its belt sheath in case he needed something to parry with.

It was a nice toy—enchanted to glow upon command, and so could buy him one hurled spell this side of insanity—and he smiled at it as he hastened on into the palace.

Behind him, Hawkblade tripped over the third member of the foreguard, the wizard who'd held the wand—ah, and *that* useful thing should be retrieved, too!—and crashed headlong to the floor, hacking so hard behind himself as he went down that sparks rang from the stones.

Elminster turned to look for the wand—and another dagger came whirling out of the darkness to strike and rebound off the one he'd just purloined, so hard that it numbed his fingers and made a sound like a bell.

"*Hold*, intruder!"

That new voice belonged to another highknight—or at least a knight—at the head of four or five heavily armored fellows. They had another wizard of war with them, too. Safely at the back of the group, of course.

Elminster sighed. If he turned back, they'd have the gods alone knew what sort of guards and traps and wards waiting to greet him, the next time he tried.

The knights rushed forward, swords out and spreading out as they came. A telltale glow moved with them, a starlight sheen in the darkness that warned any mage they were magically protected.

El sighed again. If, that is, there *was* a next time.

One spell would have to do it, then he'd be scrabbling in his pouches for the last few Harper tricks. If he was still alive enough to do anything.

"*Hold*, men of Cormyr! Down steel, all! Wizards of war, stay your spells! This is a royal command!"

That voice was as hard as swung steel and as cold as the

winter wind, and it came from behind the highknights, who swung their heads around to see whence those orders had come.

A pale glow lit the darkness of the cellars, a cold and flickering halo around a striding woman in full plate armor. Helmless and wild-haired she came, with eyes like two dark flames and arms flung wide.

The Steel Regent, looking for all the realm like her huge portrait in the Hall of Approach before the Throne Chamber; Princess Alusair Obarskyr, as she'd been in the prime of her life, long before.

She was dead, of course—must be—and a moment later the knights realized they could see through her in places, as she strode toward them.

"'Tis a trick!" one of them snarled. "A false seeming, cast by yon villain!" He pointed one gauntleted finger at Elminster and turned to resume his charge at the old man.

"Highknight Morlen Askalan," the princess snapped, still striding hard and fast, "are you loyal to the Dragon Throne or not? You heard me! Throw down your weapon, and stand where you are!"

"You're a ghost or a spell cast by this enemy mage!" the knight growled, waving his sword at her. "My oath is to the king!"

"Do none of you know me?" the apparition demanded, striding among them. A highknight swung his sword through her; it passed through her arm and breast as if through empty air, earning him only her scowl.

"You're Alusair, you are," another knight muttered. "Bedder of nobles, war-leader of the realm, fiery daughter of the Purple Dragon himself."

"And you're a *ghost*," Highknight Askalan repeated. "You wander the haunted wing of the palace, and moan how the realm has fallen since your day!"

Alusair strode right up to him, a bitter smile twisting her lips. Despite himself, Askalan flinched back from her dark gaze.

"My, my," she remarked. "Overheard and spied upon, as usual—what must a girl *do* to get a little privacy around here?"

And she strode right through him. In her wake he toppled to the passage floor with a crash, numbed and helpless, sword skittering away across the stones.

Alusair never slowed but stepped right through the weakly struggling Lorton Ironstone—who collapsed onto his face with a sigh and lay still—and walked on to Hawkblade. His struggles, too, ceased, and she dealt with the war wizard who'd come at Elminster from behind, ere she turned back to the thoroughly cowed highknights and said quietly, "I gave an order. Swords down, men. Now."

One highknight hesitated, and another burst forward to swing his blade at Elminster.

Alusair became a rushing wind that met him half a pace away from the Old Mage and sent him face-first to the floor, white-faced and shivering uncontrollably.

Stepping away from his twitching limbs, she faced the few knights who were left and gave them a glare that lasted until sword after sword was dropped.

When the clatter of the last one had died, she said, "Sit down here and await the recovery of your fellows. Do *not* follow the Sage of Shadowdale as he enters Our home, for it is also *his* home. He is always welcome here."

She bent her stare upon them until the last knight had sat himself down, then gave Elminster a wry smile.

"Thank ye, lass," he said quietly, bowing low to her. She held out her hand, and he bent and kissed it, never flinching from the cold that made the nearby watching highknights wince.

Then he rose, waved a hand at her in salute, and turned to trudge on into the undercellars.

"You're welcome," Alusair told his back. "Many have defended Cormyr. You, Elminster—more than me; more than my father; more than Vangey, damn him; more than anyone— are the one who's defended Cormyr against itself."

CHAPTER
SIX

A CHALICE, MUCH BLOOD, AND A MASKED PRINCESS

Dark dreams torment me, wizard!
Nightmares of a crown, a chalice, much blood,
And a masked princess
Can it all be born, think you, of something I ate?

said by Nargreth the Doomed King
in Act I, Scene V of the play
The Fall of the Proud House
by Darindral Haeleth, published in the Year of
Three Heroes United

I know not *why* the Open Feast's held on the score-and-sixth night of Mirtul, lass," Lord Parespur Bloodbright said testily, jerking at her arm to drag her attention back to him.

Amarune blinked at him, turning only reluctantly away from staring up at the magnificent gilded statues guarding the double doors of Dragontriumph Hall. They were, if she hadn't lost count of grand staircases, three floors above the street and just about at the south wall of the royal palace.

"It just *is*," snarled the young nobleman who'd hired her for the night, "and always has been, since the king was young. So stop asking tomfool questions, and start acting smitten with me. All I want to hear out of you is moans of desire for my manly charms and murmured thanks when I offer you something! You're being very well paid for this, remember?"

Amarune nodded hastily, gave him a smile, and moaned as requested, lips parted to let every nearby eye in the palace see her tongue. Dropping her eyelids half over her eyes, she purred like a cat, as she often did when leaning forward from the edge of the Dragonriders' Club stage—and Bloodbright brightened visibly.

"That's the way of it!" he said delightedly. "Oh, they'll be so jealous! I can't wait to see their faces—Delcastle's, most of all!"

"By my sword!" a splendidly dressed young noble exclaimed delightedly from behind them, striding around to stand in front of Bloodbright and adjusting his monocle as a deft excuse to thrust his nose practically into Amarune's bosom. "Who *is* this enchanting creature, Bloodbright? Where've you been hiding her?"

"Heh heh," her patron for the evening replied jovially, swelling up almost visibly as he started to preen. "Now, Reinlake, I can't be giving away *all* my secrets. Ladies of taste know what they like, of course, and can't help but cast their eyes at the most *rampant* stags, eh, what?"

The two young lords roared out almost identical dirty laughs and dug each other in the ribs like two drunken drovers, as Amarune smiled prettily up into Bloodbright's face and kept her own countenance serene—and her eyes steady, not rolling—through extreme effort.

She was well aware of many other eyes on her, drinking in her dark beauty. She'd been receiving such stares since back at the palace gates. Not that she wasn't used to avid looks, and more, throughout most evenings. Amarune knew she had a magnificent figure—more the result of a wasp-thin waist and a sleekly muscled body than the overly lush curves possessed by some of her fellow dancers at the Dragonriders'—and a strikingly beautiful face, thanks to eyes that were larger and darker than most. Add to that her long, swirling fall of dark hair and the graceful, flowing movements she'd worked so hard to make her unwavering habit, and she drew gazes wherever she went.

Even if Bloodbright proved to be a clumsy lover when he inevitably bedded her at the end of this long night, there were far worse ways to earn coin than to spend an evening as the hired arm-adornment of a young noble attending a palace feast. There'd be good food and better wine in her near future, as well as much to see and hear. Not just the splendors of the palace and its new-to-her gossip, but possible clients among the ambitious nobility who'd be attending. A chance to put names to faces, at least, and judge which lords she should "work" for, and which she'd probably prefer to avoid, when they sent their messengers. Only a bold few, such as Bloodbright, made it as far as the Dragonriders' while out on their evening revelries; most preferred haughtier and more exclusive establishments, and only sent envoys into more common places to do their looking for them.

Still guffawing, Lord Reinlake swept past them into the hall, and Amarune found herself being whirled along in his wake, on Bloodbright's arm through a chicane of hanging lamps and tapestries into the bright and noisy gaiety of Dragon-triumph Hall during an evening court feast.

The Open Feast, she'd been curtly told before Bloodbright had run out of patience, was called that because—out of a tra-dition so venerable its origins had been forgotten—no royalty attended, so the feasters could speak more freely.

They were certainly doing that. And enthusiastically shout-ing, singing, and making rude noises and impersonations, too. Not that Bloodbright was going to stand for her stopping long enough to really see or hear any of it yet; he was thirsty and was heading with swift urgency around the long table that dominated the room to a dimly lit archway where a cellarer was shooing servers with platters of tallglasses out into the great chamber like bees leaving a hive. Thirsty guests in the royal palace were *not* to be kept waiting.

The din in the hall was deafening. A chapbook scribbler like Flarm "Mouth of Suzail" would have described the scene around Amarune right now something like: "Over splendid food in luxurious surroundings, bright young ambitious things mingle with jaded nobles and urbane courtiers, fluted wineglasses in hand, discussing the morrow of Cormyr—and jockeying for power in that future." Amarune knew that, because those were the very words Flarm had used to describe last year's Open Feast. Tress had kept that yellowing chapbook and had produced it triumphantly for Amarune's perusal upon hearing of this night's work.

What—if Flarm could be trusted—was evidently the usual long feasting table ran like a lance down the length of

Dragontriumph Hall, lined with chairs for a formal dinner. That night, however, it was set for "catch table," where diners helped themselves to platters and moved freely about. She'd talked to some of the girls who'd been to other feasts, and knew that later, once many guests had become weary of drinking and nibbling—or drowsy thanks to overindulgence—the few who preferred to sit and eat more than circulate and talk would be joined by many more in the chairs, but at the moment almost everyone was standing and talking.

And *talking*.

By the gods, she'd heard shrieking children's fights that were quieter!

Bloodbright stopped with a smile in front of an elder servant he obviously knew, who was pouring wine from a decanter into tallglasses deftly plucked from a server's platter and offering them wordlessly to feaster after feaster, accepting dregs and empties in return with practiced and politely silent elegance.

"Fair evening, my lord!" the cellarer smiled and extended that smile with a nod in Amarune's direction, without making it a leer. "Lady!"

She smiled back at him then looked swiftly and—she hoped—longingly up at her patron, who flushed with pleasure as he took a tallglass and replied. "'Tis indeed, Jamaldro! Charsalace, is it? Ah, good, good! A glass for my lady!"

One was put into Amarune's fingers with a deft flourish, and Bloodbright smilingly propelled her away along the dim rear expanse of the hall, where knots of nobles were standing, drinks in hand, talking excitedly.

He strolled a winding way through them, obviously showing her off. Amarune kept her eyes firmly on him, an expression of ardent worship on her face, but listened hard to the snatches of converse they were passing.

". . . oh, it's haunted, all right! An entire wing of the palace! That's why they built this new one we're standing in, see?"

"*I* heard it was magic raging through it that they couldn't stop, that made them shutter yon wing and leave it abandoned—for years, now! *Surely* we've priests enough to end the hauntings in all that time, no matter *how* many there are!"

"Essard, Essard, you should find one of your servants with kin working at the palace and ply them with drink some night—your worst wine will do—and hear the *real* tales told around here! They've *tried* priests in plenty! They've even reclaimed rooms here and there, for a few months . . . but again and again they find courtiers and war wizards lying dead in its passages!"

Despite herself, despite having heard wilder rumors about the haunted wing of the palace scores of times, Amarune trembled in delicious fear.

The whole palace knew the Princess Alusair rode the halls of the haunted wing on a spectral horse. In utter silence and in full armor she went, wild-eyed and with a bloody sword in her hand, passing through walls, floors, ceilings— and foolish courtiers—freely. The touch of her sword slew, and her ghostly hand passing through you chilled you to the bone and left you shivering for days. Those she just glared at were haunted by her eyes, seeing her cold gaze again and again in their waking hours thereafter. Why—

Amarune felt a sharp pain just under her ribs. Lord Bloodbright had noticed her head turning away and had pinched her, hard. She looked swiftly back up at him—and found herself meeting an almost murderous glare.

She grimaced a swift and silent apology and hastened to move against him like a roused wanton, grinding against his hip. That restored his smile, but Amarune found herself right beside some old blowhard of a fat merchant in wine-stained velvet who'd evidently decided that this chatter about the Ghost Regent was sorely in need of some supercilious correction.

"You would do *well* to *remember*," he brayed, "that the Princess Alusair is what is popularly known as a tormenting ghost, and shares those shadowed halls with risen-from-their-graves courtiers who now walk as skeletons, decrepit skeletons, and shambling horrors—these last being the same walking dead known in less *refined* cities, such as Waterdeep, as 'zombie rotters.'"

He winced, lip curling in exaggerated disgust at such nomenclature, waved a chubby and many-ringed hand that glistened with the grease of the batter-fried prawns he'd been devouring with zealous greed, and added, "There are also a few battle wights—once palace guards—and even sword wraiths, these last being the remnants of corrupt highknights, who fly about wielding black swords. Deadly, utterly *deadly*."

"You've seen all these grisly spirits *personally*, Orstramagrus?" The younger Lord Dawntard was a sly, sardonic man, and even his friendly utterances sounded like sneers. This one was none too friendly and was delivered in a voice already slurred with drink.

The fat merchant flushed. "More than a few, young Kathkote. More than a few."

A hiss of gleeful anticipation arose among the cluster of courtiers and young nobles standing near. Even Amarune knew that reply was a deft dig, to be sure; the elder Lord Dawntard, Kathkote's father, had been a bold farfarer across the Realms in his day, whereas the son had never ventured farther from Suzail than the family hunting lodges, upcountry. Dawntard's usual companions, the younger lords of Windstag and Sornstern, chuckled aloud as they pressed closer, so as to miss nothing of Dawntard's furious reaction.

Unexpectedly, Kathkote grinned. "Oooh, cleverly said, Old Ostra, cleverly said. You *do* have some dash left in you."

Lord Broryn Windstag's face actually fell in disappointment. The big, florid, blustering scourge of stags and bold warrior had obviously been hoping for a fight, with his everpresent toady Lord Delasko Sornstern at his elbow.

A cellarer deftly steered full tallglasses of dragonslake into the hands of all three lords, pointedly serving the merchant and the courtiers from a decanter of Charsalace—a fine wine, but very far from dragonslake—so as to leave the lords preening at the silent recognition of their status.

Bloodbright seemed to have little taste for tarrying where bullying young rivals might try to snatch the mysterious lovely on his arm away from him; he whirled Amarune hastily away. Almost to the far end of the room, where the high windows of Dragontriumph Hall afforded a view of many lighted windows across the courtyard. Courtiers not exalted—or idle—enough to be invited to the Open Feast were hard at work behind those windows, in the huge, curving string of interconnected buildings known as the royal court, which shielded the royal palace on two sides from all the bustle and unwashed rest of Suzail.

Amarune had a brief glimpse of tall, dark portraits mounted on the pillars between those windows. Each was startlingly realistic and life-size. There was a masked princess wearing one crown and holding another that dripped blood, and there was a king in blood-drenched armor, rising up in his saddle at the heart of a gory battlefield to hold a gleaming chalice aloft in laughing triumph.

Stirring scenes that caught the eye and imagination. Obarskyrs, no doubt, but which ones, and why had they been painted thus?

She knew she dared not ask the man whose hip she still rode, who was starting to parade her down the other side of the long table.

Where the chatter sounded even *more* interesting.

"Ho, Marlin! I know you were hard at work on *something* to do with our shared hobby! Anything you can discuss, yet?"

"Heh, no, not yet, Mellast. Not yet. It'll be worth the wait though, believe you me."

"... ah, but that wouldn't be smugglers at all! That'd be our daring Silent Shadow!"

"Silent Shadow? Sounds like something fat old noblewomen titter over and vie to be ravished by!"

Amarune managed not to stiffen. Well, we all have our secrets ...

"Perhaps so, perhaps so. D'you mean to say you've not heard of him? Or her, for all I know!"

"Milvarune is *so* backward, my dear Jhalikoe. We stagger along from season to season hearing almost nothing of fair Cormyr except the exploits of Krimsal—quite the villain, that one. Almost like our nobles out east!"

"Oh, he's no worse than a lot of our other Cormyrean lords, believe you me; he's just more open about what he's up to—*most* of the time. Right now, he's in hiding, and no wonder, considering some of the murders and mutilations he managed this last winter."

"Ah." The envoy from Milvarune was obviously newly arrived in Cormyr. He thanked a server with a silent smile and nod for the tallglass that had just been steered into his hand. "Yet I take it this Shadow is more a thief than a slayer? More like your Skult and Vandarl?"

"Ah, so your staff *has* told you some useful things; good, good. Yet the Silent Shadow's not like Skult or Vandarl at all. That is to say, they all steal, yes, but 'Skull and Van' are thieves for hire, and good ones. You'd best beware of them; our wealthy nobles can't use either to rob fellow nobles, because these two miscreants are wise enough to refuse such tasks—but *can* freely use them to rob or harass non-noble creditors or those who get above themselves and presume to challenge nobles when it comes to competing in trade matters. The Shadow, now, is different. A loner, a thief of great daring, who works by night, purloining coins and jewelry from seemingly inaccessible nobles' bedchambers and locked tower-top rooms."

"Ah, I see! So fat old noblewomen *would* titter and coo over him!"

"Indeed! Oh, you're going to fit in here in Suzail just fine!"

Abruptly firm fingers dug like daggers into Amarune's elbow and steered her away. Lord Bloodbright, it seemed, knew just how long tarrying could continue before it became obvious eavesdropping.

They threaded their ways through gusts of laughter and around a drunken courtier noisily imitating an effeminate visiting noble of Sembia in a manner that would have earned him a death-challenge had any Sembians been within earshot, to a cluster of men speaking in low tones, almost face to face. One was the darkly handsome Lord Rothglar Illance, a lordling Amarune had been warned about. Not that she'd have failed to be on her very best behavior anyway, with Illance's tall, muscular mountain of a bodyguard, Marlazander the Mighty, standing right behind his lord, constantly peering this way and that, looking for trouble with a face of cold menace.

Bloodbright firmly led Amarune to the table, where some feasters had started to take seats. As they approached, Bloodbright went tense against Amarune, who saw the reason why a moment later.

One of the highest-ranking servants of the palace had just slipped into the chamber and was advancing in smooth haste toward them.

Or rather, was approaching a man seated at the feasting table almost right in front of them, whom Amarune only then recognized: Ganrahast, the Royal Magician of Cormyr.

Understeward Corleth Fentable bent over beside Ganrahast, murmured something, then stood smoothly back and turned away. Amarune knew that although Fentable hadn't once glanced in their direction, she and Bloodbright had been noticed, judged, and almost certainly found wanting.

She forgot about that a moment later, when Ganrahast, the leader of the wizards of war, rose from his seat wearing a frown—and hurried out.

Faster than Amarune had ever seen any war wizard move before.

Many of the nobles around were frowning, too.

Evidently the Royal Magician had been moving faster than any of them had ever seen him move before, too.

Chapter
SEVEN

Nobles, Shadows, and Deadly Doings

Curse it all, wizard!
When did this fair realm of mine become what it now is?
All nobles, shadows, and deadly doings,
With no one even pausing for naps between their villainies.

> said by Nargreth the Doomed King
> in Act I, Scene I of the play
> *The Fall of the Proud House*
> by Darindral Haeleth, published in the Year of
> Three Heroes United

But what of Baron Boldtree?"

Marlin Stormserpent made haste to drift away from that question and the excited young nobles listening to it, thankful he'd kept to his feet and had no need to rise from a chair, and so be noticed moving away.

He wanted nothing at all to do with Lord Royal Erzoured Obarskyr and his little schemes, whether the man called himself 'Baron Boldtree' or not. That one was a smilingly cold-blooded, untrustworthy danger to all nobles. Those who rode too close beside him would lose their heads alongside him, when the time came.

And it would, he had no doubt of that.

No, *this* incipient traitor prided himself on being rather more subtle than softly smiling Boldtree. Let others admire the Lord Royal or the power he was gathering unto himself, all nobles and shadows and deadly doings; the pride of House Stormserpent had other, quieter steeds to ride.

At that moment, just when he was beginning to think he'd be forever toying with the almost-empty tallglass he'd been nursing, Marlin saw what he'd been waiting for and smiled. At last.

Ganrahast's departure from the Open Feast had been gratifyingly abrupt. So would his be.

Setting his tallglass down on the feasting table, Marlin turned toward the garderobes, as if his haste was due to a need to relieve himself.

The hour *was* growing late, after all.

On his brisk way down Dragontriumph Hall, he saw something else that made him smile. Six war wizards at the feast whom old Jamaldro had unwittingly served with drugged wine—*such* a creature of careless habit, our senior cellarer, always setting out his decanters just so, long before they'd be needed, and trust the highnosed mages to want their own, oh-so-special vintage—were all slumping in their seats, as if overcome by drink.

Once he was inside the archway that led into the garderobes, where he could see out into the hall but its shadowed gloom would conceal him from those still by the table, under the lamps, Marlin turned, surveyed the Open Feast, and let his smile broaden.

Certain other guests had observed his departure and in turn had risen to depart. They were all heading his way, as they'd been paid to do. Like him, they would drift first to the garderobes and then sidle onward. Not home, but deeper into the palace.

The carelessness of whose guards was becoming simply shocking, these nights.

The noise of the feast was far behind them now.. They walked warily on into deepening, almost velvet silence. The passage was dark, and the room they were stepping into even darker.

"I've never been in this part of the palace before," someone muttered. "No guards, no war wizards . . ."

"They've few enough left of either, these days," Marlin Stormserpent told them calmly from the darkness at the back of the room. "You're late."

"We were followed," came the curt reply from a man still wiping blood from his hands. He'd killed before, but butchering a war wizard had to be done in haste, before the mage could get out a spell or send some magical cry for aid. "We've taken care of our little shadow."

"Darrake Harnwood?"

"Yes. We put his head down a garderobe shaft."

"Good." Stormserpent was pleased and let them hear it. "However, every killing is someone who will be discovered, probably sooner rather than later. So let's be about matters."

"We're all here," someone else said simply. "I counted."

"I trust all of you counted the coins I paid you, too?" Marlin asked coolly, and without waiting for a reply told the men standing close around him, "The undead of the haunted wing are real, but very few. If you come with me and do what I've paid you to do, destroying the handful or so of skeletons and wraiths you'll meet, you'll have done Cormyr a great service."

"Why are there undead in the royal palace at all?" someone muttered. "Have the war wizards grown so feeble as all that?"

Marlin smiled. "The war wizards *command* the undead, using them as guardians to keep everyone out of the haunted wing—where the Obarskyrs keep most of the wealth they seize from citizens, the dark magic they've collected over the centuries, and . . . certain prisoners. Nobles and commoners who have become too great a challenge to the Crown."

"Belnar? Thol Morand?"

"Among others. And unless you want to join them, you must all keep as silent as the tomb—ha ha—about what you've done, until I can make sure *all* the undead are gone, or you'll be seen in the city not as heroes but as the war wizards will portray you: traitors plotting against the Dragon Throne."

"Ganrahast is so stlarning *suspicious*," someone snapped. "He sees traitors behind every door and around every corner."

"The war wizards," someone else said gloomily. "The doom of the realm and its real rulers. *Always*, when there's trouble, it's the war wizards."

"A threat to every Cormyrean—even the royal family," another agreed.

"The sooner they're all killed off," Marlin told his hirelings smoothly, "in a series of *accidental* demises too deft and veiled to raise any general alarm, the better."

That brought nods, and he added quietly, "Now come. Into the haunted wing. Swords out, all."

Great arched doors had been locked across the main passage, but there was an easy way around them, through a room whose connecting doors were neither locked nor barred.

When they got three steps beyond that room, two skeletons strode to meet them—one a dust-shrouded, floating assembly of bones too decrepit to fit together anymore, the other newer and more intact.

Stormserpent strode straight on, raising his sword and pointing at the undead. "Hack them apart. Then shatter all the bones. No shouting, no clangings. Do this quietly."

Fear rose in him as empty eyesockets turned his way. They were dead or should be dead, not moving forward in silent menace, swords lashing out—

One of his hirelings snapped, "Quickly—before something *else* shows up!"

There followed a general rush and a frenzied hewing and hacking.

Stormserpent peered ahead into the gloom. The faint glows of old lighting spells, long unrenewed, kept the empty wing from pitch darkness, but he'd have been much happier if he'd dared bring lots of lanterns and walk along in proper brightness. In the shadows, anything could be . . .

Anything was. Another less-than-whole skeleton with a zombie—no, two zombies—lurching in its wake. Behind them, something dark, almost batlike, glided. One of the wraiths. *Real* trouble.

Marlin turned to his hirelings. "Get them!" he hissed. "There'll be more! You and you—watch behind us and our flanks!"

He was scared, all right. He could taste it, and the excitement was making him tremble. Not that he'd have dared such a thing at all if he hadn't had his amulet. An old family treasure that the gods alone remembered which errant ancestral

Stormserpent had got and from where, that was said to render the one who wore it "immune to what undead can do, beyond purely physical woundings."

Not that there was a Stormserpent alive who'd tested those claims. A visiting Sembian had confirmed there was "strong magic" on the nondescript, tarnished little pendant and had ventured the opinion that it *should* protect Marlin—but not anyone with him—against life drain, soul reaping, and other such necrotic dooms. But the Sembian had admitted that was just his guess. And it would be an idiot's death to trust over-much in a greedy outlander's guess.

The skeleton was down; one shattered bone skittered past Marlin's boots. The zombies, too, had been hewn apart by men with their teeth clenched in distaste.

The sword wraith hung back; Marlin took a step toward it and ordered, "Stand together, now. Some of these horrors can leap around."

His hirelings were only too happy to obey; they were still drawing together into a shuffling ring, holding their swords very carefully to keep from slicing each other, when what the wraith had been waiting for appeared.

Down the passage toward them came a helmed and armored warrior with gray, dead flesh, and eyes that blazed with an eerie emerald glow. More of that glow flickered and played around its arms and shanks as it stalked forward, moving far more like a living warrior than the undead they'd faced thus far.

"It's just one guardsman and what used to be a highknight," Marlin announced dismissively. "Hack yon greeneyes apart, but keep your eye on the wraith. The highknights were used to sneaking and stabbing, not facing down bands of armed men. As long as we keep at it, once it's alone, we can take it easily. Just *keep hacking.*"

He proved to be right. The hirelings hacked in frantic fear, the wight went down swiftly, literally cut apart as it fought, and the wraith tried to stab and whirl away, only to find itself pursued and hewn down.

Well, now. This was proving *easy*.

Moreover, the wraith had tried something on Marlin with its sword—a blade that had seemed almost a part of it, a thin line of shadow no different than the rest—that had numbed and chilled him for a breath-snatching moment . . . then simply had faded away. A warmth spread from his amulet and steadied him.

Well, then. Not that the heir of House Stormserpent saw any need to tell his hirelings about the amulet, nor that he felt any more emboldened then when they'd first gathered.

"We go on," he ordered. "I'm not expecting the gold to be just lying around. If we're to find it at all, we'll need time enough to really search. Let's find and destroy the rest of these walking dead."

He doubted very much they'd find any gold at all, or prisoners—being as he'd invented all of that earlier this evening, above the gleam of the silver finery on the feast table. Just as he'd invented the "ball of spellplague in the little coffer" to lure the Royal Magician away from Dragontriumph Hall. Word of which had passed from his hired informant to the ear of War Wizard Vainrence, who'd sent word on to his superior Ganrahast via the understeward of the palace . . . it was nice to know war wizards could be just as gullible as anyone else.

Not that Marlin was bothered about what these hirelings might think; very few of them were likely to live long enough for their opinions about anything to matter.

They advanced through the haunted wing in a small, tight band around him, confident now and quiet, ready for trouble.

Marlin allowed himself a small smile and the words, "Good work. I'll have more of it for you all, soon enough."

Empty promises were always a useful tool.

He had no intention of trusting in these sword-brawn swindlers after that night. Not if he could control even a few of the Nine.

The Nine. The blueflame ghosts . . .

He couldn't wait to have *them* at his beck and call, to send into danger like this on his behalf.

Very soon, he'd have two of them. The Flying Blade had

long been a treasure of his family, and he knew where the Wyverntongue Chalice was.

He could almost *taste* the power.

Lothrae had promised. Until together they controlled four or more of the Nine, those they did have would be Marlin's to command as he saw fit—and, by the Dragon Throne, there was a lot he planned to do with them before that fourth ghost was found!

Below, in the deep gloom, Marlin Stormserpent and his band of hirelings advanced cautiously along the great passage that ran down the heart of the haunted wing.

Princess Alusair turned from the rail of the balcony where she'd been watching them, as swiftly as if she'd been thrusting a sword.

"I could kill all these fools in less time than it would take you to get down yon stairs to hail them," she hissed. "Why shouldn't I? *Why*, Old Mage? Why?"

The chill emanating from her made Elminster's teeth chatter, but he stood his ground. "I know how ye feel, lass."

"Seething," she snapped. "That's how I feel, right now. So put an arm around my shoulder and soothe me, wizard. Or by my father's sword, I'll be down from this balcony and killing them all, before you can—"

"Easy, Alusair. Easy," he murmured, doing just as she'd bade him. His arm encountered nothing solid, only a terrible cold. A flesh-freezing chill that made him stagger, yet he tried to hold her comfortingly. And failed.

Alusair watched him stumble back against the nearest pillar, gray and gasping. Her face was not friendly.

"Not yet, lass," he muttered at her when he could speak again. "There'll come a time to smite these worms, to be sure. Probably not long from now."

She glared at him. "Not yet, not now, await the right time . . . how can you be so farruking *patient*, Old Mage?"

Elminster shrugged, looking back at her with eyes that blazed with the same rage that was almost choking her.

"It helps," he whispered fiercely, "to be insane."

"They seem rather disappointed to find only dark emptiness, shrouded furniture, and a distinct lack of chained maidens, imprisoned nobles, and heaps of gold," Alusair said tartly, a little later. "Poor little pillagers."

She peered down from a high balcony in the last room of the haunted wing. Young Lord Stormserpent seemed to be tugging something out of an inner pocket in the breast of his darkly fashionable jerkin. "What's he up to *now*?"

Elminster shrugged. "That's a map, so I'd say he's now going to tour the palace in search of a magic he thinks is hidden here."

"One of his precious Nine? Can't I kill him now? Really, El! *You* may not care what is stolen or despoiled in these halls, but this is my home—*I* care very much!"

Then she saw that the old wizard's hands clutched the balcony rail so hard they were white and shaking.

It seemed Elminster had discovered that he cared very much, too.

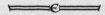

"Heartened, saer?"

"Of course," Marlin replied, smiling a real smile. "Not a man lost, and all the undead who dared stand against us destroyed with admirable ease and swiftness. We've time left to try to accomplish something that should prove much easier than facing down hauntings."

"Oh, aye?" The hiresword's voice held a subtle note of disbelief. He'd survived being hired by many overconfident patrons before—and hoped to live long enough to be hired by many more again. "So we're bound deeper into the palace?"

"Of course. I must check the accuracy of these maps and find the way to the legendary Dragonskull Chamber."

"Where the Royal Magician died?"

"That's the place," Marlin said cheerfully, consulting his map again and then waving at the armed men around him to turn down *that* side passage.

Most of Suzail knew no one dared enter the Dragonskull Chamber.

Most of Cormyr knew that name belonged to a heavily warded spellcasting chamber hidden somewhere deep in the royal palace, that was shunned because the Royal Magician Caladnei, ravaged by the Spellplague, had died inside it one night eighty years before.

Among courtiers and nobles, it was said that not even the most powerful war wizards could penetrate its mighty wards. Dragonskull still stood dark, empty, and shunned, its never-locked doors closed, because of its many warding spells. Those magics had been so twisted in the Spellplague that all spellhurlers avoided them; they still worked and were linked to so many other spells laid on the palace down the centuries that they couldn't be destroyed without a *lot* of careful, exacting quelling and dispelling—for who still alive knew or remembered all that those magics were holding up, or binding in check?

The twisted wards still roiled constantly, in a way that unsettled the minds of all mages. Marlin himself had once seen a white-faced war wizard spewing up a good meal before collapsing on his face in his own mess, and had been told the man had ended up that way by merely trying to walk across the infamous chamber—despite giving up and fleeing right back out again after only a few steps.

However, neither he nor any of these hireswords, unless they'd been lying to him—and deserved any doom they tasted, thereby—were spellcasters.

He and all Stormserpents had a very good, longstanding reason for wanting to get past the roiling wards around the Dragonskull Chamber. Unfinished family business that even in his youth had excited him. Something he'd long dreamed of taking care of . . .

Seizing the Wyverntongue Chalice.

Alone among living men—thanks to the unfortunate demises of certain of his kin, Marlin Stormserpent knew where the chalice was hidden. A secret not even Caladnei and Vangerdahast had known, something hidden, presumably, even from the very ghosts of the palace. Behind a false wall—and those tainted, roiling wards that had so effectively kept nosy war wizards at bay—in a forgotten room behind, but not actually in, the Dragonskull Chamber.

So, thanks to years of energetic and handsomely paid spies and informants, he had maps of the palace, many accounts of where the room he was seeking must be, and a strong band of armed men around him, inside the palace and moving fast.

Oh, yes, Marlin let himself smile more broadly than he'd beamed for many a day. He was trembling so much that Thirsty shifted recklessly inside the breast of his jerkin, his stinger grating along the metal plates he wore across his chest.

Lord Marlin Stormserpent, who might soon be so much more, allowed himself an eager chuckle. He could almost feel the chalice in his hands ...

CHAPTER
EIGHT

MUCH BRAZEN CREEPING ABOUT

Living in a Palace reminds one daily of all life holds:
Birth, death, grief, betrayal, theft, malice, lust, and trysting,
Bright triumph, decisions wise and otherwise,
And a whole brazen lot of creeping about and spying.

Amaelia Sandrael,
Doom at Every Hand: Forty Years in Royal Service
published in the Year of the Dozen Dwarves

Where are they heading, d'ye think?" Elminster gasped, as he fetched up against a doorframe and clung to it, fighting for breath.

Where the ghostly princess could fly, he had to walk. Even when he sprinted, he couldn't move nearly as fast as Alusair.

She'd long since taken to repeatedly racing off to check on Stormserpent's band and then returning to the Old Mage, as he panted his way along dark palace passages, hoping he'd not meet anyone.

If he did, he planned to pose as old Elgorn—with the aid of strips torn from some linens he'd purloined in the under-cellars and had just wound around most of his face in a false bandage—and tell some tale or other about discovering how long it had been since certain footings had been checked. "Mustn't let this grand place fall down about our ears, look ye!" he'd growl.

For years around the palace, he'd been old Elgorn Rhauligan, "repairer and restorer of the ever-crumbling stone, plaster, tapestries, and wood of these great buildings." Not to mention a descendant of the famous Glarasteer Rhauligan. Who didn't usually work alone, of course; Elgorn trusted in his scarcely younger sister, Stornara, to remember things and calculate stresses for him. Hardly anyone ever told her she looked like the old portrait of the Lady Bard of Shadowdale anymore, with Elminster's masking magics to make her appear as old as he.

Not that Elgorn Rhauligan was in any better shape to go rushing around the palace than Storm would be if she wore herself out racing back there from her farm kitchen in distant Shadowdale.

"Dragonskull, for all the gold in the upper treasury," Alusair answered him disgustedly. "Unless their thoughts are captivated by old and broken furniture."

Then she stiffened and lifted her head like a hound sniffing the wind. "Ganrahast and Vainrence, coming through the palace by different ways, both in a howling hurry! Both bound for the north turret . . . and Vainrence will get there first."

Elminster peered at her. "Ye can track anyone moving about the palace?"

"Of course not. Just these two, usually; I can *feel* all the magic they load themselves down with," Alusair snapped. "They often meet in a room right at the top of the north turret, where I can't go, presumably for discussions they want to keep *very* private. Want to listen in on this one? I've never seen them in such wild haste before!"

Elminster nodded thoughtfully, a fire kindling in his eyes. "I believe I do."

The eyes of the palace maid, staring ardently into his over their hungrily joined mouths, widened in sudden fear, and Lord Arclath Delcastle felt her stiffen all over.

He listened hard.

A man who was muttering to himself was trudging up the last few turns of the north turret steps before the topmost bedchamber.

Arclath left off kissing and cuddling the lass in his arms long enough to clap a swift hand over her mouth before she could so much as squeak, drag her around behind the wardrobe, and then silently—but fiercely—curse.

Last time, he'd *distinctly* heard the two wizards growl agreement that they were *never* going to climb all those stairs again, as they set off back down them.

Yet here they were again.

With furious energy, Arclath indulged himself in snarling the most flowery and fervent oaths he knew, but his profanities were utterly silent, blazing only in his mind.

Over his hand, the maid was staring at Arclath in stark terror as the wizard on the other side of the wardrobe went from murmuring to saying the clear—and distinctly irritated—words, "Come *on*, Gan. Let the courtiers see to their own tasks for once. We've *important* matters on our platters."

Arclath tried to give the chambermaid a reassuring look, but it didn't seem to work. And no wonder; they'd both recognized the voice of the wizard Vainrence, one of the most feared spellhurlers in the kingdom. The enforcer among the war wizards, the mage who could—and had—shattered the walls of a castle keep to get at traitors within.

"I heard you," another voice replied sourly from farther down the steps. The maid recognized it as well as Arclath; her eyes promptly rolled up in her head as she fell into a dead faint, sagging heavily in Arclath's arms.

On the other side of the wardrobe, the Royal Magician Ganrahast came into the bedchamber, breathing hard. The top of the north turret was a long climb.

"Yes?" he gasped.

" 'Tis urgent," Vainrence replied flatly, wasting no time on greetings.

"Always is." Gasp. "Urgent what?" Gasp.

"One of our informants just told me the nobles Rothglar Illance, Harmond Hawklin, and Seszgar Huntcrown are plotting treason. They plan to unleash what they refer to as a 'ball of spellplague' that they have locked in a small coffer, to flood the room with harmful wild magic at the Council of the Dragon."

Ganrahast didn't spend breath on a curse or a sigh. "Presumably the three are immune to its effects," he gasped, "and believe it will do harm—instantly debilitating harm—to their fellow nobles and the royal family, we mages, and courtiers."

"We war wizards, at the least," Vainrence agreed. "I can't see them as self-sacrifices to any cause. They intend to survive this unleashing."

Finding that that particular noble trio harbored treason was no news at all, but it was the first Delcastle had heard of a flying ball of spellplague. Was such a thing even possible?

"If this information is anywhere near truth," Ganrahast pointed out.

Vainrence shrugged. "Like you, I suspect the veracity of anything I'm freely told. Yet can we dare *not* take this seriously?"

"When we could be dooming the king? And most of the senior nobles of the realm with him? Hardly."

Vainrence spared himself enough time to curse. After a moment, Ganrahast joined him.

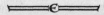

"I'll put the hilt in my mouth," Elminster whispered, settling himself on his side on the cold stone floor, "and share what my mind sees with thine, for as long as the magic holds out."

Alusair nodded and put out her hand to him.

Her touch was no more solid than a whisper, but her chill was deep, plunging him into uncontrollable shiverings in an instant.

Yet his word was his word, and she'd led him to a hidden Obarskyr dagger and offered him its magic without hesitation, so . . .

There was an instant of whirling nausea as El unleashed the spell and found it caught up in strong new wards that tore and twisted . . .

Until he could ride them, become one with them, and melt through them.

Typically unsubtle, brute force magework.

Wizards, these days . . .

Ganrahast started to pace. The windowless room near the top of the north turret held only an empty wardrobe, plain wooden bench, and a table along the wall beside it where a row of storm lanterns were kept ready, so he had plenty of room to stride.

That, the cloaking spells they'd cast on the chamber long before, and the room's deserted remoteness were why the two men liked to use it.

Vainrence was right, of course. They couldn't ignore the tip, even if it had come from someone quite likely paid to pass it on by a disguised someone else who likely intended it as misdirection. There was very little they could do about that; since the Spellplague, the mind-reaming that had once made Cormyr's wizards of war so feared—and effective—was useless.

The Crown's decreed death penalty for trying a mind-reaming was quite beside the point. Attempts by any wizard to use the reaming spells always resulted in that mage being driven to idiocy or instantly and severely spellscarred. So regardless of Foril's laws and the longtime refuge of no war wizard facing trial for what no king or courtier learned about, not a single war wizard dared mind-ream anyone—unless the mage was already dying and did it as a "last loyalty."

If things had been otherwise, a lot of sneering noble heads would probably long since have left their shoulders . . . but things weren't otherwise, and all Cormyr knew it.

"My turn," Ganrahast said quietly. "I overheard something interesting at the feast. Rumors about some nobles trying, sometime in the near future, a little foray into the haunted wing. What I could not learn—because the gossipers didn't know—was whether this was to be a lark, some sort of dare or rite of passage, or yet another attempt to get at all the treasure and prisoners and chained pleasure maidens we're supposed to keep hidden away there."

"You mean there aren't any pleasure maidens?" Vainrence joked. "Years I've been serving the Crown, *years*, man, in hopes of . . ."

"Har har *har*, Rence. Think about it. We'll double the guards on all ways in, of course. Who's behind it, that's what I'd like to know."

As everyone in the palace and most who worked in the royal court knew very well, the haunted wing of the palace really *was* haunted. Even war wizards avoided it as much as they could. The Blue Fire had twisted layers upon layers of wards cast down the centuries into dangerous magics no war wizard dared tamper with.

The Spellplague had wrought one good thing in the royal quarter of Suzail, and one thing only. No portal or any other sort of translocation magic worked properly anywhere within, into, or out of the palace, court, or royal gardens anymore, so the Crown was spared one worry. No one could magically whisk marauding monsters, would-be assassins, or small armies into the haunted wing or anywhere else near where the council would be held.

Ganrahast, Vainrence, and the most senior courtiers had already talked about raising spells to seal off the haunted wing during the council. The war wizards would have done so without wasting breath on a single word of discussion if they'd quite dared to cast wards that powerful inside the palace or had known the best web of spells to try to construct.

"The Shadovar, perhaps?"

With that quiet murmur, Vainrence voiced the longtime fear of both men: that Shadovar wizards had killed and are now impersonating the heads of many powerful noble families of Cormyr, and were now beginning to do the same with courtiers, so they'd soon gain control of the realm by stealth, without a sword being drawn or a spell hurled.

These dark thoughts had already made them suspicious of certain efforts, promoted by the War Wizard Baerold, to collect items of magic said to house the trapped essences of the Nine.

After all, Baerold just might be a Shadovar trying to use—and use up—the war wizards as his agents to get his hands on what three now-dead wizards had written of as the "blueflame ghosts" the Nine had become, which could be commanded by one who held the items that contained them, and who knew how to compel them.

Might be, but might not be, either. Ganrahast and Vainrence were the most powerful of the current wizards of war, and their spells—that fell far short of the mind-reaming of old—could find no hint of Baerold being anything more than a young, ambitious, rather romantic mage of middling skills and training. So they watched him very closely and were careful not to advance his training with any sort of alacrity.

Like most Cormyreans with ears, Ganrahast and Vainrence had heard legends of the Nine, the legendary band of adventurers destroyed more than twoscore-and-a-hundred summers earlier, when Laeral Silverhand—later famous as the Lady Mage of Waterdeep, and consort of the Blackstaff, Khelben Arunsun—was possessed by the fell Crown of Horns.

Being war wizards, they knew a little more about the Nine. Most nobles of Cormyr had heard rumors that some of the Nine still existed, trapped in magic items, and could be summoned forth from those items by those who held them—and knew how— to fight as the item-bearer's slaves.

Unless those three wizards, whose writings had been proven true in all other respects, had told the exact same lie, Ganrahast and Vainrence also knew the rumors of "blueflame ghosts that could be commanded as deadly slaves" were true.

With two men trying to pace back and forth in it, the room near the top of the north turret suddenly seemed small and crowded.

Elminster was suddenly back in darkness, the only radiance a faint glow from the ghostly face bending over him. The dagger had melted away entirely, its magic spent; his mouth held only the taste of old iron, a tang like long-shed blood.

He was cold, damnably cold . . .

The ghost of Alusair drew back from him. "Still alive, El?"

"Still alive," he mumbled through chattering teeth. "At least they're not plotting against the king, those two." Shaking his numbed arms to try to get some feeling back into them, he rolled over. "What of our greedy young robber noble and his merry band?"

"I'm going after them," Alusair announced, her eyes two dark holes in what was little more than a woman-shaped wisp of gray, a glow so faint it was barely there at all. "I won't slay them—yet. I, too, want to know what they're up to, here in my home. Yet there *is* something I must know, Old Mage."

She drifted closer to Elminster, her eyes darker still.

"Are you on Cormyr's side in this? Or still playing your larger games across the Realms, using us all like pawns on a chessboard?"

Elminster regarded her gravely. "I have *always* been on Cormyr's side, Princess. Yet, aye, I've always played those larger games, as ye put it, too. I must. There is no one else who can save the Realms."

"No one else you trust, you mean."

Elminster stared at her, and there was a tired look in his eyes. Silence stretched.

"Yes," he whispered at last. "Ye've said it true. There's no one else I can trust to save the Realms. That's my doom, lass."

As if in comment on his words, there came a faint metallic crash from behind them. It sounded as if an armored man had been hurled violently to the stone floor, two or three rooms back along the way they'd come.

Without a word Alusair whirled around and sped away, heading for the sound like a streaking arrow.

"There was a time," Elminster muttered a little testily, "when the Weave let me send eyes wherever I desired . . ."

Aye, there had been a time.

Long gone, so he stood mute, one more pillar in dim silence, and waited.

Only to blink in genuine surprise at who appeared around the corner, walking beside the flickering shadow of Alusair like an old friend, to reach out long and shapely arms to him and offer her mouth for a kiss.

Elminster obliged, feeling as elated as he was surprised.

"I trust," he said, when his lips were free to speak again, "ye'll find time and will enough to tell me thy reasons for returning so swiftly, hey? I thought we'd agreed on a strategy."

"We had," Storm agreed, "but matters changed." Her smile died swiftly, and she held out something small and round. "Behold one of the latest toys of the wizards of war."

Elminster peered at it. "An orb. Tell."

"Upon command, it captures speech and can later be made to emit what it has, ah, recorded as often as desired, for the hearing of others. The mages use it when questioning those they're suspicious of."

Elminster arched an eyebrow in the manner that meant it was a substitute for a mirthless smile. "Some war wizard is now missing this, I presume?"

"He will be when he wakes up," Storm replied, "but that may be a day or so from now. I'm afraid I hit him rather hard."

The look he went on giving her was both a silent question and the message that he wasn't in the mood for waiting much longer for answers, so she added, "I dislike being surprised by someone I am unaware of, who has obviously been following me for some time. I dislike even more men who wait until I'm sitting relieving myself to attack me."

Alusair's glow grew a little brighter. "I fear our current Crown magelings share the poor manners of much of their generation," she commented wryly.

"I doubt not thy justification for hitting a mage, nor decry thy wisdom in latching onto magic whenever possible," Elminster said. "I'm merely curious as to why ye're now back here, rather than a lot closer to Shadowdale."

"I overheard something you should hear, too," Storm replied, folding herself gracefully down onto the floor and murmuring something over the orb as she touched it. "The awakening word's graven on its underside," she announced. "You'll hear two wizards of war who were unaware of my presence."

The orb shook itself a little, and voices arose from it.

"Oho! Scared of the infamous Lady Dark Armor, are we?" A jovial, teasing man's voice.

"No, not *her*. If she still exists—if she ever did—I've not seen her." A younger, grimmer male voice.

"The Princess Alusair, then? Worth being scared of, that one, let me tell you!"

"No, it's the one called Elminster."

"Ah, the infamous Elminster! He's been living in the haunted wing for some time, you know, hiding among its many ghosts—and posing with some old hag or other as the brother and sister Rhauligan."

"Yes, yes. That's not what worries me. It's this trap they're talking about, that they've set up for him when next he shows his face in the palace. If we blunder into any part of it, it'll kill *us*, they're saying!"

"So don't go atrysting in the haunted wing, dolt! Huh. Elminster. Some 'Great Old Mage,' that one! A doddering old fool, sharp-tongued and *scared* of using magic, by the Dragon! At least watching him has been a bit of a diversion. Just what he's seeking, I haven't an earthly idea, but if the old fool is witless enough to think he can find royal treasure and get out of the palace with it undetected, he *is* an utter dunderhead."

"They . . . the word is he just killed a lot of us, and they're right out of patience with him. If he steps into the trap, it'll kill him—and it might hurl a good bit of the palace into the sky, just to make sure!"

The orb quivered again and fell silent.

Storm looked up at Elminster. "El, Alassra will be no more mad tomorrow than she is right now," she whispered. "But if you fall, neither she nor I have any hope, nor any reason to carry on. You need this, right now, more than she does—and the Realms needs you more than it does her. It can muster many Red Wizard slayers, but only a handful of men who can and have saved it time and again. And of those men, you are the only one I trust."

She took the orb and held it up to him. "Yours, El."

He took it with a wry grin. "More magic to guard my mind while I take a turn at hurling a good bit of this palace into the sky?"

"Hey, now," the ghostly princess put in sharply. "This is my *home* you're speaking of. A little less talk of hurling skyward, if you *don't* mind."

CHAPTER
NINE

IN THE NAME OF THE DRAGON

Ah lords, if you but knew
The dark villainies I've done, murders and far worse,
With loyal pride and private praise,
All in the name of the Dragon.

> said by Galaunt the Highknight
> in Act II, Scene I of the play
> *Defending the Dragon Throne*
> anonymously chapbook-published in the Year of
> the Scroll

"This is it," Marlin announced triumphantly, gazing at the life-sized bronze staring dragon skull adorning the dark double doors before him. "The Dragonskull Chamber."

Around him, his hireswords stirred restlessly, swords up and faces tense. Killing six Purple Dragon guards to reach this spot hadn't bothered them in the slightest, but they were fearful now.

Their employer surprised them then by turning away, pointing along the passage, and saying, "Now we go this way. To another room, not this one at all."

Their gasps of relief were almost audible. Marlin hid a widening smile from them as he waved some of the men past him to take the lead as they turned the first corner.

Out of long habit, not just in accordance with the firm orders he'd given them, a few of the rearguard sellswords looked back behind them as they followed Stormserpent and their fellow hireswords.

They were men whose lives depended on seeing anyone who might be behind them, but dust swirled thickly where they'd slashed their way through great hanging draperies that had been drawn across the passage, to be sure no lurking guardians, undead or otherwise, awaited them. So none of them saw who was staring down at them from the deep gloom of a distant high balcony—the faintly glowing ghost of a princess, flanked by a dark, slender man and woman.

All three were watching Stormserpent's band with eyes that burned like smoldering coals.

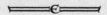

"And so the jaws begin to close. Slowly and patiently. Very patiently. There'll be no escape for you this time, old foe."

The darkly handsome man who drawled those words to no one but himself strolled across the chamber to watch another glowing, moving scene hanging silently in midair, where he'd cast it.

After observing it for some time he nodded unsmilingly, turned away, and went to a waiting decanter and tallglasses.

"This time, Elminster of Shadowdale," he told the decanter politely, "I'll wear you down. Spell by spell, ally by ally . . . one by one they'll be stripped away. Worn out, exhausted."

Manshoon poured himself a glass, held it up to catch the glow of one of his scryings, studied the hue of its contents appreciatively, and told it, "Yes, the days of your seeing all and always being two strides ahead of me are gone. Gone with the integrity of the Weave and the love of your oh-so-tolerant goddess. Gone with the lost mantle of being a Chosen. Now, Elminster, you're no better than the rest of us."

He glanced idly at another nearby glowing scene, one full of writhing tentacles and a silently shrieking victim in their coils, then walked past it. "Not that you're a toothless lion. Ah, no. I've underestimated you in the past and have been humbled for that, but not again. Never again."

The next scene showed him several wizards of war, heads together over a highly polished table in an ornate palace chamber. Manshoon did not bother to make his magic let him hear what they were so excitedly saying, but he added to the glass, "So there'll be no grand spell battle between us. No chance for you to taunt me with your cleverness one more time then somehow slip away. We'll not be seeing each other until you have no spells left worth mentioning."

He moved on, waving a hand to dissolve a scene he no longer needed. "You'll defeat this looming trap, I've no doubt. Almost certainly the one after that, too. Perhaps the third and fourth that await you. Yet I've prepared more, and I'm not going away, Sage of Shadowdale. I'll cut at you and claw at you and stab at your back, withdrawing whenever you turn to see who wishes you ill, so time and again you face nothing and no one to hurl your spells at or put a name to. And when at last you've no sleeves left to hide your tricks, then I'll strike. And I *will* strike."

He stopped in front of another silently moving image. "Marlin draws closer to the prizes we seek. Talane shall shortly do my bidding in a far more subtle ploy, for I *know*, Old Mage. Yes, this time I know. Your hoped-for apprentice—your naive young descendant—will be corrupted to my will or destroyed, not become one more of your long line of handy rescuers. Expendable, weren't they? All of them, expendable . . . just as my magelings were, in the name of the Brotherhood. As these fools who call themselves wizards of war are, in the name of the Dragon. And as the thousands you've slain or led astray down the centuries all were, in the name of Mystra. So much for your high and noble motives. You, Old Mage, are no better than I am. You never have been."

He waved his glass at no one and asked almost jovially, "And now, what are you reduced to? Stealing magic to drag your brain-burned lover back from insanity for a few moments! With the loyal lass who can't even sing anymore, let alone cast a spell worth a hedge wizard's striving, fetching and carrying for you. Whither your Harper armies now? Your scores of apprentices? The thousands who cowered to your bidding whenever you sent a glare their way? Why, I fancy my paltry agents outstrip yours. At last."

The darkly handsome man strolled on. "And I shall enjoy corrupting your little lass into joining their ranks . . . just as hope rises in you that you can count on her."

Manshoon sipped, smiled approvingly—*much* better than Arrhenish and a credit to some long-dead cellarer of this sprawling pile of a royal palace—and murmured, "And where neither she nor Talane nor Marlin will serve, I have others. Nobles and wizards of war . . . and a certain Lady Dark Armor."

The vampire who had ruled cities and citadels drank more deeply, smiled again, and added almost gently, "Nor am I less than formidable, myself. The score between us is deep, and I have thought long and hard on how best to settle it. While you, as is your wont, have wasted your time saving the Realms for others. This time, Elminster Aumar, Sage of Shadowdale, you are going *down*."

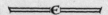

Some of his hirelings were so frightened, he could smell it, but he was paying them well and had made himself as safe as he could be. His ironguard magic should protect him against their blades, and he had other magics he could call on. He bore a potion that could quell poison, his high metal collar and gorget should foil stranglings, and a deadly secret nestled against his chest, ready to strike the moment he loosed it.

More than that, he knew just where he was going and what to do when he got there.

Yes. Unlike the many courtiers who thought the legendary Wyverntongue Chalice was hidden somewhere in or near the Dragonskull Chamber, Marlin Stormserpent knew *exactly* where it was concealed. Even the notorious Silent Shadow, if he or she came looking for it, wouldn't know that.

An Obarskyr family treasure, gifted to Queen Filfaeril by a Waterdhavian envoy not long before her death, it had been stolen from its display plinth in the Room of the Red Banner during a long-past palace feast . . . more as a drunken prank than anything else. For fear of being caught by war wizards using magic to trace the chalice, the thief had hidden it that same night elsewhere in the palace, before departing its gates.

That thief was Nethglas Stormserpent, Marlin's eldest

brother, whom Marlin remembered as a sharp-nosed, mustachioed, unpleasant shark of a man.

Nethglas had intended to boast of the theft all over Suzail to win the general acclaim of elder nobility, but quickly grew too scared of the repercussions to say a word, after war wizards seeking the chalice started mind-reaming other nobles who'd attended the feast—and those reamings ruined their minds and those of their war wizard interrogators too.

Not wanting the Stormserpents to face reprisals, or himself to be slain, imprisoned, fined, or even just banned from the palace, Nethglas publicly kept silent. He'd already boasted of what he'd done to his three brothers, but sought to mend that error by threatening them with murder if they told anyone. Elgrym, next oldest of the four brothers, told his best friend, Lord-to-be Nael Rowanmantle, anyway—and Nethglas promptly slew them both, making it look like an "unfortunate accident."

Those were the very words he'd used when next speaking privately with his two youngest brothers, Rondras and Marlin. Who took full heed of the warning and kept *very* quiet for years, until Nethglas died fighting at the side of Crown Prince Emvar Obarskyr, when the prince and all of Cormyr who'd ridden with him were slain in a Sembian ambush south of the Vast Swamp in the Year of the Silent Flute.

As the body of Nethglas was being brought back for burial in the family crypt, Marlin had quietly poisoned his older brother Rondras. Though he and Rondras detested each other, he'd done it more to get his hands on the Flying Blade—a *gorgeous* sword that also happened to be a family magic traditionally worn by the Stormserpent heir—than to become head of House Stormserpent.

Marlin had longed to hold and wield the gorgeous weapon since he was small and had thanked the gods that Nethglas had not taken the Flying Blade to war but left it safe in the vault deep under Stormserpent Towers. He promptly purloined a key to the vault, but visited the sword only rarely, to gloat over it and run a cautious fingertip down its gleaming length.

Now, though, the possibility that it held one of the ghosts of the Nine made him *really* want to have it. Not locked away, but riding his hip and under his hand all his waking hours; power he could hold.

He'd left it at home for this foray, though. No sense risking it's being seized by war wizards when he could use Thirsty instead—and his long, long dosings of paralyzing poison were done, leaving him immune to the mischance of the same stinger that should put paid to any Purple Dragon or war wizard his pet stirge could reach.

The chalice couldn't be traced by the spells of war wizards or anyone, thanks to the magic on what it was hidden within— and its own enchantments, too.

Hidden within, aye. On that night, so long ago, Nethglas had hurriedly thrust the chalice up inside the hollow head of a yawning-jawed sculpted stone dragon in the huge sculpture that dominated the Chamber of the Wyrms Ascending, a rearing statue for which that glossy-floored, crossroads chamber had been named.

Marlin had been told the stone dragon was awash with enchantments that made an endless cycle of glowing lights arise and shift hues all over it. Images of dragons seemed to melt out of it and silently spread huge wings, beating them so as to soar up to and through the vaulted ceiling above and—

"Here 'tis, saer!"

The chalice flashed as one of the hireswords turned from the dragon statue, brandishing the cup. "Just where you said—"

"*Cast down your swords, and surrender, in the name of the Dragon!*"

The echoes of that thunderous bellow rolled off distant walls behind him as Marlin blinked his way back to the here and now. His hirelings had found the Chalice stlarning near the same farruking *moment* as a night patrol of Purple Dragons had discovered them!

His men had their orders, even if they hadn't known what awaited prisoners taken in such circumstances. They were rushing the palace soldiers already, wasting no breath on shouts or war cries.

What his dead father had liked to call "a brief and bloody affray" was about to erupt.

Marlin smiled and pulled open the breast of his jerkin to let Thirsty fly free.

One distant Dragon wasn't running to meet the sellswords, but was instead trotting off down a side passage. Marlin pointed at the man the moment the poison-painted stinger of his pet stirge was safely out past his arm.

"That one!" he snapped—and Thirsty flapped off in untidy, streaking haste.

Marlin waited, ignoring the first grunts and clangs of hard-swung swords as the rushing men met. Swords flashed and thrust, a Dragon fell with a groan, and a hiresword and another Dragon guard slumped with nigh identical wet gurgles.

Marlin still stood motionless, head cocked and listening hard. Gods, this was taking *forever* . . .

Then Thirsty flapped back into view, almost nonchalantly, and fell on the neck of one of the Dragon officers, stinger lancing down hard. Marlin allowed himself another smile.

That Dragon had gone down before the alarm could be raised. No doubt the man was lying paralyzed on the floor, not far from the gong he'd been running to reach.

So sad—but then, life was a series of such sadnesses. The trick was making sure every one of them was suffered by someone else.

Thirsty was no ordinary stirge, the well-known vermin that sucked blood from cattle until sated. Rather, it liked the tastes of many victims—and was even now winging to another one.

One of Marlin's hirelings died on a Purple Dragon blade thanks to being startled at the sight of Thirsty flapping past, and the guards had already hacked down two more sell-swords—but those hirelings hadn't been idle, either. The smartly uniformed patrol had been reduced to a trio of fright-ened, surrounded men, beset by too many swords to stop.

The Dragons fought desperately, sending one of Marlin's sellswords staggering away cursing weakly, then slashing out the throat of another. Yet with the numbers they faced and the veteran skills of those seeking to slaughter them, their fates were never in doubt.

The last Dragon died spewing blood with two swords through his body.

Leaving two of Marlin's hireswords still standing and a third on his knees gasping out blood, his face twisted in pain.

As Thirsty flapped back to its master almost lazily, the two able-bodied sellswords looked to their patron for orders.

Marlin pointed at their wounded fellow. "Kill him," he said curtly.

They gave him expressionless looks for a moment, now knowing their own fates if they got hurt, then did his bidding, turning again from the corpse to learn his will.

"The sacks we brought along," Marlin told them promptly as he caught up the chalice from the floor where its death-struck recoverer had carefully placed it. "Retrieve them. Behead all of the dead, and collect the heads in the sacks; they're coming with us."

That earned him another pair of expressionless looks.

Marlin sighed. "So there's nothing left that can possibly have seen us or wag tongues about that, when the war wizards come prying with their spells and asking their foolish questions."

Chalice safely in the crook of his elbow, Marlin then applied himself to close scrutiny of his maps. By the time his two hirelings joined him with their dripping sacks, he was ready to lead them confidently away from the Chamber of the Wyrms Ascending, through a secret passage in its walls behind the rearing dragon statue.

Gods above, but the Obarskyrs had loved secret passages.

"This is heading deeper into the palace," one of the sellswords muttered, as Marlin waved them to move ahead of him. It was a safe bet that the chalice would earn them more, sold illicitly, than any sack of heads. Unless that sack had, say, the king's head in it.

"So it is," he snapped. "Rest assured that I know *exactly* what I'm doing—and what you're thinking, too, come to that."

After climbing a precipitous flight of steps right after departing the Wyrms Ascending, the passage ran straight and narrow for what seemed a very long way, obviously inside the thickness of a wall. It climbed and then descended once, presumably to hop over a connecting door, and then, for no apparent reason, took an angled bend to the left.

"Stop," Marlin murmured. Just as his most expensive map showed, part of the angled section of wall could be slid aside to reveal an older, damper stone passage. He took care to put that panel carefully back into place after they'd stepped through it, then cautioned his two men to keep as silent as possible.

Keeping quiet was, after all, only prudent when trying to sneak out of a palace.

This new hidden way had a lower ceiling than the previous ones they'd used, arches built of crude, massive stone blocks. Its walls were rougher, too, and it smelled *old*.

According to his map and the tales that had come with it, the passage linked the royal palace with the deepest winecellar of the Old Dwarf, a long-established Suzailan tavern, passing right under or between various cellars of the royal court. It had probably been dug by the Old Dwarf himself—whoever he'd been—and no doubt used often by the legendary womanizer Azoun IV to move unseen between the palace and willing wenches all across Suzail. Or Azoun's father before him, or any of the half-dozen randy Obarskyrs before that.

A plague on them all. Their day was almost done.

"Long live King Marlin, first of the Stormserpent line," Marlin murmured to himself. Then shook his head and grinned wryly.

Perhaps that would be his fate, but he doubted it. Wasn't there something about a sky full of hungry dragons returning to devour and ravage and seize Cormyr back from all humans, if no Obarskyr backside warmed the Dragon Throne?

He shrugged, glanced behind him—nothing but darkness—and devoted himself to following his cautiously striding hirelings. There'd be time enough later to ponder old legends . . .

"Later" as in after he was dead, most likely. A demise Marlin Stormserpent fervently hoped would occur in his sleep in some gigantic bed with gold-glister sheets and dozens of beautiful, willing, bare bedmaids in a suitably opulent chamber atop whatever palace he was then ruling most of the Realms from. About a century or so from now.

CHAPTER
TEN
HARDER THAN HARBOR RAIN

Idle nobles laugh and waste fair coin,
Their hands with work never they stain,
While in hold and warehouse and wagonbay,
I toil long days and nights away,
Working harder than harbor rain.

> Lune "Minstrelcloak" Ardratha
> *The Dockhand's Lament*
> first performed circa the Year of the Sheltered Viper

Arclath smiled his customary easy smile.

Both of his two unlikely friends were nervous and tired. It must be the upcoming council and their superiors shouting at them about this particular exacting preparation and that specific niggling detail. As the days dwindled down to that grand gathering, the tension behind the palace doors would rise to shrieking heights that would need far more than a mere knife to cut. These days, it always did.

Wherefore Lord Arclath Argustagus Delcastle, who prided himself on being a benevolent, enlightened noble who was considerate of his lessers—as well as being *the* airily outrageous, flamboyant flame of Suzailan fashion, though he knew some folk described him far more bluntly, "an utter fop" being one of the politer descriptions—had conducted them that evening to the Dragonriders' Club, an establishment they'd otherwise never have spent coins enough to enter, for it was both exclusive and very expensive.

These were factors he dismissed in less than an instant. His coins would be spent, not theirs, and his purse could easily cover the patronage of two hundred nervous and tired young men. Besides, those who hoarded their coins only lost them in the end to such perils as the Silent Shadow, without ever enjoying them.

"Come, Belnar! Ho, Halance!" he said merrily, turning in a whirl of his rich and splendid half cloak. "Come and stare at the best mask dancers in all Suzail!"

He reached to fling wide the doors and usher them in, but the club door guards, who knew him well, hastened to open up for the trio.

The revealed maw of revelry made Belnar and Halance both hesitate, so Arclath smilingly strode forward and led the way out of the night and into warm, welcoming hedonism. As he'd expected, they followed readily enough.

Lanterns of leaping flame were reflected from scores of polished copper wall adornments and artfully placed mirrors; a constant murmur of chatterings and chucklings washed over everything; and a thudding, piping tune was undulating and swirling sinuously from somewhere close behind the red-lit raised stage at the heart of the dimly lit sea of small—and crowded—round tables.

The Dragonriders' had been open for only two summers but had established itself firmly at the social height of the "daring" private clubs that catered to the young and rebellious, rather than oldblood money, centuries-old heritage weighing in membership, and stiff courtesies. Anyone who had coin enough could roll into the Dragonriders' to drink and talk, but no one would if they didn't also want to watch mask dancers. Or even do more than watch them by paying steep extra fees and seeking out back rooms with doors decorated by painted masks to match those worn by the dancers they'd seen on the raised stages out front—wearing *only* masks.

Arclath was much of an age with his two palace friends and knew they might be stiffly mortified—or trying to seem so—for the first few drinks, but would be hungrily watching thereafter. By the Dragon, the dancers were beautiful and skilled enough that *he* loved to watch them, and he could hire his pick of lasses anywhere in the city or enjoy the company of many an ambitious beauty for free, purely on the strength of being Lord Delcastle. Yet he loved to watch here as hungrily as the next man.

Mask dancers had been the rage in Suzail for less than three summers, but it was a fury that, as far as Arclath was concerned, could last forever. Some began their dances clothed, and others didn't bother, but always their faces were hidden behind grotesque, long-beaked, birdlike masks. These lasses danced on raised stages, *almost*—but never quite—touching the front-row patrons.

Tress was already smilingly showing the men to Arclath's usual table, right in front of the club's lone half-oval stage. She was the owner of the Dragonriders' and more properly known as "Mistress," but it had been two years since Arclath had heard even a Watch patrol address her thus. Just "Tress" she was, to everyone. She was tall, urbane, and always clad in leathers that made her resemble some bard's fancy of what a sexy, wingless, humanoid dragon might look like. But she never danced on the stage, and there was no backroom door with any mark of a dragon on it. He'd looked.

She patted Arclath's shoulder like an old friend, murmuring, "Your guests, Lord?"

"Of course," he smilingly assured her. "And I do believe they're as thirsty as you are strikingly beautiful, high lady!"

"Flatterer," she purred fondly, gliding away to fetch some decanters herself, rather than signaling her maids.

The two uneasy, blushing young men sitting beside Arclath might have bolted from their seats right back out into the street if they'd had the slightest idea how much Tress knew about them at a glance, though they'd never darkened her doors before. She caught Arclath's eye as she came back with the wine, interpreted his grin and slight shake of his head correctly, and did not address either of his companions by name.

Even as she smilingly called them "saers," and bent over them to give them their choice of wine and a pleasant view of the dragon she'd painted sinuously arising from her cleavage, the owner of the Dragonriders' knew the paler, thinner one in plain street tunic and breeches with the black curly hair was the young but dedicated Wizard of War Belnar Buckmantle. While the slightly larger, agile, and darkly handsome man in palace chamberjack's livery was Halance Dustrin Tarandar, an amiable courtier of low rank but longtime, trusted service. It was the business of many club owners to know faces and names. For one thing, it prevented husbands and wives from encountering each other unexpectedly and unpleasantly when they were availing themselves of a club's services to temporarily forget each other. For another, it kept inferiors and superiors in common service from seeing each other to the embarrassment—or worse—of both. It was also always handy to know when a senior courtier or a noble was in the house and not wanting to be recognized. It was even more useful to know when a wizard of war was visiting. Or several war wizards, especially if their faces warned that they might be ready for trouble and expecting it.

The style of Tarandar's uniform sleeve told any Suzailan who cared about such things that he was a senior chamberjack, head of a duty of eight chamberjacks, the fetch-and-carry men who ran errands, delivered messages and small items about the palace, moved furniture as required, announced guests entering a chamber, and guided visitors through the chambers of state. The crook of the smile on Tress's face told Arclath she regarded Tarandar as a fellow underappreciated and underpaid toiler in personal service to the too often ungrateful. If that smile had been a comment, it would have been "Poor lad."

Seated beside Arclath Argustagus Delcastle—in his beribboned clothing, gilded wig, curl-toed boots, and all—his two court friends looked like two of his drab, timid servants. Who suddenly, despite their wide-eyed stares at the stage, were yawning. Tired little servants of the Crown, the both of them.

"So," Arclath began, when Tress had poured each man his mumbled choice from the decanters and smilingly had withdrawn, "tell me about this Council of Dragons from the inside, as it were. Will there be wine? Dancing? And are we all going to have to put on fetching little dragon suits like the one Tress pours herself into?"

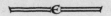

"Where's he heading *now*?" Storm murmured, as the last of Stormserpent's men vanished around that distant corner. "Not the Dragonskull, after all."

The ghostly princess lifted shapely shoulders in a shrug. "*He* certainly knows where he's going. Which is more than I do. Elminster?"

"Why do folk always think I know everything? Hey?"

"Perhaps because you've spent more centuries than I'd care to count very loudly pretending that you *do*," Storm said sharply, before Alusair could say something worse.

The grin Elminster gave them both then was one Storm Silverhand had been seeing all her life. It had probably looked very much the same riding his possibly then-beardless face when he'd been about six summers old, back in long-vanished Athalantar.

"Well," the Sage of Shadowdale said mildly, "he's obviously going to wherever the treasure he's seeking is really hidden. Somewhere nearby; near enough that he could use the Dragonskull Chamber as a navigational landmark to reach it."

"A pirate, sailing my palace in search of buried treasure." Alusair's smile was bitter.

Elminster's impish grin brightened. "That's a *very* good way to think of Cormyr's nobility. Rapacious pirates, all of them."

"A wizard would know," Alusair said over her shoulder as she departed the balcony through the nearest wall.

Storm and Elminster hastened to follow her. After all, they had to use the door.

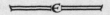

Amarune danced at the very edge of the stage, tossing her head to let her unbound hair swirl as she crawled along the polished rim like a panther, growling and purring playfully at the men—and a few women, too—gazing longingly at her from the nearby tables.

Though not a hint of it showed on her face or in her manner—she was good at that—she was slightly irritated and almightily interested in what was going on at just one of the tables.

The one right in front of her.

Whereas the Lord Delcastle and his two companions seemed not to think she had ears at all, the way they freely discussed the council so close to her.

Oh, they knew she was there, all right.

The other two couldn't keep their eyes off her, and Lord Fancybritches Delcastle, wearing his usual easy smile, was idly tossing coins to her in a steady stream, to keep her posing right in front of them.

His aim was as unerringly teasing as ever, too.

Yes, by the Dragon, the three genuinely seemed unaware she could hear all they were saying—and she was listening to them intently.

Such a gathering of nobles, after all, would mean the richest business of this season coming right into her arms, if she was able to spread word of her charms *just* right. Exclusive, that's what they'd want; something they can have that others won't be able to taste . . . something thrillingly dangerous and dirty . . .

She'd seen the chamberjack just once, when visiting the royal court to pay her taxes. He was quiet, perhaps the politest courtier she'd ever encountered, and darned handsome to boot. That's why she'd remembered him . . . Tarandar, that was his name.

The other one was a war wizard, but that was all she knew about him. Except that if he was a spy and a veteran hurler-of-spells, he was also the greatest actor in all the Realms. If he wasn't an inexperienced, thoroughly embarrassed youngling, she'd eat her mask—right now, in his lap, and without sauce.

She decided she'd much rather be decorating Tarandar's lap, instead.

As for the loudly effeminate fop across the table from them, well, he was good winking fun, but there was a reason he was mockingly known among his fellow nobles as the Fragrant

Flower of House Delcastle. Not that he preferred men in his bed, but because he was all overblown fripperies and dwelt in a Delcastle Manor that was legendary for florid, beribboned, rose-hued decor.

Tossing her hair as she caught Tarandar's eye, she parted her lips longingly, ran her tongue around them—and watched him blush. Delcastle chuckled, of course, and the chamberjack looked so overwhelmed by her displayed self that she almost burst into laughter. His tongue was actually hanging out.

She wondered what his face would look like if she told him who and what she truly was: Amarune Lyone Amalra Whitewave, an orphan from Marsember, who for some very hard-bitten years had earned her meals with her body—and thievery. A string of bold thefts every wizard of war had been publicly ordered to stop, if they could, by any and all means.

Not that anyone knew she was the Silent Shadow.

So hearing who she really was would make his face change, to be sure.

Yes, mageling, behold my bared charms. I'm your very own Silent Shadow—mask dancer, sometime forger, and busy prostitute.

The daughter of a much-respected and trusted war wizard, too, though Beltar Whitewave had been slain decades earlier in a frontier battle by hirespells working for Sembian smugglers. Those same smugglers had later knifed her mother and her brother, leaving Amarune kinless in the world. She'd fled Marsember across its rain-slick rooftops that very night, never to return. If she'd waited until morning, she was sure she'd have suffered the same fate.

So, drooling young war wizard, you think I'm for you? Well, if you've coins enough in your purse, certainly.

Yet will you ever dare take them out and proffer them? I think not.

Wormling.

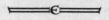

As they trotted along a dark passageway, a great crashing clangor of steel striking stone arose, ahead and below, and echoed off vaulted ceilings above them.

"Stormserpent's snakes meeting with more guards?" Storm asked, turning her shoulders and ducking to crash open a door stuck in its frame from long disuse.

It yielded, sending her staggering.

Alusair was waiting for them, glowing like a coldly amused flame.

"You could say that. They blundered into some suits of empty armor set upon pedestals as adornment, and got buried in old cracked plate for their troubles."

"Cracked?" the Bard of Shadowdale asked, as the ghost led them out onto another balcony.

"We don't waste still-serviceable armor in Cormyr," Alusair replied. "Or didn't. Things are different in the palace, these days."

"A lot of things are different, these days," Elminster muttered. "Is yon lordling going to be allowed to wander these halls all night, without challenge? There *are* still wizards of war, aren't there? And Purple Dragons, too? Cormyr still has a few of those?"

"They seldom pay much heed to what goes on in the haunted wing, Old Mage," the ghostly princess replied.

"So who does guard it?"

Alusair turned to face him, striking a pose that mocked the gestures preferred by flamboyantly foppish nobles. "Me."

They had been easy coins, but Arclath's deft rain of them was coming to an end; all three men were visibly weary. They'd downed about half a decanter each, followed by bowls of mulled broth, then sweet iced buns; even Arclath was yawning. The other two were sagging in their seats.

Abruptly they all seemed to realize they were more than half asleep and thrust themselves to their feet, clasping arms and parting. Arclath tossed a generous handful of golden lions onto the table—enough to pay for six men to enjoy five such nights, at first glance—and they were heading for the door. The lordling no doubt for his soft silk mansion bed, and the other two, by their murmured converse, back to the palace to write down some of the concerns and ideas they'd thought of across the table regarding this precious council.

Ignored, Amarune stared thoughtfully after them, holding her last pose. Saers, behold, your very own nude statue. Forgotten and discarded, like all statues, which sooner or later only incontinent birds remem—

At the door, Arclath turned on his heel and looked back.

As it happened, her pose had her standing with her arms outstretched toward him almost imploringly.

He smiled a tired smile and tossed two golden lions at her, high and hard. A good throw even for a wide-awake man.

Amarune broke her pose at the last possible instant to pluck the coins deftly out of the air. Then she bowed to him, waved thanks with the most fluid grace she could manage, whirled, and ran lightly off the stage.

She knew, without looking, that he'd stood and watched until after the swirling curtains had swallowed her.

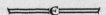

"Stormserpent's met with real guards, this time," Alusair observed with some satisfaction. "Dead ones—mere bones—but they can ply blades well enough. Hearken to the fray."

"Aye," Elminster agreed, "They'll not last long, but they'd probably destroy a few thieves. They're hacking down yon lordling's boldblades like harbor rain."

"So what's this war wizard trap that will hurl you skyward?" Storm murmured, peering warily ahead.

Elminster shrugged. "The feeling grows within me that we'll find it soon enough."

Amarune yawned again, uncontrollably. Dances as long as tonight's were always tiring, and the hot soaking bath she liked to follow them with, to keep from stiffening up on the walk home, always made her sleepy.

Then there was the walk itself and the long climb up the stairs to her lodgings at the end of it . . . yes, she was more than ready for sleep.

Yet it was one of *those* nights—the times when she found herself prowling wearily around her few cramped, dingy, rented rooms, mind too awake and excited for slumber. The council and all those nobles descending on the city, with their bodyguards and dressers and scores of other servants—what would such visitors who found their ways to the Dragonriders' find most alluring?

Well, the unobtainable, of course. If they were nobles, that meant coupling with a willing, hitherto-unknown Obarskyr princess, of course, but she couldn't give them *that*.

Or could she?

Hugging her thick, much-patched old nightrobe around herself, Amarune stared at herself in the mirror. Dark eyes stared back in smoldering challenge.

She blew herself a kiss, stone-faced, almost insolent in her inscrutability.

She was—tell truth, lass, and shame the Dragon—the best mask dancer in Suzail.

Yes, it just might work.

She'd fool no one, of course, and it'd be death to even try any sort of Obarskyr-kin claim—but she could *tease* . . .

The Princess in the Mask, she could be, hungering after the right dragon to warm *her* throne. Yes . . .

She bent to her littered desk in sudden urgency, snatched a bit of reed-weave paper out of her heap of salvaged scraps, plucked up her quill, and started scribbling. Sometimes ideas came pelting down harder than harbor rain . . .

CHAPTER
ELEVEN

TEMPTATIONS FOR MANY

Gods laugh and make cruel sport with us all,
Serving hope heaped on platters, or not any,
Leaving high noble or grim farmer alike all afire,
A-running and a-fighting hard for their heart's desire,
And chasing bright temptations many.

> Lune "Minstrelcloak" Ardratha
> *The Dockhand's Lament*
> first performed circa the Year of the Sheltered Viper

Elminster gave the undead Steel Regent of Cormyr a long, hard look. "I thought I knew these halls. Evidently not."

Not surprisingly, Alusair's answering smile was thin and ghostly. "Evidently not."

That was all she said, so after waiting vainly for more, El sighed and asked, "So just how many whirlbone traps don't I know about?"

Alusair shrugged. "Six, perhaps seven. I could be more precise if I knew just how many secrets of my family you know about." She held up a hand to forestall his reply and added, "I speak now of palace architecture only, not long-hidden heirs, bastards, scandals, and proverbial skeletons in wardrobes. We'd be here a tenday or more, I'm sure, if you started in on those."

Elminster nodded. "At least. Well, then—"

Alusair flung up both her hand and her sword in urgent unison, whirled, and was gone, leaving behind the whisper: "He's done something. The skeletons are down and done. Our Stormserpent continues to surprise. I must see."

"Go, then," Elminster murmured. "My time for flying and hurrying isn't upon us yet."

Not for the first time, he spoke to empty air. Much to Alusair's displeasure, Elminster trudged along no more swiftly than before Storm had been at his side.

The two former Chosen walked patiently, trusting in the young noble's men needing some time to plunder once they found what they were seeking. That did not suit the ghost's patience—or lack of it—at all.

The passage they were traversing ran on into unseen gloomy distances, but Elminster suddenly stopped at a stretch that looked the same as the rest of it and flung out one hand to halt Storm. Then he touched a certain stone in the wall beside him with the other.

With the briefest of stony grating sounds, a section of wall slid inward, revealing the edges of a door-sized opening. El shoved on that moving door of stones—and they pivoted aside in unison, to reveal a dark passage beyond.

Storm rolled her eyes. "Are you *still* finding them? The early Obarskyrs must have been suspicious of *everyone* in all the Realms!"

"Now, now, lass; they probably told Baerauble to see to the making of some secret passages, and he did his usual thoroughly overefficient job of it: thrice as many passages as needed, plus a *more* secret passage for exclusively royal use, not to mention an utterly secret passage for his own use—to spy on both the royal passage and the secret way that had been ordered for mere palace courtiers to trot along."

Storm regarded him with some amusement. "So he was as devious as you? I can scarce believe it! Fancy a wizard being sly!"

"Behave, stormy one," he told her fondly.

Startled, Storm fell silent. He hadn't addressed her by that term for centuries.

They padded along the new passage in companionable silence for some time ere once more starting to murmur to each other—low-voiced and often, as was their wont. They rarely mentioned Alassra. Instead, El spoke of items that held blueflame ghosts, items of *real* power, and the possibilities of seizing them to restore shattered minds. Which of course meant just one person who mattered to them both.

When he was done recounting snatches of blueflame ghost lore, El looked to Storm, seeking her willing agreement for such hunts.

She shrugged. "Why not? We're losing her."

"Hardly words of ringing eagerness," he murmured.

Storm sighed. "We've run out of easily snatched magic items, and those who guard what's left are watching and waiting for us. Our luck can't hold forever, and our skills are failing us."

"Well, there's always the possibility of recruiting someone suitable to do the snatching for us."

Storm regarded him soberly, knowing what was coming. "A blood descendant," she said flatly. "And you have at least one young, vigorous, nearby, and quite likely suitable candidate in mind: Amarune Whitewave."

At his nod, she frowned. "Just how much does she know of her heritage?"

Elminster spread his hands. "She's heard that her father's father's mother, Narnra, was said to be the daughter of the notorious Elminster, but she considers such talk mere wild legend. One claim among so many others, in the small army of women reputed to have been fathered by everyone's favorite Old Mage."

Storm smiled thinly. "You *were* busy, weren't you?"

El sighed. "So rumor has it. Now, if rumor could just turn its mighty power to making me again a worlds-striding, peerless-in-Art Chosen of Mystra, once more young, hearty-strong, and a dallier with, say, a slim hundredth of the women I'm *supposed* to have, ah, entertained . . ."

"You'd have that army and several more besides."

El gave her a wry grin, sighed heavily . . . and said no more.

In companionable silence, they walked on along lightless passages for what seemed a very long time.

Until it was Storm's turn to sigh. "This Amarune is going to be a temptation for you."

"Aye," Elminster muttered. "Try not to remind me."

"For one who knows how and has the spell, taking over bodies is so stlarning *easy*," Storm added.

El nodded. "And finding more magic around these halls that Alassra can subsume is getting harder. Pretending to inspect every crumbling inch of this palace only yields so many forgotten, free-for-the-taking baubles. The Crown of Cormyr quite reasonably wants to keep its crowns and such."

"So right now . . ."

"Right now," Elminster almost snarled, "our most pressing need is to stop young Stormserpent from getting any of these ghosts of the Nine. Our second need is to get those items ourselves. Our third is to recruit Amarune—*without* attracting the attention of whomever has been spying on us."

"The ever-vigilant wizards of war?"

"No, not those particular everpresent annoyances, this time. Someone else. Someone who hides behind Cormyr's spying mages, looking our way only fleetingly. Someone whose magic is much more powerful than theirs."

Storm stopped abruptly to stare at him.

"Someone whose magic is likely stronger than mine, too," Elminster added grimly.

She blinked. "Do—do you have any idea who it is?"

Elminster made a rude sound. "If I did, d'ye think I'd be chasing around this palace after silly young nobles?"

Whatever reply Storm Silverhand might have made was lost then, as the spell-glow those voices were coming out of flared into wildness.

And fell silent, to hang in midair in the heart of a huge room's chill darkness, flickering fitfully.

"Back into a ward that resists my spells yet, the pair of them," a cold voice sighed. "Yet those wards grow steadily fewer. Soon, old foe, there will be none left to you—and the time of my triumph will come at last."

As if in reply, the glow spat sparks. Then it faded, dwindling swiftly to . . . nothing.

Hmmph. Strong wards indeed.

"For centuries before I did," the cold voice added, "others said Elminster must die. They were right, and more than right. Old foe, you should have been swept from the fair face of Faerûn long ago."

The owner of that cold voice drifted across the vast chamber. "I should have done it myself, before you served me the same way so often. You thought you'd slain me for good, no doubt—but, as in so many other things, you were wrong. And even clever old archmages who consort with goddesses pay the price for their errors in the end. As you shall pay mine. Soon."

A pincer-ended tentacle drew open a door, and the owner of that dark and sleekly deadly appendage drifted through the revealed archway, its eyes turning on agile stalks to peer warily this way and that into the darkness as its other tentacles arched and coiled almost lazily around it.

There were no intruders to be seen. Good.

These ancient spellcasting chambers, deep in the oldest part of the royal palace, were warded more heavily than the mightiest fortress the tentacled one had ever seen or helped enspell. They were never used these days, and no scrying but his own should be able to worm a way through all their inter-woven layers of shielding—but Bane take all, the young and incompetent fools who now strutted Cormyr as its wizards of war were apt to blunder into every nook and corner out of sheer doltish curiosity . . .

Well, not there. Not yet.

"Soon, you'll pay," the floating, many-tentacled thing repeated firmly, rising up so its tentacles could hang at ease rather than trailing along the floor. "Soon. And forever."

A glow flared ahead. The cold-voiced owner of the ten-tacles snarled in sudden satisfaction then departed that body for his own, slumped waiting in a grand old chair.

It shuddered all over as he returned, then it lurched to its feet and set about weaving and hurling a spell with deft speed, ending the spell with but one cruelly whispered word, "Dance."

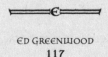

"Dance," the empty air whispered—and the ghost of the Princess Alusair arched her back in midair, writhing in agony. The shriek that burst out of her was high and shrill.

Right in front of her, eerie light had flared into being without warning, magic where there had never been magic before.

It lashed through her, clawing and slicing and searing ruthlessly before it faded. In its wake, she faded toward the floor, moaning softly, little more than a flickering, shapeless wisp ...

"What—what's wrong?" Storm snapped as Elminster suddenly stumbled against the passage wall then slid limply down it.

"Alusair," he gasped, turning a sweat-glistening face up to her. "Something ill has befallen her. She screamed."

"Is she—?"

"Dead? As in, released from undeath? Destroyed and gone? I ... think not."

He shook his head grimly as she helped him to his feet, and muttered, "The surge of magic was *very* strong."

Storm tapped her head. "In here, it's been getting much worse," she told him bitterly. "I rarely feel surges at all, anymore. For me, the Art is almost gone."

Elminster gave her a look. It was a long time before he whispered, "For me, 'tis a warm, seething treasure within me, a waiting, beckoning pit I hunger to plunge into, as easily and as often as I used to. Power I ache to wield, no matter how witless it leaves me."

He drew in a deep breath then blurted, "I need ye. To hold my mind together whenever I slake myself in the Art. We're a team, the two of us together an archwizard formidable enough to face down most foes." He put his arm around her. "Together, lass. Together we'll guard the Realms yet."

Storm's eyes shone as she smiled. "And if it refuses to be guarded, El? What then?"

"Then we tame it and teach it, until 'tis willing!"

"Well, now!" snapped a harsh young voice out of the darkness. "Impressive words indeed! A pity they'll be your last!"

Elminster and Storm had no time to roll their eyes and groan at how many times they'd heard such gloatings before.

They were too busy screaming in pain as the passage around them exploded in roaring emerald flames that flung them away like helpless scraps of rag.

"There's no way in the world they could have survived *that*," a somewhat shaken male voice offered into the smoke-reeking darkness.

Up and down the passage there was a restless din of groanings and crackings; stones cooling and complaining about it. Here and there louder crashes could be heard, as blocks of stone fell from their places to shatter on the floor below.

"Lord Ganrahast is seldom mistaken in his judgments," the harsh young voice observed, a little smugly.

"I'd be happier if I could clearly see the Sage of Shadowdale lying dead at my feet and know there was no way he could rise again to face me. Ever," a third voice observed.

"Oh, don't be such a *coward*, Mreldrake."

"I don't think I much care for those words of yours, Rendarth," Mreldrake replied stiffly. "You didn't face him and his mad Witch-Queen out in the wilds. *I* did."

"And ran like a scuttling rabbit, no doubt, and so lived to tell us all the tale," Rendarth snapped right back. "So if you're so bold and battle-hardened as all that, mighty Rorskryn, suppose you advance down the passage and find us Elminster of Shadowdale—or what's left of him. We'll need his head to bring back to Ganrahast and Vainrence, mind. Or, failing that, some bit of him large enough to identify him with certainty."

"I did in fact listen to the orders we were given, too," Rorskryn Mreldrake replied coldly. "*You* go, boldest of mages."

"As I recall," Wizard of War Andram Rendarth said in his harsh voice, "*I* was placed in command of this little trio, and I am giving you, Mreldrake, a direct order. Get down that passage and start hunting. And mind you bring back lumps of Elminster, and not the other one."

"It was a woman," the third wizard added helpfully as Mreldrake conjured light with an angry snarl. "So if you see large breasts, you're not looking at—"

Elminster had heard more than enough.

Storm—still breathing, thank all gods—was lying atop him, silent and heavy and bleeding copiously all over him, but he could readily reach and aim the wand he'd taken from Wizard of War Lorton Ironstone, after Alusair had obligingly won that earlier battle for him.

It was a wand that dealt short-term paralysis, the weapon Ironstone should have used back then, right away and without warning, instead of issuing his grand challenge. Yet lost chances were part of the fast-fading past, and it should ably serve a certain Sage of Shadowdale now.

He leveled the wand carefully and murmured the word that brought it to life. Ganrahast and Vainrence weren't training these dolts well; only utter fools stand side-by-side on a battlefield, when both are mages and face a foe they know wields magic.

There was a flash, and all three wizards toppled like trees. Mreldrake, Elminster saw sourly, had been standing behind the other two, and his fall was gentler, a hand going out to shield his face. *Not* paralyzed, to be sure.

The other two were, and Elminster thrust the wand back into his belt to snatch out the enchanted dagger. Mreldrake or no Mreldrake, Storm must be healed before all else.

As the dagger expired in a flare of light under his murmurings and crumbled to dust in his hand, he heard the faint scuffling he'd expected from where the war wizards lay.

"Before ye *quite* crawl off, Rorskryn Mreldrake," he said sharply, "suppose ye avoid my slaying ye very painfully, here and now, with a spell that will literally turn thine innards out of thy body, by answering a few questions. Truthfully, if ye know how to tell truth."

Mreldrake drew in his breath so sharply that it was almost a faint shriek.

"The wards," Elminster continued. "Ye called on the ancient wards of the palace, all around us, to strike at me just now, didn't ye?"

He waited, knowing the answer already. He'd cast some spells himself as part of those wards, a long time before, and knew very well the tingling of wards he'd worked on, all around him, being altered.

Rather than words from Mreldrake, he heard the faint scufflings of a frightened war wizard trying to crawl away without making a sound. And failing.

"Answer me," he added calmly, "or die."

A long moment passed. Elminster drew the wand from his belt again and held it warningly.

That brought results. "Y-yes," the war wizard blurted. "But it was Rendarth's idea!"

"I can scarce believe he acted on such a notion without the Royal Magician's approval," El replied as disapprovingly as any scandalized tutor. "Let us have truth, Wizard of War Mreldrake. In the name of the king. I *do* still hold a court rank in this kingdom that far outstrips thine."

"I—I—Ganrahast said we could use the wards to hide and armor us against you," Mreldrake admitted almost miserably. By the distant sound of his voice, he was slowly crawling away down the passage.

"And clever Rendarth took it upon himself to use it to augment the bolt ye three hurled at us," Elminster said heavily. "Did ye not know doing so would ruin and consume the wards immediately around us here? Leaving a gap in them, and weakening the entire web loyal wizards before ye spent centuries weaving?"

"I . . . you must be stopped. At all costs."

Elminster exploded. "Idiots! Ye three strip away centuries of defenses—warding spells ye don't even know how to replace—just to smite me! What price Cormyr's future, if ye toss it aside so readily to win one day's victory? What of the morrow, hey? Despoilers! Fools! Irresponsible children!"

The reply that came out of Rorskryn Mreldrake then *was* a sort of shriek—the sort of strangled *eep* a man-sized mouse might blurt in unthinking terror. It was followed by wild scrabblings as he clawed his way to his feet and fled headlong down the passage.

Shaking his head in exasperation, Elminster let him go. The lesson he'd take back to Ganrahast was one that had best be learned swiftly and well.

Younglings, these days. Win the day, and bother not with looking beyond the end of one's nose . . .

It was a wonder there were any realms left in the world, at all.

Wizard of War Rorskryn Mreldrake was almost sobbing from lack of breath as he panted his way around another corner, his frantic sprint falling into an awkward stumble.

He never even felt the spell that fell on him like a net, claiming his mind in mid-panic.

Before he knew it, a steel-hard grip was closing firmly on his mind.

"As it happens, wormling," a gentle whisper rolled through his head, seeming to bring with it a floating pair of dark eyes as sharp and hard as the points of two daggers, "the Sage of Shadowdale is not the only one who has taken to hiding in this large and rather well-appointed royal palace. I, too, want all thoughts of altering its wards to be crushed and quelled, promptly and completely. I am Manshoon and am even more terrible than the legends about me suggest."

The grip became a tightening cage.

"Rorskryn Mreldrake, you are mine now."

CHAPTER
TWELVE

DARKER AND DARKER

My father told me what my grandsire said before him:
That all the Realms around us, as the years pass,
Grow ever darker and darker.

Markuld Amryntur,
Twenty Summers a Dragon: One Soldier's Tale
published in the Year of the Splendors Burning

The darkly handsome man made his latest acquisition abruptly turn and slam himself face-first against the wall.

Wizard of War Rorskryn Mreldrake groaned dazedly, staggered back from the wall, and reeled a little as he resumed his swift, gasping trot along the passage.

Manshoon arched a critical eyebrow. His control over this wormling was complete, but weak tools do poor work. This coward Mreldrake was a wizard of war, yes, and a pair of somewhat useful hands, too, but no great prize. Certainly not up to the task he needed done.

Mreldrake, Rendarth, and Nalander must all vanish or be silenced, soon, to send the right message to the Royal Magician and his trusted second that doing anything at all to the palace wards was a *very* bad idea. Then it would be time to put Ganrahast and Vainrence to sleep before they got any other clever ideas. Moreover, removing them without causing their deaths would leave the wizards of war in headless confusion for some time—time he intended to stretch for as long as possible—ere a new chain of command was settled and accepted.

First, however, the more pressing task.

The energetic young Stormserpent was about to fall afoul of the usual treachery, and must be rescued from it.

It wouldn't do to have the items he bore that were linked to the Nine fall into the wrong hands and plunge all Suzail into a tiresome battle as the war wizards and various ambitious nobles and mages—including both shadow-commanded and independent Sembians, to say nothing of all the wolves-for-hire in Westgate—got wind of something worth seizing and tried to take it for themselves.

No, the overbold young fool of a noble needed rescuing. A swift and forceful saving that would require someone far more competent than Mreldrake. Someone who knew the palace well and served Cormyr—or at least her vision of it—with fierce loyalty. Someone undead, whom he commanded.

The death knight who was called "Lady Dark Armor" in the dark tales whispered in back palace rooms. Targrael, whose twisted mind was already his.

Smiling, Manshoon murmured a spell and bent his will down into chill, dusty darkness.

Down, down into a certain old, seldom-visited tomb deep in the palace.

Down to where someone smiled in her endless unbreathing, unthinking oblivion, and stirred . . .

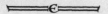

Targrael smiled in the darkness.

Awake again, after too long asleep. She was aware of another mind, folded around her own and watching her. Strong and dark and terrible, a mind that had mastered her before . . .

Abruptly her attention was forced away from that lurking presence to the point of her own nose. To the slab of smooth, unbroken stone just beyond it.

"I am the last lady highknight, and the best," she whispered fiercely to the lid of the closed coffin above her.

There had been a time when, yes, she'd been as insane as your average gibbering wizard, but that was past; Targrael knew quite well she was beyond death, and what she'd become.

And she'd found it quite suited her coldly ruthless self.

Death was a curious thing. Neither precious Caladnei nor shiningly heroic Alusair had perished in the ways everyone thought they had—not that she'd found any trace of Caladnei, yet, around the palace. Alusair was a different matter . . .

Targrael found herself quivering with rage at the mere memory and forced herself once more down into cold calm.

Patience. Stately patience.

I am, after all, Cormyr. Its sole true guardian; the Forest Kingdom and everyone in it depends on me, though they know it not.

Wherefore I tirelessly—her lips curled in scornful amusement at that, for she was either lost in oblivion or awake and unsleeping—lurk in and around Suzail, slaying all who displease me. I decide who shall flourish and rule or fall in the Forest Kingdom. As the years pass and the vigilance of the realm fades and its foes grow darker and darker, I play no small part in hurling back Sembian and Shadovar interests seeking to covertly conquer the realm by their usual means: magically influencing, bribing, or blackmailing various nobles. They'd have succeeded long before, but for me—and that gives me the right, as Cormyr's most effective protector, to decide just what Cormyr should be and will become.

Three failures, only. Three who've resisted me. The intruders from Shadowdale, the wizard Elminster and the wench Storm . . . Bah. It is to sneer.

Her one attempt to destroy them should have been ease itself but had not gone well. Alusair had suddenly been there, all fierce menace, barring her way with the announcement that the two were under her protection and Targrael would harm them at her own peril.

She'd rightfully sneered at that, of course, but Alusair had taken her by the throat and had done something that had seared her very undeath.

Targrael's throat pained her still, months later. Her voice had become a hoarse, hissing whisper, and she burst anew into ghostly flames about her throat whenever upset.

So she took bitter care indeed when in the palace, avoiding the ghost of the princess and those two thieves from Shadowdale as much as possible, and doing more watching than slaying.

Cold flames were licking about her throat now, though, as excitement rose icy and fierce within her.

Cormyr must be defended.

Targrael thrust up the lid of the stone coffin she'd been lying in, stretched stiff arms, and drew her sword.

The room around her was dark, empty, and unguarded—nigh forgotten, even at times when the royal court offices all around were bustling. Dusty and little regarded, like too many reminders of the kingdom's past.

She climbed out of the raised coffin and put its lid back into place.

There. The Tomb of the Loyal Dragon looked as good as new.

She'd long ago tossed out the crumbling bones of the long-dead soldier interred there, and had made it her favorite hiding place. The idiot weaklings who called themselves Purple Dragons and senior courtiers and wizards of war these days hadn't noticed, of course.

Targrael felt her lip curling. The darkness in her head was giving her orders without speaking, sending her marching off through the darkened passages of the royal court's upper floors. Stalking slowly at first, blade held close to her chest as she stumbled into walls and closed doors.

She was no clumsy, lurching zombie, but she was seeing much more than dark, empty passages. In her mind were unfolding scenes of a band of hireswords, plundering the royal palace!

A band she was to aid and guard, or at least the man who led it: the young noble Marlin Stormserpent.

He had seized two precious things, and she was to see he kept them and his life. So he could wreak great change upon Cormyr.

She would be part of it. She would have a hand in the destiny of Cormyr.

At last.

She'd not miss her chance again . . .

"The way ahead is barred, saer," one of his two surviving hirelings muttered warningly, shifting the gore-dripping sack that rode on his shoulder.

"I am aware of that," Marlin replied firmly. "Matters have been arranged."

It had been a long, boring trudge through cold darkness toward a faint glimmer of light.

They were almost at that light, a lantern hanging from an overhead hook in the Old Dwarf's deepest winecellar. On the other side of the old and massive steel gate that walled off the end of the passage, where the lantern was, stood a row of massive oak casks, each in its own cradle.

His trusted, long-serving "dirty work" accomplice, Verrin, was waiting under that lantern, smirking at him. Just where Verrin was supposed to be.

Marlin stiffened. Not enough for anyone to see, but enough that Thirsty stirred restlessly inside his jerkin. Something was very wrong.

For one thing, the spell-warded steel gate was still down and locked in place. The Spellplague had twisted its wards like so many others, and wisps of wild magic were eddying around its wide-spaced bars as they had done for years, casting eerie glows on everyone's face.

For another thing, Verrin wasn't alone.

That "everyone" included a tall man who was standing with Verrin: Marlazander, the head bodyguard of Marlin's longtime rival, Rothglar Illance.

As Marlin came to an expressionless halt, the chalice in one hand and his drawn sword in the other, his two hirelings with their sacks of severed heads flanking him, Marlazander put one large hand on Verrin's shoulder, sneered at Marlin, and said gloatingly, "The problem with trusting in hirelings is keeping them bought. Or rather, *your* problem. Once more it seems Rothglar Illance is more than a little less miserly than Marlin Stormserpent."

Marlin sighed. "If no more noble."

He sent Thirsty flying forth again, making the little trill that told his pet to fell all strangers. It swooped through the bars while Verrin and Marlazander were still staring.

The bodyguard hurriedly stepped back, shoving Verrin away to give himself room, and drew steel.

His swing, despite being aided with his startled curse, missed the stirge entirely. Yet Thirsty wasn't heading for him. It zigged, zagged—and struck, deftly lancing Verrin's throat.

The man started to topple, clutching at his throat in a vain and stiffening-fingered attempt to stop his lifeblood jetting everywhere. Thirsty was already whirling away, darting between two casks where Marlazander couldn't hope to reach or follow.

The bodyguard was still cursing and turning, trying to see where the stirge would swoop, when a tall, slender figure stepped out from between another two casks to confront him.

It was female—or had been, when it was alive. The remains of a woman clad in black leather war-harness, bareheaded, her face white with death in some places and fetchingly streaked with mold in others. She held a sword almost carelessly in her hand.

"Another swaggering, foolishly arrogant noble's pawn," she murmured, surveying Marlazander the Mighty and letting him feel the weight of a sneer. "They're almost as annoying as their noble masters. Almost."

Marlazander sprang at her, slashing at her viciously in one of the best attacks he'd ever learned. It was parried and turned aside with a flick of her blade—as was his next and his next. She danced around him, toying with him like an armsmaster— and when his first fury of increasingly frantic attacks started to falter along with his wind, she disarmed him with casual ease.

And slid her blade past his frantically snatched-out daggers and into his throat, an unruffled moment later.

Before he was finished falling and dying, she'd strolled to the limp, gory mess that was Verrin and had cut a ring of keys from his belt. Wiping her sword clean on a dry part of his breeches, she tossed the ring of keys through its bars to Marlin, saluted him with her blade—as he and his hirelings gaped at her, aghast—and stepped back between the casks again.

Who—who *was* that? The Silent Shadow? Some long-dead agent controlled by another noble House?

"I'll be long gone by the time you get that gate up," Targrael told the young noble mockingly as she continued to retreat into the shadows. "Waste no time hunting me, for you'll not find me. Nor is there really any need to hunt me. As you can see, I'm dead already."

It took Marlin some time to manage to swallow, find his voice, and dare to ask, "W-who are you?"

He was answered from deep darkness far away across the cellar by coldly mocking laughter.

Manshoon chuckled despite himself. Gods, but she was *evil*. He should be able to resist this sort of behavior, all this mocking, prancing villainy, when his mind was riding and commanding hers, but . . . somehow . . .

She enjoyed it so and made him enjoy it. More than he had in centuries.

Centuries . . . too many passing years, drifting past darker and darker, too many friends and lovers and useful allies gone with them . . .

Enough reverie. To work again.

To this little minx Targrael . . .

Still smiling, he bent his mind once more upon hers, in firm command, and felt her heed and obey.

Back to your tomb, Lady Dark Armor. Until just the right moment to take care of the Lords Ganrahast and Vainrence.

It would not be long in coming.

In the meantime, there were two other minds to ride and

their pairs of eyes to spy through. Being a manipulative mastermind was busy work.

Work that he loved—every sinister moment of it.

The former Night King of Westgate and incipient Emperor of Cormyr—and Sembia, and the Dales, and wherever else he could conquer, once he mustered the might of the Forest Kingdom for real battle—turned to his floating, conjured scrying-scenes.

Back to the beloved work at hand. First the stirge, and then Talane . . .

They were thankfully deep in Stormserpent Towers now, and Thirsty had obediently soared up into the darkness of the room's vaulted ceiling a short while before, unseen by his two hireswords.

Just a few more deeds to do, and he could relax.

Marlin stood a good many paces back from the sellswords, lounging against a doorpost. They were both keeping wary eyes on him as they obeyed his latest orders, tossing the sacks of severed heads down into the roaring flames of the main tower's furnace.

They expected to be shoved in after the heads, of course, but he smiled sardonically at them and displayed empty hands whenever they whirled around from the flames to give him hard and suspicious glares.

His smile broadened when one of them did something to his belt that made a ward rise with the usual faint singing sound. Its glow, before it faded into invisibility, was flat gray; a steelshield ward. Stretching like a wall right across the room between Marlin and his two hirelings, it would prevent the passage of any crossbow bolts, spears, or hurled darts or axes.

"Don't you *trust* me?" he asked them in his best guise of wide-eyed innocence.

"No," one of them replied bluntly.

"Wise of you," Marlin commented before he gave the warbling whistle that brought Thirsty swooping down to sting them both.

The paralysis hit them before they could finish cursing, but not before they both crashed to a Stormserpent rug that had seen much better days.

Marlin strolled to a handy table, leisurely divested himself of the chalice and his sword belt, then removed a few rings from his fingers, and daggers from various sheaths up his sleeves and down one boot. Kicking off the boots, he unbuckled his waist belt and let his breeches fall.

Thus metal-free, he strolled through the ward and proceeded to kick the two helpless, paralyzed men into the furnace, one after the other.

Then he turned his back on the cloud of sparks swirling up, walked back through the ward, and took up the chalice to gaze at it admiringly.

Thirsty returned to his shoulder, rubbing affectionately against his cheek and neck, and he stroked it as he smiled at the chalice.

He must remember to let the stirge drink deep before the night was out. That fat she-dumpling of a cook he'd seen helping out in the kitchens, perhaps? Or should he hire someone and quell fears about the household for a while?

Ah, decisions, decisions ...

He gazed at the Wyverntongue Chalice and let himself gloat. Yes, the night had been a triumph, to be sure.

So inside this large and elegant old metal cup was all that was left of an adventurer who'd once been among the most powerful in all the Realms. A hundred and fifty summers earlier, more or less, it had all come to a sudden end for the Nine, when Laeral Silverhand—later the Lady Mage of Waterdeep, alongside the infamous Blackstaff, Khelben Arunsun—had been possessed by the Crown of Horns. A god, or what was left of one.

And the Flying Blade held another of the Nine.

Thanks to much coin spent on various adventuring bands far less accomplished than the Nine—adventurers who were all since dead, thanks to *more* Stormserpent coin—Marlin knew how to command a blueflame ghost.

And knew where there was a warded spellcasting chamber in which he could test his control over said ghosts, without even Ganrahast detecting what he was up to.

Moreover, until Lothrae produced two ghosts of his own, a certain Marlin Stormserpent was free to proceed with his own, *ahem*, "dastardly plots."

He chuckled, watching the ward—visible again, as it died—flicker and start to fail as the belt that it was grounded in started to melt. Hot places, furnaces.

Then he turned, hefting the chalice lovingly in his hand, and started the long walk through Stormserpent Towers to get the Flying Blade.

Through one of the many tall windows that he passed, the first glimmerings of dawn were lightening the last failing gloom of the night.

A new day was coming, and it was high time for the fun to begin.

"Ambition has felled so many, young Stormserpent," Manshoon purred. "It has even humbled Fzoul of the Too Many Gods and the strutting, preening Chosen of Mystra, Elminster of Shadowdale not least among them. I've tripped over my own ambitions a time or two, myself. Have a care now, King Marlin, Secret Lord of Westgate or whatever you strive to first become, that ambition not cause *your* swift and premature fall. Oh, no. I need you to last until *I* deem you expendable."

CHAPTER
THIRTEEN

NOTHING TO LAUGH AT, AT ALL

Lords high and low, if you learn one thing today,
Heed this: murderers who kill at will among us, yet remain
Dark-masked, unknown, no matter who they conveniently happen to slay,
Are nothing for any lass or jack to laugh at, at all.

> said by Paradur the Sage
> in Act I, Scene II of the play
> *Too Many Skulls Underfoot*
> anonymously chapbook published in the Year of
> Seven Sisters

Amarune came awake quickly, her mind singing with
alarm. There it was again, and definitely not in her
dreams. Another stealthy sound. Nearby.

She'd fallen asleep at her scribbling, head down on the litter
of papers on her desk. No ink all over her cheek this time; that
was one good thing. All was dark. Her little candle lamp—only
a stub to begin with—had guttered out.

So where—?

Ah, there it was yet again. That time, despite the pitch
darkness all around, she knew where it was coming from and
what it was.

Someone was using the blade of a knife to try to force open
her shutters.

Very quietly.

"That won't work," she announced calmly, moving as
soundlessly as she could from where she'd spoken to stand at
one side of the closed shutters, the spear from under her bed
ready in her hand.

"Got you awake, didn't it?" a rough and familiar voice
replied calmly from the night outside the window. "I've work

for you, Rune. It's Ruthgul, if you haven't marked my dulcet tones yet. I'm alone."

"What *sort* of work?"

Thieves in the city who weren't careful didn't live long enough to accumulate hard-bitten pasts.

Not that thievery didn't run in her blood, if skill at thievery *could* run in the blood. Most tales insisted she'd been the daughter of the legendary Old Mage of Shadowdale, Elminster.

"Need a false contract signed," Ruthgul growled, breaking into her thoughts—and just why had she been thinking about *that*, anyway? Ye gods, what nex—

"Copy a signing I've brought, onto it," he added. "Match the ink close, if you can."

Amarune made a sound that was half a sigh and half a chuckle, undid the catches on her shutters, and unhooded the faint, cracked glowstone fragment that lived on the table beside the window. Its light was barely brighter than the darkness, and no wonder; it had been broken when she'd stolen it, and that had been long, long before.

In the days when she'd had far more coins than she did now, but cared nothing for how many more days she might live to spend them in.

She shook that thought aside and lifted the iron bars that held the shutters closed.

"In," she commanded, the pull cords of her two ready crossbows in her hand. Ruthgul had always been honest with her, but his first lie might well be her last surprise, as the saying went.

The scarred and grizzled old man outside handed her his knife, hilt first, then held out empty hands for her inspection. She caught hold of one and hauled him half into the room, then stopped, pinning him across the sill, to make sure he was alone and not readying some hidden weapon.

The knotted cord he'd climbed swung freely in the night air outside; she could see there was no other weight on it. Nor, so far as she could see, was anyone lurking above—and Ruthgul always worked alone. Nearby rooftops seemed empty of lurking figures, and every window she could see was dark and tightly shuttered, as was both prudent and usual.

Under her firm hand, Ruthgul kept still. There was a satchel covered with short planks strapped to his back, to protect the documents he'd told her about, and though he almost certainly had a blade in either boot and probably a strangling cord somewhere, she could see nothing ready to menace her.

"In," she commanded tersely, and plucked up one shutter bar, holding it ready to brain him with. Ruthgul landed on the floor, grunted, then got up and took hold of the other shutter bar, moving slowly to reassure her.

He turned, drew her shutters closed, put the bar in its place, and did up the catches. Then he held out his hand for the other bar.

Amarune gave it to him, holding the spear steady at his throat. He sighed, mumbled something about trust being rarer and rarer these days, and finished bolting her shutters.

Then he kneeled down, spreading his hands again to show he wasn't reaching for any weapon. Slowly worming his way out of the satchel straps, he slid his burden off his back.

"The contract," he muttered, "is an agreement—"

"I *don't* want to know."

Their usual phrases. Ruthgul uncovered just the signature of one document and let her look at it long and hard. An ordinary ink, as far as she could tell. She lit her last precious candle to check its hue closely.

"Four lions," she decreed flatly.

Ruthgul knew better than to haggle. He fished out a purse from somewhere amid his filthy rags and leathers—it wasn't the one riding his belt—and slowly set forth four gold coins in an arc around her candle lamp, each one sticking to his middle finger until he set it down soundlessly and twisted firmly.

Then he used the purse and her glowstone to hold open the document bearing the signature, and uncovered the contract for her to sign.

Or rather, to peer closely at the rush paper it was written on. Then again at the signature.

Amarune fetched several bottles of ink, the right quills, and some scraps of paper, to practice a few swashes. Ruthgul waited in patient silence. His hands had once been young and strong and unsmashed enough to do such work himself; he knew what was necessary, and he knew the true measure of her skill, too.

She caught up the edge of her robe and wiped her forehead. She'd be sweating before she was done.

Then she sat back to breathe slowly, as if falling asleep in her chair, and let her hand mimic the signature again and again, until it *flowed*.

Ruthgul nodded approvingly and waited.

She signed it with a smooth, swift flourish, then sat back to mop away sweat again.

Perfect, or so it seemed to her eye—and she judged such things as critically as any miser of a coinlender.

The grizzled old man sat still as stone, waiting for the ink to dry. He let Amarune decide when the contract was ready to be covered again, and let her restore both documents to the wrappings he'd brought them in, too, and return them to the satchel.

"Thanks, lass," he said, sitting back and away from her.

"You are welcome," she said firmly.

"Better I go," Ruthgul said. "I'll be needing the rest of my falcons . . ."

The blade that thrust into the room through the shutters at that moment was much longer than Ruthgul's knife, and gleamed very brightly.

"Not this night, thank you," Amarune said firmly in its direction, raising her voice a trifle. "I have business unfolding in here already."

"Will it have unfolded completely and be done, if I return in two hours?" The speaker was female, sharp-tongued, and unfamiliar.

Amarune rolled her eyes. "What price my slumber, this night?"

"I'll pay double. Just a little copying."

"Two hours," Amarune agreed and heard the voice outside echo those words in confirmation, already sounding fainter and more distant.

Only then did she notice that Ruthgul was cowering on the floor, both hands over his mouth.

She joined him down there, close enough to whisper in his ear, "What?"

"'Tis *her!*" he said fiercely, eyes wide with fear.

"*Which* her? She and I aren't the only females in Suzail this night, look you."

"She whose name you just . . ." Ruthgul gestured frantically at the satchel then looked wildly around what little he could see of her dimly lit room. "I've got to get out and away—!"

"Oh, *Ruthgul,*" Amarune sighed into his ear, her exasperation as quiet as she could make it. "Let me get some boots on and lead you out through the cellars. It links up behind the cobbler's, with Tathlin's—the message runner's—two doors down. He'll probably charge you a lion, though, to wear one of his caps and capes and go out with one of his lads. So you *will* be needing the rest of your falcons."

"Farruk," he snarled.

"No, you haven't brought enough for that," she replied brightly, crawling quickly out of his reach.

He glared at her. Then, slowly, face twisting as wry humor won out over angry fear, he managed a grin.

A grin that wavered into confused disbelief as Amarune calmly took off the cloth belt of her robe and let the garment fall open.

"I'm going to blindfold you," she murmured, stepping past him, and did so, tying her worn and raveled belt securely over his eyes. He offered no resistance as she gently guided him up to his knees.

"Try to remove that, and die," she added, as softly as any lover.

The grizzled old man nodded carefully.

"Crawl forward," Amarune murmured into his ear then. "Straight as an arrow and slowly, so as not to blunder into me.

Without my guidance, there are several places ahead on our journey where you could easily meet your death. *Very easily.*"

"Understood," he muttered. Then, satchel carefully clutched close, he started crawling cautiously after her.

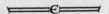

Amarune swallowed again. Fear was making her throat very dry.

She hoped her face was as impassive as she was trying to keep it. Her rooms had never seemed smaller or more tawdry.

She hated and feared her newest client and suspected the woman knew that—and was amused.

Only two lions gleamed on her desk between them.

On the other side of it stood the woman who'd put them there. Someone Amarune knew she'd never seen before; someone lean, lithe, and clad in black leathers that covered her from head to the pointed tips of her boots, hooding her face in a mask that left only her mouth and large, lion-bright yellow eyes visible. Someone who'd given her name as Talane and held a drawn sword in her hand.

It was a blade that drank all light, reflecting back not the slightest gleam, and emanated a silent something that made Amarune feel ill even from across the desk.

Its bearer was every bit as agile as Amarune and probably far deadlier in any fight. If she happened to want the Dragonriders' best mask dancer dead, Amarune was doomed.

"I've offered you fair coin," Talane purred, "and really don't believe you're in any position to bargain with me, *Silent Shadow.* Or do you prefer to be called Amarune Lyone Amalra Whitewave? Only daughter of Beltar, last of your blood, whom the Helhondreths and the Ilmbrights would dearly love to find. They want their gems back, little Rune."

Amarune stared at her visitor, not knowing what to say, fighting to keep her face as calm as stone.

She knows. She knows all about me. But how?

"Oh, I know you don't have that chest of waterstars," Talane added. "I do. Pity they blamed Beltar for that little theft; he was more useful to me alive. Almost as useful as you're now going to be, little Rune."

Her voice became softer, yet somehow more vicious. "One word from me and Cormyr's proud wizards of war will be turning your mind inside out, learning all your little secrets and leaving you a drooling idiot as the price of their schooling. Which means you accept *that* fate—or you'll be doing my bidding at prices *I* set henceforth, doing little tasks all over fair Suzail. I've amassed quite a list of little tasks, some of them too dirty for my hands to be seen anywhere near them. Quite a list; I hope you can flourish on mere scraps of sleep."

She backed away. "I'll come with the first of such tasks four nights from now. Feel honored, little Rune; you are my new 'dirtyhands,' and I don't choose such agents lightly."

"Honored," Amarune repeated flatly.

Talane's mouth twisted in something that was more sneer than smile. "Four nights," she murmured, and she backed right out the window—and was gone, falling from view in eerie silence.

Something made Amarune hang back from rushing to where her shutters were swinging gently in the first gray hints of coming dawn.

She knew, somehow, that her unwanted new client would be nowhere to be seen. Certainly not as a sprawled, crumpled corpse on the cobbles below.

If Talane was flying, wriggling, or sheer-wall-climbing away right now in her real shape, and was in truth some sort of horrid monster, Amarune knew she should learn that as swiftly as possible . . . but in truth, didn't want to know anything about it at all.

So she stood where she was, panting as if she'd run miles. Panting in fear that wouldn't go away.

Why did life have to get darker and darker and more and more complicated? Why couldn't it be like all heartsong chapbooks, where every last mask dancer had a dashingly handsome noble lord fall in love with her, whisk her away to his castle to lavish countless riches on her, marry her, and dwell with her there happily ever after?

"Farruk," she whispered into the familiar darkness around her. It made, as usual, no reply.

No matter how much she tossed and turned, her bedclothes drenched and twisted around her as she fought with them and conjured up scene after scene of discovery and doom in her mind, sleep was nowhere to be found.

Which meant she'd be wan-eyed and weary indeed when next she took to the Dragonriders' stage. Which in turn meant she'd be earning disapproving frowns from Tress, and far fewer coins than usual.

"Farruk farruk farruk farruk *farruk*," Amarune hissed at her ceiling, more despairing than angry, rolling onto her back and flinging her damp linens aside. "What am I going to *do*?"

Something swam promptly back into her mind. The grinning face of Arclath Delcastle, that airy, idle, free-from-all-troubles nobleman. Heir of his House, which meant he hadn't a care in the world and would never have to work a moment in his life or spend an instant thinking about where any coins he'd need might come from.

She should hate him for that—*did* hate his ruder moments of jesting and smirking coin-flicking at her most intimate spots, and his everpresent carefree jauntiness—but somehow . . .

Angrily she thrust him aside, tried to think of this Talane and who she might be, how to discover who she was and somehow use that to get free of her—only to have young Lord Delcastle pop right back up to grin at her, nose to nose, winking and smirking as he always did. As if he could be of any use in . . .

She stiffened and then whistled in astonishment, long and low. Perhaps he *could* be of use, at that. Clearly he fancied her, if only as a night's conquest; that should give her some sort of reins to lead him by.

As the old nobles' saying went, "Dancers are meant to be used." Well, so are young noblemen who can be led around by their manhoods.

But how, precisely?

Well . . .

Wouldn't Lord Arclath Argustagus Delcastle himself know that best?

She'd have to interest him, have to become one of his enthusiastic little whims . . . a whim he clung to for long enough to deal with Talane.

Which meant she must *not* seduce him—at least, not right away—but lead him in a merry little dance. A rather *long* merry little dance . . .

Chapter
FOURTEEN

Justice, Order, and Refinement

You seek a world of justice, order, and refinement?
My lords, you *do* know where you are, do you not?
I fear you're standing in the wrong world entirely!

> said by Ammaura the Maid
> in Act I, Scene II of the play
> *The Harrowing of House Drauth*
> anonymously chapbook-published in the Year of
> the Splendors Burning

Elminster stared down at all the sprawled and headless bodies for a long and silent time. The only movement he made was to fling out one arm as a barrier when Storm joined him, an arm that then pointed at the floor. It was awash in a dark, sticky carpet of drying blood.

"Should I—?" she asked, pointing past the bodies.

He shook his head. "Whatever Stormserpent came for—the long-lost Wyverntongue Chalice, most likely—is gone, and him with it. We've come too late."

He turned back a few paces, moved purposefully to the wall, did something that revealed another hidden door, and waved Storm toward it.

Obediently she ducked through it. "We're departing before the war wizards—and whatever Purple Dragons still survive in the palace—get here to blame us for this?"

"Exactly," Elminster said shortly. "We've failed. Standing and staring won't mend that."

He set a brisk pace down the old and narrow secret passage he'd ushered Storm into; the strong smell of ancient and flourishing mildew grew stronger as they advanced.

"Just the two of us can't do this anymore, lass," he added grimly, as the passage split and he headed to the left without slowing, leaving the mildew reek behind. "And it's time to stop fooling ourselves that we can."

"Do 'this'?"

"Save the Realms."

"So we go now to find some comfy chairs and sit back to watch the world fall apart?" Storm asked softly, arching an eyebrow in devastating mimicry of his longtime mannerism.

El sighed, came to an abrupt stop, and spun to face her. "It's time to recruit successors to take over the task of saving the Realms. We need new hands and sharp eyes and vigor."

Storm studied his face. "You mean it."

He nodded mutely, and they stared into each other's eyes for a time. During which both silently found astonishment at how shaken this late arrival—this one theft not prevented—had left them.

Devastated and close to tears.

Storm nodded slowly, her gaze never leaving his. "Defending Cormyr from behind the scenes—even in the days when Vangerdahast prowled these halls like a sly old lion, meddling and manipulating and thinking *he* was protecting Cormyr—was what we *did*," she whispered. "What we excelled at. The cornerstone of the Realms that should be, a world of justice and order and refinement . . ."

Elminster sliced the air impatiently with the edge of his hand, as if to chop aside her words. "We start training my unwitting descendant Amarune. Right now."

Storm shook her head slowly, wincing. "It will take some time," she murmured.

"Time we have," Elminster snapped, "*if* we start right now. Shall ye approach her first, or should Elminster the Terrible frighten and enrage her?"

Storm frowned. "I'll try luring her a bit, first. *Then* you can frighten and enrage her, if it becomes needful. In the meantime, start hunting up more suitable magic for feeding Alassra. In a palace so full of decaying and forgotten magical gewgaws, even after all your foraging, there must yet be *something*."

"Heh. Lass, this place holds entire war wizard armories—walled away and ward-guarded, mind ye—full of enchanted baubles. This current crew of Cormyr's most puissant guardian mages knows not the worth or working of half of them. Yet seizing any magic of Cormyr is going to upset Alusair."

Storm smiled tightly. "*Everything* upsets Alusair."

"Aye, but lass, lass, forget this not: given what we've become, if she catches us at the wrong time and uses all her power, she can readily destroy us."

Storm shrugged. "I doubt it. The gods are seldom that merciful."

That feeble jest did not bring a chuckle from Elminster or even a smile.

After a moment, she added, "And didn't something or someone in these halls just come close to destroying her?"

The Old Mage nodded grimly. They shared another long look, then a mutual sigh—and with one accord turned and began the long trudge back out of the haunted wing, toward one of the older secret ways out of the royal palace. One that was least likely to be guarded by current and puissant Purple Dragons or wizards of war.

Amarune Whitewave was somewhere in the city outside the palace and wasn't likely to be invited inside anytime soon.

Not unless King Foril developed a sudden taste for skilled mask dancers.

Six passages later, El stopped in midstride, glared at a certain stone in the passage wall as if it personally offended him, then bent down to the floor, felt among the stones where wall and floor met, and drew a small block out from between its fellows with a little grunt of satisfaction.

Behind it proved to be a flat, rusty iron coffer that El persuaded to open with one firm bounce of his fist. Inside was a little pendant on a fine chain, such as a court lady might wear, a mask, and two gleaming steel vials, firmly stoppered and sealed. El passed all but the pendant to Storm. "Nightseeing mask and two healing vials; ye carry them."

He put the pendant around his neck; it vanished entirely beneath his beard.

Storm pointed at where she knew it was. "So what does that do?"

"Read passing surface thoughts. Nothing like a mind-ream, mind, but it should help me tell how many guards are standing on the other side of a door, or the like, as we go on from here. Back when Vangerdahast was building up the wizards of war to be what he wanted them to be, they established scores of identical caches all over the palace to aid them as they rooted out disloyal courtiers."

He straightened up and pointed at the stone that had first caught his eye. "See yon slanting chisel mark? That tells ye to look low, if you're in a rough-walled passage like this one."

Storm nodded. "Harpers told me to look for an inverted T of chisel-scars."

"Ah, those were the caches that held poison-quelling as well as healing. They were for fighting nobles," El informed her gruffly. "Not so many of them survive, and they were fewer to begin with. I remember—"

He stiffened then and fell silent, raising a hand sharply to command silence. Storm gave it.

A moment later, from beyond the wall on the other side of the passage—a wall that must be *very* thin—they heard a door open and a sneering voice speak in a loud and sudden pounce of triumph.

"And how brightly doth the spark of Tarandar shine across all the watching Realms this fair evening?"

El knew that voice. He put a finger on the pendant and felt the dark, hot flood of malice in the thoughts from the other side of the wall. So the sneering and sarcastic Master of Revels really was every bit as pompous and nasty as the wagging tongues of palace servants made him out to be.

Khaladan Mallowfaer, it was said, never did a lick of work and never stopped spying on his lessers, needling them, and decrying their work, either.

Just then, all gild braid and crisply uniformed magnificence, he had stepped out of nowhere into the path of . . .

El frowned and fought hard to steer the pendant away from Mallowfaer's malice toward the other nearby mind . . .

. . . a weary Halance Tarandar, just as the senior chamberjack had started the long walk from his little cubbyhole of an office toward home and bed.

All these preparations for the council—plans, revisions, and new plans to sweep away the thrice-approved, thrice-modified revisions . . .

Halance was anxious to get some sleep before he had to present himself at the court—too soon, by the racing moon, too soon!—all over again for the next day's work. However, the man who stood sneeringly under his nose, wearing his usual unpleasantly mocking smile, was eleven rungs above any senior chamberjack in the exacting ladder of palace rank, so Tarandar managed a smile.

"Tired, saer."

"What?" Mallowfaer was playfully jovial. "How so? With all the—*ahem*—powers at your disposal?"

"Had to use those powers in my dealings with a certain noble lord, just now, to keep the arrangements right for the big day, and Cormyr safe, saer."

"Oh? *Which* certain noble lord?"

"Not at liberty to say, saer. Sorry. Standing orders of Lord Ganrahast, saer; I'm sure you understand."

The Master of Revels flushed a deep crimson that Elminster could *feel* through the pendant.

The whole palace knew Mallowfaer feared the Mage Royal and all war wizards, and deeply resented them and anyone else who had the authority to keep secrets from him, or to order others to do so. Every courtier who'd worked more than a few days at court knew the Master of Revels would never dare speak to Ganrahast. So Halance could be certain his words would never be checked for falsehood.

And Mallowfaer knew the darkly handsome young courtier standing so deferentially before him, eyes carefully downcast, understood full well the depths of his cowardice.

So he stepped aside with a wordless snarl and stalked away, whirling around three paces later to see if he could catch young Tarandar smirking.

The unseen Elminster rolled his eyes.

Rather than smirking, Mallowfaer had almost caught Halance yawning.

Gods, the senior chamberjack was thinking, but Mallowfaer is predictable . . .

It was a measure of Halance's weariness that his feet had taken him down a side stair before he was quite finished with that thought. He passed the door guard at the foot of the stair with a trading of silent nods and went out into the night.

Elminster stayed with the chamberjack's mind, hoping to learn something of the council preparations.

Halance Tarandar was stumbling-tired, but smiling.

Arclath Argustagus Delcastle was an exhausting friend.

His thoughts rushed through some of the airy nonsense Arclath had declaimed to the Realms around . . . then, for some odd reason, Tarandar found himself in another memory. He was staring into the dark eyes of that mask dancer at the club, posed as still as a statue in front of their table. Her arms had been flung wide to display all he was supposed to stare at . . . yet it was her eyes he remembered.

Because they'd been watching him intently.

Then Halance Tarandar realized what the subtle changes in her gaze had meant, and stopped in midstride, a little chill finding its way down his back.

She'd been listening to their every word.

Why?

"She's my kin, all right," Elminster muttered to Storm, letting go of the pendant. "Taking as much interest in doings at court as we do. Too much interest for her continued health, as it happens; yon courtier, a kindly and overworked young chamberjack, has just realized how much attention she was paying to them when young Lord Delcastle took him and a friend out to the club she dances at. Right now he's wondering whom she's working for, or what scheme she's hatching herself. He'll report as much to Delcastle, too, but thankfully for her—and us—he's too falling-down tired to do it yet. We should be able to get to her first."

"And bring Ganrahast and Vainrence and all their keen wizards down on her head?" Storm asked warningly.

El gave her a scowl. "She's young and of my blood," he growled. "She should welcome a little adventure."

"A little, yes," Storm replied. "I'm not so sure she'll stay smilingly welcoming when half the realm comes after her. We're used to it, remember?"

"Hmmph. Better for Cormyr if all its younglings happily take on anything the world hurls at them."

"You're sounding like a gruff old noble," the silver-haired bard teased him.

"I'm *feeling* like a gruff old noble," Elminster snapped back. "Distinctly underappreciated and beset by suspicious wizards of war at every stride I take. Not to mention experiencing a glut of foes that's flourishing, not diminishing."

Storm shrugged. "As I said, we're used to that. Ride easy, El. Yes, you had to destroy more wizards and highknights than Cormyr should lose, but it hasn't gotten really dark yet, for us or for young Amarune."

"That," the Sage of Shadowdale muttered, "is precisely what's souring me. I've a feeling this is going to go very bad."

"And I have a feeling you're not going to be disappointed," Storm sighed, putting a comforting arm around his shoulders.

He gave her another scowl, but it faded into something close to a wry grin.

Ere he shook his head and told her, "Just two of us, lass, until we secure Amarune's loyalty and get her competent enough to do what we do *and* keep herself alive. Then we'll be three. Not enough, not near enough."

The air around them dimmed, then, as an enchantment on the cache abruptly took hold of them both.

Ganrahast had cast trap spells on the remaining caches that slowed every movement of someone who violated a cache without murmuring the correct password or wearing the right sort of enchanted ring.

Elminster and Storm had time to recognize what was happening and start to say so to each other, eyes meeting in dismay . . . but they lacked even a moment more to do anything about it.

"Such a simple trap! It seems the Chosen of Mystra are mighty no longer. So you are brought low at last, old foe. *At last.*"

The glow of the conjured spell-scene was by far the brightest light in the vast and gloomy cavern. In its heart, Elminster and Storm stood despondently facing each other in a secret passage deep in the royal palace, their faces grim as they started to speak words so slowly it would take them hours to finish.

"At last," the beholder said again, smiling crookedly.

It was a very big smile, because the eye tyrant was as large across as the front door of any grand mansion. It had tentacles, some of them ending in hands of three opposed pincers, as well as eyestalks. The mind the tentacled hulk had begun life with was not the mind that still inhabited it.

It spent almost all of its time alone—and like many a loner who had not held that role lifelong, by choice, it spoke aloud to itself often.

"Yet the time to strike is not quite yet. Not with all the magics still tied to you. I've no wish to be destroyed alongside you in the fury of their unleashing. Your slaying must befall at *just* the right time. So I shall watch and wait still more. Yet now I know my wait will—*finally*—not be long."

The eye tyrant smiled. "As your torment deepens, will you save the kingdom you so love, the rock you stand on when saving all the Realms one more time—or will you let that rock crumble and shatter to save the madwoman you love?"

It drifted across the cavern to a floating cluster of small, glowing spheres, each one a scrying eye that was busily showing its own moving, silent scene of a different place in the Realms. Sounds would arise from those images only if the beholder willed matters so.

At that time, it seemed to prefer the sound of its own voice.

"I need not even muster an attack on Cormyr, so feeble have you become. The pieces already in play upon the board will serve well enough. Soon, soon will come my revenge—and at last, at *long* last, Elminster of Shadowdale will die a final death."

The tentacled terror drifted back to the large, three-dimensional image of Elminster and Storm, frozen in the narrow passage.

"And you will die, Elminster, knowing it is I who have slain you," the beholder whispered, almost fondly.

It gave the cavern around a dry little chuckle. "Soon, soon . . ."

Halance fought again to keep his jaws shut. He could *not* seem to stop yawning.

Gods, but he was tired—with a whole day of work ahead of him, a day that bid fair to be a very full one, too.

Behind the dark weight of weariness, the chamberjack never felt the cold, cruel presence that was watching him from afar, lurking deep in his own mind.

Around him, the royal court was abuzz. Not just with the ever-mounting confusion and endless rearrangements for the council—coming down on them all very soon—but at what had befallen in the palace the previous night.

The uproar was bringing war wizards in all haste from every corner of the realm, a worried-looking Understeward Corleth

Fentable had murmured to Halance. More than a dozen Purple Dragons dead—and Belnar Buckmantle, too. Murdered at their posts by unknown intruders who'd beheaded most of them and had departed by some secret way that had the highknights as well as the war wizards mightily upset.

Fentable had looked more than worried, come to that. He'd looked sick . . . and he happened to be one superior that Halance liked, trusted, and respected. The man must know things he wasn't allowed to tell underlings, to make him look that way.

Halance shook his head. Things always happened all at once, stlarn it. When everyone was already too busy to tend to them properly. "Beshaba's kiss," the older courtiers called it. Mischance, farruking, ever-irritating mischance . . .

Manshoon smiled darkly. Mischance or artful manipulation.

Halance yawned again. He *had* to find Arclath and warn him that the mask dancer had been listening to their talk the night before and might well be the paid informant of some noble client or other.

Yet he hadn't time to be seeking nobles across the fair city, with all the daily moving of furniture and linens and replacement of oil lamps to be done.

Not with all the extra council preparations on his desk, the untidy heap of fresh scrawled notes from Fentable and Mallowfaer and the gods alone knew who else about this, that, and the other little details.

Now prepare the lure . . .

Note, make a note; Halance snatched up a fresh scrap of parchment from the pile given him to make his senior chamberjack notes, and a quill from his stand, and wrote hastily, "Tell Arclath Delcastle, Belnar murdered. Also, the dancer in the Dragonriders' was listening to all we said."

"Tarandar," Mallowfaer bellowed from down the hall. "The new chairs and stools are being unloaded at Zorsin's dock right now! I've sent Emmur and Darlakan for wagons, but get yourself down there to see they don't break or mar every last piece in their loading!"

Right on cue. As anticipated and planned.

"Saer!" Halance shouted back. "I hear! And I'm on my way!"

Hurry, chamberjack. Hasten; mustn't be late. Neither Mallowfaer nor my agent who waits for you should be kept waiting.

He dashed to the door, then spun around, strode back to his desk to snatch up the still-wet note, and ran.

For a wagon, it was a long way to Zorsin's dock, but not such a long route for one hurrying man. Which meant . . .

He had a fair idea of where Arclath would be. The Eel or the Dragonriders' Club or possibly Saklarra's Wonderful Willing Wenches if our young Lord Delcastle was feeling particularly frisky.

If the Fragrant Flower of House Delcastle happened to be elsewhere . . . well, there were half-a-dozen inspections and negotiations regarding the upcoming council that a senior chamberjack could parlay into depart-the-court forays. Yet telling Arclath soonest would be best and would get it off his desk and out of the way, the better to devote all his attention to all the council details . . .

Into his head, then, came a brief, bewildering vision. It seemed as if a beholder was staring at him fixedly, through an eerie glow, with a dark cavern all around it. A *beholder?*

Gods, he was having waking nightmares! This farruking *council!*

Shaking his head, Halance Tarandar hastened down one last hall, ducked past the guards with a smile and nod, and hurried into the streets, crossing the promenade and turning immediately into his favorite alley.

He never even saw the hand that struck him down.

CHAPTER
FIFTEEN

ENTER A LORD, LAUGHING

Why if the realm needs saving from villainous king or tyrannical wizard of war
We need new heroes to be our Dragon! Look yonder!
Enter a lord, laughing—and behold, we have a new hero to admire,
Until his dark heart in turn is revealed.

> said by Goodman Ruskar Manycoats
> in Act II, Scene I of the play
> *The Galloping Knight of Cormyr*
> anonymously published In the Year of the Halls
> Unhaunted

In the sumptuous heart of pink-walled Delcastle Manor, there
were rooms most visitors never saw. Rooms whose pink-
plastered walls were sculpted into semblances of thickly clustered
roses climbing the paneling and entwining above doors.

Lord Arclath Argustagus Delcastle would have shuddered
to see such decor in someone else's home, but in his mother's
rooms, he was used to it.

Or so he repeatedly told himself.

It was a long-standing family rule that blood members of
House Delcastle arriving home should present themselves to
his mother—or to her personal maid on the rare occasions
when Darantha had been ordered to intercept him—so, as he
had done so many times before, Arclath took his dashing self up
the soaring stairs from the entry hall and through several ornate
chambers into the land of sickly roses. Sweeping past the usual
impassive guards, he glided into his mother's receiving room.

Where the Lady Marantine Delcastle gave him her best
well-fed-cat smile. She was sprawled on a daybed whose blood
red silks complemented the roses beautifully—but clashed
horribly with the flame orange sleeping silks she wore, open to

somewhere well below her waist. Not to mention shriekingly discordant with the emerald-dyed fur wrap she'd thrown oh-so-elegantly around her shoulders.

The hour had crept from very late to very early, but Lady Delcastle was wide awake and practically purring as she languidly ate scorched-orange-peel chocolates and sipped from a tallglass of amberglath "sweetwine" liqueur. Unless she'd found some unusual new diversion to leave her in such a mood, it meant she was very much enjoying the afterglow of being pleasured by three of her strapping "chamberjacks."

"Well met, Mother," Arclath gave her his cheerful, smoothly sardonic greeting. "Are your oiled ones gone?"

She gave him one of her best sneers. "Don't belittle my playthings, Arkle dear. They're more men than you'll ever be."

"How so?" he asked, strolling to her decanter-covered side-board and regarding her in the mirror above it.

"Don't you prefer boys?"

Arclath shrugged. "No, as it happens. Aren't those *your* tastes, Mother?"

She waved a dismissive hand. "No, unobservant fool, I want *men*. Men who fight and kill and come to me reeking of sweat and blood and danger. *Real* men."

"Lord Delcastle," Arclath observed calmly, selecting a decanter and a clean tallglass, "is a real man."

His mother's shrug was far more dramatic than his. "He was, once. Now he's too drowned in drink to be much of anything."

It was an open secret in Suzail that Arclath's father, Lord Parandur Delcastle, was a habitual drunkard who spent his days walled away in his favorite turret in Delcastle Manor, drinking.

"And so?"

"And so, nothing. Disposing of him would make *you* Lord Delcastle—and you are even less of a man."

"And would I be a man if I came to you reeking of sweat and blood and danger?" Arclath asked calmly.

His mother laughed throatily. "Oh, yes. Not that such a celebratiory moment is all that likely to befall, is it?"

"Not all that likely," Arclath agreed, setting the decanter down again and sipping the vintage he'd chosen. "Pleasant dreams, Mother."

He strolled out, back into the dimly lit passage—where a hard-faced House guard stood watching him, a loaded and ready crossbow aimed at Arclath's breast.

The younger Lord Delcastle raised an eyebrow. "Has heir-hunting season begun, Trezmur?"

"Orders," came the curt reply. "Sons have murdered mothers before."

"And will again, I fear," Arclath replied, strolling away down the passage with his tallglass in hand. "Yet not this son. Such a deed would be entirely too . . . noble. I seek other delights in life."

It was a good thing one of those delights wasn't sleeping, he thought to himself, knowing just how soon he'd be up again and out of the bed that was waiting for him.

Two passages later, when he arrived at his own chambers, he handed the now-empty tallglass to the doorjack waiting there, went inside, and firmly closed the door.

Only after the inner door beyond that first one had closed behind him did he add aloud to what he'd told Trezmur, "And when at last I discover the delights I should be seeking, life can truly begin."

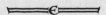

Bright early morning was flooding through windows that thankfully weren't framed in sculpted roses. Not that Arclath was lounging and enjoying the view.

He was at his usual desk, looking over documents, deeds, and an ever-rising pile of cross-strapped-between-boards parchments; the endless scrip of family investments and business dealings.

Around him, the front chambers of Delcastle Manor were bustling, as various family factors, clerks, scribes, and coin-stewards hastened up to him to receive their directions among his crisp stream of orders.

They might have been concealing yawns, but their smiles were genuine; the sooner they were done, the sooner their time was theirs, and once Lord Delcastle left his chair, their days were ordered for them, their tasks clear.

As he spoke, the factors bowed and bustled out, one by one; trade agents get about early, or inevitably find themselves picking over leavings spurned by others.

Soon enough, Arclath followed them, spiking his quill and deeming his day's work done.

Catching up his favorite gem-handled cane, he gave the clerks an airy wave and swaggered out into the streets, twirling his spike-ended stick like a carefree child.

These days, success meant departing Delcastle Manor before his mother, exhausted by her parade of hired lovers, awakened and began her daily tyranny. And today, if the gods smiled, would be a string of successes.

With deft skill, Arclath speared a warm bun from a baker's tray being rushed past, and before the runner could even start to snarl a curse, tossed the man a lion—enough to pay for four such trays, buns and all.

The bun was hot and greasy, the spiced meat inside it splendid on his tongue but threatening to leave his chin glistening.

"Ravenous, Lord?" a hot-nuts vendor called.

"Not at all!" Arclath replied heartily, not slowing. "Merely keeping in training! And how is the trade in roasted jawcrackers this fine morn?"

"Hot, Lord—hot! Get them hot while I have 'em!"

"Words my mother lives by!" He sauntered on, already hailing the next vendor to indulge in more silly repartee as he tossed a coin to a dirty barefoot child, danced a little flounce-and-flair with her as if she'd been a highborn lady, then with a wave left her and went on, very much the noble dandy at play.

He was heading for The Eel Revealed, an eatery specializing in cheese-and-eel pies, fiery fortified wines, and oiled young lasses who served them both. A welcoming refuge for the famished stomach in the dear dawn hours . . .

She was the sleekest and swiftest of the serving maids, and his favorite. Wherefore she added a wink to her most ardent smile and twirled in front of him to make her skirt swirl fetchnignly to reveal her thigh-garter as she set down his platter in front of him.

"Ah, *thank* you, Emsra!" Lord Arclath Delcastle was at his whimsical airiest. "You know how to make a man's insides roil in delicious pleasure! Just as I—a time or two, when at my *most* heroic—can claim to know how to do the same to the right maid!"

Emsra tittered as she removed the dome from the steaming platter with a deft flourish, revealing a heap of succulent eels and morels in sardragon sauce. Or so the menu claimed.

She'd heard all of his lordship's favorite lines before, but it was the playful-as-a-child way he delivered them that still smote her into mirth. There were nobles she hid in the kitchens from and nobles she served with stiff, silent care—but if there'd been more nobles like him, she'd have rushed eagerly forward to greet all nobles and cheerfully would have seen to their every little want.

Around them, The Eel Revealed was growing quiet. The rush of early diners who were departing the city on business or had to get to their shops or to market or to meet and make deals at the docks or in various offices was done, and those who struck work early for highsunfeast hadn't yet done so.

Wherefore all the serving maids lounged around Lord Delcastle's table, sharing in the laughter. Not out of greedy desire to get a coin or two for their troubles—for they knew from experience they'd get those, regardless—but because this man had a way about him that lifted hearts and set folk to laughter and made the day brighter.

"Sausages," Varimbra purred in Arclath's ear then, setting a small side platter down at his elbow. "Compliments of Laethla, who desires your opinion of this new spicing she's trying."

He looked up with a smile to find the women ringing his table all beaming at him, resplendent in their glow-painted suns and high-heeled boots as they struck poses—out of sheer habit.

"Would any of you care to join me?" he asked, and he meant it. "Surely you've worked up hunger? I'm not trying to get anyone in trouble, but—"

But the smiles fell right off their faces, leaving only concern behind, and it had nothing to do with his offer. All of the maids stared over his shoulder at the same cause.

A cause that approached him rapidly.

Arclath could move swiftly when he had to, and sprang from his chair, snatching up a hot sausage just in case, even before he turned.

To behold, striding toward his table with their eyes fixed on him, a frightened palace messenger and a suspicious-faced veteran lady war wizard he'd seen about the palace once or twice.

"Sausage?" he offered politely, holding it out to her with a bow—and receiving only silence in return.

From the messenger it was the silence of open-mouthed bafflement; from the war wizard it looked more like cold scorn.

Arclath shrugged, put the end of the spurned sausage into his own mouth, bit down, and started to chew.

He had plenty of time to study the stocky, aging war wizard as she bore down on him, and did not fail to notice she had a wand out and ready. She also had a cold-eyed, thin-lipped face like a horse, and a body that seemed to bulge with more muscles than one of your larger palace guards.

"Lord Arclath Delcastle, I will have words with you," she announced.

Hmm. A cold voice, too, and probably very keen wits.

Arclath sensed the serving maids melting away from around him and turned in smooth haste to tell Varimbra, "Please convey my compliments to Laethla. Peppery, and therefore should result in many drinks being bought and downed. I like it and would be pleased to pay her for this platter and the same again at my next visit."

When he turned back to face the wizard of war, she was standing right in front of him. And contriving somehow, though she was a head shorter than he was, to seem to *loom* over him.

He sketched the briefest of bows. "Well met, Lady—?"

She snorted. "Glathra by name. No lady. Spare me your honey-tongued flatteries."

She turned her head and gave the messenger beside her a stern look—and he silently stretched out his hand and proffered a parchment note, holding it up and open for Arclath to read but drawing it back and away when, out of sheer habit, he reached to take it.

Arclath demonstrated that not just lady war wizards could dispense dirty looks, and the messenger blanched, swallowed, and advanced the note again. Arclath didn't reach for it this time, but merely applied himself to silently reading it.

"Tell Arclath Delcastle, Belnar murdered. Also, the dancer in the Dragonriders' was listening to all we said." Halance's handwriting. Freshly written, and smudged in one corner, as if handled before dry.

Belnar *murdered?*

He raised his eyes questioningly to Glathra, who snapped, "Just what *was* 'all we said,' and why were *you* to be so swiftly and urgently told of this killing, Lord Delcastle?"

"If 'Belnar' is Belnar Buckmantle, Lady," Arclath said stiffly, "he was my friend. Halance can tell you that."

"Halance Tarandar's headless body has just been found in an alley." Her voice was grim. "He was carrying this note. The Crown desires to know just who 'we' are or were *and* what was said. I'm not accustomed to repeating myself, Lord Delcastle."

Arclath stared at her, too shocked to give her the sort of stinging rebuke that most nobles would have greeted such words with. Belnar and Halance—? But only last night, we were ...

The war wizard was watching him like a hawk.

Arclath bent to take up another sausage. As its greasy magnificence flooded his mouth, he thought back over what had been said across his table at the club.

His eyes narrowed, and he nodded slowly. Glathra took

a step forward but said not a word. She knew control as well as bluster.

"The 'we' were Halance, Belnar, and me," he told her. "We're friends. Not conspirators, Lady Glathra, not schemers after profit. Just friends."

The sausage, somehow, was gone. He plucked up another and bit into it. Gods, they were good.

"They were both," he added, chewing, "consumed with the tumult of preparing for the coming council, and I was being sympathetic . . . merely that, *not* rat-hunting details of security. So, yes, there was much talk of the unfolding arrangements, and more about the probable troubles there'd be with this noble and that, various opportunistic visitors likely to come to town because of the gathering . . . spies of Sembia, of course . . ."

"And did Tarandar or Buckmantle seem particularly interested in anything? Some matter they shared an interest in, perhaps?"

Arclath grinned weakly. "The charms of the mask dancer who was performing practically in our laps. I don't think either of them have had much time recently for, ah, dalliance."

Glathra nodded. "You," she told the messenger beside her, as she almost snatched Halance's note from his hands, "will accompany Lord Delcastle in finding this dancer, identifying her, and bringing her to me. I shall be back at the palace, watching you both from afar."

Without pause she turned back to Delcastle and added crisply, "And you shall find her before you do anything else in your life, and bring her safely to me. *Not* dallying with lasses or over drinks, and not taking time to exchange witticisms with your idle friends. Nothing is more important than this, in your life from now on. *Nothing.*"

Delcastle sketched a florid bow. "Though I must observe that I've been given commands more politely in my time, I cannot find it in myself to disagree with so charming and fiercely Crown-loyal a lady. I shall obey and strive to—"

"Save it. You don't want my old and unlovely bones in your bed anyhail," the war wizard interrupted curtly and turned away.

Delcastle gave the messenger an almost comical look of injured innocence, shrugged, and announced grandly, "Come! We have a kingdom to save!"

He scooped a handful of gold coins from his purse and flung them on the table, turned with a swirl of his cloak, and strode for the door, the messenger on his heels.

Glathra watched them go. When they were quite gone, she allowed herself a loud sigh.

"Nobles," she snorted. "Unruly children, every last one of them."

She eyed the gold coins on the table. Surely he'd left enough to pay handsomely for a dozen such meals, or more.

And this one would all go to waste . . .

Her eyes fell on the nearest platter, just as a delicious smell of spicy, juicy, hot sausages wafted up to her.

Her stomach rumbled.

Slowly, hesitantly, she reached out.

That sausage proved to be every bit as good as it smelled, and in two ravenous bites was gone.

There were more.

Gods above, when had she last eaten?

As the serving maids drifted back into view, eyeing her doubtfully, the war wizard firmly sat down in Arclath's still-warm chair and helped herself to the main platter.

Those sausages still beckoned, but she hadn't had eels done properly for an age. They disdained sardragon sauce as "Marsembian glop" in the palace kitchens.

Uhmmm. They didn't in the Eel's kitchen.

The messenger's name was Delnor, and he looked guilty as they sat down at Arclath's usual table in the Dragonriders', hesitantly darting uncertain glances this way and that.

The stages were empty, and there was no sign of even one alluring dancer, masked or otherwise. Nor anyone leering, cheering, or tossing coins. Of early morning hours, the

Dragonriders' Club offered members and their guests only tankards of strong broth and baths in scented water.

Aside from Delnor and the noble lord across from him, who was smilingly signaling that tankards be brought to them, the only patrons were a handful of drunkards and the wealthy and truly lazy, relaxing as servants—some their own and some provided by the club, but looking nothing like the sort of beautiful lasses who might at some other hour preen and pose unclad on a stage for anyone—bathed and shaved them. Delnor also saw washing, styling, and cutting of hair, and even some cleaning and mending of clothing and boots.

"So," Arclath asked airily, "is the Lady Glathra always that much of a dragon? Or was she fond of Belnar? Or Halance?"

Delnor flinched as if he'd been slapped, flushed, then mumbled, "N-no. I think not, anyway. No. There were other ... violent deaths in the palace last night. Uh, rumors abound that, ah, nobles were involved. *And* the ghosts that haunt the palace. Oh, and they're saying the Silent Shadow is going to steal things, and old dead wizards—like Vangerdahast—may have been roused to walk the palace and make trouble by someone with an old grudge against Cormyr."

"'Someone'?"

"Uh, Elminster the Doomed, some are saying. Or crazy old Sembian lords on their deathbeds. You know ... someone." Delnor waved a hand dismissively then dared to really look for the first time into the eyes of the noble lord sitting with him. "Just talk. You ... you care about any of this?"

"I know not what your general opinion of the nobility is, friend Delnor," Arclath Delcastle replied, "but I assure you I am indeed interested in who killed my friends."

One of his hands went to the hilt of his sword. "*Very* interested."

Chapter
SIXTEEN

Something of an Uproar

My lord king, pray pay no heed to flames at the windows,
Nor the heads on pikes outside the door.
A foul traitor hath done a dark deed, shamefully goading those
Who've now roused something of an uproar.

> said by Arkrashos the Sage
> in Act I, Scene VI of the play *Old King Sorrowhelm*
> by Stornald Merritree first published in the Year
> of the Scroll

The broth was good. Not to mention hot enough to burn tongues.

As the two men sipped cautiously from their tankards, Arclath's firm demands of the serving maids were reluctantly obeyed; the owner of the club was summoned from her bed somewhere in the labyrinthine loft overhead.

Eyes hooded from the clinging edge of sleep, barefoot and clad in a very old and well-worn robe that looked as if it had once been someone's rather magnificent carpet, Tress looked somewhat different than the vision in dark and clinging leather Arclath was used to.

She gave him a rather unfriendly look, yawned, and asked pointedly, "You required my servile presence, Lord?"

Delnor buried his face behind his tankard, trying to look as if he weren't there. Arclath gravely tendered his apologies for rousing Tress at such an hour and asked her the name of the dancer who'd performed for him the previous evening, and if it would be possible to speak with her. Immediately.

"No," Tress said simply. "She's not here."

"And her name would be—?"

"The Mysterious Dancer You Seek," Tress announced flatly. "She'll be performing on yon stage again at dusk tonight and thereafter until near dawn, unless trade's too paltry to make it worth her pay." She yawned again.

Arclath dipped into another purse—Delnor blinked; just how many did the man have, anyway?—scooped out a heaping handful of gold coins, and held it up. "Her real name?" he asked quietly.

Tress frowned and shook her head. "I won't give, Lord Delcastle. I'm sorry, but unless you have a Crown warrant or someone I know to be a senior war wizard asking that for you, you won't learn it from me. I must protect my girls."

"So must we," Arclath murmured, waving a hand to indicate he and Delnor were a team.

Tress snorted. "Against getting cold from being all alone when they're bare in their beds?"

She turned away, adding over her shoulder, "Come back at dusk and ask her yourself. You'll need all those coins and more, if I know her. Her company can be had at competitive rates, but her name she guards—and why shouldn't she?"

Arclath and Delnor exchanged glances, shook their heads at each other soberly, then looked up at Tress and tendered their thanks.

She merely nodded, looking as if she was sliding right back into sleep again, while still on her feet. They rose, bowed to her, took a last swig of broth each, and made for the door.

Tress roused herself. "Your coins, Lord!" she said sharply, pointing at the pile on the table.

Arclath gave her a smile and a wave. "Consider them a donation for your hospitality, and some fumbling reparation for so clumsily attempting to bribe you," he said lightly, and he departed the club, Delnor smiling apologetically in his wake.

Tress watched the door close behind them and shook her head. "Now just *what* was all that about?" she asked softly. "Stlarn it."

"Nobles are crazy," the maid who'd awakened her offered helpfully.

Tress sighed. "So they are, Leece. So they are." She padded back toward the loft stairs. "Yet they always have been—and they don't all come to my club with callow young palace messengers every morn, asking after my best dancer." She sighed again. "I have a bad feeling about this."

The magic faded at last, leaving the long-bearded wizard and the curvaceous silver-haired woman free to curse heartily.

They did so with enthusiasm, though Elminster spat out his words at a trot.

"We've lost the night and some of the morning," Storm added, lengthening her stride to keep up with him.

"I *know* that, stormy one," El snarled. "I also know just how careless I was to fall afoul of a dolt-simple war wizards' trap, so ye can refrain from commenting on *that*, too!"

"Hmm. Someone's very touchy this morning," Storm told the ceiling.

Elminster made a rude sound popular with small boys, turned a corner, and started along the corridor even faster.

"What if she turns willful and impatient?" Elminster asked suddenly, as they rushed along the damp and dark passage together. He shook his head. "She could do so much damage . . ."

Storm snorted. "And we, down the years, have not?"

"Ye know what I mean, lass. Goes wrong, like Sammaster and—well, too many others. The Realms could be in *real* trouble."

Storm put a hand on Elminster's shoulder. His muscles were as tight as drawn bowstrings. "Then we'll have to destroy her," she said softly. "As we've had to destroy bright weapons we forged before. The needs of the Realms demand, and we must meet those needs."

"And *then* what? How shall we find a successor if she's gone?"

Storm grinned. "Again, needs demand. You'll just have to father some new ones, won't you?"

"Ah, thanks for that broth," Delnor said hesitantly, once the door of the Dragonriders' Club had closed behind them, leaving the two men standing in the starting-to-get-noisy street. "Very good, that was."

Arclath shrugged. "Tables are like beds; far better shared." In unspoken accord they set off along the promenade together, walking at a leisurely pace, as he added, "So tell me more of this tumult at the palace—does the king seem agitated? Or Ganrahast? Or is it mainly courtiers fussing and hand-wringing as they contemplate favorite possible dooms?"

Delnor winced and flushed simultaneously. "You know the palace well."

"Well enough to spot a palace messenger looking for a way not to answer me directly, yes." Arclath grinned. "So give, friend Delnor. Worry not; I won't be asking you for guard deployments or whom our wizards of war are most attentively going to be farscrying. Just the general mood, and who's setting it ... or trying to."

They'd been strolling around the great arc of the promenade in no particular haste but were already within sight of where it met the city wall in one of Suzail's great gates. Arclath turned to walk into the nearest side street, entertaining the vague notion of heading to the harbor, when a fanfare of war-horns rang out at the east gate.

As the flourish had intended them to, they stopped to watch. A large group of armsmen on matching horses came riding into the city, a great clattering of many hooves echoing off the gate arch. The riders surrounded a string of richly appointed coaches.

"A noble coming to the council," Delnor said uncertainly, peering at the pennants fluttering from lance points.

One glance at those banners had told Arclath the identity of the arriving party. "Lord Daeclander Illance," he volunteered. "Arriving early—as he does for all court events he deems too important to ignore—so as to have plenty of time for tasting the, ah, pleasures of Suzail and transacting as much shady business as he thinks he can get away with before the war wizards and highknights actually start sitting in his lap to listen in."

He grinned. "I imagine Rothglar will be more than a little annoyed. He has to rein himself in a trifle and behave when his father's in town. Daeclander has so run out of patience with his eldest son that disowning him might well be a positive pleasure. It's not as though Velyandra's birthed him only a few sons; Rothglar has eight brothers, last time I checked."

The riders started to fan out, to form a broad front across the promenade to create the maximum inconvenience for others and stir up as much notice as possible; Arclath sighed in disgust and led Delnor firmly into a side street. "We'll turn south at the next street crossing," he murmured, and they did—but soon detoured hastily back westward at the intersection after that, as a dung wagon came rumbling toward them, bringing its reek with it.

"I *knew* there was a reason I usually tarry at the Eel until the highsun patrons start to flood in," Arclath declaimed— and then swore as a second dung wagon came their way, goading them into ducking up the nearest alley.

It was wide and relatively uncluttered and clean-smelling, as Suzailan alleys went—they could tell without looking for tall landmarks that they were close to the palace and far from the Westwall slums—but the courtier and the lordling soon came to an abrupt halt as a *third* dung wagon rumbled into the muddy midyard of the city block that the alley had led them to, and came to a creaking stop, blocking their path.

The drover drew a knife from his boot and with its pommel struck a two-toned chime next to his head—and Arclath and Delnor were mildly interested to observe that this signal bore immediate fruit. Many sleepy figures promptly shuffled out of the lofty back balcony doorways or stout back doors of the surrounding shoulder-to-stone-shoulder tallhouses, down a rickety variety of back stairs, and out through various locked or latched gates at the bottom of those stairs to proffer a coin each to the drover—copper thumbs—and then empty their buckets of nightsoil.

Delnor looked pained. "Let's go another way. This could take *forever*."

Arclath started to nod—then stiffened, plucked imperiously at the palace messenger's arm, and pointed.

One of the weary figures who had just lowered her emptied bucket was the very dancer they were seeking. He said as much, hissing out the words.

"You're sure?" Delnor muttered excitedly.

"I *have* seen her without her mask, more than once," Arclath said, nodding. "I'm sure."

Unaware of their scrutiny, she turned and stumbled sleepily out of their sight behind the dung wagon. They hastened after her, but when they rounded the reeking wagon, there was no sign of her among the trudging neighbors.

"She must dwell hard by, in one of these," Arclath said, peering up and all around. Then he started purposefully for the nearest door.

Delnor ran two swift steps, hesitated, then dared to lay hands on a noble lord, and held him firmly back.

"We *can't* scour out a score or more tallhouses," he protested. "Most folk won't even answer their doors; are you going to try to break them all down? And what'll you tell the Watch? I'm Lord Arclath Delcastle, and I'm searching for a mask dancer because I—uh, because I—"

Arclath nodded. "Your point is made." He stared up at the surrounding balconies once more, sighed, then asked briskly, "The club, tonight, then? Dusktide?"

Delnor agreed, then stifled a yawn of his own. As the dung wagon rumbled off along the alley again, he waved farewell, then turned and started trudging in the direction of the royal court.

Arclath watched him go then caught sight of a young lad trailing past with an empty nightsoil bucket.

"Lad!" he called and held up a copper coin.

The boy stopped, and Arclath tossed it to him. Watching it

get snatched deftly out of the air, he said, "A silver falcon to go with that if you bring me a hire coach right speedily."

The boy stared at him for the moment it took to judge Arclath's fine clothes and sword then grinned and sprinted off, tossing the bucket over his gate as he went.

He was back before Arclath reached the mouth of the alley, a small coach clattering in his wake.

Coin, Arclath reflected ruefully for about the hundredth time thus far that month, can work wonders.

The coach was a swift one; he soon overtook Delnor and called up to the drover to stop.

"Don't you have all sorts of Crown errands and inspections to do?" He grinned, beckoning Delnor to enter the conveyance with a grand flourish.

The messenger's mouth fell open, and he shied back. "Yes, but not in a *coach*! I can't be spending Crown coins like that!"

"You're not," Arclath said sweetly. "*I* am."

Delnor blinked. "Uh—ah—yes, but—but everyone will think you're buying my approvals and Crown business!"

"They already do. You're a courtier, remember?"

Delnor sighed, shrugged, and climbed into the coach. "That's . . . overly cynical," he murmured.

"That's Cormyrean," Arclath corrected airily. "We border *Sembia*, by the gods! We'd have to be barking mad not to be cynical!"

Mockingly Delnor made a halfhearted barking sound by way of reply—but broke off abruptly as he saw a shopkeeper staring curiously at him.

By the gods, indeed.

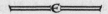

Storm peered out of the secret passage again, then drew back her head and slid the panel closed in calm, smooth haste.

"Court and palace certainly seem to be in something of an uproar," she observed.

Elminster nodded silently, looking tired and less than pleased.

As they'd worked their way through the cellars, heading south from palace to court, seeking a way they could depart either royal building unobserved to slip into Suzail for some Amarune-hunting, neither of them had failed to notice the large and frequent armed patrols of Purple Dragons who were suddenly tramping tirelessly through the halls of both vast buildings—or standing alertly, guarding most secret passage entrances.

To say nothing of the many grim-faced trios and quartets of war wizards searching this room and that.

"They've found the bodies," Elminster growled. "And that, plus the inevitable rumors of assassins and worse being prepared for the council—or by or for the nobles now gathering in the city before Foril's little get-together—is causing all of this sudden burst of vigilance."

"Well," Storm replied, "our long-standing palace identities won't serve us any longer; they know the Rhauligans are Elminster the mage-murderer and the notorious Harper who walks with him, now. Do we burn one of the baubles you took from those three ward-meddlers, to look like two courtiers or palace maids? They probably won't be too suspicious of two dirty, work-worn lasses!"

"Frightened and suspicious mages usually suspect everyone of everything," Elminster reminded her darkly, "and everyone of being someone else than they appear to be. They use magic for disguises, so of course they think everyone else does, too."

"Oh, stop being so cheerful," Storm said serenely. "If they're going to pounce on us, they'll pounce on us. It's not as if we haven't spent years being Elgorn and Stornara Rhauligan, repairers and restorers of the ever-crumbling stone, plaster, tapestries, and wood of these great buildings."

"Descended, moreover," Elminster joined in, almost chanting, "from the famous highknight hero, Glarasteer Rhauligan."

They snorted in unison—and the Sage of Shadowdale held up one hand with a grin, drew a ring from his belt pouch, and announced, "Many minds, approaching fast. So we burn a bauble, as ye suggested. Thy typical wizard of war may be darned suspicious when he sees Royal Magician Ganrahast and his trusted Vainrence striding along a passage—but he'll hesitate before he blasts them, I'll wager."

He frowned, there was a flash from inside his fist as the ring vanished, and a brief tingling sensation crept over them both.

Storm held up one of her hands. It had gone hairy. "Hmmph. *Not* an improvement, I must say," she commented. "I get to be Vainrence, of course."

"Of course. I'll tender ye my apologies later," El replied, turning back from the door that led into the overly bustling hall beyond, and seeking a passage he knew to be older, moldier, and usually quieter.

It was still all of those things and led them out into a dark and deserted room where disused furniture was shrouded in dust wraps.

"An old tablecloth of Rhigaerd's, if I'm not mistaken," Elminster murmured, peering at one of them. "Aye, there's the stain where—"

"*Hold, intruders!*"

The shout from behind them was loud and sharp.

"Hold what?" Storm asked mildly, reaching out two rather eager hands—only to find that she was about to embrace several onrushing spear points.

"I *thought* I heard voices!" one of the Purple Dragons at the other ends of those weapons snarled excitedly.

An entire patrol of Dragons trotted forward, clanking and clanging as they hastily drew daggers or swords and rushed to menace the newly discovered perils to the Crown.

The Royal Magician and his Lord Warder Vainrence stood calmly waiting as a ring of glittering spears swiftly formed around them.

"Halt!" the patrol commander barked at them, unnecessarily.

The two immobile men exchanged glances with each other then turned to reply in laconic unison, "Aye, still halted."

"Who—oh, by the Dragon!" The swordcaptain knew their faces and was suddenly looking decidedly ill. "M-my apologies, Lords!"

"Accepted," Elminster replied with dignity. "Now continue your patrol, Swordcaptain. The enemies of Cormyr are, I fear, everywhere."

"Closer than you think," an angry voice said sharply. "Arrest them!"

The furious speaker strode into the room. "I'm Wizard of War Rorskryn Mreldrake," he snapped, "and these two men are impostors, using magic to seem to be the Lords Ganrahast and Vainrence!"

Purple Dragons stared at him then swiftly and frowningly back at the two men standing quietly in the midst of their ring of spears.

"I have just now come straight from converse with those two lords—the *real* ones," Mreldrake added, "and as you can all see, these two are dressed as the Royal Magician and Lord Warder were garbed a day back, *not* as they now are."

The Purple Dragons stiffened, three of them—who'd evidently seen Ganrahast and Vainrence not long ago—starting to frown and nod.

The possibly false Vainrence cast a calm look at his companion, who shook his head ever so slightly before sighing and announcing, "Yon mage is mistaken, but in the interest of sparing the lives of diligent Purple Dragons, we'll not resist. Obey your orders, Swordcaptain."

"I . . . I shall," that officer said grimly. "Seek to work no magic as we conduct the pair of you into the presence of some wizards of war who will then interrogate you. 'Bring us anyone suspicious,' they told me . . . and you certainly are."

"No doubt. I also have no doubt whatsoever that when he hears of this, the king," the possibly false Ganrahast informed the Purple Dragon darkly, "will not be pleased."

"You tell the wizards that," the swordcaptain replied evenly. "They may even believe you."

Chapter
SEVENTEEN
Wizards Go to War

Lock the door, let loose the hounds,
Our lives will be peaceful no more.
Trust in no laws nor all daily rounds,
The wizards are going to war.

> from the Cormyrean ballad
> *Our Wizards of War* (composer unknown)
> first heard in Suzail, circa the Year of the Turret

Meldrake gave the Purple Dragons a nod and an unpleasant smile and disappeared rather hastily back through the door he'd come from.

The swordcaptain looked at the two lords who might not be lords and pointed imperiously at another door, one that stood open. "Walk that way, saers. We'll be escorting you—and won't hesitate to make holes in you with our spears, so try nothing foolish."

"I rarely do," the possible Ganrahast impostor informed the man with dignity as they set off, the Dragons shifting position to keep their prisoners menaced before and behind by leveled spears.

After a few strides he added, "I require your name, Swordcaptain."

"Yet will receive only disappointing silence," came the prompt reply. "I don't take orders from prisoners."

The perhaps-false Royal Magician stopped and spun around to face the officer directly, ignoring the spears that thrust at him warningly. "In the name of the king," he barked, "yield unto me your *name!*"

The officer hesitated.

"As you seem to be a stickler for orders," Vainrence put in softly, "suppose you obey one of the standing ones."

"We're required to give our names to Dragons of superior rank, certain courtiers, and . . . uh," the swordcaptain replied, wincing. "Ah, Lord Ganrahast, I am Paereth Vandurn. *Swordcaptain* Paereth Vandurn." He regained his gruff confidence almost visibly, thrusting his chin forward. "So, who are the two of you—really?"

The prisoner who might or might not be Lord Vainrence thrust a spear aside with one hand to wag a disapproving finger at the swordcaptain. "You're less than polite, Slamburn, and I'll tell this war wizard so! Lead us to him!"

"I am *not*—," the swordcaptain began heatedly, but he stopped as he saw smirks appear and as hastily vanish from the faces of more than a few of his men.

Drawing a deep breath, he managed a brittle smile and said, "But of course, Lord Warder. If you'll kindly proceed through yon door, obeying the directions of the *nice* men in uniform holding the spears pointed at you, you shall have your opportunity to speak to a war wizard soon enough. For the greater glory of Cormyr, of course."

"For some years," Elminster informed Vandurn haughtily, "those very words have been mine to speak: 'for the greater glory of Cormyr.'"

"Ahhh, *good*," the officer replied heavily, his smile becoming decidedly desperate. "*Very* good. The door, now, is just this way . . ."

On the far side of the ring of spears from the swordcaptain, someone among the stone-faced Dragons snickered.

"Who did that?" Vandurn snapped. "*Who?* I'll be requiring some nam—"

He broke off and fell silent just a moment too late.

The Royal Magician began the laughter, and the Lord Warder swelled it with hearty guffaws, but at least two Dragons joined in—and then they all did, mirth ringing around the passage.

With one exception. In the heart of it all, a certain

crimson-to-the-ears swordcaptain clenched his jaws and silently steamed.

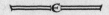

Talane. That name echoed like a curse in her mind, the chant of some dark seer desiring her doom ... *Talane.*

One night, and she was undone. One night—no, less than half an hour—and her life had been shattered, her freedom gone.

She was caught in the ruthless talons of someone she didn't even know.

Amarune felt exhausted. Bone weary. With a full night facing her.

Disheartened, the bards called it. When singing about someone else. She wished that was who felt that way, instead of her: someone else.

She pushed open the side door of the club and slipped inside. It was hours before she'd have to be up on that stage, but this was her usual routine, and what most Dragonriders' dancers did: come early, soak in a long bath, dry off slowly in a warm room and have her hair done by Taerlene or Mrarie, eat a hearty meal, and then sink into a nice long nap. All of it behind the club's closed doors, so she'd be safe inside, not having to run the gauntlet of leering admirers that would await her if she arrived later.

The dressing room was silent and empty. She frowned. Usually four or five of her fellow dancers who followed the same routine made it there before her ...

There was something in her accustomed chair. A large sack, it looked to be. Laundry, dumped here by one of the maids, getting interrupted?

The door swung closed behind her with its usual slight squeal—and then her chair spun around by itself to face her.

Or, no—the man sitting in it had turned it with a kick, to face her and warm her with his easy smile.

No sack, after all. The Lord Arclath Delcastle was lounging in her chair.

"Well met," he said brightly, his smile growing even broader.

Amarune was too startled to be polite. "What are *you* doing here?" she blurted.

"Waiting for you, obviously. I paid your fellow dancers some rather large sums to be primped at the Gilded Feather today, to leave the room clear for me. For us."

The Gilded Feather was the most expensive pretty-parlor in all Suzail. Though it was only a street away, Amarune had never been inside it. Its noble patrons tended to sneer at mask dancers, and its staff did rather more than sneer.

"*Us?*"

Gods above, *no*. Trapped by the mysterious Talane, and now this.

Oh, he'd been nice enough to her, and all nobles were crazed, but . . . stlarn it, she and probably most of Suzail thought the prancing fop Arclath Delcastle preferred *men* in bed and admired women merely as diversions.

But it seemed as if he was going to turn out to be another nightmare. One of the "obsessed" who stalked dancers and made dangerous nuisances of themselves until they had to be dealt with. Not that dealing with noble heirs was easy.

Well, farruk the Purple Dragon, she was going to deal with him, right away! It would cost her lots of forgone coins in the years ahead, but—

Whether or not it dissuaded him, she was going to beat the natal innards out of him! He'd be a laughingstock if he went to the Robes about her, so the worst that could happen would be her arrest—which would at least get her away from the spying of Talane and out of that bitch's reach, and perhaps win her a little time to think of a way to flee *that* trap.

Without another word or wild thought, Amarune set her teeth and went for him, hands like claws and knees ready to drive in hard and see if she could dent that *ridiculous* codpiece he was wearing.

"Lady!" he said reproachfully, ducking and twisting with surprising speed—and lashing out a hand to ensnare one of her wrists.

Successfully. Gods, but he was strong!

She clawed at him with her free hand, catching a nail on something.

"Lady," the lordling panted, wriggling like an eel under her, his free hand grabbing at hers, "I don't want you to misunderstand my—uhh!—motives. I'm not here to—ah!—assault your—uh!—charms!"

He caught hold of her other wrist. With a shriek, Amarune slammed herself down on him, pelvis riding his belt buckle bruisingly, so she could get close enough to bite him. And managed it. Hard.

He roared out a less-than-coherent curse of pain as she wrenched her hands free and clawed at him again, raking at his face.

"*Easy*, wench!" he snarled, slamming a forearm across the side of her head hard enough to twist her half off him into dazed darkness. "I might *need* some of these limbs in the years ahead, you know!"

"You should've thought of that—," Amarune panted at him as light and sound came back to her in a throbbing rush that left her head ringing, and she tried to claw at him again viciously, "before you—"

"Sat down in a chair in an empty room, after paying for the privilege?" he snapped. "Stop this! By Tempus, lass, leave *off*! I just want to ask you—uhhh!—some questions!"

"Oh, like how many of your friends will I pleasure for a cut price? Or will I let Lord Delcastle's pet hired wizard give me feathers and a tail for the night, so you can ride a peacock at last? A peacock on a peacock? *Hey?*"

Right out of breath from that outburst, Amarune had to put her head down, shuddering, to snatch air as they struggled. Under her, the noble straightened one arm and thrust her up and away from him.

Gods, he's strong. If he *really* loses his temper . . .

Amarune twisted, slapped at him, and tried to jerk free all at once—and Delcastle's hand slid from a tight grip on her shoulder to a good hard grip on her left breast.

Farruk! That *hurt!*

"Sorry!" he blurted hastily, letting go. Amarune back-handed him one across the face as hard as she could, then used her other hand to do it again, rocking the chair.

"No," he groaned as she slammed an elbow into his ribs, "not those sort of questions! H-heed me, lass! You—unhh—you were listening to all we said, my friends and I, when you were dancing for us! Whom did you tell?"

"Tell *what?*" Amarune snarled into his face. "You think I'm some sort of spy?"

"Yes, but I need to know for who—uh, whom! The nobles behind the murders at the palace?"

"*What?*" Amarune lost her temper utterly, sheer rage almost choking her. "You think I—"

Words failed her. Shrieking, she clawed Delcastle's belt dagger out of its sheath and stabbed at him, the blade going wide as his forearms slammed against hers in a desperate parry. Before she could try again he'd clutched her dagger wrist, fingers tightening this time.

Sobbing in pain—he was crushing her wrist, he was *crushing* it!—she flung all of her trembling weight and strength behind trying to drive it down into his throat, before ...

Just as Delcastle kicked out desperately, trying to make the point of the dagger miss the throat it was just about to slice—the door banged open.

The blade missed its mark as the chair lurched sideways, giving Amarune a momentary glimpse of Tress looking horrified, with some of the club bouncers right behind her, before they all rushed forward.

A moment later, Amarune's head rang from a furious slap. Tress tore the dagger away from her even as that blow landed.

"Are you *mad?*" the owner of the Dragonriders' shrieked into Amarune's ear. "D'you know what will *happen* to us—to the Dragonriders'—if you kill a noble? Girl, you're fired—*fired!* Get out of here at once, or I'll call the Watch and let this noble set the Black Robes on you!"

"A-a moment," a battered Arclath groaned hastily from beneath Amarune. "Good Lady Tress, I fear you misunderstand. I *paid* this, ah, *highly* professional dancer to do this!"

Sudden silence fell, and the club bouncers stopped trying to haul Amarune off the man under her and hurl her bodily up at the waiting ceiling.

Tress stared at what she could see of Lord Delcastle, then at the panting, obviously furious Amarune atop him.

"Isn't she a peerless actress?" Arclath managed to croak, waving his free—and bleeding—hand at the dumbfounded, on-the-verge-of-tears Amarune. "Superb, eh?"

Tress returned her stare to him, incredulity warring with disgust across her face. To hide her own similar expression, Amarune dropped her head to stare at the floor, her disheveled tresses falling over her face.

"You . . . you *welcome* being beaten and overmastered, Lord?"

"By the right high-spirited lass, yes," Arclath assured the club owner almost eagerly, his bright smile returning. "My friends and I saw this one yestereve, and I knew she was the one for us; I came asking for her this morn, you'll recall. Now, please believe me, I did *not* intend to imperil her position here, and she did not want to trammel the routine of this night's mask dancing . . . wherefore we sought to transact the seeing-to of my needs here and now. Please accept my apologies for the misunderstanding and the upset this has caused. The arrangements—and therefore all fault—are entirely mine. I'll happily pay for any damages; your dancer has been *magnificent*, far outstripping even my high expectations!"

Tress stared at him for a while longer before turning her gaze to Amarune.

"Is . . . is this true, Rune?" she asked in obvious disbelief, but seeing the offered road out of this for them all.

Struggling not to cry, bewildered and seeing nothing but traps yawning on all roads she might choose ahead, Amarune managed to lift her chin and say, "Y-yes."

Tress sighed a long sigh, closing her eyes for a moment, then gave a polite nod to the torn and bleeding noble in the chair.

"Please accept *my* apologies for the interruption, Lord Delcastle. Pray proceed."

Without another word she ushered the half-grinning bouncers out, not seeing Amarune open her mouth and raise a hand to protest—only to freeze and stay silent.

When the door had closed again, Amarune glared at the man still beneath her and hissed bitterly, "So now you have a hold over me, just as you sought! What's this all about, anyhail? What foolish game are you playing?"

"No game," Arclath murmured, rising from the chair but with gentle courtesy holding out a hand to assist her in standing rather than being dumped on the floor as he did so, as if she were his equal.

When he faced her, however, standing very close to her so that their noses almost touched, his smile was gone.

"You were listening to us while we talked, my friends and I," he murmured, his voice low and his eyes boring into hers. "Why? Whom did you tell what we said about the council—or will you tell?"

"No one," Amarune hissed back scornfully. "Who would care?"

He regarded her thoughtfully. "I can call to mind a score of nobles who will be hungry indeed for every detail," he said slowly. "How much will it cost for your silence?"

"Why do you ask?" she whispered bitterly. "Whatever answer I give, having me killed will be cheaper, won't it? For a silence you can truly trust in?"

Arclath stared at her expressionlessly, then bent, plucked up his knife from the floor where Tress had flung it down, and handed it to Amarune, hilt first.

"I trust you right now," he told her quietly, pointing at the dagger and then at his throat, before leaning forward to offer it, undefended. "Completely."

They stared at each other, Amarune trembling—until she slapped his dagger back into his hand and snarled, "I need a drink."

The door behind them promptly opened, and Tress stepped in with a tray that held a decanter and three metal goblets.

"Thought you'd say that," she told them with a nonchalant smile, obviously not caring that they'd know she'd been listening at the door. "Compliments of the house."

Arclath and Amarune exchanged glances. Then, slowly, they both started to chuckle.

The passage was a long one, and the moment the laughter died away, the furious swordcaptain set a brisk pace along it, forcing his prisoners almost into a trot. He speeded up still more as they approached a darkened stretch, where by some servant's oversight no lamps glimmered in the sconces that in an earlier age had held torches.

Into the gloom they plunged, Vandurn snarling orders, and his men beginning to pant, the prisoners stumbling as they were prodded into greater haste.

"Get going!" the swordcaptain barked at everyone. "I've half a mind—"

"Well, that's true," Vainrence agreed loudly, drawing snorts of mirth from several of the nearest Dragons.

Then it happened.

There was a sudden burst of light around the Royal Magician's head, and a smaller one abruptly flamed into being around the brow of Lord Vainrence, wildly whirling and crackling bolts of light out of nowhere that stabbed from one man to the other, brightening into a shared nimbus.

"Stop that!" the swordcaptain roared. "Stop it at once!"

Then he saw his prisoners were staggering and clutching their heads as they sagged, clearly as taken aback by the sudden magic as he and all his men were.

The eerie light snarled louder than Vandurn could, drowning out his shouted orders with a louder voice, a panting madwoman's voice that soared and wavered in lost, mournful pain as it thundered up and down the passage: "El! Oh, my Elminster! Where are you? I need you! I'm dying . . . dying! Elminsterrrrrrrrrr!" The last word became a shriek, a raw animal cry of agony and need that sent everyone to their knees, clutching their ears as that scream raced through their heads and ran around and around in their minds, howling in desperation and keening in despair ... keening ...

When at last it faded, Swordcaptain Vandurn lay senseless on his back, his sweat-drenched face staring at nothing. Around him, most of his Dragons were the same, sprawled and motionless; the remainder were curled up and sobbing or groaning, spears fallen and forgotten.

Elminster and Storm stared at each other, their own faces wet and wild.

"Well?" Storm panted, bosom heaving; her Vainrence guise was melting away with every sobbing breath.

"Go to her," Elminster snapped, snatching things of magic from inside his robes and pouches at his belt in almost feverish haste. "As fast as you can, and feed her everything you have to! Then get back here!"

"But, El—"

"Go! I'll be fine here. *Something's* happened to her, and we must find out what. Go! Use the Dalestride; the time for stealth is past."

"It'll be guarded," Storm warned breathlessly. The Dalestride was a portal linking the Room of the Watchful Sentinel with a certain glade just west of Mistledale. Reinforced by Caladnei, it had survived the Spellplague, and King Foril and his wizards of war and highknights knew all about it; it was never unguarded.

"Good." Elminster's sudden smile was as ruthless as that of an old and hungry wolf. "I'm glad of that." Almost hungrily he added, "I'll go with you to open the way."

"If they stand against us—Alusair and Foril, Ganrahast and Vainrence—"

"The wise ones will stand aside and live," the Sage of Shadowdale told her grimly, snatching her hand and starting to stride back down the passage. "The fools will taste consequences ... and Cormyr will be the stronger."

CHAPTER
EIGHTEEN

TALONS AND PEACOCKS AND WORSE

Bright fire races round my face again,
Burning through my little brain,
I may soon make many die if I
Hear one more stlarned-fool jaunty verse
Of sparkling-sharp talons, and peacocks, and worse.

from the ballad *Old Lord Ratturbury*
composed by Lalanth Tarntapple
Bard Wayward of Suzail
in the Year of the Forged Sigil

Marlin Stormserpent loved the Old King's Favorite. Oh, it was stiffly expensive, even to a wealthy noble heir, but it was also one of the most glittering lounges on the promenade, a place to see and be seen in. Not to mention that the food was good, the wine even better.

Moreover, it had been a very useful place to dine in, down the years. Upper-rung courtiers frequented such eateries—fattening themselves on the public purse, stlarn them—and by listening to the excited converse going on around him without seeming to do so, he learned a lot about what was currently afoot in Crown matters. Without all those expensive bribes and even-more-costly spies.

So the younger Lord Stormserpent had made it his custom to take highsunfeast at the Favorite most days, despite the cost. It wasn't as exclusive as, say, Darcleir's, derided by the lowborn as "the House of Peacocks" for all the flamboyantly dressed nobility to be found there daily, but the gossip of courtiers tended to be more intriguing than the usual airily empty boasting—or endless complaining about new ways and those who forged them—of nobles. Even when House

Stormserpent couldn't profit from what its heir overheard, Marlin learned a lot of interesting things.

Just now, for instance, word was spreading like wildfire around Suzail of some mysterious invading army that had been slaughtering people in the palace. Parts of which—the table to his right was whispering loudly enough to be heard down the far end of the room—had been, as a result, sealed off to everyone.

"Filled with scores of dismembered corpses," an underclerk of protocol hissed excitedly.

"The floors ankle deep in pools of congealing blood!" a gentleman usher hissed back.

Not to be outdone, the two cellarers at the table to Marlin's immediate left wanted most of the room to overhear just how upset Understeward Corleth Fentable was. The man was driving them—to say nothing of the high chatelaine and the clerk of the shield—into seething rages with his prohibitions on anyone opening *this* door or walking down *that* passage.

"If we aren't allowed to go a few more places in the palace, the king'll find nothing but well water in the glasses set out at this council—and nothing for him and his oh-so-exalted peacocks of guests to nibble on but boiled potatoes with a side of horse mash!"

As the specifics of just what parts of the palace had been made off-limits were excitedly discussed, Marlin had to hide a smile behind his ornate goblet of best Berduskan dark.

Everyone was being kept away from the palace-end of the passage he'd recently used, and the vicinity of the Dragonskull and the Wyrms Ascending.

Which meant that the stalwart wizards of war didn't know what to do. They'd searched that part of the palace from top to bottom, found nothing useful, and had decided to hide their futility behind the usual cloak of mystery.

So sea and sky were clear, as the sailors liked to say; a certain heir of House Stormserpent could freely use that passage to get back into the palace, take his two items of the Nine to the Dragonskull Chamber, and see if he could summon two flaming ghosts out of them to obey him.

Marlin got rid of his smile, drained his goblet and set it down, and rose, tossing just enough coins onto the table. It was time to fetch a certain sword and a particular chalice and do a little testing. And then . . .

Well, then it would be high time to set about transforming Cormyr to his liking.

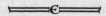

Manshoon turned away from casting careful spells on a thing of tentacles and strolled across the cavern to another of his glowing scenes.

For some months, through a variety of minds he could eavesdrop upon, he'd taken to lurking around Stormserpent Towers.

There were larger and grander noble mansions in Suzail where louder preening peacocks dwelt, and there had never been any particular shortage of idiot nobles desiring to overthrow the Obarskyrs or work smaller treasons . . . but there was something *interesting* about the Stormserpents. Young and ambitious Marlin Stormserpent in particular.

Perhaps it was the feeling that something long-brewing and uncontrollable was soon going to break forth, regardless of what befell Cormyr in the process. Marlin was heir of his House and one of an all-too-common sort of noble heir. Purringly handsome and bright-witted—but only about a tenth as brilliant as he considered himself to be. All such tended to be more rash than wise and more ambitious than competent . . . but that was part of what made spying on them entertaining.

So Manshoon wormed his way into the mind of servant after servant at the Towers until he could skulk, listen, and watch at will—riding the unwitting mount of his choice as just one more black shadow in a mansion that had become largely unlit, sheet-shrouded, and neglected. Oh, yes; long before he'd taken any interest in it, House Stormserpent had become a mere shadow of its former self.

Marlin's father was long dead, leaving real power in the hands of his widow Narmitra. Who hated everything about

Suzailan high society and court intrigue and was letting her brother-in-law Mhedalakh play patriarch because she knew Marlin hated it all, too, and would prefer the freedom to pursue his own interests as long as Mhedalakh could totter along.

It amused her vastly—just as it did Manshoon—that Mhedalakh's feeble wits and his being neither the head of his House nor its heir frustrated other nobles no end. The Stormserpents couldn't be bound by any agreements old Mhedalakh made, and fellow nobles couldn't use him as a reliable source of information about the family nor as a bearer of proposals, agreements, or opinions to any Stormserpent.

There was nothing foolish nor slow-witted about the Lady Narmitra. No peacock, she.

It had been almost immediately clear to Manshoon that Marlin, whether he admitted it to himself or not, was more than a little afraid of her.

Even before Manshoon had stolen into his mind, the young lord's occasional murmurings to himself revealed all too clearly that Marlin suspected his mother knew what he'd done to Rondras but said nothing because she had always liked him far more than his brothers—and because she was, in turn, a shade scared of him.

And so they danced, mother and son, in a slow and endless duel of barbed comments, deployments of servants, and tacit accords.

Manshoon observed all their little ruses and conversational gambits with frequent delight. It was better than a play.

For his part, Marlin dealt with his mother cordially but firmly, and early on obtained her promise to keep out of certain towers of the house, which were to be his alone. Manshoon admired the lordling's patience over that. For a long time after obtaining that promise, Marlin did nothing at home that Lady Stormserpent would find at all suspicious—so she could, and did, pry and spy in "his" towers many times only to find nothing worth the looking and eventually lose interest.

At long last, Marlin Stormserpent's long-awaited breaking forth might just be about to happen. He'd returned home in a hurry, and was bustling about getting the Flying Blade and the chalice out of hiding with a distinct air of glee.

Marlin took off his customary sword belt and weapon, replacing it with the enchanted one, then put on an oversized dark jerkin, thrusting into its breast both the chalice and the notes he'd assembled on how to compel and call forth the blueflame ghosts.

Then he went looking around Stormserpent Towers for the two men he trusted most in the world. The bodyguards he'd hired, rewarded well, and worked closely with the past six or seven seasons.

"The two men," Manshoon murmured as Marlin rushed off down a passage, paying the dark and motionless form of the House servant whose mind Manshoon was riding no heed at all, "who are *almost* as personally loyal to you as you believe them to be."

He shook his head. Marlin Stormserpent had thus far been very fortunate in the trust he'd placed in his servants. Far luckier than most nobles.

And just how long would that luck hold out, hmm?

An insistent chiming wrenched Manshoon's attention away from Stormserpent Towers and back to another of the floating scenes in his cavern. He peered at it for a moment, thrusting his nose forward like the beak of an eager hawk, and slowly smiled.

Well, now.

Mreldrake was close enough . . . and this was almost better than he could have hoped for.

A battle that should take care of another generous handful of these irritating and meddlesome wizards of war and highknights—and at the end of it, Storm Silverhand would be gone again, leaving the Sage of Shadowdale standing alone.

Just where Manshoon wanted him.

Yes, this should be *good* . . .

In midsmile his eye fell upon another glowing scene, and mirth faded into thoughtfulness in an instant.

Then he nodded to himself. It was high time to remove the head wizards from circulation in the Palace, before they had a chance to do anything dangerous. Such as waking up enough to provide some organization and leadership for their magelings, once news of the battle with Elminster reached them.

So what were they up to, just now? Kordran was one of his dupes, so it would be simple to eavesdrop.

Manshoon let his mind descend into the quavering pool of fear that was Kordran's mind, at the moment. From there, he would be close enough to leap into Vainrence, probably undetected...

"I—uh—I—Lords, I—we—"

Wizard of War Aumanas Kordran was as white as new-fallen winter snow and quivering with terror under his streaming mask of sweat, his eyes large and staring.

Abruptly those eyes rolled up in his head, and he slumped to the floor like the proverbial sack of potatoes. A large, limp sack of potatoes.

Ganrahast and Vainrence exchanged weary glances. Their shared opinion of the terrified young war wizard was not a high one, and his report had been neither coherent nor conclusive. Moreover, it was the second time he'd responded to their increasingly sharp questioning by collapsing.

"Leave him," the Mage Royal said curtly.

Vainrence nodded. "Orders?"

Ganrahast said promptly, "Set a guard over the palace-end of that passage: Nelezmur, Tomarr, Baerendrith, and Helharbras. No doubt all manner of curious courtiers will come sidling up to have a peek at what's so horrible, the moment word of my more general order gets around."

Vainrence smiled a trifle bitterly. "And that order is?"

"No courtier nor visitor is to be allowed within earshot of the Chamber of the Wyrms Ascending until specific orders to the contrary are proclaimed by the king or by me," Ganrahast replied. "And any unfamiliar person seen in the palace is to be retreated from and reported to me—even if they claim to be royalty or an envoy or a ghost or a highknight."

Vainrence nodded and made for the door.

Ganrahast watched him open it, look out, and acquire the near-smile that meant something had met with Vainrence's approval.

Something had. The guards had been facing the closed door from the other side of the passage, spaced apart from each other and to either side of the door a good distance away, not pressed against the door trying to listen.

Vainrence beckoned to the courtier he saw beyond the far-thest guard, standing by another, open door farther along the passage—and murmuring instructions to a steady stream of scurrying servants. It was Understeward Fentable, who bowed his head and hastened forward to hear Vainrence's will.

As Vainrence started to repeat Ganrahast's orders to the courtier, the Mage Royal turned away and stalked across the room to stare grimly down at the sprawled and senseless Kordran.

It hadn't been much of an interrogation. Perhaps something was awry with the man's wits.

So with that dark possibility raised, what did they *really* know of these latest murders?

If some sort of resident undead had done the slayings, why now—when it had supposedly been haunting the palace for years?

What deeper darkness was it going to herald or goad into happening?

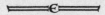

In the darkness of his cavern, Manshoon smiled. Clinging lightly to a small part of Lord Warder Vainrence's mind, he sent his will plunging somewhere else, into a mind darker, colder, and deeper.

Awaken, my Lady Dark Armor. A little task awaits . . .

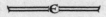

Hurrying along a passage in the darker, damper depths of the royal palace, Ganrahast and Vainrence stiffened in unison and exchanged anxious frowns. An age-old alarm spell had interrupted them, unfolding in their minds like a forgotten door. An unwelcome surprise telling them one of the caskets in the royal crypt had been broken open!

Now fresh tumult was unfolding in their minds. A second Obarskyr coffin had just been breached.

"Should we warn Mallowfaer?" Vainrence snapped.

Ganrahast emitted a very un-Royal Magician-like snort. "Lot of good *that* will do."

His second-in-command smiled. "Heh. Point made. Well, then, shall we warn Fentable?"

"Time enough for that later—when we know what we're warning him about."

They turned the last corner, wands raised and ready and shielding spells spun into being in front of them. A thief's poisoned dart could be a very nasty greeting.

The passage stood empty, and the doors of the crypt were closed.

They exchanged silent glances. Undead, within?

Ganrahast drew a rod he'd hoped never to have to use from its sheath down his leg, and Vainrence activated one of his rings.

At a nod from his superior, the Lord Warder unsealed the doors.

Then he opened them, wand up again, to reveal . . . darkness. Still and silent darkness.

The two mages looked up and down the passage, then at the ceiling, then peered at the ceiling inside the crypt. Nothing.

Ganrahast held up one hand with a ring pulsing on it as seeking magic stole forth, and waited tensely as it found . . . nothing.

The two men exchanged doubtful looks again. Then, hesitantly, they stepped into the crypt, wands held ready.

The silence held. Nothing moved, nothing seemed out of place—*hold*!

The royal crypt was not visited often, but to both men it seemed the coffins and the few relics on the shelves along the back wall were undisturbed, everything very much as it had been the last time they'd been there.

With one exception that was making them both peer again into every corner of the crypt and check the ceiling once more.

One casket—an old and rather plain, massive one, probably one of the kings not long after Duar—stood open, its unbroken lid laid neatly on the floor beside it.

The two senior war wizards peered suspiciously around at all the silent, undisturbed coffins. Nothing moved, and there was no sound but that of their own breathing.

Cautiously—very cautiously—they moved forward, Vainrence at the fore and Ganrahast shooting glances here, there, and everywhere around the crypt and back out the open doors at the empty passage they'd come from.

There was nothing in the stone casket but unmoving, shrouded bones, under a thick cloak of dust.

Vainrence put one hand slowly into the burial cavity, the ring on his smallest finger blazing a steady, unchanged white. No undeath there. Nothing stirred at his intrusion, and he felt no tingling of awakening magic.

Withdrawing his hand, he stepped back and looked at the Royal Magician who had taken a pendant out from under his robes and was holding it up, turning toward this wall of the crypt and then that. It, too, glowed a faint, steady white.

They traded suspicious frowns, then without a word strode to stand back-to-back and started to search all over the crypt, Ganrahast moving cautiously to look here and there, and Vainrence guarding his back.

Still nothing.

There was certainly no intruder—not an invisible one, and not a ghost. The wards that prevented all translocations were still pulsing strongly around them; the magic alive in the crypt was so strong and swirling that they had no hope of telling what spells, if any, had been used there recently . . . still less, longer ago.

The alarm spells had told of two disturbed burials, yet there was only one open coffin. With nothing missing or disturbed, if that dust could be trusted. Still, there were simple, everyday spells to settle shrouds of dust on things . . .

"Your guess?" Ganrahast asked calmly.

Vainrence shrugged. "Some long-ago spell to lift a casket lid? Either it started to fade and was written so as to function before its energy ebbed too much for it to do so, or something among all the wards and shieldings in here triggered it?"

"That," Ganrahast murmured, "seems entirely too convenient. Not to mention overly benign."

"So I feel, too," Vainrence agreed. "I await your better explanation, Mage Royal."

In the silence that followed, they traded wry grins.

Then Ganrahast shrugged. "Let's shift this lid back where it should be and see what that does to the alarms; reset, gone off and gone, or still awake and insisting an intrusion has occurred."

The coffin was old; there were certainly no spells to levitate the lid. They staggered under the weight of the carved stone slab momentarily, grunting and huffing to heave it high enough to restore it to the top of its casket—and only then saw a fresh piece of parchment on the floor under where the lid had lain. There was writing on it.

Vainrence stooped. "You are doomed," he read aloud.

As he spoke, the lid of the closed casket beside them lifted just enough for magic to be triggered from within it.

There was a singing sound, as if an idle hand had slashed across the highest strings of a harp—and the two war wizards stiffened in unison.

To stand frozen, unseeing and unbreathing in the midst of their own new and pale auras.

"Well, well," Targrael murmured, lifting with casual ease the lid she'd lain concealed under and climbing gracefully out from atop the bones she'd been relaxing on during the blunderings of these two. "These old Obarskyr trinkets still serve quite effectively. Unlike the realm's wizards of war, these days."

Ganrahast and Vainrence stood mute and immobile, caught in stasis. Targrael smiled at them almost fondly.

"Pair of prize idiots."

She examined Ganrahast's nearest hand then plucked the ring she wanted from its finger—it took a strong tug, but she'd known the stasis would hold and really cared not if she broke the man's finger; he had plenty more—and donned it.

No doubt he could trace its whereabouts when he was capable of doing anything again. That might well be a very long time later, however.

The faint beginnings of a smile twisting her lips, Targrael put each of the stasis-frozen men into his own opened coffin and restored the two lids to their proper places.

"Ineffectual dolts. That'll keep you. Once I use this *useful* little ring to seal the crypt, no one will think to look here for you until the next Obarskyr dies. Whereupon they'll hopefully be too upset and concerned with the succession to dare to go around opening up royal coffins to peek at moldering contents."

With a chuckle, the undead highknight departed that silent chamber, her dark cloak swirling.

Chapter
NINETEEN

Expecting Much Blood

He is a fool who sends any realm into war
With eyes full of glory and thoughts of easy victory.
His thinking should instead be of loss,
And his days and nights spent expecting much blood.

> Mardrukh Noraeyn, Sage of Zazesspur
> *Mardrukh's Musings*
> published in the Year of the Sheltered Viper

S torm slowed a little, to try to catch her breath. It wouldn't do to try to talk pleasantly to hostile guards if she was panting so hard she couldn't even gasp out words.

Inevitably, Elminster ran into her from behind, head-butting her rump and propelling her helplessly around the last corner.

Where she was promptly greeted by far too many cold, vigilant stares.

She found herself smiling wryly, despite the looming danger. It seemed that the Room of the Watchful Sentinel was very well named.

Architecturally small and unimportant, a mere antechamber off the far larger and grander Starander's Hall, it was guarded day and night to prevent covert departures—and unwelcome incursions—by way of the small, flickering doorway that stood in its northeast corner, bereft of surrounding walls or even a physical door or frame.

The Dalestride Portal's usual guardians were fourteen. Two Highknights, eight battletested Purple Dragons, and four Wizards of War.

Right now, there were more guards than that just in the passage outside—and they had set, unfriendly faces and ready weapons. The passage ahead of Storm looked like a crowded forest, with every tree a waiting sentinel expecting battle, and with eyes fixed on her.

Still breathing hard from her brisk run through the palace and from the brief tussle that had punctuated that journey, Storm turned her walk into a stroll as she approached the row of waiting spear points.

Beyond those leveled spears, several wands were aimed her way, and she could see some dart-firing bowguns held in highknight fists, too.

"El," she murmured, "this is going to be messy. There's no way I can force passage through this many—"

"Keep moving. Duck aside against the wall, if they let fly at ye from inside the room once ye try to enter," Elminster muttered from behind her, where he was lurching along bent over, an arm held up to shield his face.

Storm lacked both breath and will to point out to him that he was fooling no one; any Purple Dragon or war wizard who'd been warned to watch out for Elminster of Shadowdale or any other old, bearded, male stranger walking the palace would know at a glance exactly what was scuttling along in Storm's wake.

"I don't *want* to kill or maim scores of good and loyal folk of Cormyr," Storm hissed over her shoulder. "These are our allies, remember; those who stand for justice and—"

"I've not forgotten that. Don't believe what ye're about to see, overhead," Elminster warned her. "I still have a little magic to spend."

Storm nodded, eyeing bowguns being aimed carefully at her throat—as the ceiling of the passage came down with a roar.

The passage shook, a hanging lamp starting to swing wildly. Dust billowed, swallowing many of the arrayed guardians—who shouted in fear and started sprinting wildly along the passage.

Right at Storm.

"El," she snapped, reaching for her sword, "I—"

Darts came streaking at her, and there was a sudden snarl of crimson flame as a wand spat in her direction.

The flames rushed at her, expanding with the usual terrifying speed—only to fall silent and begin to spin in a great pinwheel right in front of her that . . . that . . .

"El, what're you *doing?*"

There came an all-too-familiar chuckle from behind her. "*How* many times have ye asked me that, lass? Down the passing centuries?"

"Don't remind me," Storm replied sharply, sword up and out and seeking foes she couldn't see. "How many times have you destroyed bits and pieces of palaces? Or castles?"

"I don't keep track," came the gruff reply. "Always seemed a mite childish, all this keeping score. Those who do tend to be those I dislike. Now, don't step forward, whatever ye do. The results would be . . . unpleasant."

"You're sending what they hurl right back at them, aren't you?"

"Wise lass; I am indeed. And I'm destroying no palaces this day—at least, that's my present intention. Yon collapse was no collapse at all."

"But if you try to scare them away, those who'll flee will come running right into our laps!"

"Oh? Has thy lap greeted anyone, yet?"

"No, but—"

"More years ago than I care to remember," the Sage of Shadowdale announced, straightening out of his crouch with a brief wince, "ye may recall I had a hand in crafting some of the wards cast here. Without the Weave, I can't twist them much now—there are *so* many later castings—but in some places I can temporarily cause a room or passage to, ah, adjoin another that's really halfway across the palace. Wherefore—heh—a lot of guardians, whether fearful or enthusiastic, are now sprinting along the torchwalk outside the Hall of the Warrior King, heading for the royal court at a pace that shouldn't break *too* many necks, if the door at the end of that passage is as flimsy as I remember it being. I do hope they've repaired the little bridge over the silverfin pond, or more than a few loyal defenders of Cormyr are shortly going to wind up rather wet."

Storm smirked, despite herself. "How far do your magics reach? Into the Room of the Watchful Sentinel itself—or are all the honor guard undoubtedly waiting for us in there going to be standing untouched, crowded to the very walls, and itching to fell Elminster, infamous enemy of the Dragon Crown?"

The Sage of Shadowdale favored her with one of his more sour looks. "D'ye think I started spinning spells yestermorn?"

"No," Storm replied dryly, "I believe you only started thinking of your own neck about then. Yes?"

"Stormy one, when did ye start wanting to take all the fun out of things? Eh?"

A man in ankle-length robes came staggering out of the roiling dust just then, a wand in one shaking hand starting to spit sparks, so Storm ducked into a low lunge that gave her reach enough to shove him into the wall.

The young and startled wizard of war rebounded off it hard, head lolling and wand cartwheeling away, so Storm didn't bother braining him with her sword hilt. She just glided out of the way and let the handy, hard flagstones feed him that fate instead.

"Yon overbold unfortunate wasn't one of those waiting for us in the passage," Elminster remarked, "so I'd say the portal guardians are coming out after us. Time to send my shield of return spell in to greet them—and let them harm themselves with everything they hurl at it. I am, after all, a hand that brings about the fitting justice of the gods."

"We all were, we Chosen," Storm reminded him sadly. "When Mystra still spoke to us and the Weave still sang."

"Not now, lass," Elminster grunted. "I'm busy." The walls and ceiling ahead of them seemed to shudder, as the very air around them seemed to snarl and then whirl and rush loudly.

"Keep thy sword up and handy," he added a little grimly a shrieking moment or two later. What sounded like the wail of a gale-force wind was rising around them, as the Sage of Shadowdale wrestled his magic sideways and through a doorway that wasn't made to accommodate it—at the same time as a dozen or more mages inside the room beyond that door hurled their own spells at the pinwheel of intruding magic, seeking to destroy it.

Elminster's face was suddenly drenched with sweat, so much of it that his nose dripped a stream like a village tap and his beard became a small waterfall.

"El?" Storm asked sharply, eyeing him as he went pale. "Is there anything I could—should—do?"

"No," the Old Mage snapped. "Not unless ye—"

A section of the passage wall ahead of them screamed like an agonized child and abruptly burst into shattered shards of stone that crashed into the far wall with force enough to rock and heave some of the flagstones beneath their boots. Amid the hail of falling stone descending that far wall was at least one wet and broken crimson thing that had been a man.

Much of the wall that had separated the Room of the Watchful Sentinel from the passage was missing. The room itself seemed to be full of glowing smoke lit by frequent flashes and bursts of howling radiance—and to hold the turning pinwheel of Elminster's shielding magic.

Abruptly, somewhere in the distant midair of the room's interior, something blinding bright exploded, hurling off great streamers of flame and sparks.

"A wand!" Storm snapped, having seen wands destroyed by wild magical backlashes before. "Do you think the Dalestride can—?"

"Withstand all they're trying to hurl at us?" Elminster replied, throwing an arm around her from behind and dragging her hastily back. "Drop thy blade—*now!*"

Storm was several centuries too old to argue with him or question such an order. She flung away her sword as if it were burning her hand, turned in a smooth shifting of her hips, and started to run with him down the passage to where it met—

Behind them, a blast erupted that snatched them both off their feet, smote their ringing ears so hard that all sound abruptly went away, and flung them headlong down the passage, well past the intersection and through a servant's door that gave way in an instant of wild, high groaning of rent wood and whirling splinters, onto a table where a cream sauce studded with mushroom and smelling strongly of nutmeg was being ladled over thick steaks of spit-seared lion on gold plates.

Undercooks screamed or at least flung up their hands, wild-eyed, and opened their mouths wide, as the Sage of Shadowdale and the tall and curvaceous silver-haired woman at his side crashed breast-first down onto the hot sauce and slid the length of the table . . . straight into the ample backside of Nestur Laklantur, Royal Cook of the Low Kitchen, as he stood bent over at the end of the table, carefully applying garnishes to platters of dishes on an adjacent counter.

Struck hard, Laklantur plunged helplessly face-first into a glazed and steaming manymeats pudding he'd spent hours preparing, and rose up roaring in scalded pain and rage, ready to turn and rend whoever had *dared*—

He had managed only to half turn and snatch up the nearest ladle to serve as his weapon of retribution when Storm's sword arrived.

It raced like an arrow, pommel first and surrounded by a winking cloud of sparks. The outraged cook had no time to dodge or duck nor even to draw breath to frame an appropriately scorching oath of wrath ere the ladle numbed his hand with its clanging departure. His life was saved by its deflection of the sword, and the cloud of sparks left the ricocheting steel to become a crawling fan of blue fire that transformed the stamped copper sheeting of the kitchen ceiling into a sheet of solid sapphire.

Laklantur and various maids and kitchen jacks stared up at it in astonishment and then either fainted or fled.

A good long breath before the sheet cracked into a thousand shards and fell, with a crash that sent cauldrons rolling and lids and cleavers ringing all over the kitchen.

And left a dazed wizard and former bard rolling slowly over, coated in sapphire dust and lumpy cream sauce, to stare at each other and then back the way they'd been hurled.

They were in time to see a wizard of war part the roiling dust with an impatient wand blast and glare in their direction.

In the suddenly clear air they saw that the Room of the Watchful Sentinel now extended into the passage and right up to the kitchen doors. Though it held much heaped rubble, adorned with more than a few silent and sprawled bodies, the Dalestride Portal stood glowing and unharmed—behind a grim dozen wizards of the Crown and half that many Purple Dragons.

"Those two, on yon table!" the wizard of war with the wand barked, looking at the Portal guardians and then pointing at Elminster and Storm. "They did this! They imperil the palace and us all, the king included. Slay them."

"Now, now, impetuous Cormyrean," Manshoon murmured, smiling into the glows of his scrying scene. "Not just yet. I shall fell Elminster of Shadowdale when the moment is right. A killing I perform at the time I choose. None other shall come between us."

He worked a magic that sent the glows roiling more brightly and added, "After more than two centuries, I deserve that much."

A moment later, his spell took hold, sending his awareness plunging down into the warm, dark depths of a mind more twisted than most. A mind he was becoming all too familiar with.

The mind of Wizard of War Rorskryn Mreldrake, who was hastening along a passage to a particular door, one of the most powerful magical scepters in all the palace in his hand.

"Mystra, She Who Is Fallen, certainly enjoyed the dramatic last-moment appearance and rescue," Manshoon purred, "and I begin to feel why."

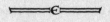

Storm looked around wildly. "Where'd my swor—oh." She snatched up her weapon. It looked unharmed . . . but promptly crumbled into glittering dust with a curious sigh, leaving her holding only a hilt.

She dropped it in disgust, shot a glance at the warily advancing Purple Dragons and the wizards behind them— who were carefully aiming wands at her over the armored shoulders of those warriors—then ducked down again to join Elminster on the floor.

"Might I suggest running away?" she murmured in his ear. "*Now?*"

"Ye can," the Sage of Shadowdale grunted, rolling over and clambering up to his knees, "but running is a deed my knees grow less and less fond of as the years pass. How many still stand against us?"

"Too many, and the Dragons are almost upon us," Storm told him grimly. "I don't see any highknights or bowguns, but—"

"They charged to the fore, of course," El replied, "and so are now pelting along that passage halfway across the palace. Well, now . . ."

He produced a wand. "Paralyzes," he announced. "I still have the thought-prying pendant, too, but that's about all. The retreat ye suggest might indeed be prudent, if I can recall what lies on the other side of the Low Kitchens. Quite a warren of ramps and stairs, in *that* direction, and—"

"*Elminster!*" Storm snapped warningly as a Purple Dragon loomed up over them. Elminster calmly called up the wand's powers, and the warrior stiffened in midlunge and toppled forward, crashing down at them.

Only to fetch up against the heavy table, his frozen, helpless body forming a shield.

"Right, lass, let's be off," the Sage of Shadowdale said gruffly. "We—"

Startled cries erupted beyond the paralyzed Dragon, as bright light burst into being and washed over the room. At its height the cries ended in midblurt, leaving only eerie silence as the radiance faded again.

Storm flung herself sideways into a roll that brought her out beyond the table and two toppled stools to where she could look down the former passage at the distant glow of the Dalestride.

She was in time to see Wizard of War Rorskryn Mreldrake standing in a hitherto-closed doorway in another back corner of the Room of the Watchful Sentinel. He held a still-flickering scepter in his hand and was staring around at the guardians in front of him with an uneasy smile on his face.

Those men—every last Purple Dragon and wizard of them—had fallen on their faces and were lying still and silent.

Mreldrake took a swift and uncertain couple of steps into the room, craning and peering to make sure none of them were moving, then spun around and hastened back out the door he'd come through, closing it behind him.

"It seems we have an unexpected ally," Storm whispered. "Or the wizards of war are harboring a traitor who just decided the time was right for a little treason."

Elminster shoved the paralyzed Dragon aside with a grunt of effort and crawled quickly to the next nearest warrior. "Senseless—not dead," he muttered. "They'll be gone for most of a day, unless someone casts spells to revive them."

He shot Storm a look. "I'll take care of our traitor, if I can catch up to him. Ye get to Alassra before the inevitable horde of guards arrives to see who's been blasting down walls in the palace."

Storm nodded, raced to Elminster, and swept an arm around him to give him a brief, fierce kiss, then snatched up the fallen Dragon's sword and sprinted for the glowing portal.

Halfway there she bent over a fallen wizard and tugged hard, rolling the body over. She came up with his cloak, and two strides farther on scooped up a fallen wand. It was a short run from there to where she could pluck a second wand from another outstretched hand.

Casting a brief look back over her shoulder at Elminster— he was on his feet and gave her a cheery wave—she raced for the glowing portal and plunged through its silent white fires without hesitation.

The palace was suddenly gone, and she was running on soft, sinking nothing, in the heart of a bright blue void that stretched endlessly and silently away in all directions, a void that just as abruptly vanished in a flash of bright light that became the low, bright sunlight of late afternoon lancing through trees.

A certain freshness in the air and a cool breeze coming down from the north told her she was east of the Thunder Peaks. Mistledale should be just ahead, with the broad straight wagonway of the Moonsea Ride just out of sight behind and below yon trees, and there'd undoubtedly be a sentinel of some sort keeping watch over this side of the Dalestride, being as it connected with the heart of the royal palace of Suzail, and—

Storm looked around wildly and swerved toward the nearest trees as she did so. Guards of realms with wild borders often have bows or spells to hurl, and lone women running with drawn swords in their hands could hardly fail to evoke a certain apprehension in even the laziest of sleepy sentinels …

"Hold!" an annoyed male voice snapped from somewhere behind her, right on cue. Storm ran even faster, turning sharply to meet the trees even sooner, and tore open her jerkin with her free hand as she went, ducking low.

"*Halt*, I said!" the guardian shouted, sounding angrier. "Are you *deaf*, woman?"

Storm found a tree and caught hold of it, spending all the haste of her run in a swing around it that brought her back facing the glade she'd just fled.

A young, stern-looking wizard of war flanked by two Purple Dragons with longbows in their hands was striding toward her, and he was frowning. Behind them, this side of the portal cast no glows at all; instead, it looked like endlessly rippling empty air.

"No," she panted, giving all three men a good look at her bared and bobbing front. "I'm just—a certain none-too-noble lord seeks my virtue! Lord Wizard, I dare not tarry!"

"But—but this way is guarded at the palace end! How did you get through?"

"Please, Lord, the guardians of the Dalestride let me through! Lord Warder Vainrence ordered them to and said he'd take care of—of the one chasing me! *Please*, Lord, I must be *away* from here!"

The Dragons were staring only at what she was displaying, but the wizard was reddening and looking away. "How do I know you speak truth?" he asked, sounding exasperated.

"Vainrence'll sure tell you, I'm thinking," one of the Dragons muttered, "when he takes your report."

At that, the wizard went very red and waved wildly at Storm. "Get you gone!" he commanded. "Just get—go!"

"T-thank you, kind lords!" Storm babbled, swinging around the tree again and sprinting headlong into the woods. There was a stream nearby, she remembered, and a little wade up it would cover her tracks, if anyone changed his mind about permitting her departure.

As she went, she rolled her eyes. As the centuries passed, her acting seemed to be getting more than a little rusty, but men weren't changing much.

Chapter
TWENTY

When Vengeful Ghosts Walk

Young men so proud, and foolish, and bold,
Pray ye hear and heed well when I talk.
There's no doom old, no night so cold,
As a night when vengeful ghosts walk.

> from the ballad *A Little Dark Wisdom*
> composed by Tamyth Larandree Lady Minstrel of
> Mintarn
> in the Year of the Blackened Moon

"You're armed for *real* trouble? Good, good."

Marlin was gleeful.

In fact, the young lordling was actually rubbing his hands.

Manshoon rolled his eyes. Not even Fzoul at his gloating worst had been *that* unsubtle.

The lordling's two bodyguards stood awaiting further orders. Ormantor said nothing, as usual. That tall, broad-shouldered mountain of muscle seldom said much of anything at all. Gaskur, however—nondescript, forgettable-looking Gaskur, Marlin's fetcher and carrier and trade agent and nigh everything else, whose service had enabled the younger Lord Stormserpent to accomplish everything he'd managed thus far—was clearly worried.

"Where are we bound, Lord?" he murmured.

Marlin grinned like one of his nieces' well-fed cats. "No, no, Gask, better you not know. Safer, that way."

Manshoon managed not to roll his eyes again. Stupider, rather—you obviously *don't* know, lordling.

Gaskur obviously thought so, too, though he knew better

than to say so. A flicker of Ormantor's eyes betrayed his similar judgment.

"Come!" Marlin said eagerly. "Glory awaits!"

Unheard in his cavern, Manshoon smiled mirthlessly. It was time to have some fun, flex a few tentacles, and slay the guards set to watch over the secret passage—so foolish young Lord Stormserpent could reach the Dragonskull Chamber and test his secret weapons. If they held the blue-flame ghosts and young Marlin could control them, they would be formidable weapons indeed.

And if he could not control them, young Lord Stormserpent's ambitions would come to a swift and painful end.

"Glory, lordling," Manshoon murmured into the glow, "awaits."

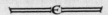

Elminster came to a certain place in the passage and stopped. An old ward should be waiting right in front of him, and as he was—admit it—less than what he'd once been, what he did next should be done cautiously.

He stretched forth a hand gingerly into the empty air.

Which remained empty, though a whispering awakened all around him and raced away along the dark stones into the distance.

He took a cautious step forward, and—nothing else happened. Good.

He took another. Still nothing. Six more strides brought him to the stone he knew, which moved under his hand and let him step into the wall and avoid awakening the spell-trap that awaited another few steps along the passage.

It had been long centuries since the royal crypt had been guarded by bored Purple Dragons, but it was still protected by other things, and bore alarm magics that might alert someone in the palace above, if anyone up there still had the wits to be alerted by anything.

He was beginning to doubt that.

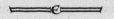

The air in Dragonskull Chamber wasn't as stale as it should have been, and the darkness wasn't as dark. Even the stillness wasn't still; it pulsed and swirled and *flowed* in an endless, soundless tumult that could be clearly felt.

The twisted wards were alive and restless, and although they made him feel rather sick, Marlin Stormserpent was glad of that. It meant the war wizards—even the Mage Royal, Ganrahast—couldn't see him from afar or know he was there or what he was doing.

Which was good indeed, considering that what he was doing would undoubtedly be seen as high treason.

"I'm experimenting freely," he murmured. No, that excuse sounded lame even to his ears; he couldn't imagine even the youngest Crownsworn mage or courtier believing it.

Wherefore he'd best be doing what he'd come to do swiftly, and get back to his bodyguards before they drank the deepest winecellar of the Old Dwarf dry. Even shunned rooms of the palace must have patrols stalk by their doors from time to time.

Marlin drew in a deep, excited breath, brought forth the chalice with one hand and his handful of parchment notes with the other, and awakened one of his rings to give him light enough to read.

That reminded him that he was wearing the Flying Blade and would perhaps be wiser to set it aside and try to deal with one ghost at a time.

The room around him was as empty as ever, most of its walls lost in the evershifting darkness—but it was clearly bare of furniture. So he laid his sword belt on the floor a few paces away, the scabbarded sword atop it, and stood so he could face it while he worked on the chalice.

His notes were few the casting or ritual, or whatever it was properly called was short and simple.

Which meant he couldn't delay any longer. Sudden fear uncoiling in his throat, Marlin held up the chalice, peered at his notes again, then said firmly, "*Arruthro.*"

The word seemed to roll away across vast distances, though it seemed no louder than it should have been—and at a stroke, the room was darker, the air singing with sudden tension. He looked around in case something was slithering or creeping out of the darkness to come up behind him, but saw nothing.

"*Tar lammitruh arondur halamoata*," he added, loudly and slowly. He had no idea what language—if it was a language— he was speaking, but it sounded old and grand and menacing. Very menacing.

The room went colder still.

"*Tan thom tanlartar*," he read out—and flinched as the chalice in his hand erupted in weird blue fire. Raging flames that raced down his arm to the elbow and then wreathed it and the chalice in an endless, soundless conflagration. That held no heat at all and caused him no pain, only a disturbing, bone-deep tingling.

"*Larasse larasse thulea*," he added.

And shivered in the sudden icy chill—as the blue flames sprang from the chalice in a flood, like a gigantic snake or eel pouring forth from the goblet to the floor and then rebounding up again, growing larger and taller … man-high. With a darkness at their heart that slowly became a man. A man standing facing him and smiling, clad in a dark and nondescript leather war-harness. Boots, sword, and dagger. Dark eyes with those blue flames dancing in their depths—and a ceaselessly burning shroud of blue flames around the man's body that ignited nothing, charred nothing, and seemed to cause the man no pain at all.

As he shifted his stance, one hand falling to his sword hilt and the other coming to rest on his belt, and smilingly faced Marlin Stormserpent.

Who asked carefully, "You obey me, y-yes?"

The man nodded curtly. "I do. And will."

The lordling let out a breath he hadn't known he was holding and asked, "And you are?"

"Treth Halonter. The best warrior of the Nine, or was … before Myrkul."

"Before Myrkul?" A dead god, something to do with the

dead. Old Lord Bones, that was what the ballads called him. "Before you died?"

"Before Myrkul did this to us and bent us to his love of death." The ghost's smile never wavered.

Marlin peered hastily at his notes. "Is there—what must I avoid doing to prevent you turning on me?"

"Nothing. We know and obey the one who summons us forth."

"And you'll, uh, go back into the chalice when I say the right words?"

"Or just command me to. Myrkul was not interested in allowing me to deceive, betray, or turn on you. This is no fireside faerie tale, man. I am your slave."

Marlin glanced at his sword, still lying where he had left it.

"How many of the Nine can I command at once?"

Halonter shrugged. "I know not. Are you given to fits of madness?"

In the depths of young Lord Stormserpent's mind, Manshoon smiled.

This was going to be *fun*.

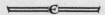

Marlin discovered he wasn't just drenched in sweat; he was shaking with exhaustion. The two cold smiles facing him felt crushingly heavy, as if he was staggering under the weight of two suits of armor at once.

Those unwavering smiles belonged to the two who stood facing him wreathed in glowing blue flames that burned nothing—but drank energies from living beings they touched, if they willed it so. Or so they claimed.

Two blueflame ghosts who could stride through stone walls at will, but nothing living. If he commanded them to, they could literally walk right through the walls of the palace— leaving them whole and unmarred—and out into Suzail. Again, so they said.

Not that he had any way of proving wrong anything they said, except by watching as they tried to follow his orders. He would order them to walk through the wards and the walls beyond them, in a breath or two, and see.

He'd already commanded them both back into the sword and the cup he'd brought them forth from, and had brought them out again. They assured him they could sense where those items were, no matter how far he took them, and would return to them, but "go into them" only if he was present to command them. Unless or until his command over them was broken by someone else.

How that could be done, or by whom, they did not know—or, again, said they did not. Marlin knew he had no way of catching them in falsehoods until it was too late ... and he was beginning to fervently wish they'd stop smiling.

Relve Langral had been the rogue among the Nine and was far more talkative than Halonter. According to him, the dark god Myrkul had corrupted them; they were now ruthless and uncaring, gleefully enjoying killing and any chance to do harm. "We are insane and beyond death," Relve had announced calmly. Smiling that terrible smile all the while.

They had been awakened from their imprisonments before, and had then heard themselves termed "blueflame ghosts," but said they were nothing like the *real* ghosts they'd met and fought when the Nine were adventuring.

They'd said more, too. "We cannot and will not destroy each other, nor will we attempt to. It's one of the few commandments you can give us that we must ignore."

"And the others are?"

"Still unknown to us—and, I gather, to you, too," Relve had replied promptly—and, of course, smilingly.

Marlin drew in another breath and wiped his dripping forehead with the back of his hand. "Then hear my first command to you. Somewhere in this city around you—we stand in the palace in Suzail, Cormyr—there is a man by the name of Seszgar Huntcrown. The one I seek is nobly born and the heir of House Huntcrown, in the unlikely event you find someone else by that name. You are to go forth from here—through the walls—to find him without delay, slay him, and return to me. I will not then be here but in my home, not far from here in this same city. Go. Go now."

In smiling silence, the two flaming men—or ghosts, or whatever they were—drew their swords, slashed the air around them a time or two as if working stiffness from their limbs, and started toward him.

Marlin watched them come, mouth dry, and it was only when they were a mere stride away that he retreated, clutching at his belt dagger and trying in terror to remember what in all the odd powers of the various rings he wore might save him against two ruthless slayers who could suck the life out of him with a mere touch.

He was still stumbling back, trying to think of something to stammer to keep them at bay, when they strode past him with their fierce smiles, cold contempt for him in their eyes, and . . . through the nearest wall, as softly as any maiden's whisper.

And the blue flames were gone from the Dragonskull Chamber, leaving Marlin Stormserpent whimpering and shaking.

Farruking Tempus forfend! So he could control them . . . or were they merely humoring him?

Stlarn. He swallowed hard, his mouth as dry as he imagined any howling desert to be, and tried to quell his shaking.

He had to get out of there, notes and chalice and all, and back home before some sneering fool of a war wizard found him.

Home, to await a horrible doom—was there *anything* in the family vaults he could protect himself with? Anything?— or to learn that this little test had become a success, and he was rid of a longtime foe.

Not that Seszgar Huntcrown was one whit as important as Seszgar Huntcrown believed himself to be. However, he'd hated Seszgar because the Huntcrown heir had bullied and humiliated him when they were both young, and still sneered at him.

Moreover, Seszgar would be no loss to anyone. And, over-confident as he was, he was all too apt to trust in his formidable skill with a blade and go swaggering out alone, dismissing his bodyguards, and so could more easily be caught alone than most other nobles.

The two ghosts of the Nine scared Marlin, but they might know almost nothing about Suzail—and all they knew about their quarry was his name, his nobility, and that he was probably carousing somewhere in Suzail. Marlin didn't want to lose these useful weapons before they accomplished anything at all, by setting them a task that would keep them scouring the city until every last war wizard in the realm descended on them hurling blasting spells.

Smiling, they'd marched right out, wreathed in their ceaseless blue flames, but that meant nothing. After all, what did he really know about them, aside from a few lines of speculation from various dead men, and what they'd told him themselves?

What did he really know about them at all?

Suddenly shaking worse than ever, Marlin snatched up his sword belt in feverish haste, wanting to be gone.

He fled from the room a breath later, and the death knight Targrael detached herself from the darkness of the wall and glided after him, unnoticed and as silently as she knew how.

Manshoon was smiling in the depths of both of their minds.

He was learning at last. Even if it was only to fear, young Lord Stormserpent was learning at last.

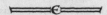

Manshoon made his Lady Dark Armor lurk silently, well in the wake of what his newly bold lordling had unleashed.

Ahead of her, two men whose bodies blazed blue stalked the dark streets of Suzail in menacing silence, keeping together.

Langral and Halonter of the Nine were quite capable at reading the will of the one commanding them, when they stood close and those thoughts were fierce—and young and fearful Marlin Stormserpent had wanted them to stay together.

Well enough; that suited both of them. They were busy finding Seszgar Huntcrown, and it was proving to be slow work.

Every few paces they came upon someone hurrying along who couldn't outrun them, or who blundered out of a door or alley too preoccupied with something else to notice blue enshrouding flames in time to run.

"Have ye seen the noble Seszgar Huntcrown?" Relve would ask.

"Recently?" Treth would add, leaning forward to rumble that word.

Usually the answer was a stammered denial, sometimes of even knowing what Lord Huntcrown looked like. Less than helpful—but then, their orders had come from a noble, and nobles weren't known for sparing underlings work or calling on overmuch thought when crafting orders in the first place.

No matter what answer Langral and Halonter got, they promptly slew the answerer if there were no nearby witnesses, or just stalked on in search of someone else if there were.

It was a good thing night hadn't fallen all that long before. Questioning and butchering their way across Suzail might take most of the dark hours. They briefly entertained the notion of keeping count of how many killings would be necessary before they found Huntcrown, but hadn't thought of it until after they'd slain six—or was it eight?—already. Suzailans died quickly these days.

In Targrael's head, and managing to read the thoughts of the two men in flames faintly through endless and silently snarling blue fire, Manshoon smiled. He'd noticed the very same thing.

Belgryn Murenstur blinked. Well, now . . . 'twasn't every night you saw the likes of *that*. Wreathed in flames they were, from head to toe, two men with drawn swords, striding along the street as if they felt nothing at all.

"Ho, man!" the shorter one called—to *him* Belgryn realized. And blinked again, coming to a sudden halt in his rush to be home. In another two paces, he'd have walked right into them, flames and all.

"Have ye seen the noble Seszgar Huntcrown?"

"Recently?" the taller flaming one added, in a deeper voice. They were both smiling.

Were those swords in their hands wet? As in, with *blood*?

With a rush of relief, Belgryn realized he had. "Yes, yes, I just laid eyes on him, as it happens—and all he carouses with, too. They were going into the Bold Archer and were more than a bit merry."

Something was happening in his head . . . as if he was being *watched* from the dark corners of his own mind. Yes, a dark, coldly smiling presence, Manshoon by name, that he promptly forgot all about.

He blinked again. The shorter man, wreathed in flames he didn't seem to feel, was thrusting himself closer to Belgryn to ask another question.

"What is this Bold Archer? A tavern?"

"A club. Uh, four streets back, you can't miss it—"

Belgryn was turning to point when he saw the swords come up.

"Ye will take us there," the taller flaming man rumbled, still wearing his smile. "Now."

"I—uh, I'm in some haste to be ho—," Belgryn started to stammer.

And abruptly stopped, because the swords rising to menace his throat *were* wet with blood, and because a door had just been flung open down the street, letting light spill out onto the cobbles.

Even before whoever moved to stand in that light started to scream, Belgryn saw clearly what was lying in the street where the two flaming men had just come from: two sprawled bodies that had blood running in slow, dark ribbons out from under them.

Two citizens of Suzail that the flaming men now smilingly flanking him had just slain.

CHAPTER
TWENTY-ONE
A NIGHT OF SWORDS AND BLOOD

I see men screaming and running,
And many things swept away,
After it begins as so much tumult does:
In a night of swords and blood.

said by Yarauva the Blue Seer
in Act I, Scene I of the play *New Thrones for Old*
anonymously published in the Year of the Haunting

After one long look that he knew had left him hotly blushing, Delnor kept his eyes on the rush-strewn floor as he hastened through the tables of the Dragonriders' Club. By the Diligence of Torm, when had the trip grown so long?

He was acutely conscious of his palace messenger's uniform, and of the dozens—scores—of eyes that must be following him as he made his way right up to the front table where Lord Delcastle was lounging.

In the brightest lights of the stage right above Arclath's easy smile, the same mask dancer was performing—with an air of defiance, no less!—posing and pirouetting around a glossy-smooth prowboard that had been thrust into the edge of the stage. It allowed her to move her body out until it overhung the wine-sipping noble.

Delnor firmly closed his eyes and groped his way the last few steps to the empty chair across from Arclath, who considerately removed his feet from it in the last instant before the crimson-faced palace messenger sat down both heavily and with great relief.

"Well met," came the noble's sardonic greeting as Delnor

thankfully closed his hand around a proffered flaretop goblet and drank deeply. "What news?"

The mask dancer thrust her face in the new arrival's direction for long enough to tender Delnor a brief, hard stare before returning to deftly catching Arclath's steady stream of tossed coins out of the air, and putting them into dozens of small clips she'd braided into her long hair. Delnor saw her attach a gleaming golden lion then whirl away to smile at the next table, long hair swirling and sleek hips . . .

He swallowed again and looked away into the darkness—straight into the expressionless gaze of Tress, who was standing with her arms folded, keeping steady watch over her prized dancer and Lord Delcastle's front table from a dark alcove beside the stage.

Delnor gave the club owner a weak, wavering smile and transferred his gaze to Arclath, who leaned forward through the sudden din of music that arose just then to accompany the dancers—a merry rhythm of longhorn, lute, tantan, and handdrum, being played somewhere above their heads and coming down through holes around the pillars—to murmur, "So, now, what banners have you seen coming through the gates? What word has reached the palace of this or that noble's arrival for this Council of the Dragon?"

For his part, Delnor was almost itching with curiosity as to what the Lord Delcastle had learned about the eavesdropping dancer, who was at that moment almost insolently performing right above them again. *Something* had obviously happened between them.

He risked the swiftest of glances up at the dancer—long enough to see quite vividly that she wore only sparkles, sweat, and her mask—and resigned himself to hearing about it later. Leaning forward until his nose was perhaps a finger's length from Arclath Delcastle's, he started muttering names across the table.

When a noble wants to hear which fellow nobles have come to town, and is paying for the drinks, the duty of a lowly courtier is clear.

" . . . And so she opened her arms for meeeee!" Broryn Windstag roared, off-key and more shouting than singing but too drunk to care.

Spreading his arms wide in a dramatic flourish, he crashed bodily through the doors of the Dragonriders' Club as his fellow nobles stumbled on through the next verse of the song, words slurred and half-forgotten. Lord Dawntard was drunk, but then Dawntard was *always* drunk. Delasko Sornstern was the soberest of the three, but that wasn't saying much, and he was drinking hard to try to overtake his hero Windstag in the race to oblivion.

Arclath peered hard back over his shoulder at the disturbance. Windstag, Dawntard, and Sornstern. Trouble. The crowd of loud roisterers with them were either their bodyguards or the hangers-on that any nobles who spend coins like water in the finer taverns of Suzail will attract, when said nobles will cheerfully buy anyone who howls approval at them wine—flagons and skins and bottle after bottle of wine.

"Full *trouble!*" Tress snapped, striding out of her alcove to wave a warning to all of her bodyguards. By then Windstag had spotted the reason he'd just gotten up from the floor—the bare-bodied dancers up on the distant stage. He promptly kicked a chair out of the way with a wicked grin, with no heed at all for what might become of its half-drunk occupant.

When the others at that table shouted at him angrily, he flung the half-full bottle in his hand into the face of the loudest one, then used that freed hand to pluck up the table and overturn it on all their heads, roaring with laughter.

Men sprang up on all sides, some of them just bolting away from the unfolding trouble, and others to find room to snatch out sword or dagger.

"Hah, so it's *blades*, is it?" Dawntard snarled. "Well, we know *that* game!" Behind him, a dozen bodyguards and wellwishers drew steel in singing unison.

"That table, that one, and *that* one!" Windstag bellowed, pointing at the three tables closest to the stage—at one of which Delnor sat, huddled in his seat and staring at the drunken nobles in open-mouthed horror. "They're *ours*, now! Get clear of them, or *die!*"

Arclath was waiting, with sword out and a rather dangerous smile growing across his face. Windstag's roar brought the wealthy merchants at the other two tables to their feet, too, some of them busily snapping orders to their own bodyguards.

"The Watch!" Tress barked at someone. "Get the Watch! *Now!*"

Then Windstag let loose a wordless shout of exultation and charged.

Dawntard and Sornstern hastily joined in, and all the intruders were trotting and lurching forward, shouting and hacking furiously and wildly at everyone and everything in their way. Someone threw a chair, someone else hastily drained a bottle and then hurled it—and the Dragonriders' erupted.

On the stage, some of the mask dancers screamed and fled, others cowered, and the one at the front with the coins in her hair, bare as she was, crouched down behind the prowboard as if it were a castle rampart and she were a warrior awaiting the right moment to spring over it into battle.

A merchant screamed and gurgled as he was hacked at, another shrieked as a sword seeking his life sheared away one of his ears, and bottles shattered against pillars and tables, showering the surging men with glass as patrons slipped, fell, swore, and stabbed at each other.

A large, much-scarred sailor went down, a richly dressed merchant staggered away weakly spewing out both his dinner and all the wine he'd drunk, and a club bouncer threw a chair at a noble he couldn't reach, felling two bodyguards who got in its way.

As if that had been a signal, the air was suddenly full of hurtling chairs. With many wounded groaning and sagging, men slugged each other with fists and bottles and dagger pommels, bodyguards rushed to hurl aside anyone who got too close to their clients, and tables got upended.

Merchants were fleeing in all directions, and Tress and her staff seemed to have vanished. Resistance melted away from in front of Windstag and Dawntard and their hard-faced bodyguards.

Leaving a panting, wild-eyed palace messenger, a few merchants who were more angry than frightened, and the coolly unruffled Lord Arclath Delcastle between the sword-swinging intruders and the stage.

"Stand aside, unwashed vermin!" Windstag roared.

"Go home, drunken disgraces!" Delcastle snapped back. "You stain the families you belong to, and will answer to the king for it!"

"Yes!" Delnor shouted desperately. "Leave this place, in the name of the king!"

Ignoring Delcastle, Windstag sneered at the palace messenger. "And who are *you* to call on the Crown for aid? Jumped-up commonborn lout! When our day comes, we'll not have to put up with the likes of you! We'll just order you beheaded and sit and sip wine and watch from the farruking palace windows as you scream and wet yourselves and die!"

"Since when," Arclath Delcastle inquired icily, "did *your* drunken lawlessness have anything at all to do with anyone's rank or birth? Windstag, you're a bully and a coward, and—"

With a wordless roar of rage, Broryn Windstag went for Delcastle, six bodyguards at his side. Almost casually one of them tripped Delnor, and he hit the floor hard, gurgling out a vain plea. Arclath Delcastle cursed as he ducked, darted, and slashed as swiftly as any mask dancer, buying himself room to spring up onto the stage.

"That was a *palace messenger*, you fool," he spat at Windstag. "You'd better start for the docks right now, before—"

"Before *what*?" Kathkote Dawntard sneered. "You think a noble lord will face the *slightest* punishment for felling some palace lackey who dared to offer us violence? Without every noble in all Cormyr rising to rid themselves of all courtiers—and any Obarskyr foolish enough to stand up for such dross, too?"

"Not that we should leave any noble witnesses to this little unpleasantness," Windstag snarled. "Kill him!"

He was pointing at Delcastle.

"Carve him apart, so there won't be enough left for even the keenest war wizard to enspell and interrogate, then snatch the dancer and bring her. Search those rooms back there, and haul out all the other dancers, too! I find I've a hunger for more than *dancing*!"

There was a general shout of mirth as everyone joined in his bawled laughter, and men with drawn swords rushed the stage.

Across which Lord Arclath Delcastle raced and spun and sprang and hacked like a wild thing, seeking to just stay alive.

One man reeled back, blinded by a blood-spurting cut across the forehead; another clutched at his punched throat and crashed to his knees, choking; and a third staggered back and fell heavily off the stage, clawing at where Delcastle's slender sword had burst through his shoulder.

But by then Delcastle battled a vicious storm of steel, beset on all sides by men made wild by drink and wilder by bloodlust and eagerness to impress their noble masters.

"A rescue!" he shouted, parrying desperately. "Anyone! A rescue!"

A man in front of him shrieked and fell, his toes pinned to the floor by a dagger that hadn't been there a moment earlier. Then the man beside him toppled, his eyes bulging in astonished pain, as something very hard struck him in the back of the head.

By the time that man fell, Delcastle's attackers were turning to see who his ally was—the person the beset lordling was already grinning at as he went right on fencing for his life.

It was the mask dancer—who wore only sparkles, sweat, and copious spatters of blood—none of it her own. She'd tossed aside her mask, her hair swirling free, and there was a blood-drenched, dripping sword in one of her hands and a clean dagger clutched pommel-foremost in the other.

She faced them, panting—and promptly sliced the face of a bodyguard who'd foolishly lowered his sword to leer at her.

"Kill her!" Windstag roared drunkenly. "I can rut with her corpse!"

Heads turned as his men stared at him in disbelief, even in the midst of furiously clanging steel.

"W-well," the nude dancer hissed at him, "now that we all know how *certain* noble lords prefer to spend their dallying time . . ."

"Get her! Get her! *Get her!*" an enraged Windstag bellowed loudly enough to make the roofbeams echo. "Kill them both! Kill them *all!*"

He sprang onto the stage, his bodyguards hastening to follow. Windstag and his men came up from behind the men fighting Arclath Delcastle and crashed into them, shoving them helplessly forward in sprawling chaos.

For just a moment, through a gap in all the onrushing bodies, Lord Delcastle caught sight of Delnor's senseless, staring face.

Then it was gone behind the looming brawn of men trying to kill him, and he was fighting for his life again.

And somewhere behind him, so was she, this Amarune whose name he'd only just learned.

Just in time for them both to lose their lives together, it seemed, when such trifles would no longer matter. Ever.

In the darkest back corner of the royal crypt, three levels below any part of the palace where the sun ever reached, the lone old wizard stiffened, his eyes momentarily flashing blue fire.

"*Something's* happened," Elminster said grimly. "Something's been awakened. Strong magic, old magic. Hmmph. Like me."

All around where he was sitting loomed huge stone Obarskyr sarcophagi, where dead kings, queens, princes, and princesses of Cormyr crumbled slowly and silently into dust. The magic in this place lay like heavy armor, deadening his senses to all but the strongest disturbances but hiding him very effectively from any war wizard who might seek to lessen the task of all those diligent Purple Dragons by casting the right sort of seeking spell.

Someone among these latter-day wizards of war must know the right sort of seeking spell or how to look it up in an old grimoire. If they read anything at all, anymore . . .

It happened again, a surge in the magic within and around him that was like a great silent shout, sending him wincing and shuddering back against the nearest stone coffin.

A powerful unleashing . . . but what?

There had been a time when he could have walked within a day's ride of Suzail and would have known in an instant *precisely* what had been done, when anything that powerful disturbed the Weave. Aye, there had been a time . . .

"I *can't* save the Realms anymore," he whispered into the gloom. "Not alone."

Sudden tears made the glows around him swim and slide. "I can't even protect *Cormyr*, stlarn it! The ghosts of the Nine could, aye, if properly commanded—but I need them to heal Alassra. So which will it be? The land? Or my lady?"

The silent darkness offered no answer, and Elminster was damned and blasted if he could decide on one just then.

He couldn't sit and hide there any longer; he had to *think*. To do that, he needed room to walk and pretend he was still smoking his old pipe and . . . and to stop pretending about a lot of things.

The dead around him were dust, their days done, and so were his. He just hadn't had the good sense to die yet and leave all his cares and causes behind, hand the endless fight on to someone else young and vigorous and having even the slightest hope of winning some new vict—

Aye, that was it, right there. *Hope.*

That was the rarest treasure for him, these days. Fading, forlorn hope. Hope that his Alassra could be herself again, hope that . . . that . . .

Oh, for the love of Mystra, he *had to get out of there*!

In a whirlwind of lurching haste he was out of the crypt and hurrying along dark and deserted passages, moving more from memory than by sight, heading for the nearest way out of the palace and into the night air.

He had to ... had to ... what *was* he going to do?

Wheezing, he climbed a stair, coming out onto another level that was thankfully dark and empty. Well, and so it should be: if he'd been commanding the wizards and soldiers of this place, he'd have had many more pressing matters to deal with than some old man who might or might not be a thief!

Mayhap they had nothing else at all to worry their heads over, but somehow he could scarce believe that. That they might choose not to *see* some looming crisis or other, before it lifted its fanged head in their faces and bit them, that he could believe, oh aye, and—

At the head of the next stair, he walked straight into a man rushing past.

A man in robes who staggered and cursed, turned, stared, and snarled, "You!"

Smiles of the gods, it was Wizard of War Rorskryn Mreldrake!

"My pleasure," Elminster assured him firmly, lunging forward to where he could trip the younger man off balance.

He did so, leaving Mreldrake winded and staggering— then knocked him cold with an elbow up under his jaw before the war wizard could think of some suitably nasty spell to cast.

Elminster guided the senseless Mreldrake in a long, loose-limbed sag down the wall to the floor, relieved him of a certain formidable scepter, then hastily departed that passage, breathing hard. He was obviously out of practice at stealing out of palaces.

But then, he was out of practice at a lot of things.

"Amarune!" Arclath called, kicking, punching, and hacking at downed and furiously struggling men before they could clamber back to their feet. "To me! Back-to-back—we'll make a stand!"

Those words were still coming out of his mouth when something long and shapely hurtled past his left shoulder. It was Amarune, feet first—slamming into Windstag's chest and bearing him back off the stage, staring and agape, arms and legs splayed out comically.

He struck the floor below with a crash that shook the club from end to end and left Windstag stunned and winded, his limbs jouncing as limply as a cloth doll's. Amarune sprang up from atop him and raced off down the room, leaving Arclath alone and surrounded on the stage.

He leaped after her, landing on the littered floor at a hard run, sprinting for the distant street doors with more than a dozen men after him. Bare and beautiful, the long-legged dancer vaulted the bar ahead and vanished from view behind it.

Why hadn't she made for the doors? Was there a cellar way out? Or a strong-cellar below that she could barricade herself in? Was—

Amarune bobbed back up again, face set in a snarl of anger, and started hurling bottles hard and accurately at noble and bodyguard faces alike. Arclath ducked low, staggering but not slowing, but needn't have bothered; none of them came spinning his way.

He saw a man go down behind a wild spray of wine, and another man's head snap back as a hard-thrown bottle caromed off it . . . and then they all seemed to forget Arclath and charged at the bar, roaring for her blood.

The dancer kept right on throwing as they came, bright anger on her face. Five men down, six . . . then the foremost were at the bar and hacking at it wildly with their blades, trying to drive her back so they could clamber over it, and—

A door slammed open not far from the bar, and Tress came storming into the room with the mustered Dragonriders' staff right behind her, a motley array of improvised weapons in their hands. A swift breath later, the street doors beside the bar burst open to let hard-faced Purple Dragons pour into the room with their swords drawn.

"A rescue! A rescue!" Amarune shouted, pointing straight at Dawntard and Sornstern. "Yon three nobles just felled a palace messenger and tried to kill Lord Delcastle!"

Tress brought the Dragonriders' staff to a hasty halt. The bodyguards and hangers-on were slower to stop but soon faltered under the cold glares of advancing Purple Dragons.

Back by the stage, three bodyguards were helping a groaning, groggy Windstag to his feet, his arms about their shoulders.

"*Which* three nobles?" the patrol swordcaptain snapped at Amarune.

She pointed. When her finger reached Kathkote Dawntard, he sneered, "Hah! The word of some lewd dancing wench against the sworn testimony of lords of the realm?"

"I, too, am a lord of the realm," Arclath Delcastle snapped, "and my words will support every one of hers against you."

"Ah, but there's just one of you, and these lying low-life riffraff who will, of course utter any falsehood against a noble, against *three* of us," Dawntard jeered, pointing rather unsteadily at Delasko Sornstern and the staggering Broryn Windstag.

The Purple Dragon swordcaptain had heard enough. "Him senseless and you so drunk you can barely stand? I think we'll be needing our wizards of war to peer into your minds before I believe you!"

Dawntard paled and raised his sword threateningly. The Dragon officer gestured disgustedly to one of his men, who had stolen around to stand behind Dawntard. The soldier obediently and efficiently used the pommel of his belt dagger to club the sneering noble to the ground.

"Saer Swordcaptain, I'm ready to freely answer all questions," Arclath offered affably, shooting Windstag a stare of challenge.

"Uh, urh . . . so am I," that noble said sullenly. "We . . . we were drunk, is the truth of it." He looked around, wincing at all the blood among the sprawled bodies, and added reluctantly, "The House of Windstag will make amends for all of this, Swordcaptain. We were in the wrong."

Then he gave Arclath a long and murderous look.

The Purple Dragon officer wagged a finger. "I *saw* that, O most noble heir of Windstag. Should anything befall Lord Delcastle, I'll know who to set the wizards to questioning."

Windstag's reply was short, emphatic, and extremely rude.

CHAPTER
TWENTY-TWO
HANDS CLASPED OVER A DECANTER

The best deals I ever made in all my long life
Were not signed on parchment and thrice-checked
By sober, world-wise merchants.
No. They were all, look you, hands clasped over a decanter.

> Ammarantus Gaerld,
> *Twoscore Mansions and Counting:*
> *A Successful Merchant's Life*
> published in the Year of the Risen Elfkin

The two door guards were enthusiastically discussing their chances with the prettiest of the junior chambermaids when the bent old man in ragged clothes shuffled between them, gave them both a pleasant nod, and stepped out of the palace into the night.

The younger guard stiffened, but his older companion—after a swift, craning look that told him the departing man was empty-handed—nodded back and said affably, "The gods grant ye a fair night and a pleasant one."

The reply to that was a silent, smiling wave, ere the old man trudged off, bent over and moving none too swiftly.

"You just let him go!" the younger guard hissed then. "That was this Rhauligan we're supposed to—"

"Supposed to promptly usher out of the palace if we see him," the older guard growled. "And that's just what we did. Aye?"

The bent figure dwindled into the distance down the well-lit promenade.

"It . . . it doesn't feel right, what we did," the younger guard protested as the old man vanished from sight somewhere in the night gloom.

"What doesn't feel right is some of these overly hasty and bullying orders our younger war wizards are all too fond of giving," the older one replied heavily. "A little too eager to command, they are, and a lot too lazy to think through consequences before they open their mouths. Some of them need to get their fingers burned and learn a little wisdom. Hopefully, before this council dumps some *real* trouble into their laps."

"You think it'll go ill, then?"

The veteran Purple Dragon's answer took the form of a long, meaningful look.

Both Dragons might have felt rather differently if they'd been able to see old Elgorn Rhauligan at that moment. He'd straightened up and was striding along far faster and more steadily than when he'd shuffled his way between them.

Elminster was in a hurry as he headed into the heart of the city.

"H-here," Belgryn Murenstur said in a rush, turning to face the two burning men and hastily backing away, even as he indicated the carved hanging sign of the woman poised on a forest rock with bent bow above the heads of many snapping wolves. "The Bold Archer!"

"Thank ye, goodman," the shorter of the two replied. "Strangely enough, reading plain Common is something we can manage for ourselves."

The taller man made a swift movement toward Belgryn, but his companion shook his head. "We need to leave one witness, Treth."

He looked back at Belgryn. "Go in and see if Huntcrown's still in there. Warn him—or anyone—that we're here, and ye will die. Very slowly."

"We'll slice off thy tongue first," the taller man murmured almost gently. "Then thy nose. Then one thumb, and then the other . . ."

"Enough, Treth. He's starting to shake," the shorter man interrupted—and lunged forward to slap Belgryn across the face so hard that the proprietor of Murenstur's Imported Vintages banged his head on the front wall of the club, lost his breath, and ended up blinking dazedly into the man's wide, endless smile.

"Just go inside, see if Huntcrown's in there, and come right back out and tell us so. Through *this* door, not some other way, or Treth will begin his little surgeries the moment we find ye. Which won't be long."

The presence inside him rose up to fill him with dark confidence, and Belgryn found himself nodding furiously and rushing almost eagerly inside the Bold Archer.

In the space of three swiftly gulped breaths, he was back out again, eyes wide with terror. All his dark confidence, wherever it had come from, was gone.

"Y-yes," he stammered. "He's the one in the jerkin with the horned shoulders and black musterdelvys with white luster-stars all down it. Fair hair, green eyes, sharpish nose. H-has at least six bodyguards with him."

Those fierce smiles never wavered. "Good," the taller man wreathed in blue flames rumbled. "I've never liked bodyguards."

"There—," Belgryn started to blurt then fell silent.

"Yes?" the shorter burning man asked silkily.

"There . . . there are a lot of other nobles in there, saers, and all of them have bodyguards."

"Thy concern," the taller man told Belgryn, "is touching. Live, then, man."

He clapped Belgryn on the shoulder—a light, brief touch that scorched nothing but left the wine merchant chilled to the bone and shivering uncontrollably—and strode past into the Bold Archer.

The other man in flames waved to Belgryn and hastened into the club on the heels of his blazing companion.

Belgryn knew he should run away, far and fast. When he could master his trembling enough to keep his feet, he dashed as far as the other side of the street, where his reeling made him bounce hard off the wall of a shuttered-for-the-night bakery. Panting, he turned as something made him stop and turn to look back at the Archer.

Faint shouts came through the club's doors—an inner and an outer pair, of heavy, copper-sheathed duskwood—followed by the unmistakable ring of steel, of swords crossed in anger. There came a scream, some crashes, and more clangs of clashing blades.

Then the doors banged open and richly dressed men were streaming out, white-faced and frantic, clawing at each other to find freedom enough to flee into the night. The tall, blue-flame-shrouded warrior came bounding along in their wake, lunging and slashing. Men were screaming and choking and falling on their faces as he killed them, never slowing as he raced on down the street after some of those who'd fled, as fast as a storm wind, catching men up and butchering them viciously, all the way.

By then, Belgryn Murenstur was almost too busy spewing out everything he'd downed earlier in the evening all over the nearest wall to see the sea of blood and heaped bodies that was briefly visible through the doors of the Archer, ere they swung closed again.

Almost.

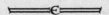

Arclath and Amarune stared rather wearily at each other across the table. Around them, Tress was bustling about, firmly directing her staff in the ongoing cleanup of the Dragonriders' Club, which by Dragons' orders was shuttered for the rest of the night. Someone had found Amarune's robe for her and someone else's slippers to go with it.

Various Purple Dragons and war wizards—they'd lost track of exactly how many but retained the impression that "various" was a rather large number—had asked Arclath and Amarune many, many questions about the events of the evening and their previous experiences, if any, involving the younger Lords

Windstag, Dawntard, and Sornstern. From time to time, the lord and the dancer had been separated, so their stories could be compared—and, it seemed, had matched. Those questions had all been fairly friendly and civil ... but there had been a *lot* of them. Not to mention more than a few spells gravely cast their way, and carefully expressionless men eyeing them thoughtfully.

Wherefore the decanter that Tress had wordlessly deposited on the table between them was deeply appreciated.

In silence they'd begun to pass it back and forth across the table, taking turns to sip, and murmuring questions of their own.

Not the probing sorts of queries they'd just finished—at least, they fervently *hoped* they were finished—answering, but the short, simple exchanges of two people getting to know each other better.

A guarded trust, of a sort, was slowly growing between them, because they'd been through danger together and had stood up for each other ... and because, it seemed, they genuinely liked each other.

"Noble lord," Amarune murmured, "I need an ally. Not a lover. A friend."

"I, too, have need of one of those," the elegant lordling told her, his gaze bright and level.

Slowly, hesitantly, their hands went out ... and clasped over the decanter.

The first wild-eyed man rushing past the Sage of Shadowdale awakened his interest, and the second an urgent desire to get out of the way to avoid being knocked down. When a third, fourth, and fifth pounded pantingly past before he could regain his balance against a handy wall, Elminster's interest had grown to a bright flame.

"What news? What're ye running from?" he called to the next few running men. All of them young, all well dressed, more than a few bleeding from what looked to be sword cuts ... "Where's the war?"

"B-bold Archer," one of them gasped in reply, stumbling and almost falling. He caromed off the wall beside Elminster, nearly taking the old man to the cobbles with him, but clawed at the stone with frantic fingertips, enough to keep upright, and ran on. "Men in flames!" he shouted back over his shoulder. "Killing everyone!"

"Men in flames?" Elminster inquired aloud, feigning more astonishment than he really felt.

"Aye," the next pair of running men panted; El recognized one as a noble he'd recently seen peering out of a coach on the promenade, though he knew not the youngling's House or heritage. "Blue flames!"

Ah, of course. Stormserpent had unleashed his new toys. Clearing his throat, Elminster squared his shoulders, drew in a deep breath, and set off for the Bold Archer with as much speed as he could manage, leaving the rest of the frightened nobles and their bodyguards to flee past him in peace.

If that was quite the right way to put it . . .

Gods, but he was getting old. Hastening for just a block or so had him limping for real, his weary old bones complaining with every lurching stride.

Luckily for the safety of the good folk of Suzail, almost all Purple Dragon patrols could move faster than he could. One of them rushed out of a side street and past him in swords-out, fearless haste.

He did not have to see the signboard to know which building up ahead they'd all vanished into. For one thing, a second patrol was hurrying up from another direction, and for another, Dragons from the first one were reemerging to take up watch by the doors, as more of their fellows reappeared to rush excitedly everywhere looking for witnesses and, no doubt, the guilty.

Elminster slowed. No horns were being sounded, which meant no fighting was still going on inside. Which meant, judging by the behavior of the Dragons, that there were plenty of bodies but no sign of any live and present murderers, flaming blue or otherwise.

Which in turn meant 'twas time for this old sack of bones to hang back, stay in hiding, and listen.

"Alassra," he muttered to himself as he sought the handiest alley, "forgive me. I love ye—but I love this realm, too. I can't stop meddling in its affairs, trying to defend it against those who'd tear it asunder, guarding it against itself. I just can't."

The alley was well situated to watch the front doors of the Archer from, and even came furnished with a handy heap of discarded crates that the hired refuse-wagons hadn't yet arrived to take away.

As he slid in behind them, relaxing against the rough and dirty wall with a satisfied sigh, one of his hands started to tremble all by itself, some of his fingers burning like they were afire, and others . . . going numb.

Elminster looked at it disgustedly. "This hand used to hurl down dragons and castles with equal ease."

He stared at his fingers grimly. At least they still moved in obedience when he waggled them. Though two of them, it seemed, couldn't curl up tightly anymore.

No more snatching things away from foes or keeping a tight grip on anything at all.

Stlarn it.

"This last century has not been kind," he told the darkness quietly. "I'm getting too old for this now . . ."

His entire hand had gone numb.

"Oh, Mystra, that it has come to this . . ."

Arclath and Amarune looked up in startlement. A breathless Purple Dragon was staggering past them across the main room of the Dragonriders' Club, gasping, "Swordcaptain? Swordcaptain Tannath?"

The patrol leader came out onto the stage from where he'd been examining the dancers' dressing rooms. "Aye, Telsword?"

"Your patrol's needed at the Bold Archer. There've been murders there, lots of them! Nobles, too!"

All over the club, Dragons started to move.

"Swordcaptain Dralkin sent me. Wants you there faster than possible, he said," the telsword added with the last of his air, weaving to a chair to lean on it and gasp for breath.

Arclath and Amarune stared at each other across the table.

"You stay here," the noble muttered, thrusting the decanter in Amarune's direction.

By the orders Tannath was bellowing, he'd decided to leave none of his men at the Dragonriders' and wanted "every last jack" of them out the door with him *immediately*.

"And I became your servant when, Lord Delcastle?" Amarune very quietly asked Arclath's unhearing back as he rushed across the room to join the soldiers.

With a shrug of farewell to Tress and a swift swig that drained the last liquid fire out of the decanter, Amarune ran to the bar. Snatching up a cloak from the litter of unclaimed clothing from the fled and fallen that had been gathered there, she whirled it about her shoulders to cover her skimpy robe and ran out into the night, right on the heels of the noble and the slowest of the Dragons.

Tress watched her best dancer go, shaking her head. Then she turned back to survey the damage to her club. Again.

Sigh. Mustn't let yon blood dry and the stain *really* set in . . .

Elminster sighed. Either this was a very slow night for Dragons walking patrol in Suzail, or the butchery inside yon club was truly impressive.

War wizards were still arriving—pairs and trios, each with a sword-jangling Purple Dragon escort—and hurrying into the Bold Archer.

From which the Dragons would soon emerge to stand talking with their bored, pebble-kicking soldiers who'd arrived earlier, and wait.

Presumably for the growing assembly of wizards inside to decide something or finish casting something—or fall asleep.

Gods, what did the callow young idiots who called themselves wizards of war *do*, these days? What could *possibly* be taking them so long?

Or were they all spewing their guts out in shock and disgust at the sight of so much carnage? By all the gods that still walked, weren't jacks or lasses who joined the war wizards *expecting* much blood in their lives ahead?

If not, why not? Were they all utterly ignorant of the world they strode around in?

Elminster sourly abandoned asking silent questions that the alley around him couldn't answer.

After all, who was he to demand answers about anything, an archmage who couldn't control his own trembling fingers?

He'd have to go and see and hear for himself. Using yon alleyway refuse hatch, for instance.

He glided over to it, found it ajar, shook his head anew at the carelessness of Cormyr's guardians, and listened hard.

About the length of his arm away from him, two swordcaptains had just begun to confer.

Swordcaptain Tannath was out of breath and none too happy. "Well, Dralkin? I got here as fast as I could; where's the fire?"

"Out," Dralkin said grimly, standing just inside the innermost door of the Bold Archer. All the lanterns had been lit and allowed to blaze up full; the room was bright, and every man could see the pool of blood that began at his boots and stretched away into a wrack of furniture and torn, draped bodies like a sticky crimson lake. "This would be what bards like to call 'the bloody aftermath.' Just before they start spewing up their suppers."

Tannath was dispassionately scanning the severed limbs and hacked and staring faces. "I'd say more than a few noble families are going to be howling for vengeance come morning."

"Aye, and our heads for not preventing it before it befell, when they can't find anyone else handy to blame," Dralkin agreed. "The spellhurlers have just cleared out to concoct something to head them all off. Not to mention to try to decide—though *how* a man decides such a thing, I wouldn't know—if some plague of marauding madness has befallen Suzail this night."

"Right, I'll ask the obvious one," Tannath asked heavily, his breath back. "Who did this?"

Dralkin shrugged. He caught sight of Arclath and Amarune's pale and set faces at the rear of Tannath's patrol, but went right ahead and said what he'd been going to say anyway.

"We've talked to two men who ran like stags before a forest fire and got away alive. They say two men who never stopped smiling, with blue flames that scorched nothing burning all over them all the time, did all this. They told everyone they were here to carve up Lord Seszgar Huntcrown—and did. His body's missing, though Wizard of War Scorlound took away a finger he thinks was Huntcrown's."

"So these two flame-enchanted slayers hauled their prize carved meat back to whoever sent them, to prove they'd done the deed, and earned their fee," Tannath said grimly.

"Of course. That's not what's riding me right now, though," Dralkin replied. "Here's why I want you upset and brooding, too: With all the nobles who want to get here camped in Suzail for this council, is this just the beginning? How many are these flaming murderers going to be sent to harvest, hey?"

Chapter
TWENTY-THREE

To Dream a Little Dream of Being King

Him? Fear not, he's gone off with eyes aflame,
Chest to pound, his laughter to make rafters ring,
As he prepares once more for his favorite game:
To dream a little dream of being king.

said by Asult the Cobbler
in Act II, Scene II of the play *Mad Mrodran's Fate*
anonymously chapbook published in the Year of
the Dauntless Dwarves

Gaskur's face was carefully expressionless as he admitted the three tardy nobles, but he led them up the back ways of Stormserpent Towers in almost undignified haste. On another occasion that might have earned him kicks and curses from the young Lords Windstag, Dawntard, and Sornstern, but not in the common mood that governed them just now.

Their hasty departure from the Dragonriders' Club had been followed by a near-race to Staghaven House, the Windstag family mansion, to shelter in its garden summerhouse until the Dragons who'd skulked along behind them from the club gave up and turned back to report their whereabouts. Then the three had taken the tunnel under the street that led from Staghaven's walled grounds to the Windstag-owned luxury stables, and from there down more than one back lane to reach Stormserpent Towers.

The journey had taken more than time enough for their anger to cool into fear, self-cursing, and worry—not just of missing out on Stormserpent's delicious schemes, but for stern consequences or at least annoyingly hampering war wizard suspicion ahead for themselves.

"*There* you are!" their host snapped as they came into the room in an untidy rush, Gaskur closing the doors behind them as he withdrew. "Too busy drinking to attend covert little meetings of treason on time?"

"Sorry, Marlin," came a swift reply that left the room blinking in astonishment; none of the six nobles who heard it had harbored the slightest inkling Kathkote Dawntard even knew *how* to apologize—to anyone.

"Aye," Broryn Windstag mumbled. "The family purse'll be much lighter by highsun tomorrow, once the Dragons show up at Staghaven House."

Sornstern was nodding; the three lordlings were the very picture of apologetic and chastened nobility.

Marlin Stormserpent sighed and turned from the board where he'd been filling himself a tallglass from his favorite decanter. "What happened?"

The explanation was an untidy collaborative affair that made the heir of House Stonestable snort loudly—and the other two nobles seated around Stormserpent's table roll their eyes a time or two.

For his part, Stormserpent drained his glass at a gulp and had to refill it. When their mumblings died away, he barked, "None of you were so drunk or angry as to threaten retribution on the Dragons or Delcastle when you gained more power, did you? *Did you?*"

"No," all three of the late arrivals replied with puzzled frowns, genuinely believing they hadn't—and, luckily for them, therefore sounding convincing.

Marlin Stormserpent shook his head in exasperation and waved them toward his decanters. "Sit. Lack of self-governance—and tardiness—once court and palace are aware of us, will cost you your heads, so consider what you've just been through a warning to be remembered and heeded. Now, where were we?"

With Marlin still on his feet pacing excitedly, there were— or would be, once the tardy trio got their glasses filled—six nobles around the table, all young heirs of lesser Houses. That is, scions of families who had long been frustrated that larger clans, such as the royal Houses of Crownsilver and Truesilver, and perennially masterful wealthy schemers like the Illances, always crowded them out of all real power.

Most of the lesser nobility had quietly striven for centuries—against several handfuls of Obarskyr kings—to force the Dragon Throne to give them "their due." Marlin's conspirators, however, were largely drawn from newbloods, families ennobled after the exilings of House Bleth and the dispossessions of the Cormaerils and others.

Young and wealthy nobles can find sycophants and toadies in plenty, but friends among their fellow nobles are rarer to come by and harder to keep, among all the feuding, pride, and burning ambition. Nobles tend to cling fiercely to the few real friends they do make—and friendships had inevitably complicated Marlin's choice of conspirators. Choosing a man he wanted might well bring along a second one he might not have ever chosen to trust with secrets that could cost noble necks.

Yet among the young heirs of Houses available in the realm, Marlin judged he'd done about as well as he could, if he wanted to retain any semblance of dominance at all in enterprises that could lead to swift graves if handled poorly. He had no stomach at all for recruiting stronger fellows who'd thrust him aside into the role of lackey—or scapegoat—once success was near.

They were all in their seats; Marlin sipped from his glass and studied them, his face once more a smoothly unreadable mask decorated by the faintest of smiles.

Windstag was a good blade and better hunter, but the sort of big, florid, blustering hothead that could all too easily land them all in disaster—and, there beside him, Sornstern was a nothing, Windstag's toady. Dawntard, though sly and a drunkard, had swift and sharp wits and could steer Windstag where none of the rest of them could.

Dawntard could be trouble, though; trouble for Marlin himself. The sort who waited for weakness and then betrayed fellows to step forward and seize the spoils for himself. So were Handragon and Ormblade, for that matter; he must take great care to keep the three of them opposed to each other, not working together.

Irlin Stonestable was sour-faced and dour of outlook, one who'd endure and do what was needful and no more—but stand like stubborn stone for the cause, when others would slip away and run.

Mellast Ormblade he still could not read as much as he wanted to, nor had he means enough to blackmail. The man was the worst snob among them, but a saturnine, sophisticated, smooth-tongued diplomat, who just might deserve to look down his nose at almost everyone else in all the realm.

Marlin knew a bit more about Sacrast Handragon, whose family's fortunes had fared perhaps the most poorly of them all—but what he knew made him firmly resolved to treat Handragon with wary respect. The man had the face of a statue when he wanted to, and iron self-control his every waking moment, it seemed. Swift and ruthless when that would benefit him, and a superb diplomat and actor all the time.

Aye, Ormblade and Handragon would bear watching. Hard and constantly too.

He smiled, raised his glass, and announced, "It's time, friends, for me to impart some truths."

By the gods, how he loved watching men stiffen in fear, waiting for his next words! This must be how it felt to be king.

Marlin waved a dismissive hand at the paling faces and stiffenings around the table, and let his smile broaden.

"Have no fears! This is *not* a moment of betrayal, I assure you. Rather, it is when I demonstrate my deepest trust in you by revealing my dearest secret: the very thing that made me dare to think a small, loyal-to-each-other band of true nobles could succeed in remaking—in rescuing—the land we all love. Before I reveal it, let me reassure you once again that no war wizard—not even the Mage Royal himself—can eavesdrop on us here. I have assembled magics they cannot hope to master or win past."

He waited a moment, seeing by their burning stares that he had their interest, all right. No superior and sneering detachment rode any face around the table just then.

"I have a weapon in my keeping that legend trumpets often but very few folk suspect truly exists. One we can use to conquer Cormyr when the time is right. Friends—fellow conspirators—I have a hold over someone I will not name nor breathe any hint of where this someone is hidden. Someone whom spells protect me from revealing by coercion, spells that I can use to kill in torment any who seek to coerce me. Lords, I control . . . a long-imprisoned Obarskyr!"

A wordless, hastily stifled murmur—almost a gasp—arose. Then silence. The silence of men leaning forward eager to hear, excited and delighted.

"We must work out the details of my grand—and, yes, treasonous—scheme together, in meetings to follow this one. Yet here is its general outline. Agents I've been training—with, from time to time, your assistance—will deal with any courtiers who learn too much about us as we proceed. Our work shall be to eliminate living Obarskyrs—without betraying our own identities, and as much as possible delaying anyone seeing this goal of royal elimination—until we can present the one who's under my hand as the sole remaining true Obarskyr!"

He fell silent to let them burst out with their questions.

"Coronation," Stonestable murmured. "And then?"

Marlin gave them all a warm and friendly smile. "At my covert bidding, this new king will name me Lord Chancellor and Marshall Supreme of the Realm—and appoint all of you to the other major offices of the kingdom."

"And then?" That was Handragon, his voice soft and almost lazy.

"And then," Marlin purred, "Cormyr will be ours, and we can all settle all the scores we want to. I have my little list, and I'm sure all of you do, too. I expect much blood."

The Sage of Shadowdale sank down into a crouch in the reeking alleyway, peered through the best of the many gaps in the untidy heap of rotten crates between him and the crowd of Purple Dragons milling about in front of the Bold Archer, and listened hard.

Not so much to the Dragons, for he'd heard Dragons who knew little but were being grandly the-entire-realm-rests-on-my-proudly-uniformed-shoulders about it more than a time or two before.

No, he was intent on the two persons in the little throng who weren't wearing Dragon uniforms: Lord Arclath Delcastle and the dancer who was with him, her cloak swirling open at every step and trying to take her robe with it. Amarune Whitewave, pride of the Dragonriders' Club. His descendant.

Hopefully his successor.

She was keeping silent and staying at Delcastle's side, as the young lordling asked questions of various Purple Dragons. He got some curt answers from the lowest-ranking, and a few "I know not" shrugs, but Dralkin's telsword answered his query with a blunt, "Who are you two? And why are you here, instead of keeping back beyond our sentinels?"

Arclath smiled. "I," he informed the Dragon officer loftily, "am Lord Delcastle, and I am charged by the war wizards to learn as much as I can about what's happened here."

The telsword regarded him expressionlessly for a moment and then raised his arm to point at the barely clad Amarune. "And her?"

"She," Arclath replied grandly, sweeping an arm around his ill-cloaked companion, "is with me!"

"Just for the evening?" another Dragon asked cynically from behind them. Arclath whirled around to confront the man, but couldn't tell which of the six or seven impassive veteran Dragons standing there had spoken.

He turned back to Amarune to say something supportive—and saw she was both pale and trembling with weariness. The excitement of the fray and seeing bloody death was wearing off or hitting home or whatever such things did. There was only one gallant thing to do.

"Lady fair," he announced, "Suzail seems all too full of brawling nobles—and worse—this night. Menaces who may well reappear, despite the vigilance of these dedicated Dragons. Pray, allow me to escort you safely to your place of rest!"

Amarune eyed him for only a moment ere shaking her head wearily. "No, Lord Delcastle, not there. The kindness of an escort back to the Dragonriders' forthwith, however, I'll not refuse."

"But of course!" Arclath replied with a smile, bowing low. Far wealthier and more respectable women didn't want lords to know where they lived—neither location nor depth of squalor. Well enough.

"I can promise you, Lady Dragonrider, that you'll be *quite* safe. There won't be just one upright and well-bred man guarding you; there'll be me, my title, and my honor—so that's three!"

Amarune rolled her eyes amid amused snorts from several of the Dragons. "I'm *not* Lady anyth—oh, never mind."

"Of *course* not," Arclath told her jovially. "I barely ever use my mind at all!"

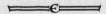

Heralded by a louder chorus of snorts, the two of them set off back down the street. Elminster kept his eyes on the Dragons and was not surprised to see the telsword point at one of his men and then at the departing noble's back.

That Dragon nodded and started to drift off down the street after the lord and the dancer, walking casually to a nearby doorway and standing in its shadow until Amarune looked back. When she was done doing so and the pair walked on, Delcastle airily declaiming something about local architecture, the Dragon strode a little way down the street into another, deeper doorway to await their next look back.

Throughout all of this, the rest of the Dragons studiously failed to notice their departing fellow, returning instead to their aimless back-and-forth strolling and muttered conversations.

Elminster let them get well and truly into these before he slid out from behind the crates and walked slowly out of the alley, hunched over, affecting a rolling limp, and paying the milling Dragons not even a glance. They returned the favor.

So as the Dragon skulked down the street from doorway to doorway, a hunched and limping old man followed him.

Around the curve of shuttered shopfronts, as the street bent in a southerly direction, all four went.

Elminster considered the Dragon's shadowing about as subtle as a series of warhorn blasts, but Arclath, at least, never looked back.

Neither did the Purple Dragon, so when the Dragonriders' was a little more than a city block away, the stooped old man limped a little faster.

Which meant that he calmly caught up to the Purple Dragon in the space of a few breaths to murmur in the man's ear, "Have my apologies, loyal blade, but I fear common thuggery is about all I can manage, these days."

"Err—uh?" the startled soldier grunted intelligently, turning to face Elminster—and receiving a well-worn dagger pommel hard and squarely right between his eyes.

As the senseless Dragon slumped heavily into Elminster's arms, leaving him staggering under the sudden weight, Lord Arclath Delcastle decided it was finally time to look suspiciously behind him.

However, all he saw was a drunken Purple Dragon staggering down to a wavering chin-first meeting with the cobbles, a sight that evidently didn't strike him as suspicious at all.

As he shrugged, opened the door of the Dragonriders' Club, and waved Amarune inside with another low and florid bow, Elminster rolled the Dragon against the nearest wall, out of the way of any wagons or carts, and ducked into the nearest alley that came furnished with a handy heap of refuse to hide behind. After all his years, he knew the night streets of Suzail *very* well.

With a grunt or two, El leaned his weary limbs against the alley wall and settled down to wait for Amarune to reappear.

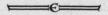

"Pleased, Lord?"

"Indeed, Gaskur. It went well," Marlin replied, making the gesture that told Gaskur he was dismissed for the night.

Smiling, the younger Lord Stormserpent watched his servant vanish down the back stair, then strode into his own rooms and started locking and securing doors.

He was just about done when blue flames erupted from a nearby wall, as the two ghosts of the Nine stepped into the room with dripping bundles in their hands. The thief, Langral, plunged one hand into his bundle—someone's cloak, darkened with blood—and drew forth a head that stared blindly past Marlin's shoulder, features frozen in terror.

The face of Seszgar Huntcrown; its look of fear was certainly preferable to its usual sneer.

Satisfaction became triumph. Deed done, that swiftly and easily.

"Take all that to the furnace," Marlin commanded, staring hard into their cold smiles and repeatedly visualizing the room, the way there, and tossing their bundles down into the flames. If the writings spoke truth, they should be able to see what he was thinking in his eyes. "Then return here to me without delay."

After what seemed like a long time, the two flaming men nodded, turned, and walked through his wall . . . at just the right spot for the shortest journey to the furnace.

Marlin surveyed the trails of blood they'd left behind, then went to his board—his private one, far better stocked than the one most guests ever saw—selected a flask of Rhaenian dark he'd noticed going cloudy, and used it to sluice away the blood. Gaskur could scrub away the faint results in the morning.

"Farewell, Lord Huntcrown," he murmured. "My, my, the dismembered bodies are piling up. I must remember to have Gaskur rake the bones out of the furnace ashes before a servant who might report them to Mother sees to that little chore."

He selected a clean flagon and the decanter that held his latest preferred throatslake: Dragonfire Dew, a fiery amber vintage from somewhere barbarous in upland Turmish. Cleansed throat and nose, kindled a fire below, and left a taste like cherries and blackroot on the tongue between. Ahhh . . .

He was well into his second flagon when his blueflame ghosts returned. He set it down, took up the Flying Blade and the chalice, and told them, "Well done."

Did those wide, steady, cold smiles waver a little when he began to will them back into their prisons?

It was hard, that much was certain, thrusting back an imponderable darkness in his mind that might have been their silent resistance or might just have been the weight of the magic. He was sweating when he was done—but he managed it, setting blade and cup, flickering an angry blue, on the table in a room suddenly empty of grinning, blazing men.

Right. I am the master of Langral and Halonter . . . and soon, of many thousands more.

Taking up his flagon, Marlin made for his bedchamber. High time to snore a little and dream of being a mighty and ruthless king of Cormyr.

As he unbuckled and shrugged off garments and kicked them away across the floor, Marlin sipped more Dragonfire Dew and pondered the part of his scheme he'd neglected to tell his fellow nobles.

He controlled no long-lost Obarskyr, but he was going to *make* one.

His two blueflame ghosts—they were hardly ghosts, really, but he liked the phrase—would one by one, at his direction, slay all the highknights and war wizards. He'd replace those dear departed with his hirelings, one by one as they fell, until the Obarskyrs had no one attending them who was truly loyal.

Then, of course, it would be their turn. He'd slay them all, every last living Obarskyr, and then present one of the Nine he commanded—Halonter looked the more Azoun-kingly of the two—to Cormyr as a "true Obarskyr" from the past.

Throughout all of that, he'd keep his fellow conspirators handy, up to their blood-besmirched elbows in the killings and ready to be framed as scapegoat "traitors"—and slain before they could implicate *him*—at any point in the proceedings where other Cormyreans became suspicious or any of his deeds got inconveniently witnessed.

Even if Lothrae produced more of the Nine and wanted to call a halt to his use of his two . . . well, Lothrae would hardly be eager to pass up the chance to rule Cormyr from behind the scenes.

It was, after all, one of the richest kingdoms in all the Realms.

Chapter
TWENTY-FOUR

A Storm in Shadowdale

These I have learned to watch for, and beware:
Fires atop Ghaethluntar, ships sailing the skies of the Moonsea,
Beholders seen in the Ghost Holds, black-hued elves seen anywhere,
And a Storm in Shadowdale.

Nestrel Mharrokh, Sage of Saerloon,
Old Pages from an Old Sage
published in the Year of the Elven Swords Returned

It had been a glorious day in Shadowdale, but the sun was lowering in the deep forest of the hills around the dale. Long shafts of light stabbed in under the trees to gild ferns and set aglow the broad leaves of the asthen-thorn and halabramble bushes that cloaked the toppled trunks of fallen forest giants.

Storm Silverhand crossed a glade like a slow and patient shadow, making as little noise as possible. She'd meant to be there much earlier, but the need for stealth and leaving no clear trail conquered all else. She'd draped the wizard's cloak over her distinctive hair to make herself a cowled, anonymous figure.

Twice she'd sunk to her fingertips to crouch in motionless silence as foresters with ready bows came stalking through the trees, following the trapline trails aseeking dinner. Their bows were more to keep off bears and worse than to bring down game, but it seemed there was always one who'd loose a shaft first and worry about what it had hit later.

It had been years since Storm had been the Bard of Shadowdale in anything more than legend; she farmed her land and mothered Harpers under her roof no more. The folk of the dale would think her a ghost or a shapeshifter or perhaps an accursed reminder of the Spellplague—and try to put an arrow through her or set their dogs on her, as likely as not.

And it had been years since such violence would have been a passing annoyance to her and no more. Increasingly she was more forlorn grim wisdom than mighty power. Alone, most of the time, too, though that bothered her less and less.

From the glade, it was a short way up through close-standing trunks and rising rocks to where a shoulder of rock reared out of the trees, moss-girt and dark with seeping moisture. Cracks and crevices aplenty gaped in its flank, some impressively large. Two were big enough to be termed "caves" to a passing man's eye.

One, she knew, was a niche that went in no deeper than the length of a short man lying down. The other was her destination.

Or would be, after she'd turned at the last tree to look back and bide silent, listening long enough to make sure no one was following her.

Storm held still as gentle breezes stirred leaves above and around, until the birds started to call and flit about unconcernedly again, and she decided no one was on her trail. Whereupon she set the cloak down on the toes of her nondescript old boots, shrugged off her robe, undid the jerkin beneath it and doffed it, wrapped the cloak around herself, donned her clothing again over it—and strode straight to that deeper cavemouth.

Where she stopped, put her left foot carefully on a little ledge about shin-high up one side of the jagged opening, and kicked off, to leap forward into the darkness, taking care not to put her other foot down anywhere on the rocks by the lip.

As a result, the spring-spear mechanism remained still as she ducked past it, rather than slamming its long metal boar spear right through her body.

Several human skulls—that she'd helped gather, a lifetime ago—adorned the narrow and uneven floor of the natural cleft she was suddenly standing in, that ran deeper into the solid rock. Mere warnings.

She strode past them and into the *real* guardian of the cave, hoping its magics hadn't decayed enough to kill her.

Harper mages had woven it long before, Elminster among them; a magical field to keep intruders out of this waystop hidehold in the forest. The Blue Fire had turned the ward into a roiling chaos that made living bodies shudder and terrified most who felt its touch, but the menaces it offered were meant to scare, not slay. If, that is, they still worked as intended and hadn't become something worse.

First came the blistering heat that robbed her of breath and drenched her in sweat in two steps. Storm closed her eyes to keep her eyeballs from cooking, gasped for air through clenched teeth, and forced her way on.

On, as the inferno grew and all her garments hissed, the moisture baked and blasted out of them, into—in mid-stride—icy cold, a chill that froze the sweat on her skin and plunged her into helpless shivering. A cold that seared nostrils and lungs, stabbing at her like countless spikes—Storm had nearly died, too many years earlier, on hundreds of sharp-pointed metal needles, and knew what that felt like—then faded into the next part of the ward, the curtain she disliked the most.

Mouths formed in the air all around her, maws she didn't bother to open her eyes to see, blind eel-like tentacles that saw her without eyes. Worms ending in jaws with great long fangs that struck at her like snakes, then bit and tore, savaging her as she hastened on, trying to get through them without losing overmuch blood. The maws hissed and roared or gloated wetly nigh her ears as they drooled *her* gore . . . as Storm stumbled across what she'd been expecting to find, heavy chain that clanked and skirled on stone beneath her.

The manacles, lying discarded on the passage floor. She kicked them and plucked them up, through all the vicious biting, and clung to them as she fought her way on.

Then the biting mouths and their roaring were behind her, and she was walking in air that crackled and snapped as many small lightnings stabbed at her, raking their snarling forks across her skin, her muscles trembling in their grip, spasming and cramping painfully as she lurched on.

Out of that torment into another, a nightmare of half-formed, shadowy coils that tugged at Storm, tightening like so many ghostly yet solid snakes of titanic size, coils that *always*, despite her upflung and clawing hands, managed to encircle her throat and start to strangle her, until she was walking arched over almost backward, caught beyond sobbing or gasping for breath, fighting through gathering dimness to—win free and snap back upright into a last torture of sharp, unseen points that jabbed at her eyes, solid shards of air that struck only at eyes and throat and mouth . . . to let go of her at last, leaving Storm staggering forward spitting blood from her many-times-stung tongue to regain breath and balance in the widening mouth of a cavern.

Alone and almost blind in near darkness, the only light coming from faint, fitful pulsings of the roiling ward behind her, Storm gasped and stretched and panted, seeking an end to her trembling as she tore off robe and jerkin again, to take off the war wizard cloak so she could wrap it firmly around the manacles and keep them from clinking.

After what seemed a very long time, she felt her body would obey her again. Not bothering to dress again, Storm caught up her clothes, the magics she'd brought, and the muffled manacles, and strode through the deepening darkness for a long way, across the level stone floor of a great cavern, until a faint glow became visible ahead.

She headed for it, and it became several glows, close together and down low and flickering feebly, at about the same time as the smooth stone under her boots started to slope down and the faint echoes of her progress changed, making it clear that the unseen ceiling of the cavern was descending as she went on, to hang close above her, the cave narrowing, descending, and getting damper.

And starting to stink, too. Not the smell of decay or earth or stone, but the musky stench of an unwashed and filthy human.

Then, at last, Storm reached the source of the glows and the reek.

Her sister Alassra, once queen of Aglarond and forever infamous in legend as the mad Witch-Queen and slaughterer of Red Wizards, the Simbul, was sitting alone, naked and filthy, with her feet in a pool. The water that fed it dripped down the cave walls in a dozen ceaseless flows.

Still shapely under the filth, still silver-haired, Alassra looked perhaps a lush and well-preserved forty-odd winters—but also, by the same scrutiny, seemed an utterly mad, keening wreck.

Gibbering and drooling wordlessly, she rocked and swayed back and forth, eyes staring wildly but seeing nothing.

A long, heavy chain that Storm knew ended in a shackle around her sister's ankle rose out of the water past her, to end at a massive metal ring set deep into the rock. It had been forged by dwarves but enspelled by Elminster and all of Alassra's sisters who could work magic powerful enough, its links bearing Alassra's blood slaked in her silver fire, let out in wounds they'd gently made. It called to her across the world, a ceaseless whisper she could ignore when lucid, but that lured her slowly but irresistibly whenever her mind collapsed. A binding she could easily remove but would not want to; the only comfort and companion she would crave. When her mind was in ruins, it could make her feel wanted and not alone, as long as she embraced it.

It was doing that right now.

So Alassra wasn't dying or under attack. She was just . . . more mindless than ever before.

Storm set down the magics and her discarded clothing, laid the manacles on the garments and unwrapped them with infinite care to avoid telltale rattlings, then left those shackles lying, draped the magical cloak around her neck, and went to her sister, embracing her wordlessly.

The Simbul stiffened in alarm and wonder then gasped in pleasure as she felt the cloak against her skin where it was pressed between them.

The cloak began to glow—the same eerie blue as the blue fire from the skies had been—as her body started to absorb its enchantments. Alassra clawed and clutched at it like a desperate, starving thing.

Her gasps became moans of pleasure then groans of release as her arms tightened around Storm, and she kissed her sister with dreadful hunger.

"El!" she cried, in a raw, rough-from-disuse voice. "El?"

"Sister," Storm said gently between kisses, " 'tis me: Astorma. Ethena."

"*Esheena*," the Simbul hissed in mingled disappointment and gratefulness, relaxing as awareness returned. The wild fire faded from her eyes, and she stared into Storm's gaze as they lay on the wet rock nose to nose.

Then she wrinkled her nose.

"*Faugh!*" she spat. "I *stink!*"

And she flung herself into the water, dragging Storm with her.

The pool was every whit as cold as Storm had expected, numbing her instantly. She'd be chilled for a day or more, thanks to her soaked breeches and boots, but that was a worry for later.

At the moment, Alassra was laughing with delight amid water aglow as the last of the cloak's magic passed into her and it crumbled to nothingness. "Did you bring some soap? Or one of those new Sembian scents?"

Storm made a face. "Do I look as if I want to stink like a cartload of jungle flowers crushed into the blended lees of an extensive wine cellar?"

"You," her sister said happily, "look like you can and do shrug off everything and serenely take from life what you seek, letting all else drift away without getting bothered over it."

She spread her limbs and floated, submerged except for her face. "*Thank* you, Storm. Thank you for myself back . . . for a little while. So, what's afoot in the wider world outside this hidehold? What are you up to? And El—where's he right now, and what foolishness is driving his deeds?"

"Meddling in Cormyr, as usual," Storm replied. "He sent me because he wants all the fun for himself."

"Hah, *as usual*," her sister told the cavern ceiling. "He always tries to keep me away from the best moments, too. I'd have slain thrice the Red Wizards, down the years, if he wasn't always—"

"Alassra," Storm told her with mock severity, hauling herself out of the water and hissing at the chill she felt as streams of it ran from her to rejoin the pool, "you haven't left two-thirds of the Red Wizards alive, so far as any of us can tell, at any time since you started defending Aglarond. You *couldn't* have claimed three times the Thayan lives you did. Trust me."

"Oh?" Alassra grinned archly. "Why start now, after all these years? Tell me more news. Not about El—you're helping him, of course—but of the wider Realms. Any kings toppled? Dragons tearing cities apart? Realms obliberated by angry dueling archwizards?"

"Oh, all of those," Storm chuckled, running both hands through her hair to shed fresh streams of water as she cast a swift glance back at the manacles and the rest of the magic she'd brought. "Where to begin?"

"Thay, of course," her sister said promptly. "I always want to hear what calamities have befallen the Thayans lately. Why, alathant so partresper I . . . what's kaladash, ah—"

Their eyes met, and the wildness was back in the Simbul's. And a moment of desperation, too, almost of pleading, before they rolled up in her head. Then they sank half-closed, making her look sleepy.

"S-sister—," she managed, in one last struggling entreaty.

Storm plunged grimly back into the pool and reached for her sister as Alassra started to slip under, babbling in earnest.

That hadn't lasted long.

Mystra damn it all.

Storm tugged her feebly thrashing sister—who was starting to bark like a dog—up out of the water, rolling her far enough away from it that only a determined crawl—and Alassra was beyond doing *anything* in a manner that might be termed "determined"—could get her back to a swift drowning before Storm returned.

Then she crawled back to her cloak and the manacles, water running from her soaked breeches and boots in floods that thoroughly drenched the sloping stone beneath her knees.

Storm shackled her sister to the wall ring, wrists crossed and hands behind head. That put most of her back in the water again—but unless something tore Alassra's arms from their sockets, the short length of the manacles would keep her face clear of the surface.

Giving Storm time enough to gather plenty of wood for a large fire and rocks to warm around it, to get herself and her sister dry.

Drenched and dripping, jerkin in hand to bundle twigs in, she lowered her head and trudged grimly back out through the ward again.

She hadn't expected the cloak to win Alassra's sanity back for long—its enchantments were relatively feeble, after all—but it had lasted a much shorter time than she'd expected.

Which was, as they said, bad. Storm hadn't brought all that many enchanted gewgaws with her.

Huh. El had better liberate a *lot* of magic from the royal palace or the nobles of Cormyr coming to council, if he ever wanted to see his beloved sane again.

Once Lass was over the initial frenzy, the rage that always accompanied her slide back into idiocy—and who wouldn't scream and fight, knowing they were sinking back into *that?*—she'd be fine. A survivor who'd fight like a tiger to cling to life. The ankle-chain didn't keep her from the water; it kept her from walking out of the cave, absorbing the ward as she went.

Even chained a long way from it, she was unwittingly reaching out and leeching its power, draining it ever-so-slowly to keep herself alive. Water, she had, and food she needed not, as long as she had magic to drink from afar . . .

Yet if ever Lass got out to wander the vast forest that surrounded the Dales and cloaked most of the land between Sembia and the Moonsea, she'd be just one more clever prowling beast awaiting fearful foresters' arrows. And the jaws and claws of larger, stronger prowling beasts.

Those were watchmens' manacles, recent Cormyrean forge-work stolen from down in the Dale. They neither had nor needed keys, and locked or opened by sliding complex catches on both shackles at once, something that could be done easily except by anyone wearing them, the cuffs being rigid. Unless they were put on a shapeshifter, or someone who had tentacles, that is . . .

Well, Lass had always hated malaugrym and doppel-gangers and anything with tentacles; she was hardly likely to work any magic that could give her such features, even if she did somehow regain sanity enough to work any magic at all.

Those thoughts took Storm back out through the tor-ments of the field—she really noticed, then, how much feebler they had become—into the forest where full night had fallen, bringing a darkness that would be deep indeed until the clouds thinned and let the moon shine down.

Which made the tiny, leaping orange glows over to her right all the more noticeable. She couldn't see the fire, only the light it was throwing up onto the leaves of overhanging trees; a campfire in one of the hollows on the edge of Shadowdale, where travelers who lacked coin for inns or wanted not to be seen down in the dale often spent nights.

They might be merely passing through, or they could be trouble. Which meant she could not ignore them.

As silently as she knew how—which was *very* slowly, in this poor light—Storm crept closer to the flames.

There were eight well-armed, fierce-looking adventurers in the hollow. Three were huddled asleep in their cloaks; two stood watch with their backs to trees, facing out into the night; and a trio were muttering together as they banked their fire with clods of earth. Their talk told Storm they were trouble, all right.

"Harper's Hill," one was saying. "Three different men down in the dale said he'll be thereabouts, if he's to be found at all."

"I heard he lurks around Storm Silverhand's farm—with her and a lot o' ghosts and the like," another put in.

"Nay," said the last of the three. "Ulth and I searched there a day back. No crops sown this year, and a garden run wild. The house stands open and empty. They say in the dale the Lady Storm walks out of the woods when she pleases—mayhap twice a year, now, no more—and no one knows when she'll appear or why. Never stays more than a night, seems to avoid her farm, then is gone into the trees again."

"Crazed, all of them," the first man offered, spitting thoughtfully into the fire. "Been thus a long time, now."

"So what do we do if we can't find Elminster?" the second man asked, sounding younger and less assured than the other two. "Search the backside of every tree between here and Sembia? That's a *lot* of forest!"

"Yes," the first man told him firmly. "Search we will—not trees, idiot, but every last cave in all the forest. Yet I doubt it'll come to that. Once we find a hint of magic, we'll have found Elminster."

Storm sighed soundlessly and backed away. Right past the sentinel she'd passed on her way in—just as unnoticed as during her arrival.

She would have to deal with them before she headed back to Suzail . . . or Alassra would be dead with half-a-dozen arrows in her before this lot were done looking for El.

Who would just have to deal with the council on his own, Cormyr fall or Cormyr stand.

Oh, Mother Mystra, come back to us.

That fierce prayer was answered by the utter silence she'd been expecting.

The empty silence she'd heard for a hundred years.

Chapter
TWENTY-FIVE
WELL EARNED

This crown? These scars?
This pegleg? The hand of steel?
The dark, endless hunger to kill everyone around me?
Well earned, Sardusk. Every one of them, well earned.

> said by Garangor, King Darkheart
> in Act III, Scene I of
> *Darkheart's Fall, and the Price of It*
> by Amrathgus Taerl, Bard of Daerlun;
> from *A Belt of Stars: Plays for Players*, published in
> the Year of the Splendors Burning

Marlin poured himself another glass from his favorite decanter and nodded approvingly.

This Jharakphred *was* the best artist for hire in Suzail, it seemed.

A nervous, simpering little runt of a man, to be sure, as he stood there holding the protective cloth covers he'd just stripped from the two portraits he'd painted—but the best.

There was no arguing with the two boards lying flat on Marlin's table. They weren't just good likenesses of Lord Draskos Crownsilver and Lord Gariskar Dauntinghorn—they *were* old Draskos and Daunter.

"You like them?" the artist asked nervously, misinterpreting Marlin's silence. "I followed both lords for days, until they told their bodyguards to run me off. With cudgels." He rubbed at some bruises, reflectively, then left off to add proudly, "I think I got them right, though. Very true to life."

"Very," Marlin agreed with a smile, stepping forward to hand the man the promised fee. "Well earned."

Jharakphred beamed, bowed deeply to his noble patron with the heavy pouch of gold clutched in both hands, turned away—and never saw Marlin's smile widen into a beam to match his own as two men blazing with silent blue flames from head to toe stepped out from behind tapestries both before and behind the artist and ran him through.

"Take him to the furnace," Marlin ordered, plucking the gold back out of convulsing claws that would never hold a brush again, as the impaled man gurgled and shuddered on two swords at once. "You know the way. Mop up every last spot of blood 'twixt here and there, then return to me."

His will more than his words compelled the two silent slayers, but Marlin enjoyed giving orders. Besides, he needed the practice. It wouldn't do to sound less than regal when the time came.

Soon.

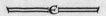

What seemed a very short while later, silent blue flames erupted out of the nearest wall. Marlin smiled and, as both Langral and Halonter emerged, beckoned them over to the pair of portraits.

"These men . . . would you know them, across a room or down a dark street? Look well, until you will."

He pointed at the painting on the left, so vivid and lifelike that it might have been the living man it depicted, somehow rolled out flat on Marlin's table.

A burly, fierce-looking lord, going white at the temples but possessed of a warrior's confidence and rugged good looks, staring hard out of the painted board at anyone viewing it, with a frowning challenge in his ice blue eyes. "Lord Draskos Crownsilver, patriarch of the Crownsilvers."

Then Marlin waved at the other picture. A faintly smiling, smoothly handsome, dark-haired man with steel gray eyes, this one. A sleek, dangerous old sea lion. "Lord Gariskar Daunting-horn. Like the other, head of his family."

The two flaming men—or ghosts or whatever they were—stood in silence looking down at the two portraits for a long time, ere they both finally nodded.

Marlin smiled again. "When I compel you to," he told them, "you'll enter whatever club or inn or wing of the royal court I direct you to and kill them. Bearing their bodies away with you to a place I'll tell you of, so they cannot be found and brought back to life."

And as they nodded once more, eyes on his, he bent his will on them, forcing them back into the chalice and the Flying Blade again.

It was still a struggle but an easier one this time; when he was done, a single swipe of his fingers sufficed to wipe the sweat from his brow.

Then he reached for the handy decanter of his favorite wine, seeing with approval that his steward had freshly filled it since the morning, and pondered his plan.

If his coerced slayers slew these two key senior nobles during the council, he'd at one stroke remove the most capable and stubborn resistance to any change in rulership, plunge the realm into uncertainty and turmoil, and lure any investigating highknights and war wizards within reach of the deadly blades of Langral and Halonter.

The flower of House Stormserpent sipped thoughtfully. And smiled again.

It was high time to take himself back to the Old King's Favorite to survey the fresh crop of nobles arriving early for the council.

There might well be some other nobles fair Cormyr would profit from the removal of. To say nothing of the fortunes of one Marlin Stormserpent.

Once settled at his usual table, Marlin made haste to hide his face behind a full goblet of something refreshing, so as to not to be so obviously listening to the talk rising excitedly all around him.

Word spread as swiftly as ever in Suzail. The Purple Dragons on watch were all in an uproar; that young and sneering braggart Seszgar Huntcrown had been murdered in a club, along with all his blades—servants, bodyguards, and hangers-on, every jack of them—by two mysterious slayers who did their deadly and unlawful work wreathed in constant blue flames!

That would bring out the wizards of war after morning-feast on the morrow, to be sure. Or so ran the shared opinion of the nobles dining and drinking—mainly drinking, at such a late hour—in the Favorite.

There were far more lords in the place than usual, Marlin noticed; the city was starting to fill up with nobles who spent much of their time at their upcountry keeps and hunting lodges.

They knew they could find good food and properly fawning service at the Favorite at that hour, without all the din and roistering of more common clubs—and without most of the perils of such places, too. Most nobles mistrusted their fellow lords even more than they disdained commoners and hated Crown and court; even there, in the Favorite, they'd brought their wizards along for protection. Their House wizards, most of them, though a few had hired outlander mages as bodyguards. That was only to be expected; it was commonly accepted but officially unconfirmed truth that the war wizards trained, influenced, and even infiltrated the ranks of the House wizards, and spied on all noble-hired spellhurlers anyway. So there would always be some nobles whose mistrust of their House wizard overcame any miserly instincts.

Marlin smiled wryly to himself, recalling what courtiers called such lords. "Incipient traitors." Well, for their part, nobles had far less polite terms for most courtiers.

Lord Haelwing, two tables away from Marlin, was one of those mistrustful nobles, it seemed, and had no doubt given his bodyguard wizard some blunt and specific orders before pro-ceeding to the Old King's Favorite and commencing to drink himself into insensibility.

So the mage, a Sembian of slim mustache and cold eyes hight Oskrul Meddanthyr, was seated at the table beside the drunkenly snoring heap of his employer. A table acquiring an interested audience of young nobles and wealthy pretenders to nobility, who had eagerly seized the opportunity to ply a talkative wizard with drinks and question him about the unfolding ways of the world.

Marlin listened as the Sembian became increasingly loquacious, as drink after drink took hold. Grand tale after grand tale was rolling out of Meddanthyr, and even the nobles' bodyguards had started to listen.

"Oh," he was saying to one would-be noble, leaning forward to favor the table with an unlovely smile, "the Harpers *officially* disbanded. That is, the head Harpers announced the dissolution and then set about very publicly butchering many Harpers whom they knew to really be agents of various evil groups who'd infiltrated Those Who Harp."

Meddanthyr sipped from his jack, smiled again, and added, "Yet I very much doubt it will surprise any of you to learn that the Harpers did not, in fact, cease to exist. An extremely secretive, underground fellowship of some two dozen Harpers continued—as they do to this very day. In fact, my friends—"

The wizard thrust his head forward and lowered his voice dramatically, to add in a menacing whisper, "*the Harpers are rebuilding . . .*"

"WhooOOoohoo!" young Lord Anvilstone piped up, imitating a ghost's frightening wail as he wiggled all his fingers in mock apprehension.

"They're sitting among us right now," his friend Lord Mrelburn put in sarcastically. "Under the tables, everybody!"

There were snorts and derisive chuckles, in the heart of which someone muttered, "Fear a lot of lasses and fancy-boys sitting half-naked over harps? Not farruking likely!"

"Here, now," an older lord said quellingly, "I can hear wild nonsense about the Harpers any time! Leave off; we've got a wizard here, and for once it's not one of Ganrahast's watchful toadies. *I* want to hear about magic, old magic out of legend—and what out of all those tales has *real* spells and suchlike behind it that we should be seeking or being wary of or that might be here in Cormyr under our noses."

A general rumble and roar of assent greeted these words, and Marlin decided to seize this chance to steer the Sembian's tongue before he downed any more drinks and veered toward the fanciful or incoherent.

"Hey, now!" he called firmly, before Meddanthyr could decide what tale of magic to tell first. "If it's to be magic spoken of, I want to hear about the Nine—the Crown of Horns, Laeral before the Blackstaff 'saved' her right into his bed, and the shattering of that fellowship. Two of whom had interests hereabouts, I've heard. We know what befell Laeral, but whatever happened to the rest of them?"

Meddanthyr turned to face Marlin for just long enough to dispense a shrug. "Dead, some of them. Fled away, others—I know not where, but they were veteran adventurers, mind; they may well have had other names and faces prepared to step behind, to live out their days in plain view but not known for who they really were. And they could have had all manner of spells and enchanted items, aye, though Laeral was their strongest spellhurler, by far. I've heard of nothing linking any of them or their doings to Cormyr after the Crown of Horns took her and she turned on them all. But as to powerful magic, three of them shared a fate that should be of interest to you."

The Sembian sampled the fresh jack that Marlin's signal had just set in front of him, set it down again with a sigh of nigh tipsy contentment, and added, "Three of them got trapped and bound into magic items."

A murmur of interest rippled around the table, and the old lord nodded and beamed triumphantly, as if he'd already heard something of this and was very pleased he'd be hearing more.

Meddanthyr waited for someone to answer the cue, and one of the younger and more impatient lordlings obliged. "Well? Who did it, and why, and what're they like? Curse you for being so secretive, wizard!"

The Sembian smiled. "Secrets are what wizards deal in, Lord Mhorauk. No one knows who did it, which is to say there are so many competing stories and accusations that we can be certain of nothing beyond most of them being pure fancy. Someone very powerful in Art, obviously—and any answer to your 'why' will have to wait until we know that 'who,' or we'll be merely spinning new fancies. Yet I can tell you a little of what they're like . . . and will."

He sought to sip from his jack again, discovered it empty in an almost mournful pantomime, then waited in satisfaction as three irritated lords all signaled to the Favorite's hovering maids to refill it.

A trio of jacks were swiftly set before the Sembian, who in priestly pious manner both smiled his thanks and contrived to look surprised at the same time.

"Right now," he said, leaning forward and lowering his voice to gather all nearby ears to his words, "somewhere in the Realms, there are three metal objects—a sword, a rather grand chalice, and a largish hand axe, most of the writings say—that are the prisons of three of the Nine. Anyone who has hold of one of these can order the trapped one to come forth from it, or send them back in, and when they are out of it can compel them as exactingly as a willing and eager slave. A servant who'll never disobey, tire, hesitate, nor feel pain, and so can never fail for reasons of weakness or treachery."

Meddanthyr held up a finger in warning and added softly, "You can know these slaves by their flames. At all times when outside their items, they are wreathed in leaping blue flames that burn no one and nothing and consume them not. So it is written, by several wizards and sages who saw them nigh a century ago. They've not been seen since, at least by anyone who survived to write or speak of it. The three objects that imprison these three of the Nine, I should add, do not themselves flame."

He fell silent, leaving the table waiting for more, but sat back and spread his hands to silently indicate what he'd said was all.

An excited babble arose, all of the men asking or telling each other the same thing: the murderers of Huntcrown had been wreathed in flames, hadn't they?

"And how sure are you, of all of this?" Marlin asked through that chatter, making his voice sharp as well as loud, hoping to goad. He succeeded.

The Sembian turned to glare at him and snapped back, "Wise men know they can never be sure of *anything* when it comes to the Art, saer, but I know what I've just said to be true—and also know I'm surer of matters magical, large and small, than you'll ever be. I'm well aware that nobles are reared to belittle their lessers and to think all who lack titles *are* their lessers, but such thinking is *wrong*, and those who cling to it all pay stiff prices for doing so, sooner or later. Be guided accordingly—or ignore me and be just one more noble fool. I'm a wizard; I've met many noble fools. They're not nearly as special as they believe themselves to be."

Marlin waved aside this blustering with casual impatience. "But *three* adventurers? *Three*, and no one's found even *one* of them?"

Meddanthyr shrugged. "They may never be found. Buried and lost, or lying at the bottom of the sea, perhaps—or found by some dragon, who'll keep the chalice, the blade, and the hand axe in his hoard and never call forth the adventurers from them!"

"That's true enough," Marlin agreed, sitting back to let other questions come, and the wizard burble on about other things.

Finding a largish hand axe was a tall order for one young noble, but he could call on six nobles to do the seeking—and thereby draw attention to themselves and not him—just as soon as he returned to Stormserpent Towers.

Though they were still breathless from climbing the stairs of Marlin's turret in such haste, Delasko Sornstern and Sacrast Handragon looked not just excited at Marlin's news. They seemed delighted.

Marlin Stormserpent turned back to triumphantly telling his table of conspirators all he could remember of what the talkative wizard in the Favorite had said . . . and he could recall almost *everything*.

"That axe must be found!" he added, bringing his fist down on the table. "Find it, seize it, and bring it here! I—there's, ah, a spell I'll have to awaken, to call forth the slayer inside it to do our bidding!"

Your bidding, more than one noble around the table thought, but that thought made their faces slip only momentarily, for Marlin was watching them closely.

Eager enthusiasm was what they strove to show. With one exception.

"But *how?*" Irlin Stonestable asked sourly. "There must be a lot of hand axes in Suzail!"

"Call on the nobles who've come to town for the council, in their rooms," Marlin snapped. "Say you want to *really* get to know them and strike up friendships. Bring your House wizards along with you` to sniff out magic with spells they cast before you go in to meet any lords. Your mages only have to pay attention to hand axes, remember."

"Or things that look like something else, but that their spell *sees* as a hand axe," Handragon pointed out.

"Yes!" Stormserpent agreed excitedly, whirling to point at Handragon. "Well thought! Well thought!"

There were nods around the table, ranging from Sornstern's gleeful one to Broryn Windstag's grimmer agreement.

Every lordling in the room knew Huntcrown's flaming slayers must be two of the three Nine survivors who were bound into items, and it followed that the sword and the chalice must already be in the hands of someone in Suzail who knew how to use them. Stormserpent's outburst had just left them all with the strong suspicion that he was that "someone."

The someone who commanded two flaming men or ghosts who'd slay anyone he chose. Any young noble lord he took a dislike to, for instance.

"Just the hand axe?" Stonestable asked confusedly. "You already know who has the sword and the chalice?"

"The *palace* does," Marlin snapped, after a hesitation that was just a whisker too long. "The war wizards keep them both hidden, or I'd have had them already, and we'd be using them to make inconveniently nosy wizards and courtiers— and, the Felldragon forfend, nobles, too—disappear for good. Our good gain, that is."

He was almost babbling. "But *enough* talk for now! This news overrides all! Get up and get out there, everyone! There's a hand axe to be found!"

Chairs scraped back and lordlings clapped hands to the hilts of their blades out of long habit as his words rang around their ears. Then there was a general rush down the stairs as everyone hastened to do his bidding.

Or go back to bed.

At the moment, he cared not which.

Behind their departing backs, Marlin was busy wincing at the slip he'd made. He turned to seek his favorite decanter again.

If some of them said too much, and wizards of war came around poking long noses into the affairs of House Stormserpent, could they tell that the sword at his hip or an innocent chalice held a blueflame ghost inside it?

They'd not noticed the one or the other—even under their very noses, in their own palace—all these years, but then, they hadn't really been looking, had they?

What did they spend most of their time *really* watching instead?

Chapter
Twenty-Six
Driving Wizards to Drink

Wizards can rule a battlefield, pry into minds o'er a realm,
And find traitors, but enslave all doing so. So I make it my
business to do as warriors do: keep safe our wizards
And butcher all others. When no war makes spells needful,
the realm can be kept quite safe by driving wizards to drink.

> Markuld Amryntur,
> *Twenty Summers a Dragon: One Soldier's Tale*
> published in the Year of the Splendors Burning

There were more guards than usual stationed about the
Palace—and no wonder, with the Council almost upon
Suzail, a flamboyant riot of nobles freshly arrived in the city,
and more lords on the way.

Nevertheless, Lady Highknight Targrael made her way up
two floors and across the vast building with casual, almost con-
temptuous ease. With Ganrahast and Vainrence missing, their
wizards lacked both orders and attention for much else but
finding their commanders—and as they'd long since scoured
the palace several times over, most were now seeking elsewhere.

Which meant borrowing long-dead Queen Gantharla's double-
ended dagger from where it hung in the Blackrood Chamber was
largely a matter of strolling there, plucking up the nearest chair
to stand on, and tugging the weapon free of some old and brittle
leather thongs that bound it on display, high on the wall.

Those bindings collapsed into swirling dust, and the deed
was done. Chair back where it should be, and strolling away,
with the young, yawning guard in the passage outside the door
none the wiser.

The dagger was a beautiful, slender thing—elven; all

flowing lines, deceptively delicate shape, and razor-sharpness, even after all this time—and rode in Targrael's hand well.

She hefted it, smiling to herself, and murmured, "Elminster must die."

The black-armored death knight was still triumphantly uttering that last word when the secret door she was reaching for swung wide—and she and the armored Purple Dragon who'd opened it from the other side found themselves staring at each other.

"Hold!" he snapped, striding through the doorway and bringing the spear in his hand up to point at her breast. Its tip glowed with a hue that told Targrael its magic could destroy her. His shield came up, too. "Drop that steel and hands to the ceiling, you! Your name?"

A lionar, by his badge. Whatever next? What was a *lionar* doing stalking about the palace with a spear and shield?

"Having the temerity to challenge me, that's what," she murmured aloud as she ignored his order . . . and their locked stares both grew colder.

"Your *name!*" he snapped loudly and insistently.

Targrael sighed. This was becoming tiresome, and he was getting a very good look at her.

"Lady Highknight, to you," she told him coldly, "and *I'll* give the orders here, Lionar. Point that spear elsewhere or pay the price."

The spear was suddenly almost up her nose. "*You're* no highkni—"

"Enough," Targrael snarled disgustedly, calling forth what sages liked to call "unholy flames," right into his face—and sidestepping as she did so, to avoid any desperate spearcast. She held Gantharla's dagger behind herself and didn't bother to draw her sword. Not when his despairing howl would be over in another moment, and by then she'd be through the secret door and have it closed behind her.

Leaving the luckless lionar down for days, or worse. If he awakened at all, he'd be raving about his unfortunate encounter with one of the palace ghosts.

Pesky things, ghosts.

A lone chuckle bubbled forth in the great cavern deep in the heart of the palace undercellars. Ah, Targrael . . .

Once, the cave had been Baerauble's most secret spell-hurling chamber, where the founding archwizard of the human realm of Cormyr had conducted his boldest magical experiments.

Some of those castings had gone *very* awry, and it had become a place of crawling wild magic. Best abandoned, behind heavy wards to keep the unwary from blundering into deadly peril or venturing spells of their own that might bring most of the palace down on their heads in shattered ruin.

Wild magic had lurked there for centuries until the Spellplague had boiled it away and had left the great cave yawning empty, awaiting anyone's arrival.

That arrival had befallen, and the anyone who stood there chuckling was a man who intended to soon rule Cormyr and more.

A man whose archwizardry would have given Baerauble himself pause, who stood alone yet rode the minds of many others.

Both in the cavern and in the depths of Targrael's mind, Manshoon chuckled again.

Ah, but his Lady Dark Armor was a treat. He'd almost been seduced by his enjoyment of her coldly malicious mind into keeping her active too long. At an ever-increasing risk of losing her to the spells of frightened wizards of war as they *finally* awakened to the growing perils all around, as nobles poured into Suzail, the day of the council rushed nearer, conspirators plotted busily on all sides, blueflame ghosts stalked the streets slaying at will, and Elminster strolled the passages of their own palace uncaptured.

They were still an utter chaos of incompetent, overly officious fools, but they were starting to face life without Ganrahast and his faithful hound of a Lord Warder and—at last—trying to make some decisions themselves.

The wrong ones, thus far, and all of them too late, but even idiot magelings can't help but notice a beautiful, elegant, and very dead woman striding around their palace in black armor of archaic style, defying all orders . . . and even idiot magelings can aim and trigger wands.

Yes, it was more than time to send Targrael back to her slumber to await the day when he'd need her again.

He'd need others, too, at least one war wizard among them, so it was time to also withdraw from the minds of Talane, Rorskryn Mreldrake, and various Stormserpent servants as if he'd never been there at all.

Which was something he—perhaps he alone—could do.

A certain Emperor Manshoon would need all his useful tools after Elminster was dead and he'd dealt with the pitiful remnants of Cormyr's past; what was left of the wizards of war, of Vangerdahast, and of Alusair the Ghost Princess.

Then it would be time to rule, and truly loyal agents would be *most* useful.

Until then, no one would ever know they'd ever been his creatures at all.

"Not for me the clumsy mind-reamings of Cormyr that so often drive wizards of war and those they violate into madness," Manshoon told the dark emptiness around him, as his beckoning finger brought a decanter and a great crystal goblet floating out of the darkness to his hands. "Vampire I may be, but I am before all else a *real* archwizard; I ride minds and depart them leaving no traces that lesser fools can find."

Simple truth, not vainglorious boasting; he had worked hard on crafting spells while others played tyrant or meddler. He could do things no mage of Cormyr could even hope to achieve through magic. Hah, he could do things most would think impossible.

Manshoon unstoppered the decanter and poured, savoring the delicate scent of the rare and ancient elven vintage wafting up from the goblet.

Very soon, Targrael would step through yonder door and put into his hand the enchanted dagger that he could compel into magical flight to swoop and fell Elminster from behind, if a fight with the Old Mage should erupt before the old fool's carefully plotted doom befell him.

Once the dagger was his, he could send the death knight back to well-earned rest. He no longer needed her to guard this cavern, as he had it ringed with undead beholders under his command, and he'd fully mastered a living beholder body of his own—and blasting *that* mind had been a feat to celebrate—to occupy whenever he pleased.

Or if someone destroyed the human body he was using.

Manshoon scowled at that thought, remembering who had slain more of his bodies than anyone else, down the centuries ... and had played with him, as an unwitting tool, even more often.

"Elminster," he whispered gleefully, "you *will* die. Very soon now."

Soon indeed, for as he'd intended and so patiently arranged, the Sage of Shadowdale was alone.

Elminster's lover had gone howling mad again, and his lone remaining loyal ally and healer, Storm, was off to Shadowdale to see to her. Where both silver-haired bitches would die or be kept too busy fighting to cling to their lives to return to Suzail in time to help the kindly old Sage of Shadowdale. What he'd made his dupe Mreldrake tell the Highknight Starbridge should ensure as much.

That diligent hammer of Cormyr's foes should even now be scouring the dale for signs of Elminster and his two silver-haired wenches, believing those three were preparing to magically attack King Foril just after his council.

Manshoon sipped and nodded appreciatively. Yes, his plans were unfolding nicely.

He would use Talane to kill Gaskur, the mind he'd most often inhabited and of necessity altered, in Stormserpent Towers—after enspelling Gaskur to look like Ruthgul. Scrying to make sure Amarune Whitewave saw Ruthgul dead, he'd then dissolve his spell so she'd witness her dead client "melting back" into Gaskur, a man she should not know.

That little ruse should frighten her into repudiating Elminster rather than agreeing to work with the Old Mage.

Not that she had much aptitude for magic. Whitewave was very little more than an accomplished thief, and could be slain with ease—but she was far more useful as Elminster's tormentor. If she repudiated her ancestor, it would crush the old fool more than anything Manshoon himself could do.

And Elminster must suffer.

Rejection or betrayal at the hands of everyone the Sage of Shadowdale depended on should bring on that suffering nicely, before an unexpected longtime foe—the oft bested and belittled Manshoon—revealed himself and killed the old goat.

Manshoon smiled at his decanter. "And when Elminster is dead and these hands have slain him, I'll be out from under his shadow at last," he told it. Then he noticed it seemed to have half-emptied itself rather quickly.

He shook his head. That was the problem with decanters ...

It was time to bid farewell to the mind of Marlin Stormserpent, too. A young fool doomed by his own ambitions, yet thus far playing his useful—if unwitting—part.

"I have loosed him like a wild arrow among the court and nobility of Cormyr, to see how many lives he can reap before he's brought down," he purred. "Whereupon someone else will seize the blueflame ghosts and use them against *their* rivals and foes ... and so on."

Watching *that* bloody, ongoing game would be great entertainment.

Wherefore it was almost time for young Stormserpent's guide Lothrae to fall silent—which meant, of course, a certain meddling Manshoon would be departing the mind of Understeward Corleth Fentable, too.

Something moved in the distant darkness, a boldly striding, curvaceous shadow. Targrael, there at last and offering him the double-bladed dagger precisely as he was compelling her to—with one of its points held against her own throat and her other arm behind her, so he could destroy her with ease with the gentlest of shoves.

"It's not just a matter of avoiding detection as the wizards of war start prying in earnest, just before the council," he told her with a smile as he took the proffered dagger. "I'll soon be too busy to move my pawns around, with nobles galore arriving in a great flood of highborn scorn and pomposity. My attention will be on a series of subtle mind-invasions of lords and ladies of the realm, to decide who will be my future tools, and who—in a land burdened with *far* too many troublesome nobles—is swiftly expendable."

"Of *course*, Lord," Targrael murmured, going to her knees before him.

Manshoon smiled down at her, seeing in her mind as well as her eyes that if he wasn't compelling her to this subservience, she'd be trying to swiftly and savagely slay him right now.

"Let's get you back to your nice cold tomb to await more slavery to me," he murmured, letting go of decanter and goblet.

Both floated contentedly where they were, in midair, as Manshoon drew his Lady Dark Armor to her feet and waved her away on her last stroll through the palace—for a while.

A part of his awareness went with her, riding and compelling her, but her part was done; almost all of Manshoon's attention was back on what he'd conjured at the center of the cavern; his scrying scenes, his many eyes on Cormyr.

In a wider ring outside their glows, his living beholder slaves hung still and silent in the air, eyestalks hanging as limp as the fronds of dead plants. He'd given some of them bone-shearing pincers, too. They were ready to be unleashed up into the palace whenever necessary to make Foril's courtiers, wizards, and guards alike *very* busy.

Or sent out to guard the ways into this cavern, relieving their undead counterparts, his death tyrants, to spread slaughter and mayhem in the halls and chambers of state above.

Yet that was the same brute force approach that had failed Manshoon time and time again down the centuries, before Fzoul—and, gods blast the man, a certain Sage of Shadowdale—had taught him patience.

Not to mention deftness and subtlety. Never use a mace to smash what an apparently random breeze could topple.

Wherefore it was time to watch and learn and do the right

subtle things, as befitted a future Emperor of Cormyr, Sembia, Westgate, and Amn, too. Or wherever he chose to rule.

Oh, there were formidable foes standing in his way, to be sure ... but there was only one Manshoon.

"One Emperor but many bodies," he murmured. "None of them the copies of myself Elminster could so easily find and destroy. Neither he nor the foes of my future will be able to recognize me as easily as the Sage of Shadowdale did. That's one mistake behind me now, forever."

The nearest of his scrying scenes was a view of a small and nondescript office among a trail of similar offices at the rear of the palace, where Sir Eskrel Starbridge was sitting sourly behind his desk.

Manshoon sent his mind racing out. He'd prepared the highknight's mind already, and his arrivals had become deft; Starbridge should feel only a slight irritation, if Manshoon did nothing but eavesdrop on the thoughts rushing past ...

The desk was, as usual, littered with scraps of paper covered with encoded scrawls. Starbridge gazed at them idly as he listened to the last of his agents and contacts reporting in. Two more senior highknights had been slain in as many days, leaving Eskrel Starbridge right where he'd dreaded ending up—behind that desk.

The desk had a spell on it cast by the legendary Vangerdahast, one barely understood by his successors. That spell empowered a faint, almost ghostly voice to speak to whoever sat at the desk, all the way from distant Shadowdale, where the stone linked to the spell on the desk had been carried on mission. Through the link, Starbridge's predecessor had given commands to that northern dale and had heard reports. All of them, like the one just ending, saying the same thing.

Shadowdale had been hunted high and low for any sign of the legendary Old Mage, but it seemed Elminster couldn't be found at the moment.

Bah. Shared failure was no easier to swallow than a personal failing.

Not that sitting exasperated in this stuffy little room was going to mend anything.

"Must I do everything myself?" Starbridge growled. "Am I doomed to spend my life surrounded by blundering incompetents?"

At least two of the wizards and highknights crowded into the office stiffened, but most grinned wryly, and young Baerengard even dared to jest, "Well, you *did* choose to dwell in Cormyr, sir."

Starbridge gave the youngling a sour look. When he'd been Baerengard's age, idiots this callow would never have been considered for the mantle of highknight, but these dozen-some filling his office were almost all the highknights the Forest Kingdom had left. Untrustworthy, insolent puppies.

"*I* will lead an expedition to hunt down Elminster," he declared. "I'll take nigh all of you, plus a few of the more competent wizards of war—those with brains enough not to get themselves killed if they try something so difficult as camping, and who're capable of enough basic civility that we can stomach their company. Those here in this room, for instance. We leave tonight."

Several highknights stirred as if they wanted to speak, but only one plunged into dispute with him. Young Narulph, of course.

"I think an expedition is far less than wise—is, in fact, a very bad idea, given that Ganrahast and Vainrence still can't be found. Is it right and prudent that we depart the palace at this time, when the Obarskyrs may need our aid at any moment, with all the nobles of the realm gathering here for the council?"

Highknights had always owned the right to speak bluntly to superiors—even the reigning monarch or regent—without fear of reprisal, and the open debate this fostered had time and again served the realm well, but Starbridge had little time for Narulph's usual "Do nothing is best" stance.

"I'll have none of that," he snarled. "If the roof above our heads fell in and killed us all right now, there are still plenty of wizards of war left to defend Cormyr. Some of them—Arbrace,

Belandroon, and Hawksar, to name three—are even almost as competent as they themselves think they are."

The handful of mages present all grinned at that.

"If we're not here to save their precious little behinds for them, *again*," Starbridge added, before Narulph could think of some other idiocy to spout, "perhaps—just perhaps—they'll grow some backbone, and we'll all discover they're good for something besides strutting around muttering darkly about how the realm would fall every tenday or so, but for their oh-so-secret efforts."

One wizard lost his smile, another snorted back laughter, and the rest winced.

"Anyone *else*?" Starbridge barked. "Speak out now, because once we're at work, I'll take a *very* dim view of anyone trying to confound the results I'm seeking, or deciding on their own to just *change* things a little."

No one said a word. Not even the sullen-looking Narulph.

"Right," Starbridge said heavily. "Hear then my orders: Everyone is to depart the palace, starting now and leaving by ones and twos. We'll all meet again—before highsun, if you want to stay a highknight—at the Stone Goat paddock marker out on Jester's Green. Mounts, provisions, weathercloaks, and all have been gathered ready there long since, under guard. Fetch only the weapons you most want with you, and tell no one where you're going or what you're about. If anyone follows you to the Goat, *I'll* deal with them. Swift, now! The sooner gone, the sooner back again—whereupon Narulph here will be able to sleep on his bed of fears a little less fitfully. Dismissed."

Everyone broke into chatter and headed for the door, and Sir Starbridge rose from his chair with an air of quiet satisfaction. He'd be in a saddle soon, rather than this gods-stlarned chair behind this triple-be-damned desk, and that was worth any number of urgent all-hands missions.

So, where had he put that blasted cloak?

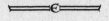

Manshoon turned away from both Starbridge's mind and that scrying, enjoying the same satisfaction that the gruff head highknight was feeling.

Another deft manipulation bearing fruit, another piece in the building mosaic . . .

On to the next piece, over there in *that* scene . . .

Shrouded in the gloom where moonlight was feeble, the muddy midyard was deserted.

Or almost deserted. It was furnished with a few small, moving shadows.

It was the same city mid-yard where Arclath Delcastle and the Crown messenger Delnor had seen a certain mask dancer carrying her nightsoil bucket to a dung wagon.

There were no wagons in the yard at the moment. The prowling shadows belonged to cats out hunting—and a few furtive, smaller, scuttling things that darted from crevices across the yard's few strips of uneven cobbles to handy heaps of fallen refuse, then on into tangled, thorny clumps of weeds, in hopes none of the cats would manage a successful pounce.

High above the midyard, a much larger shadow moved. The size of shadow that would attract the interest of Purple Dragons on Watch duty, had there been any in the midyard.

Dark, lithe, and somehow feminine, it swung down from the roof to hang against a stretch of house wall where it could peer at a certain dark, shuttered window.

Amarune's window.

After a long, silent time of watching and listening, it slipped silently back up onto the roof again.

Where almost immediately there arose a brief disturbance, a choked-off sound of startlement—and a body plunged from that rooftop to splat and bounce heavily on the cobbles, its throat slit.

CHAPTER
TWENTY-SEVEN
BLOOD ON THE ROOFTOPS

Blood on the rooftops, you say?
Stlarn them! Why can't they fight down here
On the honest cobbles, like all the other
Bloodthirsty idiots?
Why do your younglings always have to be *different*?

said by Delgar the Old Warrior
in Act I, Scene I of *War Comes to Spanglamar*
by Imbrel Hawksoun, published in
Hawksoun's Many Musings in the Year of the Secret

I thank you, Lord Delcastle," Amarune murmured gravely, sliding into Arclath's arms to look into his eyes from very near, expecting him to want at least a kiss, "and remain mindful of . . . the debt I owe you. Yet if you have any kind regard for me at all, I would ask that you depart this place now and let me go my own way until at least dusk on the morrow, when—"

Arclath was already using the arm that wasn't around her to push open the Dragonriders' street doors. Amarune broke off abruptly at what she saw inside.

At the look on her face, Arclath spun around to see what was the matter, letting the door start to swing closed again, and in so doing whirled Amarune away from what she was facing. With the briefest of angry growls, Amarune swung him around again and forward into the club.

Where amid a quiet cluster of Purple Dragons and servants still cleaning up and a few tables of newly arrived drinkers, Tress was helping a rather tipsy-looking man to his feet. Not one of the nobles who'd brawled so messily in the club earlier, but a rather haughty-looking wizard of war in full palace robes who had evidently just risen from a table and sprawled on his face and was showing signs of doing so again the moment he lost the deft support of the womanly shoulder under one of his armpits.

"Thank you, wench," he was growling rather blearily at Tress. "Know that you have aided a ver' important wizard of the court, who enjoys the ear and confidence of the king himself! Wizard of War Rorskryn Mreldrake am I, and urkgh . . . I'm going to be *sick*, s'what I'm—"

He promptly demonstrated the truth of his words, with force and enthusiasm.

Arclath and Amarune both raised their eyes to the ceiling in disgust and parted to glide well aside as Tress steered her burden firmly through his own filth and straight to the door.

Two steps away from which the weaving, green-faced Mreldrake caught sight of Amarune, gave her a nasty grin, pointed one shaking finger, and spat maliciously, "*You*! You're the Silent Shadow, you are!"

"I've skulked in the dark long enough," Elminster growled under his breath. "Time to play the befuddled old man and walk right in there and get to hear just what terms our jaunty young lordling is on with the most important lass in the worl—"

Playing a stooped graybeard to the hilt, he was still three age-shuffling strides away from the doors of the Dragonriders' Club and starting to reach for the nearest smooth-worn door handle, when Amarune Whitewave burst out of those doors, sprinting like the wind, with the bellowed "Stop! Stop and stand!" shout of a Purple Dragon pursuing her.

Elminster blinked, straightened up far too hastily for the decrepit elder he was trying to portray—and slipped. Which left him unable to get out of the way.

Amarune did not try to get out of the way either.

Even as he flung his arms wide to fight for balance, she slammed into him, running hard. The impact snatched the

Sage of Shadowdale off his feet and dashed him down on the cobbles in a crash that drove all the wind out of him and brought sharp and instant pain. As she trampled him and ran on, not slowing in the slightest.

Leaving the man who had been the mightiest Chosen of Mystra flat on his back on the cold cobblestones of the street, half-dazed and struggling to breathe through what felt like broken ribs. He couldn't even think of a spell to hurl, not that he had wind enough left to cast anything . . .

He couldn't even roll over, let alone crawl aside, as a fresh tempest burst out of the Dragonriders' and roared over him, a storm of hard-running Purple Dragons with lungs far healthier than his own, swords glittering in their fists, and *very* heavy boots.

He did, in their wake, manage a groan or two.

One of which caught the attention of a telsword who obviously hadn't been given orders to pursue the fleeing woman. Coming out of the club to stand and watch the chase dwindling into the night, he glanced down at the sound of pain then bent to lend the huddled old man a hand.

"Come on, old drunkard! You can't lie here; you'll get trampled, you will!"

"I'm *not* drunk," Elminster snarled through his pain. Ribs gone, to be sure. "I'm *hurt*. Some woman ran right through me."

"Which way did she go?" the telsword snapped back, excited in an instant.

"Down the street," Elminster replied dryly. "If she turned off it, I didn't see. I was too busy lying stunned to notice."

"All right, *all* right, old jester." The telsword sighed, helping Elminster to sit up against the club wall. He peered down at the weathered old face out of sheer veterans' habit—and frowned. "Have I seen you before? Who are you?"

"No one important, anymore," Elminster said gruffly. "Just another old man."

"Oh? Living on the streets?"

"When I can't make it home before dark."

"Oh, so you have a home, then."

"Aye."

"So, graybeard, how do you usually spend your days?"

"Growing older," Elminster told him wryly. "And ye?"

It was almost dawn, and a weary and heartsick Amarune Whitewave didn't know what to do.

She was standing in a dark street surrounded by grim-faced Purple Dragons, listening to Lord Arclath Delcastle glibly explain to them all once more that the dancer couldn't *possibly* be the Silent Shadow, because she'd been with him more than once when that notorious thief had performed a daring theft, and that she must have fled out of sheer fear of being enspelled by a drunken wizard of war. Not only was he of noble birth, he himself had suffered thefts at the hands of the Shadow, and so, believe me . . .

Oh, gods. And he was *again*, oh-so-gallantly, offering to escort Amarune home.

She wanted to hit him. Or lose herself to sobbing in the warm comfort of his arms, and . . . she didn't know what she wanted to do.

And she *couldn't* stop yawning.

The Dragons believed him, nodding and looking at her with faces a little less unfriendly, and lowering the swords that had been pointed her way.

Which meant they'd soon leave her alone with him. A young and spirited noble lord who suddenly knew, whatever his clever tongue was saying to them that moment, that she was the Silent Shadow.

She remembered full well she'd stolen from him more than once. So, obviously, did he. Should she just deny all and claim the wizard must have mistaken her for someone else? Finding proof wouldn't be easy—so long as he didn't come upon Ruthgul or any of her other clients, and tie what they said to where she lived—but driving away his suspicions would be harder still. Suspicion always died a slow death.

"Go with the Lord Delcastle, lass," a Purple Dragon was saying in her ear now, kind but firm. "He'll see you safe home."

That's just what he could *not* do—but she dared not admit it.

Wearily she nodded, half-numb, and accepted Arclath's attentive arm.

All she could think of doing was wandering the streets of Suzail until full day ran him out of time and into the jaws of some important business or appointment or other that he dared not miss. If her legs held out that long and she could keep her eyes open, that is . . .

"Trust me," Arclath murmured, giving her that bright grin that she couldn't tell if she loved or hated. "Dawn will be breaking soon enough. If you don't happen to live next door or in the rafters above us, we'll have time to see it—and sober, too!"

The stench at the end of the alley was indescribable. "Man-strangling" wasn't a strong enough description. Nor was "forty sick snails lying dead in their own fresh vomit," or "the heaped wet offerings of a hairy garrison all in the throes of the runs, brought on by eating lots of candy and mustard."

El tried all of those and some far more colorful ones on for size as he winced and hobbled his way down the greasy, narrowing, and increasingly refuse-choked way. Even the rats avoided that end of the alley, and the smell had long before forced the boarding-up and mud-sealing of all the windows opening onto it.

Alone in the graying tail end of night, the Sage of Shadowdale set his teeth and lurched on. His many bruises were stiffening, and his ribs felt on fire. He'd fallen twice, many alleys before, but it had been worth it to persuade the young and fastidious Dragon tailing him that he really was an old crazed-wits living on the streets, and make the man turn back. The soldier had fallen at least once, too, and Elminster hoped the young dolt's bright uniform was so besmirched that he was gagging.

Nevertheless, the filth had its uses. Not the least of which was safeguarding what he was retrieving. At the end of the alley was a fly-swarming heap of dung, old topped by fresh, beneath a cracked tile protruding from the wall.

El tugged the tile out—it came away in pieces, just like last time, brown and dripping—and thrust his fingers into the hole it had come from. There was a cavity in one side of that hole, within the thickness of the wall, and—aye!—the reassuring smooth hardness was there. Or rather, hardnesses, five of them. He closed his filthy fingers around the uppermost and then the lowest, drew them both forth, and shoved the tile back into place, piece by piece.

When he was done, the vials, guarded against rust by their own magic, were entirely hidden in fresh, wet dung.

El sighed, wiped his hands on random nearby walls until matters had been reduced to what might delicately be termed "smeared," then trudged back up the alley until he could find space enough to set the vials down on bare stone, spit on his hands so as to clean them enough to thrust them under his robe to reach his clout, and arrange himself so as to let fly all over the vials, washing them . . . well, not clean, but a lot cleaner.

So he could twist the uppermost open—an enchanted cap rather than a cork; well, the Art advanced in little things as well as large—and drink its contents down.

It tasted like cold, clear, mint sugar water, soothing all the way down . . . and brought in its wake that surging, warming thrill of healing, the banishment of the fire in his ribs, the stiffnesses, and all the small aches and pains he'd acquired since the last time he'd had to crawl down that alley.

When all of that was gone, El stood up straight, squared his shoulders, then thrust both vials—the lower one was reassuringly heavy with good Cormyrean coins he'd soon be needing—into his under-robe pouch and started for the street again. He felt whole and strong. Not to mention wealthier.

"See?" Arclath told her as triumphantly as if he were personally responsible. "I told you! Behold, dawn!"

Amarune nodded wearily, stumbling. Only his arm through hers was holding her up. For what seemed like hours they'd been walking the streets of Suzail together, a Purple Dragon plodding along behind tailing them as Amarune led her inanely chattering escort on a random meander across the city, waiting for his anger to rise.

Dreading the moment when Arclath stopped, refusing to go along with her obvious deception any longer and protesting that she was leading him astray. A protest that would reveal that he already knew where she dwelt.

A moment that hadn't yet come, though there was a gleam in his eye that she was beginning to think meant he was grinning inwardly at her tactic and happily going along with it.

The noble had kept up a constant, never-flagging stream of light, inane—and one-sided—converse.

"Dawn," she gasped, feeling she had to say *something*. "I'm . . . enchanted."

"And so am I!" Arclath agreed with enthusiasm. "Charmed, even! I find you the most beautiful woman to ever adorn my arm, and await that moment of full glory when you reveal to me the full sparkle of your wit, the bright edge of your tongue—in the conversational sense of course, lady fair, for I would not want even the slightest misunderstanding to lead you to take offense at a slander that was not meant, no, no, not at all!—the full grandeur, as I was saying, of your happily attentive company! At a time when you are not tired, not shocked by the horrible events of earlier this night, and not grieving the loss of your longtime and staunchly loyal employer! In short, when you can be your full and engaging self! When you can—"

"Somehow *shut* you *up*," Amarune snarled, in spite of herself. "Gods above, do all nobles carry themselves through their every waking moment of life on rivers of babbling *drivel*?"

"In a word, Lady: yes." Arclath's grin told her he wasn't abashed in the slightest. "So, how would you contemplate shutting me up? No violence, please, you know how I *abhor* viol—"

"Yes, I noticed you abhorring it right skillfully, earlier," Amarune sighed. "Though I probably owe you my life a time or six. So have my thanks, Lord Delcastle, and I'm done trying to deceive you. I no longer care if you learn where I live."

"My lady! Has that been your concern, all this time? That I might discover the whereabouts of your abode? Has preventing that dark secret—though how it can truly be dark, I fail to conceive—been the pursuit that now has you nigh staggering with weariness?"

"It has," Amarune said grimly. "Let's go. This way."

"Lady, your every command is my fond wish!"

"Really? How is it that you're still alive, then?"

"Amarune Whitewave, you're *snarling*!"

"Mask dancers snarl all the time, Lord Delcastle. Want to know what else we can do?"

"*Lady*, I thought you'd *never* be so *bold*! Of *course* I—"

"Of *course* you do," Amarune said with the most withering sarcasm she could muster as she turned a familiar corner and headed into an even more familiar midyard that ... seemed to be swarming with Purple Dragons.

Several of those officers were already giving them hard stares, and—gods above!—there were Dragons searching every alley, balcony, and outside stair in sight. There were even Dragons up on her roof.

Not to mention a large, grim cluster of them standing over ... no. Oh, no.

A Purple Dragon moved to intercept them, two of his fellows walking to where they could surround the two. "Your names, and business here?"

"I am *Lord* Arclath Delcastle," the nobleman snapped pointedly, "and I am escorting this lady to her home, by order of a Watch officer of the Purple Dragons. And yours?"

"My what?"

"Your *name*, soldier."

"*I'll* ask the questions here for now, my lord. You can have my name for your inevitable complaint later. Now, which officer would it be who gave you this or—"

"He's telling truth, Randelo," a gravelly man's voice said rather sullenly from behind Amarune. "I can vouch for their whereabouts and deeds—seeing as they've been leading me all over Suzail for half the night." It was the Dragon who'd been following them since their departure from the club.

He was giving the young couple a rather baleful glance as he added, "Stlarning boots hurt worse'n ever. Shouldn't wonder if they're full of blood down by my toes, right now."

"Ah, the price of shining service," Arclath remarked. Turning back to their questioner, he said with dignity, "Seeing as we've just been cleared of any involvement in this unfortunate, ah, death, please withdraw from us a pace or two, so as to accord us some small measure of privacy. This is a lady of high moral standing, despite what you may think—for I have found that *far* too many Purple Dragons have low, coarse minds—and I have no intention of damaging her reputation by entering her domicile at this time of night."

That little speech earned him an eloquent eye roll and a mockingly elaborate bow from both Dragons, but they did withdraw, muttering together.

Arclath pointedly turned his back on them, shielding Amarune from their scrutiny with his broad shoulders, and murmured, "So, would you like me to leave you here, Lady, with a suspicious death—almost undoubtedly a murder—hard by wherever you live, but with the dubious safety of Purple Dragons very much in evidence everywhere? Or—?"

"Or yield myself to your tender mercies in your noble mansion?"

"I *do* have some measure of honor, Lady," Delcastle murmured, almost sadly.

They regarded each other in sober, unsmiling silence for a breath or two, before Amarune almost whispered, "Lord Delcastle, did you hear what the wizard called me?"

"The Silent Shadow? I had dismissed that from my mind. A wild, baseless accusation, that—"

"No," Amarune said firmly, suddenly finding she did not want to lie to this man. "No, it's not. I *am* the Silent Shadow, though my silence has been the quiet of inaction this past season."

She gave him a glare, suddenly defiant. "So, are you going to denounce me to yon Dragons? See me flogged, stripped of every last coin, and jailed? There'll be nobles enough wanting my blood, to be sure, and—"

"And I am not one of them," Arclath interrupted smoothly. "Putting one over on my fellow highborn is what *I* do, whenever possible. I might add that occasionally I indulge in undertakings of low moral character myself . . . and I find that this is one of those times."

He lifted a finger, almost as if he was a pompously lecturing tutor, and spoke even more softly. "So I'll keep your secret, but in return I demand a price, Lady. No, don't look at me like *that*; my price is one truthful answer, no more. Tell me plainly, now: Whom do you work for? Just who is interested in what I and Halance and Belnar were talking about, that you had to listen so hard?"

"I was interested," Amarune told him truthfully, "because I'm curious. Too curious. And I'm working for no one but myself." She hesitated, then added, "Though someone is now seeking to force the Silent Shadow to work for her, by threatening to unmask me to the Dragons. A woman every bit as agile as I am, who calls herself 'Talane.'"

"Talane," Arclath murmured, frowning. "Not a name I've heard before, but I've a feeling, by all the Watching Gods, that I'll be hearing it again."

"Swordcaptain Dralkin?" a Dragon telsword gasped then, trotting out of the night right past them. "We've found a word written in blood up on *that* rooftop."

"From where the body probably fell, yes," the swordcaptain agreed curtly, advancing from the group standing around the corpse sprawled in its pool of blood, and sending Arclath and Amarune a glare that told them clearly "move away and don't listen." When neither of them moved, he shrugged and asked the telsword curtly, "What word?"

"A strange one. Might be a name," the telsword replied. "'Talane.' In Common: T-a-l-a-n-e."

Chapter
TWENTY-EIGHT
I Used to Be a Wizard

Long ago, when the Realms was magic and magic *was* the Realms,
When Our Lady of Mystery struck awe in every heart,
And a mightier spell lurked behind every mighty spell,
Then, lad, was when I used to be a wizard.
So save me your scorn, your sneers of disbelief,
For I was hurtling down castles when your revered grandsire
Was still learning one end of a cow from the other.

> Murlanth Stormspells, Archwizard of Athkatla
> *Murlanth's Book of Elder Magic:*
> *When Mystra Ruled Us All*
> published in the Year of the Advancing Shadows

He was in another alley—which reeked almost as much as the one he'd left, but of mildew and old mold and rotting greens—out behind one of Suzail's better eateries.

At that time of night, only the slugs, snakes, and rats were likely to overhear an old man who stood there talking to himself.

Which was why Elminster had chosen it. He had thorny matters to decide on and no one to debate them with but himself.

He should not, *could* not, do what he was contemplating doing to that young woman, blood of his or not, downward dead end of a life she'd landed herself in or not. Bed of thorns or not, 'twas the bed *she'd* chosen, and not for him to . . . to do what every last king or baron or petty lordling did every day—force changes on the lives of others, to get their own way. Sometimes, for mere whim.

Yet he was not so low. No, he was lower and had been for centuries.

Yet the task—the burden—was his, his duty, and he wanted to go on.

Wanted, but could not, not alone, not old and without firm control of his magic . . .

"No, I told that Dragon truth," he growled at last. "Growing older . . . waiting to die. And if I wait too long and die without doing what's needful, it all ends right then. All my work, all the paltry few protections I've been able to give the Realms down these centuries. And that must *not* happen. Ever. The work *must* go on."

He paced a few scowling steps, setting a snake to hastily slithering away somewhere safer, then turned and snapped to the empty air, "Even if it costs one more young lass her life. Or at least the carefree, naive freedom to waste her life doing nothing much of consequence."

He walked a few more steps and whispered, "'Twill kill her."

He walked a few more.

"And I'll do it to her. I will."

Thrusting his head high, he strode off purposefully into the night.

Amarune's hands tightened like claws on her arms, and he could feel her starting to shake.

After a moment, she hissed, "I have to see who . . . who got killed."

"Lady," Arclath murmured, "is that wise?"

The glare she gave him then was fierce indeed. "It is *necessary*. Just because I didn't happen to have been born a man, it doesn't mean I was born without a brain or a life or—"

"Easy, Rune, *easy*." He turned her around, rotating them both closer to the body and somehow just not seeing Swordcaptain Dralkin's arm thrust out like a barrier—until the officer was forced to withdraw it or strike a woman—with a casual deftness that made her blink. "Now?"

She nodded. "Now."

"Deep breath and look down, then," he murmured, making the last half turn. She looked down—square into the gaping, contorted, white face of a dead man, whose throat was sliced open in a great wound that had half-severed his neck and had spilled a good-sized pond of dark and sticky blood across the cobbles. The sliced neck was bent at a horrible angle . . .

It was Ruthgul.

She turned her head away sharply, starting to really shake. The Purple Dragon swordcaptain started forward with a frown, one arm rising to reach out to her, and Arclath spun her away again, turning her in his arms until he could see her paling face.

One good look at her, and his grip on her arms tightened. "Lady," he said firmly, "you're coming home with me."

"N-no," she replied with equal firmness, twisting free of him to back quickly away and raising her voice for the Purple Dragons to hear. "I'm *not*. I am going to *my* bed, Lord, and alone. Right now."

The faces of Dralkin and several other nearby Dragons hardened—and they stepped forward every bit as swiftly and deftly as Arclath, to bar the young Lord Delcastle's way to Amarune.

He eyed their stern faces, brawn, and hands ready on sword hilts for a moment, then shrugged, smiled, and gave the dancer an airy wave. "Until your next shift, then!"

"Until then," she replied heavily—and hastened away.

Only to recoil in bewildered fear as she passed Ruthgul's body, looked down at it despite herself . . . and saw that it was magically changing into the likeness of someone *else*.

A man she didn't know at all.

Shaking her head—what, by all the gods, was going *on*? Had Ruthgul been someone else all those years, or was that someone who'd been impersonating him and had paid the price?—she ducked into a side alley and trotted hastily along it to reach the door to her abode on a side of the building the Lord Delcastle couldn't see.

Arclath regarded the stone-faced Dragons, who were forming a wall of burly uniformed flesh to prevent him following the dancer or getting a better look at the dead man—whose change he'd half-glimpsed, and confirmed from some of their reactions—with a broadening smile. Giving them a theatrical sigh, he observed, "*Women!* I'll never understand them!"

"Whereas they," Dralkin told him warningly, "understand you all too well, Lord. As, now, do we."

"Bravely challenged, good Swordcaptain," Arclath replied airily, turning with a wave of farewell to stroll off back the way he'd come, "yet you don't, you know. No one understands me! Save perhaps one person, a little."

"That would be me," a sharp voice said suddenly at his elbow.

It was a voice he knew, and it belonged to a wizard of war by the name of Glathra.

"I've listened in to a lot of what you've said and done this night," she added briskly, "so spare me all the fanciful tales and instead yield me a few plain answers."

"Not without something decent to drink," he said, giving her a courtly bow. "So beautiful an interrogator deserves no less."

"I believe we have water in the palace that doesn't have *too* many squirming things floating in it," she replied dryly, as war wizards and Purple Dragons appeared from all sides to close in around them. "Come."

"Your command is my wish, Lady," the Lord Delcastle told her lightly—*almost* mockingly—as he offered her his arm. She ignored it, but when she turned, pointed toward the distant royal palace, and started walking, he fell in beside her.

Amid the suddenly tight ring of their watchful Purple Dragon escort.

Amarune was half-expecting to find Talane waiting in her rooms, but there was no sign of her.

Or anyone.

Not even under the bed.

Her heaps of soiled clothing lay just as she'd left them, the untidy little mountain range of her laziness. By the state of them, the undisturbed dust, and the way her other minor untidynesses reigned unaltered, it didn't look as if any intruder had so much as thought of entering Amarune's rooms.

When she finally dared to believe that and relax, weariness broke over her like a harbor storm, leaving her reeling.

She staggered across the room, suddenly *very* tired—yet still scared, a rising fear that got worse as her thoughts started racing through all the possibilities of Ruthgul's murder, the drunken wizard of war who'd known who she was—did they *all* know? Why hadn't they done anything to her, then?—and Talane . . .

Amarune was shaking so hard, she was almost a shuddering by the time she clawed at a certain hiding place until a bedpost yielded and she could haul out a slender and precious flask of firewine. Taking a long pull, she reeled across the room again, flinging back her head to gasp loud and long at its fiery bite.

When she fetched up against a wall, Amarune got the stopper back in, then took the flask with her as she lurched to her bed and flung herself down on it.

"What by all the Hells am I going to *do?*" she hissed aloud.

The walls maintained their usual eloquent silence, and she sighed, let her shoulders sag in the first part of a shrug of helplessness she didn't bother to finish, then in sudden irritation pulled off her boots, one after the other, and flung them hard against the wall.

Wrenching off the cloak was harder, and she was panting by the time she whirled it into the air and watched it swirl down to the floor.

The sweat-soaked robe came off with comparative ease, and she hurled it onto the highest peak of her piled-up dirty laundry.

Whereupon the heap rose up with a grunt, and a bearded old man was smiling at her, her smallclothes still decorating his head.

Amarune stared at him then flung herself up off the bed, opening her mouth to scream—and Elminster hurled himself atop her, moving surprisingly fast for such such seemingly old bones, and thrusting two or three of her underclouts into her mouth to stifle her shrieks.

They bounced on the bed together, the old man on top and Amarune clawing at him and making muffled "mmmphs" as his bony old knees and elbows landed on various soft areas of her anatomy.

Growling, she started to swing and kick at him wildly, and the old man sighed, plucked up her—thankfully empty—copper chamberpot from where he'd found it earlier under the edge of the bed, and brained her with it.

The room spun and swam. Gods and little chanting priests, the minstrels told truth: one *does* see stars . . . sometimes . . .

Amarune fell back on her pillows, clutching her head and groaning.

Whereupon the old man got off her, caught up her cloak from the floor, and wrapped it firmly around her, pinioning her arms to her sides, and propped her up on her pillows like a firmly efficient nurse.

"I'm very sorry I had to do that to ye, lass," he announced, trundling back down to the foot of her bed and perching there, "but we *must* talk. I need ye. *Cormyr* needs ye. Hells, *the Realms* needs ye."

Amarune groaned again, trying to peer at the gaunt, white-haired intruder as she struggled free of her cloak. He made no move toward her. The moment she could move her arms freely, she clutched the cloak more tightly around her—though it was more than a little too late to guard any thin wisp of modesty she might still have possessed. He was obviously waiting for her to speak, so she did.

"Who . . . who are you?"

"Elminster," came the prompt reply. "I used to be a wizard. Yes, *that* Elminster. Well met, Great-granddaughter."

Amarune couldn't help herself. "Great *what?*"

She stared at him in the sudden silence, open-mouthed. He filled the pause by smiling and nodding, but by then she was frowning again.

"Elminster? But you *can't* be! Why—"

"'Can't'? Did I hear the word 'can't'? Amarune, do ye know *anything* about wizards, at all?"

"But how—? The goddess Mystra . . ."

"Ye will be unsurprised to learn," the old man told her in very dry tones, "that 'tis a long story. Right now, I'd rather hear just what ye—*and* young Lord Delcastle—are up to."

"Why?"

Elminster regarded his great-granddaughter with something that might have been exasperation, or just might have been new respect.

"This has been a long evening already, aye? Let's go somewhere that has good wine and decent food and talk a bit. I've found dancers like to talk. Anything to keep from doing the other things customers expect them to do, I suppose."

"So this Amarune is the famous Silent Shadow," Wizard of War Glathra Barcantle mused, sounding entirely unsurprised. "You obviously didn't know that until just now, so what made you suspicious of her? Or were you governed by a paramount interest in a mask dancer who might be willing, for coins enough, to do more for you than merely dance?"

Arclath Delcastle stared rather coolly back at his interrogator. "I've seldom seen a need to pay anyone to fill my bed, Lady Wizard. Handsome, remember? Noble? Dashing, yes?"

Glathra's expression remained coldly unimpressed.

He sighed, waved dismissively, and added, "Ne'er mind. I was interested in her for a reason you already know; I wanted to learn why she'd been listening to what Halance, Belnar, and I were discussing about the council. Particularly now that Halance and Belnar are so suddenly and violently dead. Though I grant that it's both unusual and unfashionable for nobles to be so, in this day and age, Lady Glathra, I *do* happen to be loyal to the Crown."

"We know that," she replied quietly, "and that's why I've brought you here. We have a proposition for you, Lord Delcastle."

"'We'?" Arclath asked pointedly, staring around the room. The two of them were sitting facing each other across a shining expanse of table, and the palace chamber around them was bare of all guards, war wizards, scribes, or anyone else. Just a few portraits, a tapestry or two, and a lone closed door. "Have you a twin? Or are you using the royal 'we,' and there's been a royal marriage I'm not privy to that I should be congratulating you about, Lady?"

As if his questions had been a signal, one of those tapestries was thrust aside by a firm hand, and Delcastle found himself staring into the wise old eyes and familiar face of King Foril Obarskyr of Cormyr.

The High Dragon of the Forest Kingdom was wearing a simple circlet on his brow and hunter's garb of jerkin, belt, breeches, and boots of plain leather. Of the finest make and tailored to fit his lean, trim body. A simple belt knife rode his hip, and discreet rows of plain rings—most of them enchanted, no doubt—adorned his fingers. He was smiling.

"Nothing so dramatic, Lord Delcastle," the king said dryly. "The Lady Glathra was speaking on my behalf and was aware of my presence—as, now, are you."

By then, Delcastle was out of his chair and down on one knee. Foril looked pained and waved at him to rise.

"Up, up, lad; I've servants enough to do that far too often for me as it is. I need your loyalty and your friendship, not your knees ruined on my behalf. Nobles who can be eyes and ears for me are rare and precious things in this kingdom, now as ever; we need to talk."

"Majesty," Arclath replied with a smile, rising, "it so happens that talking is one of my strengths."

"I find myself strangely unsurprised," the king told him dryly, taking up his chair and coming forward to the table.

Amarune knew The Willing Smile only by its reputation. A rundown, seedy, low-coin brothel on a formerly fashionable street in Suzail, where wrinkled old harridans and a few wide-eyed younglings desperate for quick coin entertained toothless old men desiring to deceive themselves that they were still bold lions of youth and vigor whose very names left Cormyr in awe.

She was surprised to find it a clean, quiet, and dimly lit grand house that seemed to stretch on forever, run by a matron more motherly than alluring, who obviously regarded Elminster as an old and trusted friend.

"Mother" Maraedra patted the limping graybeard on the arm when he greeted her, nodded after he murmured in her ear for a moment, and then led them through lushly carpeted halls adorned with many full-length portraits that were probably doors into the rooms of the women depicted in them, to a back room decorated like a successful but careful-with-coin family's private parlor, where a table was set for four.

Humming to herself, she shuffled through a door and returned almost immediately to set before them bowls of cubed redruth goat cheese, biscuits, and an herbed paste of oil and crushed and roasted vegetables.

Then she slipped out again, holding up a finger as if in warning to them to say nothing until her return—and again, came back into the room swiftly, this time with tallglasses, which would have done any noble House proud, and a large decanter.

Then she bowed, smiled, and backed out of the room, waving in silent farewell, and in the same gesture, as she pulled the door closed on herself, bade them converse.

Elminster gave her a low bow, waved Amarune to a chair, and poured her wine. She peered at it critically, suddenly realizing she was ravenous and thirsty, and sipped. It was *very* good wine, perhaps the nicest she'd ever tasted.

Elminster spread paste on a biscuit with a small, almost circular paddle—a knife of sorts, but it could never be used to stab anyone—and handed it to her. When she took it, he thrust a cube of cheese her way.

"I'm neither a princess nor helpless," she murmured, but

gently. He seemed to mean well, and, well . . . many old folk had curious courtesies.

"Good," he replied. "I'm counting on that. So—though it knows this not, yet—is this grand old world around us."

Munching hard, Amarune settled for raising her eyebrows in a bewildered "Are you *always* this crazed?" look.

Elminster smiled. "Ye are by now fairly certain I'm a madwits. Ye have some doubts, though they diminish, that I am who I say I am and that we're related, and ye want to know what I'm raving on about—without much wanting to have any part of it. Do I read ye right thus far?"

Amarune helped herself to more cheese and spread herself another biscuit. "Hard and steady into the harbor, so far," she agreed, fixing him with her best "This had *better* impress me" look.

"Ye are young, agile, good-looking, and no fool. So ye have figured out that the career of a thief bids fair to be a short one, and mask dancing will win ye fair coin only so long as thy looks hold out. No noble lordling until young Delcastle has shown signs of sweeping ye off the Dragonriders' stage and into his mansion with a title around thy throat, and ye face at least two dark foes and know not where to run. In short, thy young life is looking darker ahead, not shining and bright."

"Still heading hard and true for the nearest wharf," Amarune agreed grimly. "Right now, I can't even pay for this cheese—let alone the wine—without leaving myself too short to please creditors who are quite likely to treat me far more harshly than Mother Maraedra."

"I'm paying, lass. Considering what I'm going to be asking ye to do, filling thy boots with gold right up as high as thy throat won't begin to be fee enough."

"You want me to take part in one of your spells? As some sort of sacrifice? Does it involve bedding thirteen nobles at once?"

Elminster chuckled. "Nay to your last query, and 'in a manner of speaking' is a fair but also fairly useless answer to your first two questions. I want to train ye."

"As some sort of *wizard*? Sorry, but—"

"As my successor."

"Doing what, exactly?" Amarune eyed the old man across the table sidelong. She found him likeable but nothing near trustworthy. He probably *was* mad, and just how, it seemed, she was about to find out.

"I am . . . old. More than a thousand winters old. Yet I live still, because . . . I have a job to do. Ye might call it 'Meddler On Behalf of Mystra.' I wander the world meddling in things—the way kings rule, the way folk think, how they roast meals when they can get meat; all of that—to make the Realms better. Oh, and get no thanks for it, save many attempts to kill me."

"So I'd expect, if you meddle with how kings rule. So Mystra has been dead for a century, and you're giving up, is that it?"

"Almost," he whispered.

Studying him, Amarune went on munching, astonished at how quickly the cheese and biscuits seemed to have vanished. The old man had eaten, so far as she could recall, just one of each. She frowned; were they tainted with something?

"You eat the last few," she ordered.

Elminster smiled, shrugged, and started spreading himself a biscuit.

Watching him devour some cheese then the biscuit and wash them both down with wine, Amarune asked curiously, "Weren't you the one who was supposed to have been Mystra's lover, or some such?"

"Yes," Elminster agreed simply.

"So who warms your bed these days?"

"A mad queen. Not often."

Amarune shook her head then watched him refill her glass.

Well, this would make a good slumbertime tale, until she fell on her face and into the land of dreams . . .

"Tell me more," she said, sipping. Happy dancing hobgoblins, but this wine was good!

CHAPTER
TWENTY-NINE
TO FILL THY BRAIN WITH WEAPONS

Sire, I've not come to make thee laugh or sit
In smiling, easy triumphant complacency;
I come to rouse thee to war before 'tis too late,
And to fill thy brain with weapons, thy mind
With battle-planning! Ye may as well die
Doing *something* useful for the realm, at last!

Jalavarr the Jester, Act III, Scene II of
The Shunned King's Doom
by Morthran Taelinth, Bard, chapbook-published
in the Year of the Dark Goddess.

S o ye see, lass, that's the dream I'm still living for. Imparting
hope, making this little thing better and then that one, for
all, not just the rulers and the rich . . . and doing it all in the
name of Mystra."

"To keep her memory alive."

"Exactly. To keep her name and what she stood for firm
and deep in the memories of folk, so there's a chance—a ghost
of a chance, mind, but better than none—that she'll return."

"So the deeds, the fireside and tavern tales . . . ghost stories,
indeed."

"Ah, now, forget not the faithful!"

"Oh, yes, the hidden cult of Mystra-worshipers I'd have to
lead. Well, *that* would certainly make me feel special, if I went
in for such things."

Elminster gave her a sour look across the table. "Is that all ye've
been hearing, in my blathering? 'Tis not about Mystra, nor thy
power or benefits—'tis all about the dream of setting things right
in the Realms, which I and Storm Silverhand and the Simbul and
all the other Chosen devoted so much of our lives to, through the

Harpers and by other means. Even if Mystra never returns to us, we will have bettered the Realms—worth doing in itself, lass! Achievements far greater than most kings or priests ever even intend to accomplish, let alone the paltry results they manage!"

Amarune poured herself the last of the wine and sat back with a sigh, eyeing the man who claimed to be her ancestor.

"You want me to carry on with this self-appointed, never-finished work of saving the entire Realms," she said grimly. "Cast aside work I do well and take pride in, the life I've built for myself—a life I *like*, mind, no matter how low and coin-poor it may be—and do dangerous and, no doubt, often illegal things and be thought crazed by everyone, for . . . a dream. *Your* dream. The dream of a century ago, of dead gods and struggles lost and done when my mother was yet young."

Elminster smiled. "Aye. I *knew* ye'd see to the heart of it in an instant. That's my lass; blood runs true."

"I have *not* agreed to anything, old man," Amarune told him angrily.

"True, true. Yet, having seen the world more clearly, ye will. Not now, not perhaps for years yet, but . . . ye will. Ye will find ye *cannot* stand back and look away when there are wrongs that need righting and suffering that need not be and things that could be better for all and less cruel for many. We're meddlers, we cursed few. 'Tis in the blood."

"Not my blood," Amarune snapped. "I've more sense."

"Ah. That would be why ye go out brawling of evenings with Lord Arclath Delcastle," Elminster told his nigh empty tallglass dryly. "'Tis the *sensible* thing for a mask dancer to do."

Amarune flushed crimson. "I *like* Arclath. And if the king's writ means anything, it should mean lasses and jacks of Cormyr can choose their friends freely, noble or common, rich or poor, and not answer to *anyone* for it. Given years enough, it should make the realm stronger, as all citizens know each other better, and no one will sneer at a freeman or goodwife because of the name they were born with or the—"

"Ye preach to the converted, lass," Elminster murmured. "Who d'ye think fixed the wording of the writ, one night while

Foril lay snoring not a spear-length away? Took me much of the night to fake his fist, so he'd look at the changes in the morning and think he had roused himself in the night to make them, not that someone else came stealing in to set things to rights."

Amarune stared at him then said sarcastically, "And I suppose you arranged half the noble marriages of the last decade, and you secretly tempt and test every last war wizard, too?"

"Nay. Just two marriages, and I've only managed to test the loyalty of about a third of the current wizards of war—Vainrence keeps a *very* close eye on them all, and getting caught vetting his fellowship of law wands would be worse than not probing them at all."

Amarune stared across the table. "You're serious. You're farruking *serious*."

"Of course. Drink that down, lass; we're just getting started. Having swept the legs out from under the tiny stool ye are so pleased to call the life ye've built for thyself, 'tis merely my duty to fill thy brain with weapons, to help ye defend that stool so it has any chance at all of lasting a little longer. I'll be needing ye to help me find and steal certain little gewgaws that hold the ghosts of the Nine, but first, for thine own protection, ye should know the truth about this Talane ye're now haunted by . . ."

Despite the hour and the fact that Stormserpent Towers was an abode of nobility, the Purple Dragons banging on its doors were most insistent. The burden of their repeated demands was the desire to speak with Lord Marlin Stormserpent, without delay.

Sleepy, exasperated servants failed to convince the soldiers to wait until a time fashionably after morningfeast, and so in the end reluctantly roused Marlin and brought word to him that soldiers of the Crown were at his gates, would not leave, and wanted audience with him immediately.

Marlin went from surly sleepiness to wide awake and stiff with alarm in a proverbial instant. His first act was to curtly dismiss his servants, telling them he was quite capable of dressing himself.

Indeed, he was well on his way to being garbed by the time the door closed behind the last of them. Running a hand over his stubbled face and deciding not to take the time to shave, the heir of House Stormserpent stamped his feet into his boots, snatched up the scabbarded Flying Blade and buckled it on, thrust Thirsty well into the breast of his jerkin, and gave his pet's head the double tap that told it to bide quiet until he called or hauled it forth again, and took up the chalice into his hand as if he had been disturbed in the act of drinking from it.

There. Ready. He glowered at his nearest mirror ere turning and hastening down to the forehall to meet with the Dragons.

When he came down the stair, they were standing in a grim, silent little group, waiting for him.

"Well?" Marlin asked shortly, sparing no breath on greetings or even a pretense of politeness.

"We have need of your aid, Lord Stormserpent. Please come with us. Just as far as your front doors, yonder."

"Why?" Marlin snapped. "What's—?"

They said nothing, turning in unison to tramp to his doors.

Marlin glared sidelong at his silent servants then followed the Dragons.

One front door of the Towers was ajar, and there were more soldiers outside.

"So what's all this about?" Marlin asked, stepping aside to avoid being caught in the doorway with Dragons all around him.

"We need you to identify this dead man," a telsword told him gravely. "We've been told he's a servant of yours. Truth?"

By then, Marlin was gaping down at the corpse on the litter, and his face was heading for the same dead-white hue that the body sported. It was Gaskur, the man he most trusted in all the world. His personal servant for years, his trade agent . . . a huge sword cut that left his throat gaping open told anyone with eyes how he'd died.

"Who . . . who did this?" Marlin blurted, his own throat closing around sudden tears, the room seeming to silently rock around him.

A firm hand at his back steadied him, and he was vaguely aware that the soldiers who'd been watching his face with intent and suspicious frowns were relaxing, some of them looking almost pitying.

"Where did you find him?" Marlin asked, his voice quavering like that of any young lass. Hearing no reply, he shook his head fiercely and turned away.

"That is my servant, yes," he told the air blindly as he headed for the distant board across the forehall and its gleaming array of decanters. "Gaskur by name, a man true and loyal. I trusted him more than anyone."

He found the decanters and turned. "Will you join me in a toast to a good man? And for the love of all the gods, *tell me how he died!*"

"Does the word or name 'Talane' mean anything to you, Lord?" The telsword's voice was near and low down, as if the Dragon was half-kneeling so he could see Marlin's face.

Marlin opened both eyes and told him fiercely, "No. Gods, no. Never heard it before now. Who or what is Talane?"

"We'd like to know that ourselves, Lord. It was written on the roof of a many-tenants house not far south and west of here, in your man's blood. His throat was slit, as you can see, and his body hurled down from that roof into a midyard. Can you tell us why he may have been there, Lord Stormserpent? Was he out and about in the city on your bidding?"

Marlin shook his head, pouring himself a drink with hands that trembled. "He lived here in this house, and so far as I know had no kin nor friends—nor property, for that matter—in Suzail. I know little of his habits and doings when on his own time, but mark you: Gaskur was trusted, and his time off was his own, to forge and further his own life, not dance always in Stormserpent livery."

"Thank you for your assistance and for your offer," the telsword said gravely, "but we're in some haste, now. We'll leave you to your private grief and take the remains of your man with us; the wizards of war will want to examine it."

"Good," Marlin said bitterly. "You do that. And come back and tell me what they find, for if the Crown does not find someone and make them pay for this—this foul murder, loyal swords of the realm, hear me well: *I will.*"

"Lord Stormserpent, we hear and will do so. Your sentiments do him honor, and yourself as well."

And with that, the Dragons were gone in a hasty thunder of boots, leaving a shaken Marlin Stormserpent to sip liquid fire and listen to the doors of his home boom shut.

After he'd downed a flagon, refilled it, and emptied it again, one of the House servants murmured at his elbow, "Lord? Will you be wanting any—"

"Leave me be," Marlin said curtly. "I would prefer to be alone. Let no one follow where I go."

He filled the flagon once more and drained it in a single quaff that left him gasping. Slamming it down on the board, he said curtly, "Wash that," and turned away to stride blindly across the forehall toward the grand stair.

"Talane" was a mystery, perhaps a mere fancy to send the watch astray. Gaskur had almost certainly died under the treachery of one of his fellow conspirators; the most recent task of importance he'd given Gaskur was to spy on their doings and meetings for any sign of possible betrayal.

"Nobles," he hissed furiously, quoting a jest that usually left him wildfire-leaping hot. "Can't trust them even as far as you can hurl their severed heads."

By then, he was up the stair and through a door and waving sleepy servants back to their beds. A few more halls and doors, a few more locks and bars seen to, and he would be alone, all servants kept well away from him.

Back in his own rooms, he scooped Thirsty back out of his jerkin and set the stirge on a perch; Thirsty hated the magic that was about to be awakened and always demonstrated that by defecating copiously and digging claws in deep, too. Drawing and downing a hasty glass of wine from his favorite decanter,

Marlin set aside the chalice and the Flying Blade, too, caught up his bedside lantern, and headed for the uppermost room of the most ruinous tower.

Dust still lay thick over much of it, in the lantern glow. From the cloak stand he retrieved the milky glass orb, took it to the small round table, and set it atop the heavy metal goblet standing there.

Settling himself into the lopsided chair, Marlin touched the orb, murmured the word, and watched the familiar glowing cloud appear. As swiftly as if Lothrae had been waiting for him—a thought that made his eyes narrow in suspicion, for just a moment—the cloud became the image of the masked man sitting in the falcon-back chair in front of his own orb.

"Yes?" Lothrae greeted him simply.

"Master," Marlin Stormserpent began fearfully, and related Gaskur's fate and his own fears of treachery, ending with, "What should I do?"

"Stop acting weak and fearful," came the cold reply. "Stop looking over your shoulder for treachery, and attracting the suspicions of every last Purple Dragon or war wizard who may set eyes on you. Carry on as boldly and insolently as if nothing at all has happened. The way you were conducting yourself before."

Lothrae leaned forward to speak loudly and firmly. "If there's a traitor in your conspiracy, this is your best armor; he has struck against you, and behold, you are so strong that you simply ignore the blow."

The masked man spread his hands. "You can live looking behind you at every shadow, fear strangling you—but that's hardly a life worth living, is it? Continue with our plan, and the throne can one day be yours. Waver, and it shall never be. Break, and it's your life you'll be frantically seeking to cling to, not dreams of kingship. But none of this should be new to you; you should already be well aware of the choices before you and the risks woven around each of them."

"Yes, yes," Marlin agreed hastily. "Yes, I'll do that—uh, those things."

Nodding, Lothrae was abruptly gone, leaving nothing but dark and empty air above Marlin's orb.

Cursing softly, the heir of House Stormserpent restored things to their rightful places, took up his lantern, and hastened back to his own chambers.

Lothrae had spoken of the best tactic, but those bold words did nothing at all to lessen the danger. Someone who'd sat around his table plotting treason—or even a cabal of several of them, grinning at him behind their masklike faces—wanted him dead.

Taking to his bed was easy enough, but finding slumber proved harder. Fear was in him, his mind whispering peril after betrayal after knife in the dark.

Marlin tossed and turned, hissing curses through cold sweat after drenching cold sweat, fear never leaving him. He was so agitated that Thirsty took to flitting back and forth across the bedchamber, flapping from post to post of Marlin's great four-poster bed.

It was no use. He could *not* sleep. Not when there could be a dozen hired slayers prowling Stormserpent Towers at that moment, blades in hand and gentle smiles on faces, drawing nearer . . . and *nearer* . . .

"Farruking *Hells*," he snarled, thrusting himself up from the bedclothes in a fresh fury.

He staggered as his bare feet hit the floor, but yawningly steadied himself against the nearest bedpost, then made for the chalice and the Flying Blade.

When Langral and Halonter of the Nine were standing coldly facing him once more, blue flames raging endlessly about them, Marlin commanded the two ghosts to watch over him as he slept and guard his person from all intruders.

Thirsty the stirge hastily flew from the bedpost up to the loftiest corner of his highest window to perch well out of their reach.

Langral and Halonter nodded silently at those orders. Silently flaming, they took up positions over Marlin as he settled himself on his pillow once more.

He'd feared he might not be able to sleep with the blue-flame ghosts looming so close and menacing, but before he could so much as fully remember that fear, dark and falling oblivion claimed him.

And so never saw the thief and the fighter of the Nine, standing there in their flames, turn to regard each other over Marlin's faintly snoring form—and then in unison look down at him, open contempt on their faces.

"Saving the world or not," Amarune mumbled, finding her nose perilously close to the tabletop for about the tenth time, "I *can't* stop yawning."

"Of course, lass. Ye need rest. We'll talk more on this later."

Elminster produced a pouch from somewhere under his robes, and from it poured a generous stream of coins into his empty tallglass in the center of the table.

Then he rose and offered Amarune his arm. She was very thoughtful now but also stumbling-weary, and almost fell as she found her feet and took that proffered arm.

"Where—?"

"I'm escorting ye back to thy rooms, where I'll part from thee and let ye enjoy a good long sleep. As long as ye need, mind; I'll settle things with thine employer so ye'll not be greeted by swords when ye come next to dance. The Dragonriders' should be reminded that drunken wizards can and do accuse any innocent lass of being almost anyone. I'll play a sober wizard who knows better."

Amarune nodded and let the old man lead her out through the deserted halls of The Willing Smile. Not the way they'd come in, she noticed; some discreet side exit, then.

So it proved to be, when Elminster ducked behind a narrow ascending stair, pushed on a panel, and they were in the outside air.

And almost falling over someone who was leaving the same establishment by another door that faced their own—a hasty departure of a robed man who was bent over as he scuttled forward, still fastening his clothing.

The collision was a mild one but parted Amarune and El and left them hopping for balance. They turned in unison—and found themselves looking into the glare of Wizard of War Rorskryn Mreldrake.

Who flushed a deep crimson and started to stride forward, snapping threats and orders at "Two miscreants who should *both* be in our dungeons, before—"

Elminster turned his head in the teeth of this tirade and quietly asked Amarune, "Trip him for me, will ye, lass?"

Unhesitatingly she obeyed, toppling the war wizard abruptly on his face onto the cobbles, sprawled and senseless.

After staring down at the unconscious Mreldrake in sleepy astonishment for a moment, Amarune shook her head as if to clear away bewilderment and gave Elminster an almost accusative look.

"You . . . did you use a spell on me?"

"No," Elminster told her truthfully. "Nor did ye obey me because I gave an order. Ye just did the right thing when I pointed it out to ye. We of the blood of Aumar can't help ourselves, lass. Doing the right thing is what we *do*."

He patted her arm. "Oh, the Realms will be *fine* in thy hands. Just fine."

Those words left Amarune standing white-faced and slack-jawed in the street as she stared at him, at a complete loss for words.

Gently he took her arm again and started towing her home.

Chapter
THIRTY
Your Castle or Mine

Lady, will you come now and dine?
To give my best honeyed words their chance
To make thee melt, and gasp, and prance,
My fingers to free gown from spine,
Working mutual ravishment in your castle, or mine?

from the ballad *Your Castle or Mine?*
Rauleth "Rory" Treln, Minstrel of the Many Cloaks
composed in the Year of the Dark Goddess

A marune awakened in darkness, lying amid her bed-clothes. They were twisted and clammy, as if she'd spent the day wrestling with them rather than sleeping. She blinked up at the ceiling.

Gods, she felt exhausted. Ruthgul was dead, *dead* . . . and she might well be, too, the moment Talane or that Windstag noble or his bullyblades found her.

She dare not stay there.

But where could she go?

What should she do? Not just *for the moment*, but with her life?

She was a very public target at the Dragonriders' . . . but she'd need coins coming in, to live anywhere.

Redoubling her career as the Silent Shadow only under a new name *might* be very profitable just now, with Suzail full of wealthy nobles, but was stone-cold sure to be one thing. Very dangerous.

Even if there were no laws nor wizards or Purple Dragons to enforce them, and even if nobles were all careless-of-coin idiots with blunt swords who lacked House wizards or hired bodyguards, she wasn't sure if she wanted to make her living by thievery anymore.

And what did the crazy old mage who thought she was his granddaughter want with her? To "save the Realms," yes, but what did that mean? And just what would he put her through next?

Arclath's face swam into her head . . . and suddenly, in a rush that took her breath away, Amarune found herself missing his company very much.

She wanted to hear that laugh of his again, his airy gestures and all the nonsense he drawled. She . . . stlarn it, she wanted to be at his side again. Where she felt, well, not safe, but confident. Or rather, wrapped in his confidence, as if it could carry them through any danger or difficulty or unpleasantness.

Huh. And what pit of vipers would *that* be, trailing along with drawling, pranksome, idiotic Lord Delcastle?

She shook her head and gave the dimly seen ceiling a wry shrug. No matter. It seemed to be what her sleeping self had decided she wanted to do.

Her next shrug took her out of bed in a long-limbed wriggle. Stalking to her row of cloak hooks for some clean clothing, she found herself wondering if Lord Arclath Delcastle would be at Delcastle Manor at that hour.

Or if, regardless of what time of day or night she appeared at its gates, the Delcastle servants would let her in—or just sneer and slam those grand doors in her face.

Drawing a clean clout up her legs, she frowned at that. Mustn't let new vipers into their cozy little pit . . .

She smiled wryly and started thinking up grand tales of secret messages from the palace she'd be bringing him. She'd be . . . a highknight. Yes, she'd have to be.

"The words I bear are for the ears of Lord Arclath Argustagus Delcastle alone," she murmured to her mirror, keeping her face as calm as stone. "They are . . . *royal* words."

That sounded good. Almost good enough to get her in.

She grimaced and reached up to fetch the knives she strapped all over herself when being the Silent Shadow.

She had a gods-strong feeling she would be needing them.

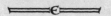

"Behold," Elminster muttered to himself, "in what minstrels are pleased to call 'the dead of night,' one Elminster of Shadowdale returns to his chosen abode and battlefield, by one of the few ways he feels able enough to use about now."

The night-lass he'd just enriched by two golden lions glided to a graceful stop in front of the two duty guards, smiled as she calmly pulled open her bodice, and announced, "Wizard of War Rorskryn Mreldrake has just lost a bet, and by way of forfeit, has paid me well to entertain you two loyal Dragons."

"Stand back, lass," the older guard replied sternly, peering warily past her into the night. "We're under strict orders to let no one pass, not stray from our posts, and keep all who have weapons a safe reach away from us."

The night-lass stepped back meekly and undid her gown.

"These are the only weapons I have," she told them slyly, gesturing down at herself.

The younger guard growled wordlessly, stepped away from the door they were guarding, and reached for her.

"I'll stand watch," his older comrade growled quickly. "Be quick."

His resolve lasted long enough for Elminster to begin to think his coins hadn't bought him passage after all, but the night-lass knew her work. One of her hands had been beckoning the older Dragon all the while, until eventually he growled and strode eagerly forward.

Wherefore Elminster stepped away from the bit of the wall he'd been pretending to be a part of for a very long time, and slipped through the door unnoticed, without a sound or any undue haste.

By the time the younger guard decided it would be prudent to at least look up from the lass—whose name he very much desired to know, for future occasions—and peer around to make sure the street was empty of a patrol or a noble's coach or two or perhaps a small approaching army, Elminster was several secret passages deep into the palace and descending some old, damp, seldom-used stairs.

He had magic to plunder, a hiding place to find, and a kingdom to save. In short, the usual . . .

Amarune drew in a deep breath, pulled her cloak more snugly around her—the moon was up, but the night had turned *cold*—and firmly clacked the knocker of the porter's door beside the gates of Delcastle Manor. Slowly and deliberately, thrice.

Almost immediately, she heard a soft, sliding sound, as if a plate on the other side of the door had been slid aside to let someone peer at her. In the shadowed gloom, she couldn't see any change in the door, but someone was there, watching and listening. There was movement behind the high, many-barred gates, too; guards, no doubt, taking up and aiming ready crossbows.

Silence stretched. She worked the knocker again.

This time, the response was a rattle of chain and a louder sliding. A square of heavy, double-layered grille revealed itself in the door at about eye level, a pair of steady eyes regarding her from behind it.

"Delcastle Manor," their owner murmured. "Your business?"

"I've come at the invitation of Lord Arclath Delcastle," Amarune replied carefully, knowing well what might be assumed about a woman walking alone and cloaked by night, and trying to sound polite, refined, and formal, "to speak with him. I am aware of the hour."

"I am sorry," the porter replied, sounding as if he really was, "but the Lord Delcastle is not now at home. Perhaps tomorrow, around highsun, I will be able to give you a different reply."

"I see," Amarune said, managing to keep her sigh quiet. "Do you know where he is?"

"Out dining. I was given to understand. Darcleir's Haven is a likelihood, but with so many friends, old and otherwise, newly arrived in Suzail, he might very well end up elsewhere. In the meantime, I regret I cannot admit guests to wait for him."

"Of course," she replied, turning away.

Where to, she was not quite sure. Nowhere at all might be safe for her, and among all these tall, formidable walls and the frequent Watch patrols, she could hardly linger on these streets of mansions and—

Lost in her thoughts, she almost walked right into a pair of gleaming boots and the dark-clad man who was wearing them, standing right in front of her in the night.

She flung herself back, clapping hand to knife—and saw that it was Arclath Delcastle, smiling a rather tired smile at her. He was just arriving home from the Haven, having grown heartily tired of the company of overpainted, oh-so-pretty venomous vipers of young and predatory noble ladies, with their honeyed threats and condescensions.

Their eyes met, and one good look at her frightened, imploring eyes told him something. Breaking into a broad grin, he swept one arm around Amarune with a loud and delighted, "*Lady* Amarune! We *must* talk! Your castle or mine?"

"Y-yours," she managed to whisper. "If it's ... convenient."

"In your company, *all* things are convenient," he replied heartily. "Open up, Lorold!"

The gates were already parting, guards coming to attention. Arclath gave them both bright smiles and nods, waved to the porter, and swept his cloaked guest past them all into the moonlit gardens beyond.

"I'm honored that you came to visit us so promptly! The family will be *so* pleased!"

He took her arm, firmly guiding her up a gentle slope of grass wet with heavy dew to a path lined with tall plantings of uruth and bedaelia. "To our right, the Delcastle bridal bower! Ahead of us, the summerhouse, and to our left, looking down across the main carriageway to the arbor, we can see in the distance the five fishponds my great-grandsire was so proud of. The Delcastle stables are justly famed for their—"

By then they were well along the floral path, and he stopped in midsentence, dropped his voice to a murmur, and asked, "Do you need shelter? A meal? A place to talk?"

"All of those, I suppose," Amarune replied, hesitantly. "To talk, mostly."

"Here, or inside, where the dragon that is my mother snorts fire and growls, devouring a steady procession of young and perfumed men entering her bedchamber?"

Amarune sighed. "Do you have a room you can call your own, with a door that locks?"

Arclath eyed her gravely. "I do. Have you a reputation left to maintain?"

Amarune snorted. "As a barepelt club dancer? I'll risk it."

"But what of *my* reputation?" he asked lightly.

"I can probably manage to moan and gasp and sob your name loudly from time to time, and thereby salvage it," she told him dryly.

Arclath rolled his eyes then grinned like an eager lad, his eyes dancing. "Then come!"

"Can we at least have drinks first?" she teased. "Isn't that the courtly way?"

"We can," he promised. "Yet never make the mistake again of thinking nobles are courtly away from court. As mistakes go, that can be one of the fatal ones."

Well, at least he was still good at one thing.

Not that breaking into the royal palace of Suzail with swift ease was apt to advance him far in any new career he'd prefer to pursue.

Panderer? Nay . . .

Elminster gave the dark and empty secret passage he was traversing his best wry grin as he hastened along it. Then he winced. Aye, he had a blister rising on his left heel. He was getting too old for waltzing young lasses home and then rushing back across too much of Suzail to seek his own hidehold, before—

Hoy, there! He stiffened, slowed, and then advanced more cautiously. The murmur of voices ahead was many-throated and excited; something had befallen.

The clack was coming through some spyholes from a room beside the passage and had the same air of alert bustle that befalls a castle before a siege; something he'd heard a time or twelvescore and remembered all too well.

Ah, *that* voice was Mallowfaer, the Master of Revels, in full pompous bluster.

Elminster rolled his eyes and glided to a cautious halt by the spyholes, taking care to keep well back from them as he peered through.

The robing-room on the other side of the wall was crowded with courtiers, and war wizards, too; facing El but half-hidden behind the shoulder of Understeward Corleth Fentable was a rather bruised-looking Rorskryn Mreldrake. The spyholes were situated behind and just above the left shoulder of Khaladan Mallowfaer, who evidently wanted to impress everyone with his authority and exacting attention to detail, but also sounded determined to demonstrate just how pompous and nasty he could be, in the process.

The burdens of his song were intertwined harmonies of exasperation at unfolding chaos, glee that the problem could not—by any stretch of verbiage he would allow—be laid at *his* door, and that he was in charge of formal protocols at the moment and could therefore decree with nigh royal authority. It seemed the palace had become aware that Ganrahast and Vainrence both seemed to be missing, with our wizards of war very alarmed about it and rushing about searching here, there, and everywhere without wanting to admit that anything at all was amiss—with the council only days away! What to do? *What* to do?

At that moment, with a sputtering roar, it became clear that Understeward Fentable's superior, the bullying, blustering, and overblown Palace Steward Rorstil Hallowdant—who was both lazy and a drunkard and therefore spent much of his time snoring somewhere, leaving things to the highly efficient and widely liked understeward, much to the relief of most courtiers—had heard quite enough of someone *else* being haughty and giving orders right and left.

"The Master of Revels," he said in a voice that had a finger-lopping-sharp edge to it, "seems to forget that *everyone* in this chamber right now is a dedicated, skilled professional, from the clerk of the shield here beside me to the underclerks of protocol yonder, all four of them. It is our *common* business to know the location and deeds of each royal personage, both before and throughout the council, from the smallest appointment to the grandest feast, and from our beloved King Foril to Lord Royal Erzoured and the Countess of Dhedluk. The Master of Revels needs only to coordinate, and *not* to command."

"Of course," Mallowfaer responded in a voice that had an edge all its own, "but the Crown Prin—"

"Crown Prince Irvel confers with *me* often. I last spoke with him—*and* with Princess Ospra, Prince Baerovus, and Princess Raedra—just before departing the Sunstatues Chamber to come here. All of them are confident the customary support of the entire palace will make this council a success, however tense matters become. I should add that even one not born to high station, the Lady Solatha Boldtree, shares this confidence and has said as much. To *me*."

"Nevertheless—"

"*Nevertheless*," the palace steward said crushingly, "we deal with functions and courtesies large and small here in this great seat of rulership, day in and day out, and shall continue to do so without any need for the Master of Revels to try to alter or gainsay the usual precedence or procedures. *I* fully expect each and every one of you to—"

Elminster shook his head and strolled on down the secret passage, Hallowdant's coldly cutting words fading behind him. He found himself both amused—he could practically complete the palace steward's speech by heart, without any need to actually hear the rest of it—and heartened. Murmurs of agreement had been backing Hallowdant in a sort of chorus.

The court was bent on their duties.

Ganrahast or no Ganrahast, things would go on. Haughty and fussy and backbiting though they were, the courtiers of Cormyr would deal with things.

King rise or king fall, regicide or nobles poisoning each other with abandon or chasing each other down the halls with gore-dripping battle-axes, the palace servants would endure. And the Forest Kingdom with them, for they *were* the kingdom. They and the carters and crofters, foresters and horsebreeders, goodwives and crafters and smiths, from the Thunder Peaks to the Stormhorns. Let Hallowdant and Mallowfaer spit and snarl; most of the other faces he'd just seen through a spyhole were both worried and excited. They were the faces of men who *cared*.

The Forest Kingdom was still strong. Whoever warmed the throne or this or that high lord's chair might change, but the kingdom would endure.

Which meant a certain Sage of Shadowdale could take the items that held the survivors of the Nine for Alassra. Cormyr would get along just fine without them.

Lord Arclath Delcastle stopped, put his hands on his hips, and sighed in exasperation.

He had arisen early this fine bright morning, checked that his slumbering guest was still sleeping—they had talked late into the night but had slept apart, Arclath showing her his private pantry and sideboard and that she could lock herself in with them, and had heard her promptly do so—taken a quick breakfast of spiced plover's eggs and hearth cakes, thrown on some suitably dandified finery, given his trusted servants firm instructions to render all reasonable aid to Amarune and to do so with respect, and taken himself off to the palace.

He had two tasks to discharge there, the lesser concerning himself and the greater concerning the news Amarune had agreed that the war wizard Glathra should hear, without delay.

His personal business was the same as many of the lesser nobles of the realm this morning. He sought to learn where his seat at council would be and which particular courtier he should look for on the day to escort him to his seat.

In Arclath's case, this lesser task also involved conveying his mother's regrets; she of course would not be attending, and was in fact sending Arclath in her stead, while his father was too drunk to even know there *was* a council.

His more pressing task—to report to the wizard Glathra that the mask dancer Amarune, the Silent Shadow, had just learned that she was the great-granddaughter of the infamous wizard Elminster, who was lurking in Suzail at that moment and wanted her to steal particular magic items for him that held the ghosts of the legendary Nine—would have been much easier if Arclath had been able to *find* Glathra.

Not that any of the wizards of war he collared seemed to know where she might be found, stlarn them.

The whole palace was in an uproar that morning, everyone rushing about terribly busy with council-related security requirements, servant deployments, and furniture rearrangements. Both the sprawling royal court and the majestic royal palace were a noisy bedlam of hurrying, calling, feverishly working folk; every last chambermaid and page seemed swept up in it all.

He was growing tired of holding his own hips. He'd much rather have his hands on Rune's, and—

Enough. Banish *that* thought until he could do something about it.

Drawing a deep breath, Lord Arclath Delcastle squared his shoulders, put a "no nonsense, please" frown on his face, and marched forward into the tumult.

He knew a few senior War Wizards by sight, and surely *some* of them must be here in the palace. He'd just keep going until he found one and ask for Glathra until he found someone who—

"*Hold,* saer!"

Arclath sighed. The challenges were going to come frequently that morning, by the looks of things. He gave the Purple Dragon guard barring his way with horizontal-held spear a patient smile, and began, "Fair morn to you, Telsword. I'm looking for Wizard of War Glathra . . ."

The man scowled, instantly suspicious. "And just why d'you want to see her, Lord?"

Oh, it was going to be a *long* morning.

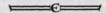

In a dark passage deep beneath the palace, Elminster came to a halt and cursed softly. On the wall ahead hung an old shield he'd watched Vangerdahast enspell, far more years earlier than he cared to remember. Its enchantments made it a silent warning of certain things arriving where nobles liked to congregate. When it started to glow, wizards of war had known to curse and hasten off to deal with whatever trouble the less loyal nobility of the Forest Kingdom were bringing to fair Suzail.

Those wizards were all dead. Which left him.

Turning to begin hastening, he got to work on the cursing part.

Chapter
THIRTY-ONE
We Must Do Whatever We Must

Love fades and death ends trust, yet we strive
Until we're dust; we go on through blood and lust,
We brave fire, fangs, gale and gust
For we must do whatever we must.

> from the ballad *We Go On*
> Marandur Erilogan of Waterdeep, bard,
> composed in the Year of the Prince

Arclath prided himself on a certain supple grace of stride, a smooth saunter that drew the eye. He'd needed it that morn to thread his way through all the rushing chamberjacks and chambermaids without too many jarring collisions.

He'd also needed all the charm and glib tongue-work he could master to fend off frequent challenges from Purple Dragons as he sought out wizard of war after wizard. The ones he did find seemed to delight in frowningly directing him this way and that.

Not that the one he was standing in front of, at the moment, was any trial on the eyes. A real beauty, with a long, glossy fall of blue-black hair—the hue they called "midnight"—and large, liquid, dark eyes to match.

"I am Lord Arclath Delcastle," he replied to her query. "What's *your* name?"

"Raereene," she replied, adding a polite smile and a calm wave of her hand that told him that his come-hither glance was wasted, and that she was more than used to the blandishments of men both young and old. "You're seeking someone?"

"One of your colleagues," Arclath told her. "A wizard of war who asked me to report to her, and gave her name as Glathra."

The young beauty nodded and pointed at a nearby door. "I know not her present whereabouts, but if you wait in yon chamber, I can promise you she'll be there soon. It's where we always find her, sooner or later."

Delcastle gave her a bow and smile of thanks, and made his way to the door. It proved to open into a little office—at the same time as an old, bearded man closed a secret panel behind himself on the far wall of the room and turned to face Arclath.

Who let the door close behind him as they stared at each other, and a crooked smile grew across the old man's face.

"Well met, Lord Delcastle," he said, going straight to a sideboard along one end of the office—ignoring its honor guard of a ceremonial suit of full armor, set up all lifelike on a stand—and selecting a decanter from the neat row atop it. "Care for a drink?"

"Who are you?" Arclath asked, waving the offer away. "A war wizard?"

"Yes," the old man replied, "and I'd like to have something of a chat with thee. I've been hearing some strange things about young Lord Stormserpent and magic and some famous adventurers known as the Nine, and I'd like to know what ye know of such matters. What're the fair nobles of the realm saying, hey?"

Delcastle stared at the old man in bewilderment. "Glathra?" he asked, frowning. "Is it you? Is this some sort of test? I've been known to enjoy little games, yes, but right now I rather lack the time—"

"Ah, nobles, nobles!" Elminster lamented mildly, sipping from the tallglass he'd just filled. "So important. Never have time for anything of consequence; so busy with feasting and dalliance and debauchery—"

Arclath sighed. "A tune I've heard more than a few times before. Saer, not now! This council must go perfectly or—"

"Or thy head'll be served up on the next feast platter? Well, if ye don't listen to me, it will go rather less than imperfectly; 'twill be a disaster, perhaps even offering the realm a regicide!"

Arclath arched an eyebrow. "My, my, so dramatic . . ."

He strolled across the room toward one of the two closed doors at its other end from the sideboard. "However, you don't seem to be the person I'm looking for, so I'll just be—" He reached out, hesitated for a moment, and then chose the handle of the right-hand door.

"Dead in about ten breaths from now," Elminster finished his sentence for him briskly, "if ye step blindly through yon door. The elder Lady Illance is changing her gown in the chamber beyond, and her guards are *very* swift with their blades. Their *poisoned* blades, may I add, despite Crown law."

Arclath whirled around. "What? They'd not *dare*! The—"

Elminster shook his head. "Ye are blind indeed, young Delcastle. Nigh every last noble at council will be breaking one Crown law or another—and they'll *all* have weapons, spells on themselves, and some sort of forbidden magic or poison about their persons. Are ye *sure* ye're a noble? Know ye *nothing*?"

Arclath stared at the old wizard, eyes narrowing. "You're . . . you're Elminster, aren't you?"

El smiled, nodded—and slumped into a rather stiff parody of a courtly bow that left Arclath rolling his eyes and grinning.

Then he shook his head, still smiling, and said, "Well, I know I can't walk around the palace asking for your advice and warnings at every second step without half-a-dozen war wizards and Dragons pouncing on us both!"

Elminster produced a grin of his own and went to the suit of armor. Plucking off its close-visored helm, he calmly emptied a dead mouse and its nest out of it, lowered it onto his head, and replied hollowly from inside it, "That's why ye're about to acquire a bodyguard. Help me on with all the rest of this clobber. Duar was about my size, I see, and he's far too long dust to be wanting it all back now."

"About your *height*, maybe, but he was twice your girth and even larger in the shoulders," Arclath sighed, "but I doubt we dare tour the palace looking for a better fit."

"I suppose not," Elminster agreed cheerfully. "Besides, this is the suit with the enchanted codpiece—and I just might need it. Ye never know."

His grotesquely broad wink left Arclath rolling his eyes again, but El was already sliding open the secret panel and waving Arclath through it. The noble stepped into the gloomy space beyond, and El followed.

The moment the panel closed behind them, the left-hand door at the end of the room swung open to reveal Glathra Barcantle and a man wearing a crown whom half Suzail knew at a glance: King Foril. They had been listening, and their faces were grim.

"So Elminster is after the Nine and believes them to be here," Glathra said gloomily.

The king nodded. "He must not gain them. Any he does find, we must take back from him. Arclath can help us with that."

"Can, yes," Glathra muttered, "but will he?"

Foril sighed. "Distasteful as it seems, it's high time to compel a few of our oh-so-loyal nobles to demonstrate their loyalty to Cormyr. Do whatever you must."

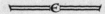

Marlin was high-hearted with excitement, but Lothrae was coldly calm.

The words had all come out in rather a babbling rush, true, in his anxiousness to inform Lothrae that a *third* member of the Nine was bound to an item, somewhere which apparently half Suzail knew about!

"Contain yourself, Marlin," Lothrae said curtly. "It will be the height of folly to rush off searching all Faerûn for magic that could be anywhere, when the council is almost upon us. We must be careful, avoid doing things that will draw both attention and suspicion, and keep our minds on seizing the right opportunity."

"But we need all the magic we can *get*," Marlin protested. "The Spellplague was unpredictable. Like a Dragon Sea windstorm, it left some things untouched *here* whilst utterly destroying castles'n'all over *there*. And it's not done yet! Things're still changing, stlarn it."

"All of this is both true—and irrelevant. The 'but the Spell-plague' argument can and has been used to justify anything and everything," Lothrae replied coldly. "Were you to advance such an argument at court, expect to be openly sneered and laughed at; for far too many years, every single argument began thus. 'But the Spellplague' *nothing.*"

"But if someone else gets the axe—"

"Then you'll know whom to kill to gain it, *without* turning all Suzail upside down and alerting much of it to your name and interests in the doing," Lothrae snapped. "And with that said, leaving it clear to both of us that you have nothing more useful to add to our shared wisdom just now, this converse is at an *end.*"

The glowing air above the orb went dark, Lothrae's image winking out, fading, and falling, all in less time than it took Marlin to draw breath to protest.

He was alone amid the dust-covered Stormserpent discards again.

Lothrae had been . . . irritated. From the outset. Not by news of the axe, so . . . what? The timing of the contact? Had he been busy or in danger of being discovered or overheard?

Marlin frowned as he restored things to the way he liked to leave them and left the room.

The orbs had come from Lothrae and were old magic. When either of the men entered the rooms where their orbs were kept, a spell cast by an outlander wizard Lothrae had hired and then murdered when his work was done made the other *feel* that a contact was about to come.

Early on, Marlin had usually felt Lothrae's approach to his orb, wherever it was, and had hastened to the disused tower of the family mansion. These days, he usually went to his orb and initiated their converses.

Was Lothrae losing interest in their alliance? Or wanting him to keep silent for a time? Or was there some danger or difficulty at Lothrae's end?

Well, the silent dust around him was hardly likely to offer him any answers. And somewhere out there, probably nearby, was a hand axe that held a secret . . .

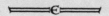

Manshoon sighed.

Marlin Stormserpent. Young. Rash. And at that moment, nigh blind with excitement.

Idiot lordling. So utterly, utterly *predictable*.

The serving maid whose mind the soon-Emperor of Cormyr was riding shrugged off the stained old sheet to give her sneer the space she felt it needed.

Young Stormserpent had just rushed past her and was dwindling down the curving stair, all oblivious to his surroundings. She probably needn't have bothered embracing the old broken statue and casting its dust sheet over them both. Just sitting still right under his nose would probably have been sufficient.

Blind idiot lordling.

"Things're still changing," she murmured, as Manshoon spoke through her. "But you grow no whit wiser, Marlin oh-so-ambitious Stormserpent. Nothing more useful to add to any shared wisdom just now, I'd say. Yet you're one of the brighter-witted lordlings of the realm. All the gods help us."

Lord Broryn Windstag was right out of breath, Sornstern was in a hardly better state, and even Kathkote Dawntard was panting and going purple. They were all wearing revel masks they'd very recently snatched down off the wall of a shrieking noblewoman's boudoir—but hadn't begun their foray with those masks, and in any case, whatever "protection" the slips of black, betrimmed silk afforded them would last only as long as they could keep out of the hands of the authorities.

Their search for the hand axe had grown increasingly frantic, and they'd had to bruise more than a few folk along the way. War wizards and Purple Dragons were after them, with the city roused; aye, it was death or exile if they didn't manage to get clear away—and stay there for long enough for doubt and planted false rumors and a few convenient "accidents" to befall key witnesses . . .

Gasping for breath as they stumbled up the back stair of an expensive address just off the promenade, with the senseless body of its guard tumbling to a stop behind them, the three started to wonder aloud at how they came to be doing it so wildly, rashly, and precipitously. Or for that matter, at all.

"Was some spell at work on our minds?" Windstag snarled.

"Well, even if one wasn't, that's got to be our claim if we get caught!" Sornstern panted, reeling against the stairpost as they reached the upper floor.

"*When* we get caught," Dawntard corrected grimly.

Still panting, they paused together to catch their breath in the passage outside the door of old Lord Murandrake's expensive rented rooms—and hesitated, exchanging wild-eyed glances.

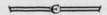

The wizard and the noble came to a spot where the dark, narrow passage ended in a meeting with a passage running left and right.

"This way, lad!" Elminster boomed cheerfully from inside his borrowed helm, turning left.

"Very well," Arclath agreed, following, "but where are we going, if I may ask?"

"Ye may," El replied brightly, "and if ye're very good, I might even tell thee. Before we get there, that is. Life is, after all, a journey rather than a—"

"Destination." Arclath sighed. "I know the hoary old sayings, too, saer. What I don't know is why I'm following you at all, when I came here to find the lady war wizard named Glathra, and . . . ah . . ."

"Tell her all about me? That I'm after the Nine, is that it? Amarune told thee?"

"She told me a lot of things," Lord Delcastle replied. "That she's your kinswoman and that you want her to help you steal certain enchanted things from the palace—which frankly puzzles me. Are you lazy, or horribly busy, or just trying to keep your hands clean? If you're as mighty an archmage as the tales all say, why not steal them yourself? Or just seize them, brushing aside our wizards of war—fallen far since the days of the legendary Vangerdahast, who was a mere pupil to you, if I've remembered rightly—as if they were so many ineffectual children?"

"My, her tongue *has* been busy," Elminster observed. "She must trust ye. Hmm; are ye lovers, perchance?"

"I'm her patron and friend, old man," Arclath replied, a trifle sharply. "It would be improper of me to take advant—"

Elminster turned and made a very rude sound in Arclath's direction. "Ye're a *noble* of *Cormyr*, lad! 'Improper' is what ye were raised to do, and haughtily! An utter dolt ye must think me, to take me for someone who'll swallow 'my morals shine' pretenses out of thy mouth! After all, a simple 'aye' or 'nay' would suffice for a man who had naught to hide."

Arclath knew he should be whipping out his sword, afire with anger, but found himself feeling far too sheepish for any such nonsense. He settled for saying simply, "We talked last night; she's very scared; she does trust me, and I touched her *not*. Truth, I swear."

Elminster dragged off the helm, revealing a face glistening with sweat, for just long enough to meet the young noble's eyes with his wise and twinkling old blue-gray ones, and reply, "I believe ye, lad."

Then the helm came down again, and from within it, the old man added, "So, aye, I'm her great-grandsire, and I want her to take my place in the harness, saving the Realms. She'll be needing help, mind; that's why I'm admitting anything at all to ye, lad, rather than just snuffing out the pride of House Delcastle, here and now. Oh, and aye, I do need to get my hands on any items that house the ghosts of any of the Nine; 'tis vitally important."

"And if, say, the Crown of Cormyr believes differently?" Arclath asked calmly as they started to move along the passage again. "And prefers these, ah, haunted magic items be retained here, in royal or war wizard hands, to defend the realm?"

"Lad, lad," came the hollow voice from within the helm, "'tis the way of all rulers, and even more so of their lackeys and toadies, to latch onto anything that just might be of value or hold power—whether they understand its consequences or know how to wield it or not—and keep it safe forever, or until their realm falls, which *always* happens first. Trust these words, from one who's ruled more realms than ye or any Obarskyr ever will, and saved this particular one we're standing in a time or two, as well: I can make better use of them than Foril or Ganrahast or all the nobles of the realm put together. Trust me."

"My dear long-departed grandfather," Arclath replied carefully, "once told me that trusting any wizard is even more foolish than trusting any noble. I have found that to be wise advice."

"Ye were well raised," Elminster agreed cheerfully. "Yet how much can any of us trust anyone, really? We'll have to talk more on this, ye and I."

He stopped at a right-angled bend in the passage, slid open another panel in the wall, and waved Arclath through it, indicating that the Lord Delcastle should precede him.

Arclath bowed and obeyed, stepping into a new and better-lit passage—where he found himself face to face with an out-of-breath War Wizard Glathra, who had just come hastening along it.

"You've been looking for me, I hear; you have news?" she snapped.

"I do," Arclath replied. "This is the wizard El—"

He turned, but the passage behind him was empty of a man in old, ill-fitting armor. He took a swift step to where the once-again-closed panel was, slid it open with only a moment's difficulty, peered up and down the passage he'd just come from, finding it—of course—empty . . . and turned back to Glathra rather helplessly.

"Well, Elminster *was* with me, and—"

"I believe you," Glathra said crisply. "If it really was Elminster and not some poser just claiming that infamous name, I'd not have wanted to trade spells with him nose to nose, anyhail. Report!"

Arclath nodded. "Well, he confirmed everything Amarune has told me: He's her great-grandsire; he was waiting for her in her lodgings yestereve to tell her so; and he wants her to save the Realms as he's been doing for centuries. Beginning with stealing some magic items that are apparently here in Suzail, and hold the ghosts of the Nine—you know about the Nine?"

"We do."

"Ah, of course. Well, as it happens, that wasn't all that I came here to tell you."

Glathra leaned forward, for all the world like a hunting dog straining at the leash to be released to pounce. "Yes?"

"I'm . . . I'm not half as capable a spy as I thought I was. I *am* loyal to the Crown, mind, just not . . . guarding the realm is not half as easy as I thought it would be. Not to mention even less fun."

Glathra's stare was hard and level. "Others before you, Lord Delcastle, have discovered as much. A few of them have even admitted it."

Chapter
THIRTY-TWO

Hunting Elminsters

Left-handed virgins now, is it?
The king has gone mad!
Next he'll have us net down the moon,
Or go out hunting Elminsters.

> Said by Orinskarr the Sentinel in
> Act I, Scene I of *Mad King Triumphant*
> by Haelana Ormkok, Lady Bard,
> first performed in the Year of the Walking Man

Watching Gods Above, was that the *time*? An exhausted Wizard of War Glathra stumbled out her usual rear door of the palace, intent only on getting home to eat something—cold roast fowl from three nights back would have to do; she was too tired to get busy at her hearth—and soak her aching feet before falling—and this night, it would *be* falling—into bed.

Almost immediately she stopped dead, because someone was standing in her way. Swordcaptain Dralkin.

"*Now* what?" she snarled, by way of greeting.

Rather stiffly, he replied, "War Wizard Glathra, I've news that might well concern the safety of the realm. I thought you'd want to know."

She closed her eyes wearily, but when she opened them again he was still standing there. "And it is?"

"Three of our younger noble lords—Windstag, Dawntard, and Sornstern—seem to be turning much of Suzail upside down right now, looking for magical hand axes. They're offering *large* coin in the taverns frequented by nobles' servants— the Rose and Dragon, the Servant Exalted, and the

Hrelto—for any hand axe brought to them that's magical when they test it, and came from any noble House. They have this chant about where they want folk to look: 'up on a wall or hidden in a bedchamber or back hall.'"

Glathra sighed heavily. "There's more, isn't there?"

"More than that," he was already adding—her query just brought a vigorous nod as he went on talking. "There've been thefts and ransackings-by-night seeking things in many nobles' mansions. Bodyguards killed or struck senseless, and many lords and ladies left seething this night at having their chambers looted."

"Farruk," Glathra said crisply. "Farewell, slumber."

She stepped around him and started to stride down the street.

"I know who's behind all this. Take me to the lodgings of the dancer Amarune Whitewave," she snapped back at him, over her shoulder. "We're hunting Elminsters."

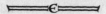

The cave was a long, narrow hovel of damp dirt, stones, and sagging old rough-tree furniture, more a hermit's cellar than a druid den. Two small, flickering oil lamps hung from a crossbranch over a rude table, and somewhere behind their glows sat a stout, broad-shouldered old man, blinking at the band of adventurers past a fearsome beak of a nose. He had a long, shaggy white beard.

The floor was an uneven, greasy, hard-trodden litter of old bones and empty nutshells, and roots thrust out of the dirt walls here, there, and everywhere; on many had been hung a pathetic collection of rotting old scraps of tapestry and paintings.

"So ye've found Elminster," wheezed the old man, "ye adventurers, and to earn thy hire would speak with me? Well, speak, then; I've naught to share, I fear, and if ye were expecting great magics or heaped gems, I'm afraid ye've come a century or so too late."

"I am Sir Eskrel Starbridge, highknight of Cormyr,"

Starbridge replied. "I've come to bring you back to Suzail with me, where your presence is . . . desired."

"L-leave Shadowdale?" the wizard quavered. "I'm—nay. Impossible."

Around Starbridge, his dozen highknights—and the five war wizards, too—stood as still as stone. Legend insisted— shouted—that this old man blinking at them had spells enough to rend kingdoms, and had done so, more than once. To say nothing of toppling castles, snatching down dragons from the sky and rending them, and transforming charging armies into smears of blood on the earth and a red mist of gore blowing away on the breeze.

Starbridge had said he would try diplomacy first. Not a one of them thought it would succeed, but, well, if there was a time for prayer, this was it.

"Elminster," Starbridge asked gently, "what keeps you here? We have woods as wild as these in Cormyr—the Forest Kingdom—and the farm on the far side of that ridge is fast disappearing beneath new saplings. What makes Shadowdale so special?"

The old man smiled. "All the Realms knows Elminster dwells here, so the fools all come to me. Fools like you."

The walls erupted, the air full of hissing arrows, quarrels, and darts.

All of which struck air that did not quite glow, a foot or so away from every one of the Cormyreans, and shattered against it to fall harmlessly to the floor. The war wizards responded almost lazily, spells lashing the walls in red-orange fire that tore into the pale, struggling forms of howling doppelgangers hiding behind the tapestries, who convulsed in agony in the heart of those flames and died.

"Your . . . servants?" Starbridge asked, in the silence that followed. "Handmaidens?"

The old man behind the table flung himself out of his chair. A highknight darted after him.

"Narulph, *stand where you are!*" Starbridge roared. "Mereld?"

"Too late to hold it in its shape," the war wizard snapped in reply, craning his neck. "Another doppelganger, shifting fast—I'll have to blast it, or it'll get away!"

Starbridge sighed in disgust. "Do it!"

He turned. "Baerengard?"

"Wizard of War Lemmeth was fast enough, sir," came the prompt reply. "The youth—Thal—was a 'ganger too. He has it held."

"Good. We question that one. Though I doubt any of them knew where Elminster is, beyond 'not here.' Stlarn it."

Manshoon smiled into the moving glows and cast a swift spell.

In midgasp the young lords Windstag, Sornstern, and Dawntard all clutched at their heads, reeled, rebounded off the walls, and bit their lips hard enough to draw blood, eyes wide and wild.

Then they shivered, shuddered, and came out of whatever had just smitten them, to blink at each other.

Nodding in grim unison, they rushed with one accord to put their shoulders to the door of the rented rooms of old Lord Murandrake.

And broke it down.

As they came crashing into a lamplit and pleasant room, an elderly man in a nightrobe started up from his chair, dropping his book of derring-do tales and his drink, as he fought to somehow pass through his seat backward to get away from them and to keep his balance at the same time.

It was a battle he lost, and swiftly. Wherefore Lord Barandror Murandrake ended up on the floor, cowering back in the cave made by his toppled chair, with three bright, sharp swords menacing him.

"An axe—d'you have an axe?" one swordsman snapped.

"A hand axe?" the second spat accusingly.

"An *enchanted* hand axe?" the third snarled.

Murandrake's quavering voice failed him, and he gabbled incoherently in his fear, but with wild wavings of his arms managed to indicate that there was *something* in the next room.

The trio of lordlings charged through the open doorway, found themselves in a luxuriously appointed bedchamber, saw a gleaming helm mounted high on one wall in pride of place with a sword and a hand axe crossed beneath it, snatched all three trophies, and stormed back to the old noble on the floor.

"These all of them?" Windstag shouted into the terrified face. When Murandrake managed a desperate nod, the young lord spun around and ran for the door.

Dawntard and Sornstern were right behind him. They fled down the stairs together, Windstag waving the axe in wild triumph.

"Another false Elminster?" Mereld muttered.

Starbridge shrugged. "We'll know soon enough. Let's see how he reacts to the moonglow."

Lemmeth nodded, drew his hands slowly apart . . . and the hollow was suddenly awash in bright, pearly white light.

Eskrel stared down into it, hard-eyed. He had a dozen highknights—aye, one of them that dolt Narulph, but still—and another three war wizards in the trees all around it, but they stayed there, awaiting Starbridge's signal.

In the meantime, they were doing the same thing as Starbridge. Staring down into a hollow where bodies were sprawled around a dead fire, with a lone figure standing over them.

The standing one was human in size and shape, and wore a battered old war-helm and motley clothing taken from the fallen, who might or might not be dead.

The figure stood still, silent, waiting for them. Gaunt and tall but stooped over as if weary or old.

"Elminster?" Starbridge asked. "Will you come with us, or be slain?"

The figure slowly spread empty hands in a gesture of surrender—or despair—and sat down on a log beside the remains of the fire.

Starbridge whistled, and the ring of men emerged from the trees and started to close in.

"You *are* Elminster?" Starbridge asked. "We'd like a word or two."

A deep growl from within the helm replied, "Oh? I'm about done with dispensing words to armed men who menace me and make demands."

It was about then that Lemmeth's conjured light showed them the menacing row of rough twigs—wands!—at the old wizard's belt. Clenching their teeth against their fear, the highknights pounced.

Hard, swift hands clawed at the wands, grabbed the seated man's arms, clawed at his garments to have off any amulets or hidden weapons, tore helm, wands, belt, and jerkin away—and the Cormyreans found themselves staring at a pair of round, firm, and very unmasculine breasts.

"Who . . . ?" Starbridge and Narulph snarled in unison, but in far different tones of voice.

Blue eyes looked fearlessly up at them, and the lips beneath them said calmly, "You, *gentle*sirs, have captured Storm."

"*There!*" Wizard of War Glathra roared as loudly as any man, pointing. "There! Take them!"

Then she, Dralkin, and the Purple Dragon patrol with them were all shouting and charging down a dark Suzail street toward the three fleeing men in the distance.

Who, it rapidly became apparent, were too winded and weary to stay ahead of the pursuit for long.

"Halt! Halt in the name of the king!" Dralkin bellowed, as the sprinting lawkeepers closed in on the running trio.

He was answered by a sudden crackling in the air, a surge of energy that brought with it the overwhelming impression of someone smiling maliciously over a glow in a vast, dark cavern. The energy rushed down on the three fleeing men—and they were gone, the street ahead of the rushing patrol empty.

"*Dung*," Glathra snapped. "Magic! I *hate* magic!"

Swordcaptain Dralkin swung his head to look at her in surprise. A wizard of war who hated magic?

Seeing the expression on her face, he decided to wait for a better time to ask her about that. On his deathbed, perhaps.

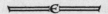

"Nice, aren't they?" Storm asked crisply, locking eyes with Highknight Narulph. Who turned a rich shade of crimson and looked away, wincing.

"Lady, they are," Mereld said swiftly, offering her his own overrobe. "Pray accept our apologies for this . . . rude handling we've given you. I'm afraid we're going to have to cast a spell or two on you, to learn the truth about what befell all these men around you, but—"

"I'll save you the trouble," Storm told him firmly. "I rang their heads for them. 'Twasn't quite a fair fight, I'll grant you—there were only eight against me, but sometimes the needs of all the Realms outweigh courtesies. Now, I've a question for you: who's in charge here? I see highknights, so you're from Cormyr—"

"*We'll* ask the questions, woman," Narulph started to growl from behind her, but an older man loomed up over the many who were still holding Storm down and said heavily, "I command here, Lady. Sir Eskrel Starbridge, now the ranking highknight of Cormyr. And you are—?"

"Storm Silverhand," came her reply. "Named Lady Highknight Protector of the Realm by Queen Filfaeril, and confirmed in that office by her husband, the fourth Azoun—which would seem to make *me* the ranking highknight of Cormyr, Starbridge—and before that ennobled as Marchioness of Immerdusk by Baerovus, when he was king. I was also Lady Envoy of the Dales to the second Palaghard, and Lady Envoy of Cormyr *to* the Dales to the second Rhigaerd." She arched her neck to look up and back behind her, and added in a murmur to Narulph, "So if I were you, sir, I'd phrase my questions rather carefully."

Hands were letting go of her in careful haste, though someone was heard to mutter, "She could have all manner of magic—"

"Yes," Storm replied with a smile. "She could, couldn't she? However, highknights and wizards of war of Cormyr, if the Forest Kingdom is anything to be proud of at all, you should dare to treat all women as ladies until you have cause to treat them in any lesser manner—not treat all strangers as dastardly foes until you know better. *I* certainly trained highknights, not to mention more than a few young noble lords, who behave in the more noble fashion. When did all of *you* go astray, I wonder?"

"Lady," Starbridge began slowly, "it is not our intent to antagonize you or offer offense, and I apologize for how matters between us have begun. Is there anything we can do to make amends?"

"Several things," Storm replied with a smile, getting to her feet. Aside from what was left of the robe and jerkin clinging to her shoulders, most of her torn clothing fell away from her, but she seemed not to notice. "Let's begin by telling me plainly what you're doing here. The last time I glanced at a map, Shadowdale was not, in fact, within the borders of Cormyr."

"Lady, we seek Elminster. We are to bring him to Suzail as swiftly as possible."

"Then you're in luck. He's there already. In the royal palace, if nothing's gone awry. And I must return to him as quickly as I can. Which brings us to the second thing you can do to make amends to me." She strode to Starbridge and held out her hand. "Yield to me your teleport ring."

Starbridge held out hands that bore no rings at all. "Lady, I have no—"

"You can dispense with lying to me, too," Storm told him crisply. "I speak of the ring in the little bag inside your tunic, that's hanging from the inside of your collar. In return, I'll tell you the name of a man in Mistledale who owes me much coin, and the word that will therefore make him freely give all of you superb fast mounts for your ride back to Cormyr."

Starbridge's face had gone flame red under the gaze of the war wizards, who were regarding him with frowns.

"How came you by a teleport ring?" Mereld asked Starbridge softly.

"It belonged to Queen Filfaeril," Storm replied before Sir Eskrel could say a word. "The highknights have had it in their keeping ever since her death, thanks to her foresight and wise wishes. And my carrying them out."

"Lady," the wizard Lemmeth said in a low voice from behind Mereld, "you'll appreciate how difficult it is for us to believe all of this."

Storm nodded. "I do. Your disbelief is quite understandable—but a serious failing in a wizard of war, wouldn't you say?"

She turned back to Starbridge. "The ring, sir."

Eskrel Starbridge seemed to be struggling with himself. He glared at her, face shifting through a variety of not-quite-readable expressions, then tore open his collar, plucked forth the little bag she'd spoken of, and produced the ring.

Storm took it stepped forward and kissed him full on the mouth, put an arm around him and waltzed her way around behind him as he was still blinking in astonishment, stepped back—and was gone.

Leaving the Cormyreans blinking at each other across a hollow full of unconscious men.

Narulph broke the silence with a sudden, angry oath. "You let her get away! Without even telling us how to get the horses!"

Starbridge shook his head slowly. "When she kissed me, his name and a word just *appeared* in my mind: 'Denneth Rhardantan,' and 'glimmerdeep.'"

He shook himself again, as if awakening, and snapped, "Get these dolts awake—they work for the Crown, so be gentle—and let's be finding the trail to Mistledale. If this council goes as ill as I fear it will, I want to be back in Cormyr before it erupts into war!"

His command all stared at him; he gave them a glare, waved his arms, and roared, "Did you hear me? *Move!*"

They moved. All except the war wizards Mereld and Lemmeth.

"Sir Highknight," Mereld asked quietly, "are you all right? What else did she do to you?"

Eskrel Starbridge stared back at them for a moment and then said, "I'm under no glamour, if that's what you fear. Put down those sticks, Lemmeth; they're not wands. She just took them from the kindling to make fools think they were seeing a wizard with wands, so they'd leave him be. She told me that, too."

He started across the hollow. "And she gave me a look into her mind," he added in a whisper. "I don't think I'll be sleeping for some while. I know now what *real* loneliness feels like."

The two war wizards stepped into his way, wearing frowns. "We'd better get you to—"

Starbridge gave them a wry grin and shook his head. "I'll be all right. You see, I know now what true love feels like, too."

"What's wrong?" Marlin Stormserpent snapped.

Windstag was too out of breath and too terrified to be coherent. He put his head down almost against Marlin's belly, gasping and shuddering. "Get us inside! Magic—don't know whose—yours?—snatched us here!"

Marlin bundled the three nobles through the door and slammed it in a whirlwind of haste, then rushed them along a dark passage, up some stairs, and into a room in Stormserpent Towers that none of the three had ever seen before. The Lords Dawntard and Sornstern promptly fainted.

Marlin gave them a grim look then snapped at Windstag, "Catch your breath, then tell me your tale."

Nodding, head down, and panting too hard to speak, Windstag fumbled in the breast of his disarranged jerkin and brought out—a glowing hand axe!

"Ha ha!" Marlin burst out, snatching it from him. "Well done! Oh, well *done!*"

And he rushed from the room, chortling in triumph.

Broryn Windstag fought to get in two gasping breaths more of air, then forced himself into a run, up and after Stormserpent.

Who was luckily still visible, racing up a narrow servants' stair in the dimly lit distance. Windstag struggled after him, lungs burning, lurching like a drunken man in his pain and weariness, but clawing his way up the stairs and keeping Marlin—or at least the glowing axe—in sight.

Stormserpent ended up in the room where he always met with them. Axe in hand, he spun around, pointed at Windstag, and commanded, "*Be still.* Don't move or speak until I'm done with the ritual."

He turned away without waiting for a reply, so Windstag lurched to his usual chair and collapsed in it. Where he leaned on the table, still gasping loudly, able to do little more than stare at Marlin Stormserpent.

Who turned away for a moment, his elbow moving as if his fingers were busy getting something out of his own clothing, then turned back to face the table and Windstag.

Holding the axe up as if saluting with it, Marlin read from a scrap of parchment that he hadn't been holding moments earlier. "*Arruthro.*"

That word seemed to roll away across a greater distance than the room could contain—and the air darkened. At first Windstag thought it was his own labored breathing that was making things seem that way, but then he felt a tension, almost a singing, in the air, too.

That *definitely* hadn't been there, before.

"*Tar lammitruh arondur halamoata,*" Stormserpent announced, speaking loudly and slowly.

The room seemed to grow colder. Windstag swallowed a curse.

"*Tan thom tanlartar,*" Marlin added—and the hand axe silently erupted in weird blue fire. Raging flames raced down his arm to the elbow and then wreathed it and the axe in an ongoing inferno that—Windstag stared—seemed to cause Stormserpent no pain at all, nor even scorch his clothing. No heat was coming from it, only a deepening chill.

"*Larasse larasse thulea*," Marlin declaimed, and the room went icy.

An instant later, the blue flames sprang from the blade of the axe, a flood of fire that arced to the floor and then rebounded up again in an upright column, a surging, rising thing that grew and grew. With a darkness at the heart of those rushing flames that slowly . . . became a man.

Chapter
THIRTY-THREE
My Hounds to Hunt You Down

I am one of those who comes howling
After the king threatens grandly. Beware!
For I have loosed my hounds to hunt you down,
And effect a capture—or worse.

> Markuld Amryntur,
> *Twenty Summers a Dragon: One Soldier's Tale*
> published in the Year of the Splendors Burning

At the sight of a man in the heart of the blue flames, Marlin Stormserpent laughed in triumph—but his mirth faltered when the flames fell to the floor with a crash, like the contents of an upended bucket of water, and were suddenly gone.

Leaving behind someone who was not wreathed in endless blue flames like Langral and Halonter had been.

Stormserpent joined Windstag in gape-mouthed, astonished staring.

Standing in his meeting room was an unlovely man in rumpled leathers who was stout—no, *fat*—and wrinkled with age and hard living. And who was staring back at him with a shrewd, measuring look.

"W-who are you? One of the Nine?" Marlin managed to ask when he found his voice again.

"Do I *look* like a bare-behind dancing girl? The Naughty Nine are all taller than me, lad, and far more shapely, too— though I'll agree they don't make cozy lasses like they used to! Nay, lad, I'm no dancer, whate'er yer preferences. I'm a bit of a trader and not much more, these days, though I guess 'tis no secret I'm a lord of Waterdeep."

"*Whaaat?*"

"Nay, nay, no need for awe and astonishment. I," the old man said sardonically, drawing himself up in mimicry of a grand ruler and striking a heroic pose, "am Mirt. Sometimes called the Moneylender, and more often—*hem*—called much worse things."

Marlin stared in disbelief, growing a frown, then swiftly tried to force the old man back into the hand axe, as he could control Langral and Halonter.

Nothing happened.

"Sit down!" he snapped. "And—and cover your eyes with your hands!"

Mirt the Moneylender lifted one bristling eyebrow. "Children's games, is it? I always *wondered* what wealthy younglings got up to when—"

"This one, a lord of Waterdeep?" Windstag sneered scornfully. "He sounds like a merchant from the docks!"

Mirt dispensed a dour look. "I *am* a merchant from the docks, loud buck! And who might ye be, with yer scorn and yer fancy clothes? Ye look like nobles, both of ye, but I know every last born noble of the city, lass and jack, an'—"

"*We* are nobles of *Cormyr*," Marlin Stormserpent snapped. "And you stand in Stormserpent Towers in the fair city of Suzail, right now. 'Now' being the Year of the Ageless One, as it happens. I doubt Waterdeep would suffer the likes of you to be among its lords these days!"

Mirt gaped at the young Lord Stormserpent and went a little pale. "Ageless One? Is—gods, is *that* how long it's been?"

"So," Windstag asked Stormserpent, "when do the flames surround him? And when can you start ordering him around like a slave? Or is he going to crumble to dust?"

"Lad," Mirt replied, before Marlin could say anything, "dust is what we're *all* going to end up as." He winced. "Dust is probably what my Asper is, right now. And Durnan, and all the others I cared for, or—"

"Oh, *shut* your *wind*," Marlin Stormserpent told the old man disgustedly. "As if we care about your doxies or friends or *anyone* from Waterdeep! On your knees!"

Mirt gave the young lord a glare and stood right where he was. "Huh. If the Realms in this year is full of the likes of ye, I don't think much of it. Or of thy sneering friend, here." He turned his disapproval on Windstag—who responded by rising and drawing his sword.

Marlin did the same, adding a menacing smile.

Mirt rolled his eyes. "And is this how converse is carried on in the Realms these days? Swords, is it? Not even a glass of something for guests? And ye call yourselves nobles!"

"We do indeed," Marlin Stormserpent told him in silken tones, stalking forward with blade in hand.

Along the other side of the table, Broryn Windstag began the same slow, armed advance.

"*Ahem*," Mirt said tentatively, taking a step backward. "I believe I did warn ye that I'm a lord of Waterdeep."

"And we quake at the news," Marlin Stormserpent sneered, hefting his blade. "*This* is what we think of lords of Waterdeep."

He spat at Mirt, though the range was considerable and he merely wetted the floor in front of the old man's worn and flopping sea boots.

Mirt raised his brows, face mild.

Windstag strode forward, menacing the Waterdhavian with his sword. "Though we *do* know how rich lords of Waterdeep are. So you can either yield up a lot of coin to us, here and now—or die."

The old man sighed.

"I don't, as it happens," he said sourly, "carry heavy sacks of coins around in my codpiece—or anywhere else under these old rags, either. All the bulges ye see are my own."

"So how much coin can you lay hands on in Suzail? And how quickly?"

"Well," Mirt wheezed, lumbering forward with an utter disregard for the sharp points of their swords, to peer at the table that displayed Marlin's map of the city, "that depends."

"On?" The decanter had caught Marlin's interest, but he stopped heading for it to see just where on the map the old man—who was standing right against the table, holding onto it for support—was looking.

"On whether or not ye fall for this," the old man said calmly, heaving up, hard—and hurling the table over onto the fine-booted toes of both noblemen.

Who shrieked in pain and dropped their swords, lost in writhing agony. Which gave Mirt plenty of time to take a heavy statuette of *Arlond Stormserpent Slaying a Dragon* from the sideboard, lurch alongside the blindly hopping, shouting Windstag, and dash the noble to the floor with a blow to the head.

Marlin, who was also hopping in pain, turned to try to fight, lost his balance, and toppled. Whereupon Arlond landed hard on his face, breaking his nose and sending him off to dreamland.

Mirt calmly drew his dagger and sliced free two bulging noble purses. "*That* quickly," he told the silent, sprawled, and copiously bleeding Marlin Stormserpent.

The royal palace of Suzail was always quieter by night than by day. Not that the servants ever slept—least of all with the council almost upon the realm—but by the dark hours the collective vigilance of guards, courtiers, and wizards of war had at least ensured that all the visiting nobles were temporarily gone, and no more of them were coming to the gates haughtily demanding things.

With morning heading for highsun, the floors above were abuzz with busy servants—though much furniture-shifting and rifling of the wine cellars had been done, and most of the chambers of state arranged, prepared, and then firmly shut up to await their coming times of need. Only the kitchens were working full tilt, with already-weary chambermaids pressed into service to help shift fresh-baked goods from the ovens to tables in nearby function rooms, thereby clearing the way so that more could be baked.

The lone armored figure stalking unseen past all this tumult in one of the better-known secret passages was weary, too. He'd filched an entire tray of sage-and-egg tarts—better a tray than just one or two, when that might rouse a search for some lurking intruder—and had eaten more than was comfortable, but this armor had room enough for a dozen trays of uneaten tarts, if he cared not how much they crumbled.

Elminster was slowly getting used to the weight and awkwardness of the armor—without its leather underpadding, it shifted loosely at his every movement and seemed to have a great abundance of sharp, jabbing edges—and had long since concluded that King Duar Obarskyr must have been more mighty bull than man.

In his postprandial discomfort, and seeking to avoid unpleasant confrontations with Purple Dragons or officious wizards, he had taken his overfull stomach and copious resulting wind down to the lower levels of the palace. Where he trudged along damper, colder passages, correctly believing he was not so likely to be noticed and thought out of place down here and challenged.

"Send no hounds to hunt me down," he muttered, belching sage and eggs.

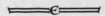

"Stop daydreaming and *attend* my words!"

This sort of bark meant Hallowdant was really angry. O Purple Dragon, preserve us all.

The man who called himself Lothrae when he was sitting masked in front of an orb talking to foolish young Stormserpent stifled a sigh and put a pleasantly attentive smile on his face. "Yes, Lord High Steward?"

Rorstil Hallowdant preened visibly. He loved it when someone pronounced his full title with *just* the right hint of reverent awe.

Lothrae wished he could enjoy toying with the buffoon, but the man *was* in office over him, and—*Great Gods Above!*

And, very suddenly—as ice raced down his spine and he felt himself breaking into a sweat—he greatly desired to be elsewhere in the palace, right then.

The ring on the next-to-smallest finger of his left hand had once belonged to the legendary Laspeera, and it had just awakened. For the very first time in all his years of wearing it.

He tried not to stare at its warning glow—silent, but so vivid and so *sudden*—then turned it on his finger to hide that radiance inside his closed hand, and cursed silently. Its warning meant someone had opened the royal crypt from the outside—but he dared not go to see who just then, with the steward literally jawing in his face, thundering order after order at him.

My, but Hallowdant was in fine form for that time of a morning. An hour at which he was usually nowhere to be seen. Lothrae tried to console himself with the thought that one of the royals must have given him a real blast, to put him in such a state and have him up and about so early . . . but that musing utterly failed to improve his own mood.

"—and *another* thing! The candles in the balcony sconces in Anglond's Great Hall are half-burnt and need replacing! *Now*, before the council is upon us and we're too busy to remember them, but need their light to fail not!"

"Ah, *yes*, Lord High Steward," he agreed hastily, starting to hasten along the hallway. "If you'll excuse me, I'll see to it and report *right* back to you for more instructions—"

"*Stand where you are, man!*" the palace steward stormed. "You'll stay still, right here, and listen! I haven't *finished* yet!"

"Lord Hallowdant, *please*," Lothrae tried again. "I really *must* relieve myself—"

Palace Steward Rorstil Hallowdant could radiate towering disgust just as devastatingly as the very best noble matriarchs; it was one of his best talents. Wordlessly he pointed over Lothrae's shoulder.

At the door of a jakes that was literally four paces away.

It was not one of the few that had secret panels in its rear wall, either, curse the luck.

Lothrae sighed, resigned himself to perhaps never knowing

who'd opened the crypt, and took his feigned need to empty his bladder into the jakes.

As the door swung closed behind him, the ring on his finger quivered and shone even more brightly, and he discovered, all of a sudden, that he truly did need to relieve himself. Badly.

In one of her favorite rooms of the palace—the nursery with the high round window she'd always loved watching the moon through—what was left of Alusair Obarskyr felt the activation of the rune, nine or so floors beneath her.

Not to mention the stirring of someone who had long been silent.

"One of Vangey's old locking runes!" she hissed, alarmed and excited—and rushed through the palace like a ghostly wind, racing to the spot.

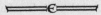

The ring's brief blue glow faded, leaving Storm Silverhand blinking in the chill darkness.

Ah, Royal Crypts are such cozy places. This one was no exception. Still, it was one spot in a Palace that, elsewhere, must resemble an agitated anthill about now, that she shouldn't have to worry about being interrupted while—

There came a faint clank and rasping of sliding metal about four paces in front of her—and then the louder sound of a heavy stone door grating open. In the dim rectangle of resulting light, Storm found herself staring at a menacing figure in full armor.

Who stumbled toward her with a muffled curse, fumbling with its skirting plates.

Thankfully, that pleasantry was uttered in a voice she recognized.

"Well met, El," she greeted her armored visitor cheerfully,

sidestepping deftly in case she startled him. Archwizards—hah, *all* wizards—were ... dangerous. Like unsheathed carving knives forgotten in a dark drawer, they could imperil all who blundered too near.

"Urrah? *Storm?*" The Sage of Shadowdale sounded astonished. "When did ye return?"

"Now," she replied simply, stepping around him to close the door. "Whence this sudden thirst for wearing armor?"

"Stops idiot wizards of war hurling spells before they stop to ask who I am," came the muffled reply. He produced something from under the skirts and thrust it at her. A tray, wobbling more than a little. "Here, hold this—and, ah, help thyself. Must get this blasted helm off."

"Savory tarts?" Storm asked, her stomach suddenly rumbling. *When* had she last eaten, anyh—

The world erupted with a white-hot roar.

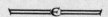

The scrying exploded in his face, but Manshoon never flinched. He let the tears stream as he smiled.

Lothrae and Mreldrake might be drooling idiots for days, but he'd managed it.

Yes.

Strike hard and fast enough, and you can fell even the mighty. Storm Silverhand should be a broken thing spattered across the back wall of the crypt, and Elminster sorely wounded.

That armor would have saved his life, but he'd be in great pain. And alone once more, as Manshoon wanted him to be.

Aye, this was much better. He busied himself casting another scrying spell to look into that crypt again as soon as possible. Spending days tainting its wards to let him through had been worth every irritating moment, after all.

"Storm?" he gasped when he knew he was Elminster again. He was lying sprawled on stone, afire with pain.

Silence was the only reply offered by the darkness.

"Oh, lass," he whispered. "Oh, no. Not like this . . ."

Mystra be with me.

Or . . . will I join her?

Elminster swam back to consciousness again. The pain was even worse, this time.

The armor was torn and crumpled where it wasn't missing. He was burned in all those bare places, yet shivering. He lay on the cold hard smoothness, feeling life run out of him . . . slow, sticky, and inexorable.

The faint glows of the tombs were gone . . . or was his sight merely dimming as he started to die?

No, there was new light.

Fey witchlight.

Alusair had arrived, and her ghostly glow with her.

"Hail, fair princess," he murmured, trying to smile.

Metal clinked and tinkled; Alusair was fighting to pluck away shards of Duar's shattered armor that kept falling through her fingers.

"Damned magic!" she hissed. "Once I could command this entire palace—and now I can't farruking pick up a stlarning *plate of armor!*"

"How . . . mighty . . . fallen," Elminster offered, choking on welling blood.

"Hey, now, Old Mage," the ghostly Steel Princess replied tenderly, her face floating perhaps a hand's length away from his, "rest easy. If you're fated to die here, at least you'll die clowning around in stolen armor—and if we kiss and cuddle as much as I can manage, you'll go in the arms of a lass trying to make love to you. Isn't that what most men want?"

"Not . . . dead . . . yet," Elminster managed. "But so damned . . . weak . . ."

Which was when a feeble whisper rose from the open door in front of them both, and something dark slithered into view. A wraith, a dark cloud barely able to lift itself far enough off the flagstones to drift, creeping like smoke toward them.

"And how d'you think *I* feel?" it asked testily.

It was a voice they both knew.

Vangerdahast.

The whisper was coming from all that was left of him. He was obviously a Dragon no longer. And just as obviously barely alive—or barely undead—too.

"Elminster," Alusair said insistently, "use the codpiece! Heal yourself, before it's too late!"

Elminster blinked at her, nodded almost absently, obeyed— a glow that brought some measure of relief promptly washing over him—and went back to staring at the dark wraith-thing on the floor. It was looking back at him with what seemed to be a lopsided grin.

"Again," the ghostly princess commanded, and Elminster obeyed, the pain ebbing still more.

"Vangerdahast?" he asked in disbelief, peering hard.

"Aye," came the growled reply. "There'd be a lot less of me if Myrmeen hadn't loved me enough to force the last of her life into me. Yet she did, so this is all that's left of Vangerdahast, once Royal Magician and Court Wizard of Cormyr. Ruler of a dark and empty closet of a crypt, these last few years. Ever since that snake who stole my ring sealed me in."

"Who?" Elminster demanded weakly. "Who did it?"

"His name," Vangerdahast hissed, "I know not. Nor did I see his face. Yet he works here at the palace—I feel the ring near too often for his station to be anything else—and schemes to bring down the Obarskyrs, and fartalks Sembians who send him coin and give him commands, and orders foolheaded young nobles to do the butchery. Which will befall at a council of some sort, by his recent talk."

Alusair and Elminster exchanged glances. "And what else did you overhear?"

"Nothing useful. I can hear only through the ring, and only for moments ere I collapse into wisps, exhausted, and must spend agonizingly long gathering myself together again."

"Is . . ." Elminster realized how helpless he felt. "Can I help ye, somehow?"

"Leave me the codpiece. I can feed on that and gather myself to carry it. I'll scare a few guards when they see a disembodied codpiece floating feebly along the passages."

Alusair chuckled. "I can carry small things, briefly; I could carry your cod."

"Then let's be going places," Vangerdahast said faintly. "How soon's this council?"

"Highsun on the morrow," El and Alusair chorused grimly.

The dark, wispy cloud that was Vangerdahast somehow managed to look disgusted.

"Always charging in at the last instant, aren't you?" he asked Elminster. "When it comes to my Cormyr, couldn't you dispense with the dramatics, for once? Just once?"

CHAPTER
THIRTY-FOUR

RUNE, RUNE, GONE AWAY

They tell me she's gone / Fled far and returning nay
Spurning our banners bright / Into the darksome night.
Vain horns calling! / Ah! Her eyes they shone,
Come what may, / I'll dream of her smile,
And artful guile. / Many a man falling!
In my heart she'll always stay / My Rune, Rune, gone away!

> from the ballad *My Dark Rune Gone Away*,
> Laramond Stillsilver, Lord Bard of Lalambril
> composed in the Year of Lost Ships

Alusair had never thought the palace cellars were so *big* before. She had very little strength and solidity left to call on, to try to drag the crawling, badly wounded Elminster along.

The chill of her touch was obviously causing him pain; he was gasping as well as shivering, his face twisted. They'd left Vangerdahast behind a long time before, or so it seemed, but, were only—what?—three passages along.

As they turned into a fourth, Alusair sighed at what they'd all been reduced to. "Are you going to last as far as where the healing magics are cached?"

"Have . . . to . . . ," Elminster snarled, ducking his head and shuddering.

"Don't die on me, Old Mage! *Don't you die on me!*"

"Die while a spirited lass has her fingers inside me? No fear! *Ahhh*, blast ye, that hurts! I'm . . . I'm too old for this!"

"Hah! Stop me vitals!" she joked.

Elminster smiled a little sadly. "Already happened, remember?"

Alusair took advantage of her spectral state to become long and thin, so she could thrust herself around ahead of him and swing her head back to face his and give him a dark look. "*Thank* you for farrukin' reminding me, *Old Mage*."

Elminster winced. "You play with sharp claws out."

"Always did," she said softly. "Would again, if I had it all to do over again. Folk *respect* sharp claws and sneer at those who are nice and kindly. Wish it were otherwise, but . . . 'tis not. Damn the gods."

"Look," Arclath told the coldly frowning wizard, "I was meeting with Lady Glathra and the king himself, and—"

"No doubt you were," the wizard of war replied grimly. "Yet the Lady Glathra has left the palace on . . . secret Crown business, and my orders are very clear. All nobles are to absent themselves from the palace until invited inside for council. No exceptions, and no excuses accepted. You have a home of your own to go to, and I'm sure you know the way there, Lord Delcastle. Your journey begins yonder."

His imperiously pointing hand indicated exterior doors that two Purple Dragons—who were not very carefully suppressing smirks—were drawing open. Arclath eyed the wall of Purple Dragons right behind the coldly firm mage, inclined his head in polite defeat, and turned for the door.

"Mind you inform Glathra—or the king—at your first sight of either of them that you conducted me out of the palace, and that I can be found at Delcastle Manor," he told the wizard, turning on his heel in the doorway to do so. "I suspect a failure on your part to do as much will not go over well—and were I you, I might risk royal displeasure, but the wrath of the Lady Glathra, now . . ."

At least one of the Purple Dragons chuckled.

Which was when there was a sudden commotion behind Arclath, and he spun around in time to see that one of the Dragons at the door had thrust a spear out to bar the path of a weathered old man in even more battered leather clothing—and the old man had jerked on the spear, hauled the soldier within reach, got him in an armlock, and spun him around to make him into a living shield against the spear of the other door guard.

"Is this the way ye greet arriving lords of Waterdeep, now?" he demanded gruffly.

The wizard of war stepped forward, reaching for a wand at his belt—and Arclath took great pleasure in clapping a hand around the mage's wrist and snapping, "Try to avoid a diplomatic disaster, Saer Wizard!"

"Stirge!" one of the Dragons behind the sputtering mage shouted suddenly, pointing out the open door.

The battered old man spun around, the Dragon under his arm struggling but being dragged with him—and lashed out with a dagger that had suddenly appeared in his hairy free hand.

Gutted and with one wing sliced through, the flapping stirge tumbled to the ground, where the old man brought a firm boot down on its head.

"Stirges? In daylight, at the very doors of the palace?" the wizard snarled, struggling to wrench his arm free of Arclath's grip.

"It's the pet of the Lord Marlin Stormserpent," Arclath informed him. "Or was."

"And what was it doing out and about?" a Dragon growled. "He sent it?"

Arclath frowned. "We can but guess." He looked the wizard straight in the eye, as they stood nose to nose, and added, "Unless you'd like to do something of *real* service to the Crown—and go and ask him?"

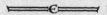

Elminster shook his vials out of his boots, then decided he didn't need them, and put them back. The healing potions Alusair had poured down him were enough. He was back to being as good as he got, these days.

"Storm," he asked the ghostly princess sadly, "what was left of her?"

"Nothing," Alusair told him. "Did you not feel her ring working? Right in the heart of the blast, it took her away somewhere. No, there wasn't a trace of her—not one drop—in the crypt."

She watched him peel off the last of the shattered armor. "Now I've one to ask you, El. Who hurled that spell at you?"

The Sage of Shadowdale shrugged. "A wizard?" he offered helpfully. "Lass, I know not. Truly."

"One of the wizards of war you didn't manage to kill recently?" Alusair asked a little coolly.

Elminster shrugged again. "Life wasn't simple a century ago, but I used to know a *little* about what was going on right around me. A little."

Manshoon frowned. Who was this gruff old man who tossed Purple Dragons about fearlessly and called himself a lord of Waterdeep? The man was just then lurching off down the promenade with the rolling gait of a sailor . . . could it be one of Elminster's disguises?

Surely not. Yet the man seemed somehow familiar. Seen long before, in, yes, Waterdeep . . .

Oh, surely not. Mirt? It couldn't be.

Or could it?

Manshoon shook his head.

It *was*, by Bane: Mirt the Moneylender. Once Mirt the Merciless, and still not a man anyone should turn his back on. He peered intently into the scene . . .

Mirt stood in the middle of a busy Suzail street and cursed bitterly.

The taverns and clubs of Cormyr's capital were deafeningly crowded bastions of revelry this day, to be sure, awash in excited nobles and their servants making merry on the eve of some grand council or other.

Every last one of them he'd managed to get a reply from was stone-cold certain it was the Year of the Ageless One. Which meant nigh a century had passed, somehow, and Asper and Durnan and nigh all the folk he'd ever known were long dead.

Naed.

Well, those two lordlings' purses would be empty long before morning, buying him what he needed to get very, very drunk.

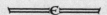

Two floors above where Alusair's healing potions had been cached, and at the far end of another wing of the vast and grandly sprawling palace, was a state chamber so remote from the great rooms of state that it was very seldom used.

Yet to those who liked crimson draperies and soft, over-stuffed beds of matching hues, the Room of the Fire Wyrm was a favorite. It had become so favored for trysts among the palace staff, in fact, that the war wizards had taken possession of its keys almost forty years earlier, and had kept it shut up ever since, except when one of them was present.

One of them was there right then. She had locked the doors from the inside after entering, and she was not alone.

Raereene was her name, and at that moment she wore only a hungry expression and her long, glossy fall of blue-black hair. The young palace server atop her, Kreane, was gasping out her name repeatedly as panting passion seized them both.

Their ardor might have more than cooled if they'd known who was watching them through the eyes of the smiling portrait of King Duar, which hung across the room, facing the great lamp-studded hanging sculpture of the fire wyrm for which the cavern was named.

Princess Alusair Obarskyr had ridden and been ridden by many panting men in her day, and her eyes were two ghostly flames of hunger and longing as Elminster came up beside her in the secret passage.

Without a word, he put his hand on where her shoulder would have been had it been solid, and he bent to look through the eyes of Duar's queen, where she'd been painted pressed happily against his shoulder.

"Gods," Alusair growled quietly, "I miss this!"

"As do I," Elminster muttered. "As do I. Yet enjoy the memories, lass; isn't that why ye made them? Hmm?"

Alusair gave him an angry glare. "*Wizards* may *decide* to 'make' memories," she hissed. "Sane folk do not."

Elminster shrugged. "No wonder all those sane folk are so forgetful, and so much evil and confusion flourishes as a result."

He bent his head and devoted himself to peering through the eyes of the portrait, enjoying the view of the lovers.

"Aren't you going to go down there?" Alusair teased, passing a hand through him.

Elminster winced, and it turned into an involuntary shiver; her "touch" had a chill that was almost heart-stopping. "And frighten or mortify them into rousing the whole palace in their terror? And *never* helping us, all the rest of their lives, befall what may? Playing the randy old goat got me a surprisingly long way a century ago, and for about a thousand years before that, but I've tired of it. And grown increasingly bad at it, too. I mean, look ye at what's left of me, lass! Who's going to be charmed by *this*?"

"Blind women with numb fingers," Alusair replied promptly.

After a moment of shared struggling to throttle mirth into silence, they sniggered together.

"Seen enough?" Alusair teased a while later.

"Nay, lass, but—forgive me—ye're too cold for me to tarry near any longer. My old bones . . ."

"I know," the ghost princess replied sadly. "I know. 'Tis why I'm watching yon lovers; they're making me feel warm. Go, then, old friend, and fare you well. New kitchen fires will be lit by now, down nigh the stableyard doors, for the baking. Take the passage along behind the ovens, and you'll feel warm enough, right soon."

"Thank ye," Elminster whispered, patting a shoulder his hand plunged through, leaving his fingers feeling like icicles.

Frowning in pain, he turned away and walked slowly along the passage.

Azuth and Mystra, if he could hand over his tasks and causes to one like Alusair! The Steel Princess as she'd been in life, that is, not the ghost she had become . . .

If only . . . nay. That way lay madness and an utter waste of his thoughts and time. He had one successor to hand, and little else to choose from.

Amarune Whitewave was what he had to work with, and she was young and strong and vigorous and . . . would have to do.

Yet she must still be won over from thinking him some sort of crazed old fool who lusted after her or who was too madwits to need heeding at all, to, well, embracing her heritage.

"I *can't* trust anyone else," he muttered aloud. "Everyone else will end up saving the Realms for *themselves* to rule."

Idly he tapped a spot on the passage wall where he'd have hidden a door if he'd been building this part of the royal palace—and a long-hidden door obligingly groaned open. To reveal a passage, complete with a spike-studded trap. A trap that had claimed a . . . war wizard, by the looks of him. Walled up for centuries and mummified into a withered, dessicated husk in his robes.

Something winked at Elminster from the throat of those robes. A pendant—enchanted, of course; that was where the glow had come from—dangling from the shriveled remnant of a neck.

"Ah," he said, brightening. "This will do, indeed. Alassra can be herself again. For a little while."

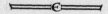

It was early evening, and it didn't seem that long since Tress had dragged Amarune out of a deep sleep and had told her to get ready and take the stage.

The snakeskins merchant was close with his coins and was one of those whose eyes burned into her flesh even as he dared not get bolder, but he'd been a good patron for three years, and seemed honest enough. His name was Raoryndar or Rindlar, or some such.

So when he'd told the others at the table Amarune was dancing above about three lordlings scouring the city menacing everyone with their swords, to yield up any hand axes they might own, she'd believed him—and promptly had left the stage, hurriedly pulled on her clothes, and hastened for Delcastle Manor.

Arclath had told her more about those three since they'd brawled in the Dragonriders' . . . he must know about it right swiftly, must—

Amarune found herself coming to a rather breathless halt in front of the gates of Delcastle Manor sooner than she'd thought she'd be. "L-Lorold?" she asked, by the hole next to the knocker. "May I speak with Arcl—the Lord Delcastle?"

The porter slid open his spy plate, and she was aware of the guards stepping forward to peer at her through the bars.

"Lady Amarune," the porter greeted her formally. "You are welcome, if you'll accept our escort to the house proper. The Lord Delcastle is at home and has given orders that you are to be admitted, if you come alone."

"I *am* alone," Amarune assured him, sighing with relief. The gates had already been unchained and opened just enough to let someone slip through, and the tallest of the guards—there were four of them, this time—was standing in that gap, beckoning her. She followed him, smiling as pleasantly to the others as if they weren't holding ready crossbows not *quite* aimed at her, on down the sweeping path that led to the looming mansion. He immediately waved her past him, then unshuttered a lantern and followed her, just to one side, holding the lantern low and shining it on the path ahead to light her way.

Either the porter had a means of signaling, or the manor guards watched for approaching lanterns, because the doors of the great house stood open between watchful guards, with a steward waiting and two housejacks waving mistballs on long poles to try to keep night insects from entering.

Wordlessly the steward smiled and bowed low to Amarune, then beckoned her and led the way within, one of the housejacks smoothly taking her cloak from her shoulders as she went.

Amarune heard the doors being shut behind her as her guiding servant hastened through the lofty entry hall, leading her to the left and avoiding the grand sweeping stairs that led up into the warmly lit great rooms above.

They passed through a door and into a darkened parlor, where the steward spoke for the first time. "Lady, are you here to see Lady Delcastle? Or the younger or elder Lord Delcastle?"

"Torold," a crisp, harsh feminine voice said out of the darkness ahead, "she's certainly not here to see *me*. At least not by my invitation. Has Arclath taken to trying to sneak his strumpets in through the *front* doors? As if they—"

"I—ah, pray pardon—," Amarune began hesitantly, at the same time as the steward turned to her, bowed low, and announced, "The Lady Marantine Delcastle!"

"Lights, dolt!" the unseen Lady Delcastle snapped, and lanterns were unhooded by a servant to reveal her standing in a wide doorway flanked by two unsmiling bodyguards in armor, glaring at Amarune and the steward.

At the same time as a door swung wide in another wall to admit light and the young scion of House Delcastle.

"Arclath!" Amarune cried. "Urgent news!"

"Amarune!" he exclaimed in delight, striding to her and reaching out in greeting.

Mother frowned at son. "Arclath? Do you *know* this wench? She looks common—*hmmph*, worse than that, either a strumpet or a thief, or both—to me!"

Arclath gave her a bright smile and said almost jovially, "I'm sure to palace courtiers *we* look strange, Mother!"

Firmly he took hold of Amarune's hand and drew her to yet another door, murmuring to the steward, "Torold, light the lamps in the receiving room for us."

"If yon wench is from the palace, *I'm* the queen of Aglarond!" Lady Delcastle declared scornfully. "You'll have nothing to do with her that I don't see and hear!"

"Suit yourself, Mother," Arclath called calmly back over a shoulder that was busy shrugging.

The receiving room had been made for a large Delcastle family to greet as large a family of guests; under the glare of Arclath's mother, Amarune felt as if she was in some sort of hall of trial, standing alone at the center of its gleaming marble floor. Arclath whirled away to a sideboard—gods, did nobles have ready rows of decanters in every room of their vast houses?—and poured her a drink, unbidden, while Amarune stood blushing and silent.

"Before you blurt out whatever's most urgent," he told her, obviously trying to set her at ease while his mother stared right through her with eyes like the points of two drawn daggers, "have a sip, and tell me what *else* is riding your mind."

Somewhat hesitantly, Amarune said, "Ah—uh—much news from city taverns and eateries of elder members of the nobility, newly arrived in Suzail for the council." She sipped, winced at the strength and fire of the strong wine, choked it down, and added, "Brawls, the chasing and slaughtering of a live pig with swords, servants being flung from upper windows, a cart set on fire . . ."

Her voice trailed away under Lady Delcastle's darkening scowl, but Arclath chuckled and waved a dismissive hand. "The usual. The elder lords indulging all of their longtime feuds and vices, many of which must seem odd or even suspicious to the rest of the realm. Right, then, out with it: the reason you came rushing here to see me."

"The coin you offered her to satisfy your animal lusts here in our house, of course," Lady Delcastle told the ceiling. "Probably on the scullery floor or over the arm of a handy lounge in *my* foreparlor." Her expressionless bodyguards seemed to *lean* toward Amarune, as if they were impatient to topple onto her and crush her.

Amarune kept her eyes on Arclath, swallowed unhappily, and sighed, knowing she was going to blurt and babble like a youngling, but not knowing how to say it better. "Three lords you know, of about your age," she began. "Windstag, Dawntard, and Sornstern. The news is all over the city; they spent last night through hunting *everywhere* for a particular axe—a hand axe! Drawing steel on folk, turning rooms out, offering coin, threatening—"

"*What?*" Arclath and his mother roared in unison.

Arclath strode toward Amarune, waving furiously at a sputtering Lady Delcastle—who was launching into a tirade about "selfish, ill-behaved young nobles"—for silence. Surprisingly, he got it.

And promptly filled it again by starting to think aloud. "Windstag, of *course*. Always up for a little mayhem, and Sornstern's his lickspittle, but Dawntard has wits to set the other two to his bidding. And those three run with four rather more formidable lordlings too: Marlin Stormserpent, Mellast Ormblade, Irlin Stonestable, and Sacrast Handragon."

"Just as I said!" Lady Delcastle snapped. "The young rakes, the reckless, care-nothing idiots who'll have all Cormyr at swords drawn—"

"*Exactly!*" Arclath roared, whirling right beside Amarune—who flinched away from him involuntarily—to stride back across the room, waving his arms angrily.

"What are they *doing*?" he snarled. "The war wizard's'll have their guts for *soup*, if the king doesn't, first! Setting the city into uproar on the very *eve* of the council!"

"Exactly," Amarune agreed, daring to interrupt because the moment seemed right. "What are they thinking?"

Arclath whirled to face her, his eyes afire. "Well, we'll have to find out, before things get any worse."

"How?" Amarune asked.

"We'll go and ask them!" he replied fiercely.

His mother laughed merrily. "And you think they'll just tell you? Because you're a fellow noble?"

Arclath whirled to face her. "No," he snarled, "because I'll be holding the point of my sword at the throat of whomever

I'm asking. I've found a man generally prefers to talk and live, rather than keep silent and die!"

He rushed out a door, reappeared almost immediately with sword and cloak in hand, and dashed across the receiving room and out the door Amarune had been brought in through.

Leaving Amarune and the Lady Marantine Delcastle to exchange startled glances and follow him.

Where they found the front doors of Delcastle Manor already open, and Arclath gone.

"Aye, the Lord has departed," one of the door guards offered in answer to Amarune's wild look around. Without a word Amarune hurried to the door, remembering only at the last moment to turn and bow in farewell to Lady Delcastle.

Where she saw a doorjack scurrying off, obviously to retrieve her cloak—and Arclath's mother looking after him, then back at Amarune. After a bare moment of hesitation, Lady Delcastle snatched her own cloak from the other doorjack and tossed it to Amarune—who caught it out of long habit of being on the stage and stared back at the noblewoman in astonishment.

There was a strange look on Lady Delcastle's face. "Keep it," she blurted. "And—and look after him!"

"Lady," Amarune replied gravely in thanks and salute, bowing low again. Then she sprang up and sprinted out into the night, the cloak swirling around her as she went.

Chapter
THIRTY-FIUE

A Great Magic Unleashed

Whenever some bright-eyed fool
Starts to talk that it's high time some great magic
Was unleashed, I itch to take myself off right smartly
Into the next realm. Or the one beyond that.

> Markuld Amryntur,
> *Twenty Summers a Dragon: One Soldier's Tale*
> published in the Year of the Splendors Burning

Mirt followed his second coinlass of the evening up a none-too-clean flight of stairs, a bottle and two metal flagons in one hand and a somewhat-gnawed leg of steaming mutton clutched in his other.

"Been a long time, lass," he told her shapely backside happily. "A *long* time . . ."

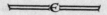

Manshoon frowned in his scrying as he watched Mirt eagerly ascending the stairs, still pondering what use to make of the infamous lord of Waterdeep.

"Well," he murmured, "he'll keep for now, at least. I have more important targets to savage."

Marlin Stormserpent was in a foul temper. He and a similarly terse Broryn Windstag were nursing headaches and huddling in bandages; they both snarlingly turned aside queries about how they'd acquired their wounds.

Marlin leaned forward to glare down his meeting table and tell his conspirators, "This is all that's left of us. Delasko and Kathkote are abed, healing, and will be for days. We must be *very* careful during the council; someone is on to us."

Before the excited talk could get going, he added sourly, "And not the war wizards, either. Someone able to hire wizards as powerful as Larak Dardulkyn."

"Windstag lives," Sacrast Handragon pointed out. "So the hunt for the hand axe succeeded?"

"It was found," Marlin replied flatly, "but proved an utter failure. We gained no slayer who'll obey us, but let loose some fat old thief of a lord of Waterdeep who obeys only himself and fled from us!"

He lurched up out of his seat and told the table grimly, "So the scheme of harming the king or the crown prince in an 'accident' when plenty of nobles are gathered for the council to take the blame will have to be abandoned."

No one looked surprised. Handragon and Ormblade confirmed for him again that they would be attending the council to represent their families, and Stormserpent asked them to watch and listen for any talk of himself or any of them or their activities—such as the hunt for the hand axe—or any denunciation of younger nobles. If the Crownsilvers or Illances or any of the other oldblood families tried to wrest even more power for themselves, they must be vigorously denounced.

"The rest of us," Marlin advised, "would do best to stay away from council. We can move swiftly, ere everyone departs the city when all the formal clack and chatter is done, to reach disaffected nobles if need arises."

Handragon smiled. "And it will."

"This will be dangerous, you know," Arclath told Amarune severely. "You shouldn't . . ."

His voice trailed away under the heat of her fierce glare, and he managed to add only, "Sorry."

"Accepted," she told him, putting a hand out from under his mother's cloak to touch his arm.

Then close around it like a claw and drag him back, pointing with her other hand even before he could start to curse.

An old man in flapping sea boots and leathers was lurching and wheezing along the street ahead in purposeful haste, bared sword in hand.

Stalking along in his wake and closing in on him fast were two figures wreathed and cloaked in crawling blue flames.

The old man cast a swift glance back over his shoulder at his pursuers, but kept going.

"Arclath Delcastle," Amarune hissed fiercely, holding onto the young lord's sword arm for all she was worth, "*don't* you throw your life away trying to fight those—"

A patrol horn sounded, and the street was suddenly full of Purple Dragons—and the bright burst of a spell that blossomed all around the two flaming men and sang a weird cacophony as it sought to harden and the men fought to get free of it.

The old man kept running, if that lurching shuffle could be termed a run.

"Come," Arclath said sharply, ducking down an alleyway that led in the direction the old man was going. "I—we—need answers."

"Doesn't everyone?" Amarune replied as they started to sprint.

His conspirators had departed, leaving Marlin Stormserpent pacing his rooms too excited—and in too much pain—to seek slumber. He contemplated forcing one of the maids to rut with him, but fancied none of them; the few he'd taken were familiar goods and hadn't been all that entrancing the first time around. No, it was time to hire a playpretty instead...

He rang for one of his trusties, and Whelandrin answered the summons. Marlin sent the impassive older man out into the streets to hire "a tall, dark, buxom lass—with most of her teeth,

mind, and *not* sporting a face like an old boot or my backside—
from the House of the Lynx, or the Lady Murmurs Yes, or
the Blackflame Curtain. Give her ten lions and the promise of
twenty more for my choice of deeds until dawn; no disfiguring,
no floggings."

Still carefully expressionless, Whelandrin bowed and took
his leave.

The old man whirled around with a snarl, blade flashing
up at Arclath's throat—but the heir of House Delcastle had
already backed out of reach.

"Keep clear!" the old man growled warningly, ere turning to
lurch another few steps—only to stumble as Amarune rolled
right in front of his shins, her dagger up warningly.

"We don't want bloodshed," Arclath said firmly, "just to
talk. I'm Lord Delcastle, and this is . . . the Lady Amarune."

"I'm still Mirt," the old man rumbled, "lord of Waterdeep.
So speak." His sword point moved from one of them to the
other with the sure, deft speed of a longtime bladesman.

"Where are you headed?"

"Stormserpent Towers," the old man snapped. "To kill the
young bull-behind who set those two flaming killers on me, so
I can command them myself—or to force him to call them off."

"Would that bull-behind be Lord Marlin Stormserpent?"

"'Marlin' I know not, but aye, the young lord in Stormserpent towers."

"Let us take care of him," Arclath said grimly. "If you go
straight to the palace and tell any wizard of war—"

"*Hah.* They wanted us well gone, remember?"

"Their spells are still your best chance at safety. If you
stand arguing with them and those two come to take you, the
wizards'll blast them out of fear for their own hides."

Mirt gave Arclath a thoughtful frown then backed away.
"It rubs me wrong to let someone else fight for me, but aye, ye
speak wisdom. I'll do that. May ye taste victory!"

As more patrol horns roared from where the flaming ghosts were confined, he lurched off in the direction of the palace, looking back warily several times.

Amarune and Arclath exchanged glances.

"I begin to admire you, Lord Delcastle," the mask dancer told him quietly. "Don't spoil it by daring to suggest I remain behind."

Arclath grinned and spread his hands. "I'd not dream of it!"

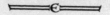

Alusair heard the scuff of swiftly moving boots behind her, and turned.

Elminster was looking grim. "Young Delcastle—ye know him?"

"Yes. You cast a tracer on him?"

"I used one of your Obarskyr baubles to let me spy on him. He's just passed through the wards of Stormserpent Towers. Young Rune is with him."

"You want to be there," the ghost said softly. "Right now. Why not cast a teleport?"

"Because I go raving mad when I work magic, that's why," El snarled.

Alusair made a sound that might have been a giggle. "And the rest of us would notice the difference in you *how*, exactly?"

Elminster gave her a baleful glare.

"Tarry a moment," she whispered, sliding past him like a chill wind.

A few moments later she returned, leading a bewildered, half-dressed Raereene—with a scared-looking Kreane right behind them.

"Teleport this man into the forehall of Stormserpent Towers," the Ghost Regent commanded crisply. "Just as carefully as you know how."

Raereene frowned. "Wh—"

"Wizards of war no longer obey royal commands?" Alusair hissed, her eyes suddenly two cold flames.

"Or mine?" quavered a thin voice from the floor below.

Raereene looked down—and recoiled.

"What ails you?" the dark spiderlike thing in front of her feet demanded. "Haven't you ever seen a Royal Magician before?"

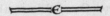

Silently Whelandrin showed a tall, dark, and buxom woman into Marlin Stormserpent's private chambers. She wore a nightcloak over high boots and a silken gown, and—

Marlin frowned. There was a taller, darker, cloaked and cowled figure right behind her, who'd just slipped something to Whelandrin; Marlin caught a glimpse of gleaming gold before his trusty was gone.

"Who are you?" he demanded, waving the girl aside with one hand while drawing his sword with the other and sweeping it up to menace his mysterious visitor.

Who threw back the cowl to reveal a sardonically smiling face. It belonged to Lord Arclath Delcastle, who was suddenly taking a swift sidestep to put a solid stone wall at his back.

"Well met," he greeted Marlin pleasantly. "You look *much* more handsome here, in proper light, than skulking around in shadows by night in the royal palace."

Stormserpent stiffened. "What're you talking about?"

"I speak of a certain chalice," Arclath murmured. "Sadly missing from its longtime hiding place. Sadly missed by some."

"War wizards?"

"Ah, I *knew* Marlin Stormserpent wasn't slow-witted. I was certain he'd grasp at once what I was speaking of, even at such an hour."

"What're you doing here?" Marlin snapped, hefting his sword meaningfully as he took a step forward.

Arclath waved an airily dismissive hand. "Merely seeking an answer or two, not a duel. Which is why I came protected by magic that will end any duel before it begins. So, no swordplay, just a few words between us, and I'll leave you to your pleasure."

He glanced at the playpretty, who was standing to one side listening to them rather fearfully.

"A few *carefully* chosen words, on my part," Arclath hinted.

"Well?" Marlin asked curtly.

"Why? Why all the secret meetings, the hunts for hand axes, the men in flames?"

"I . . . I seek a better Cormyr. I *deserve* a better Cormyr."

Arclath nodded. "As do I. Unfortunately for friendly accord between us now, that does not mean we agree on what 'better' is. You desire a Cormyr that is better *for you*. Yet you lack the vision—and honesty—to even admit this."

Marlin Stormserpent flourished his sword, snarling an insult.

Arclath sighed. "Ah, the besetting fault of the nobility— having temper tantrums whenever someone disagrees with them. *Such* shining leadership for the realm."

"And you think House Delcastle is better than House Stormserpent, I suppose?" Marlin sneered.

"I think nothing of the sort. I *know* I'm a wastrel, and freely admit it. Would such candor cost you so much? Oh, wait, I was forgetting. Candor is your greatest foe, given the laws of the realm and the presence of war wizards in it."

"How did you learn so much?" Marlin hissed.

Arclath regarded his fingertips idly and told them, "In conspiracies, someone always talks."

"Do you mind," Marlin asked coldly, "leaving my *home*, so I can enjoy my hired company?"

"Not at all," Arclath replied with a smile. "I have the answers I came for. You need not fear the dawn on my account."

"Good," Marlin snapped, ringing the bell for Whelandrin.

Arclath did not wait to be escorted. When the trusty appeared, Marlin snarled, "Make *very* sure the man you brought in is gone from our house and grounds, and the gates locked against him and all others. Be *swift*."

Whelandrin bowed and hastened away, and Marlin shot a look at the chalice and blade, wondering if he should send his slayers after Arclath.

No. Not with the lass there; no one must see him calling them forth.

With a shrug he turned to her charms, pouring his anger into being brutal to her. "Strip!" he ordered harshly.

She promptly doffed cloak and gown and started on her boots, but he grabbed her elbow in an iron-hard grip and snapped, "Leave them on, and get you to yon bed!"

She gasped in pain but managed to murmur, "My *lord*, be gentler!"

By way of reply he backhanded her across her chest with all his strength and snarled, "Get on that bed! Think of twenty golden lions, and keep your mouth shut."

"Yes, Lord," she whimpered, hurrying to obey.

"A moment, lad," an unfamiliar man's voice said sharply from the far end of the room.

Marlin spun around. "Who—"

"Call back thy slayers," his gaunt old visitor snapped. "Half the Dragons and war wizards in Suzail are fighting them right now—and being led here as they do."

By way of reply, Marlin Stormserpent sneered and strode to snatch up the Flying Blade from a sidetable. "Get out! Whoever you are, get—"

"Elminster's the name," the old man told him cheerfully as he tossed a handful of metal vials under the noble's boots.

Marlin slipped, smooth metal rolling under his feet. He made a wild grab for his sword, got it—and went down helplessly, dragging the table down atop himself.

A moment later, the Wyverntongue Chalice came down on his head, and Cormyr went away very suddenly.

"Satisfyingly solid," Elminster remarked approvingly to the woman on the bed. "Ye might want to leave now, before—"

"*It's too late?*" a coldly malicious voice said in his ear out of a sudden roiling glow, just before it claimed him in a savage roar of unleashed magic.

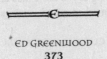

ED GREENWOOD

373

"I've business inside, look ye," the old man in battered leathers with the sword in his hand said truculently. "Stand aside."

The Purple Dragons stopped smiling tolerantly and lowered their spears to point at his chest.

"Saer wizard?" one of them called to alert the duty wizard of war behind them.

The response was a grunt and several swift thuds, as if something heavy had fallen. One Dragon started to turn.

Only to grunt in his turn and topple forward. His fellow soldier had just time to stare at him, before joining him.

"Mirt," Storm Silverhand said delightedly from behind the men she'd felled. "Come in, and be welcome! It's been *years*!"

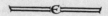

Elminster opened his eyes, feeling weak and scorched.

He was in the royal palace, in a small stone room he'd seen a time or two before. A chamber with stone benches built along two walls, closed doors in the other two, and a table in the center of the room.

Storm Silverhand was lying on it, faceup, dead or senseless. Elminster staggered to her to see which.

Her eyes opened, her gaze seeming different from Storm's, somehow, as he bent over to murmur, "Lass?"

Needlelike pincers erupted out of her to impale him.

Spewing blood, eyes wide in disbelief and pain, Elminster staggered back—and up through the body of the woman that wasn't Storm, bursting it apart like so much wet custard and rending the table and floor from beneath, came a gigantic beholder.

Large and dark it loomed, surrounded not just by its long, writhing forest of eyestalks, but by tentacles that ended in grasping pincers.

"No more meddling, Elminster," it purred in a wet, gloating voice. "No more guiding your precious Forest Kingdom this way and that, sneering as you move men about like pieces on a chessboard. All your schemes and strivings end here and now."

Two pincers snared Elminster's hands—and snipped them off at the wrists.

Blood spurted, and the old man reeled.

"Yes, the moment of my revenge has come at last, Elminster of Shadowdale. As you die your final death—your oh-so-overdue passing. All your mantles and wards and contingencies stripped away, drained, and used, down long and patient years of watching and sending you foes, and 'accidents,' and *unfortunate* concidences. *Outwitting* you, arrogant Aumar. There were more of me than you thought there were—so this last one of me will outlast *you*. Now embrace oblivion in fitting agony, knowing it is I, Manshoon, who has slain you!"

Magic lashed out from eyestalks to blast Elminster, driving him to his knees. He fought gaspingly to find breath enough to scream, his arms seared off at the shoulder, his body aflame. And failed.

"I kill you now in the name of Symgharyl, and so many of my selves, and much of the best blood of the Brotherhood. *Die*, old fool!"

More eyestalks let fly, and the kneeling man was reduced to ashes—

—that slumped down into swirling ruin, even as the eye tyrant bellowed out mighty laughter and teleported away, leaving only the rolling echoes of its mirth behind.

"Stormserpent's behind it all," Arclath panted as they sprinted for the palace together. "The flaming men—all of it. We'll just have to hope Glathra's there—or *someone* who'll listen to me!"

"I wonder where Elminster is," Amarune gasped. "He's crazed enough to step in, where our precious wizards of war won't!"

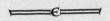

Alusair raced like a furious whirlwind. Storm rushed after her, Mirt pounding along at her heels, into a little stone room where . . . human blood and innards were spattered everywhere.

And a heap of faintly glowing enchanted trinkets she recognized, amid ashes . . . Elminster.

Or all that was left of him.

Silver fire was winking and glowing like fireflies among a swirl of ashes on the floor, and her own body winked and glowed in response; she had no doubt she was gazing at his remains.

"No," Storm whispered, lips trembling. "No. Damn you, El, not like this! Not without giving me a chance to bid you farewell! *I loved you, Elminster Aumar!* Mystra damn me, but I loved you!"

Elminster's ashes rippled over the floor and rose into a spike that became a faltering pillar . . . and took on a vaguely manlike shape.

"And I love ye, too," he whispered hollowly. "Though perhaps I should say 'What is left of me' loves ye."

He'd survived! In undeath or something like it, but—

Storm burst into tears and rushed to embrace him.

Causing him to be reduced to swirling ashes—which promptly streamed down her bodice and the rest of her, making her gasp in startled pleasure ere they raced down one of her legs to the floor. There they rose again into a little hump, from which lifted a headlike shape.

"Always wanted to do that," Elminster said in satisfaction.

Behind them arose a strange chorus of mirth. Mirt the Moneylender and the ghost of Alusair were both chuckling.

Chapter
THIRTY-SIX

A New Blade Drawn

I tell you 'tis a good day, though not for some dogs!
For behold! The long-hidden has been found,
And a new blade drawn,
Oh, there'll be blood and fun tonight!

> Said by Tarlangarr the Warrior in Act I, Scene IV of
> *Too Many Skulls Underfoot*, anonymously chapbook-
> published in the Year of the Seven Sisters

S omeone felled those guards," Arclath snarled. "Treason!
Slayers seeking the king! I—"

"Save your breath for running," Amarune puffed, "or
we'll—"

"Run right into the new ruler of Cormyr before you have
any clever plan ready?" A triumphant, liquid voice bubbled
from a dark open door ahead.

Out of it drifted something round and many-tentacled,
some of those tentacles ending in pincers. There were eyestalks
among them, too, and a huge single eye in the flying central
body, above a wide, crookedly smiling fanged maw.

"Name of the Dragon!" Arclath gasped, skidding to a halt
and throwing out an arm to stop Amarune. "It's a . . . a beholder!"

The passage exploded.

Flung headlong, Amarune was vaguely aware of Arclath
being hurled past her and a woman's voice snapping furiously,
"Not anymore, it isn't!"

Then she slammed into something very hard, and Cormyr
went away in a hurry.

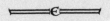

"Well done, Raereene," the manlike shape of ashes whispered as they watched a dark, wraithlike thing of tatters flee wailing from the spattered ruin of the eye tyrant's body, with the ghost of Alusair flying in hot pursuit, teeth bared.

The beautiful young wizard of war managed not to recoil, this time. She aimed the great scepter in her hands at the new menace—before the firm hands of a silver-haired woman and an old man in floppy boots and battered leathers took it away from her.

"Yon's a friend and defender of Cormyr," Mirt told her. "Don't be blasting him, now."

Storm turned. "El, your lass! Is she—?"

"Just dazed. Her young gallant's out cold, though."

Cormyr came back, confusingly. Amarune blinked up into a smiling face framed in long, flowing, silver hair. Gentle hands were cradling her.

"Y-you're Storm, aren't you? Storm Silverhand?"

"Yes."

"And you're thousands of years old."

"Not yet, Amarune. I just *feel* thousands of years old, most days."

"Whereas I *am* thousands of years old," said an eerie whisper in Amarune's ear. She turned her head and found herself nose to nose with a vague man-shape of ashes that was staring right back at her.

She fainted again.

"You're *sure* she's ready?" Storm asked wryly.

"I'm sure," Elminster snapped back. "Cast the spell."

"What spe—oh, no. El, no. You can't do this to her."

"No, I can't, not when I'm reduced to this. So ye'll have to do it."

"No, El. No, I . . . no."

"Do *ye* know of anyone else who can—and will—try to save the Realms? And if ye do, do ye trust them? *Hey?*"

Storm shook her head helplessly, looked down at Amarune—and burst into tears.

"We can't, El. We must *not*."

"There is no 'must not,' lass," El told Storm. "We must do whatever we must, or this young maid ye're trying to defend from me—and everyone else we care for—will be smashed down and slain and swept away, sooner or later—"

"Must not what?" came a soft mumble from the floor. Amarune was gazing blearily up at them. "Is . . . is that you, Great-Grandsire Elminster? Something made you . . . undead?"

"Yes, 'tis me. Though call me 'El'; we're family, lass, family! And I'm busy trying to convince thy great-grand-aunt—or whatever she is; I could never keep all those terms straight—to cast a spell that I can't, now that I'm ashes."

"What spell?"

"A spell that will let me ride thy body. Sit in thy mind and move thy limbs and voice to my bidding."

Amarune stared up at them—the eerie mask of ash and the pain-racked, silver-haired woman. As their eyes met, Storm nodded sadly, in confirmation.

Amarune went pale. "Will it hurt?" she asked hesitantly.

"Only if I make thee fall over," El replied.

"Will it . . . drive me mad?"

"No," he said firmly. "I do *not* use the clumsy mindpryings of war wizards, which drive the caster mad as often as the owner of the mind they're ruining. I promise ye, lass, that I'll treat thee like the greatest treasure, the most exalted princess, the most precious infant in all the Realms, if ye let me ride thy mind."

"And . . ." Amarune stared steadily up into the face of ash floating above her and swallowed. "And what if I have thoughts I'd rather not share with anyone? What then?"

"Those thoughts will be thine own. I'll not listen to them," Elminster assured her solemnly.

Beside him, Storm turned away so Amarune would not see the roll of her wise and weary eyes, but Rune's dark stare never strayed from the shape of ash arching over her.

"How I do I know I can trust you?" she whispered.

"Ye can't, lass. All ye can do is decide: Will ye have me—or will ye have the pryings of war wizards and madness?"

"If I choose you, what life will be left to me?"

"Just as much as I can aid thee in having," Elminster replied. "I've had centuries, but ye may not want that long. I promise thee, by the grave of thy mother, that I will not hasten thy time of dying."

"And how do you know where my mother's grave is?"

"I came too late to save her," Elminster replied, "but not too late to cast a spell on it that keeps grave robbers from despoiling her bones."

"Do it," Amarune said suddenly. "I want—I want not to have to fear war wizards or those who want Arclath dead or—or anyone else. *Do it!*"

"Thank ye, Amarune Aumar. Thank ye," Elminster replied and surged at Storm.

Who reluctantly cast a swift and simple spell, murmuring an incantation, kissing her own fingers, then putting them to Amarune's lips, breast, and loins.

"I'm sorry," she whispered as she did so. "Oh, Amarune, I'm so sorry."

The spell washed over Amarune with a faint singing sound and the briefest of flickering white glows, and was gone.

"Finally," Elminster growled, moving forward.

Storm grabbed at his arm, but her fingers passed through his ashes, stopping him not at all.

"El, no!" she hissed fiercely. "How much more can you stoop to embrace evil? This is nothing less, and daring what we must not! Yes, we're in desperate straits, but—"

"I'll ride her only briefly, to do what is needful, and then come out of her," Elminster hissed back. "Ye have my body as hostage to compel my obedience."

"Two handfuls of ashes? How can I hold *that* hostage?"

"Lass, lass, trust me. How often, down the centuries, have I failed ye?"

"I have lost count of the times," Storm replied bitterly, but the eerie shape of ashes slumped—and Amarune stirred, limbs flopping, jerked to her feet, and began a shambling, dragging walk around the room, arms flailing clumsily when they weren't dangling . . . a walk that smoothed out into more natural movements as Elminster slowly gained control.

The next circuit of the room looked like Amarune the dancer moving normally; she turned her head and carried herself as she usually did, and moved her hands as Amarune, not as an old archwizard trying to decide how a graceful young woman used her hands.

Storm Silverhand said fiercely, "You must ride her *only* when needful, and tell no one—and repay her for the use you make of her body . . . no matter how much she comes to hate us."

"Agreed," El replied solemnly in Amarune's voice but with Elminster's manner. "Now gather up my ashes in something, and we'll be out of here. So much magic has been hurled around that even wizards of war can't help but notice."

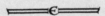

Ruthgul often thought he might not be the only grizzled old swindler in Suzail, but by the gods, he was one of the most successful.

Recently, he had even had some legitimate business errands. Which is what he was out and about seeing to at the moment, scuttling along various alleys.

He was growing increasingly astonished at what he was seeing in the streets of Suzail. Purple Dragon patrols were everywhere, and he was challenged repeatedly. Thankfully, his wagon held nothing but wine casks for various taverns, and he was searched and allowed to continue. Many times.

Returning to his wagon when it finally held nothing but empties, Ruthgul found himself astonished anew.

Amarune Whitewave was waiting for him, with a young and slightly bedraggled noble he knew by sight: Lord Arclath Delcastle. With them was a tall and strikingly beautiful silver-haired woman, who held a small coffer in her hands.

"We want to hire your wagon—and your discretion—to hide us and our friend, here, among your casks, until you've rumbled well out of the city," Amarune said crisply.

Ruthgul grimaced. "I—I'd like nothing better than to accommodate you, lass, but truth be told, I'm not *going* out of the city!"

Lord Delcastle stepped forward with a broad smile. "Ruthgul, perhaps the lady didn't make your choices clear enough."

He hefted a small cloth bag. "These gems can be yours, if you make the trip—or you can refuse and take this instead. Every finger of its bright and very sharp length." He hefted the point of his drawn sword meaningfully, smile never wavering.

Ruthgul swallowed then brightly observed that he'd just remembered he *did* have to leave the city on urgent business, *with* his wagon.

He leaned closer and added in a low growl, "But I fear for my life—or the custody of my wagon—the moment we're out of sight of the walls. What's to stop you just killing me?"

"This," Amarune told him, handing him the daintiest hand crossbow he'd ever seen, and three darts. "Ready it, aim it at one of us, and we can hopefully trust each other. So long as it doesn't go off by accident. That would be bad, see?"

Arclath and Amarune stood in the dappled sunlight of deep, mossy greenery and dark and massive leaning trees on the edge of the King's Forest with a weary Storm between them, her arms about their shoulders, watching Ruthgul's wagon rumble away.

"As promised," Storm murmured to Amarune. "Welcome back."

Amarune nodded a little shakily. "That was . . . it's going to take a lot of getting used to. When will—?"

"El be in your mind again? Only when it's needful."

"I should be on that wagon," Arclath growled. "The council . . ."

"Will unfold just fine without you. Mirt will speak for House Delcastle, and Raereene is watchful, with the Princess Alusair to spy for her."

Arclath sighed. "I very much want to know what the two of you are doing in Cormyr at all."

Storm nodded. "Trying to accomplish three things: One, save Cormyr from its present troubles—Stormserpent's treason, but also those behind him—plus other villainy that's gathering around this council and awaiting a good time to strike."

She looked meaningfully at Amarune. "Two, find a successor to take over the task of saving Cormyr and the rest of the Realms."

Amarune went pale. "I . . . I'm not sure I'm ready . . . or worthy."

"Good," Storm said with a sudden smile. "That reassures me greatly; you'll do fine. Three, gather up all magic items we can, to use them to do a good and necessary thing."

"Which is—?"

"Later, Arclath. I need a few answers, first. Where does Arclath Delcastle stand? What is Amarune to you, really? And whom do you serve first: yourself, the Delcastles, the Crown of Cormyr, or—?"

Arclath stared at Storm Silverhand for a moment then said slowly, "I regard Amarune as a *friend*. One I am honored to have, not a playpretty or someone to, ah, exploit. My lady, if she'll have me. And *yes*, after standing for her, I stand for Cormyr."

Storm smiled again. "And Rune, what matters most to you, right now?"

Amarune blushed, looked down, and told the toes of her boots, "Arclath's regard. After that, the loss of the life I had. If the war wizards know I'm the Silent Shadow . . ."

"And becoming mistress to a lord whose name may or may not be Delcastle seems less than attractive?"

"Lady Storm," Arclath said sharply, "those words try both my honor and that of this lady!"

"No doubt," Storm replied calmly. "Yet being as you leap to her defense, Lord Delcastle, I ask you: if the authorities know her past, what will Amarune do?"

A noble hand waved dismissively. "In half a day I could see her well placed in service to a dozen noble families, if she wishes."

Amarune's face told all the King's Forest around them how little this suggestion pleased her, and Arclath added hastily, "Or I have influence enough—with some *very* highly placed persons—to get her into the palace."

Amarune gave him a sidelong glance. "Oh? War wizards and palace guards like to watch barepelt lasses dance?"

Arclath nodded then reddened. "Yes, and . . . ah, other things."

Amarune's stare sharpened. "So what is a woman who does those 'other things' around the palace called? Bedwarmer? Bedmaid? Or something lower and ruder?"

Arclath winced, then said carefully, "Lady, I did not mean to give offense. I—oh, gods blast, I'm less than good at this . . ."

"Oh, I'd not say that," Amarune replied calmly. "So, would you expect to be a frequent patron of mine? Or will I be nightly facing a long line of snooty old courtiers?"

Some hours of walking later, Storm turned to Arclath a little wearily. "Are you leading us to the old royal hunting lodge?"

Arclath shook his head. "I know a better place. We want to be properly cozy, if war's coming to Cormyr in the next month or so."

Amarune whirled to face him, almost knocking Storm headlong into a bog. "*Is* war coming to Cormyr in the next month or so?"

Arclath smiled crookedly. "We'll just have to see, lass. We'll just have to see." He reached out to caress her hair. "In the meantime, this strong and noble body of mine—"

"Is getting hungry and will want to eat well before dark," Storm said firmly. "Even lust-smitten young nobles have to eat. So while I'm certain this 'better place' of yours has a bed the two of you will waste no time in bouncing on, I trust it also boasts hearth, and firewood, and a good cooking cauldron or two. Oh, and a ladle; I've grown tired of scalding my stirring finger."

"Gods," Arclath murmured, "this bids fair to echo traveling with my old nursemaid."

Amarune glanced at Storm, then gave him a rueful smile. "You have *no* idea."

"Do you regret what you agreed to?" Storm whispered. "Shall I try to have someone undo what I did, and free you from his riding?" She pulled the coffer from her bodice and held it up meaningfully.

"*Yes*," Arclath said forcefully.

Amarune wagged a finger at him and said fiercely, "My decision and *my* business, Lord Delcastle. Not yours."

She looked at Storm. "No. I . . . I saw something of his mind, during the . . . the eternity we spent sharing. I . . . gods, there's a lot to be done! Let's be getting on with it!"

Storm smiled at her—and started to weep silently, her eyes shining through her tears.

"Well done, Amarune," she whispered. "Oh, well done!"

They embraced.

Over Storm's shoulder, Amarune caught sight of Arclath's face. He looked so anxious that she snorted and added dryly, "Arclath, I do believe we'll manage to find a little time together first. Just find us that bed."

EPILOGUE

So ye think ye've grown wise in the ways of this world?
Never again to know surprise, no more astonished?
Guess again, moss-covered old sage! We've new marvels
For thee here! Gods will dance, old and new!
Will ye, I wonder, master the new tune?

> Said by the Unseen Ghost in Act II, Scene IV
> of *Azuth Meets Magic*, anonymous,
> chapbook-published often before inclusion in
> *Roray's Old Plays* by Eldran Roray of Waterdeep,
> in the Year of the Doomguard.

Elminster?

Storm awoke and lay still in the near-darkness. The banked hearth beside her was giving out feeble flickers, and as usual she was toasting on her side nearest to it and chilled on the part of her that faced away.

Elminster?

There it was again. In her head.

A voice she knew.

A voice she'd not heard for almost a hundred years.

A voice she'd never thought to hear again.

She gathered her will, finding herself on the verge of tears. *Mystra? Mother Goddess, is that you?*

Storm! Daughter, is Elminster with you?

It was her mother, but fainter, the singing blue fire diminished. Different.

Well, of course it would be. The Weave was gone; how could Mystra *not* be different?

He is, and he is not. Storm sent her words into the familiar blue warmth and felt them taken in as they always had been.

He was slain but can ride a willing host.

Send him to me. You and I will confer later.

It was Mystra. It was!

Trembling, almost unable to breathe, Storm crawled to the bed and opened the coffer.

Arclath came awake in an instant, grabbing at his sword. She flung herself on him and kissed him to quell all questions, holding him down with all her strength as Elminster's ashes flowed up the young dancer and into her.

And Amarune rose, unspeaking, smiled down at them with Elminster's eyes—eyes that danced with joy—and went out into the night.

The tale of Elminster continues in
Bury Elminster Deep

ABOUT THE AUTHOR

Ed Greenwood is the creator of the FORGOTTEN REALMS® fantasy setting, an award-winning game designer, and a best-selling author whose fantasy novels have sold millions of copies worldwide in more than thirty languages.

Once hailed as "the Canadian author of the great American novel," Ed is a large, bearded, jolly Canadian librarian who lives in an old farmhouse crammed with over 80,000 books in the Ontario countryside, and is often mistaken for Santa Claus in disguise. Many gamers think he resembles Elminster, but Ed insists he did not model the Old Mage on himself.

Ed was elected to the Academy of Adventure Gaming Art & Design Hall of Fame in 2003, and has been a judge for the World Fantasy Awards. His most popular series include the Knights of Myth Drannor trilogy and the Elminster Saga published by Wizards of the Coast, the Band of Four series from Tor Books, and the Falconfar books from Solaris.

MANY ROADS LEAD TO NEVERWINTER

RETURN WITH
GAUNTLGRYM

Neverwinter Saga, Book I
R.A. Salvatore

NEVERWINTER

Neverwinter Saga, Book II
R.A. Salvatore
October 2011

CONTINUE THE ADVENTURE WITH
BRIMSTONE ANGELS

Legends of Neverwinter
Erin M. Evans
November 2011

LOOK FOR THESE OTHER EXCITING NEW RELEASES IN 2011

Neverwinter for PC
The Legend of Drizzt™ cooperative board game
Neverwinter Campaign Setting

HOW WILL YOU RETURN?

Find these great products at your favorite
bookseller or game shop.

DungeonsandDragons.com

DUNGEONS & DRAGONS

An ancient time, an ancient place . . .
When magic fills the world and terrible monsters roam the wilderness . . .
It is a time of heroes, of legends, of dungeons and dragons . . .

THE MARK OF
NERATH
Bill Slavicsek
Available now

THE SEAL OF
KARGA KUL
Alex Irvine
Available now

UNTOLD
ADVENTURES
Short stories by Alan Dean Foster, Kevin J. Anderson,
Jay Lake, Mike Resnick, and more
June 2011

THE LAST
GARRISON
Matthew Beard
December 2011

Bringing the world of Dungeons & Dragons alive,
find these great novels at your favorite bookseller.
Also available as eBooks.

DungeonsandDragons.com

THE ABYSSAL PLAGUE

From the molten core of a dead universe

Hunger

Spills a seed of evil

Fury

So pure, so concentrated, so infectious

Hate

Its corruption will span worlds

The Temple of Yellow Skulls

Don Bassingthwaite

Sword of the Gods

Bruce Cordell

Under the Crimson Sun

Keith R.A. DeCandido

June 2011

Oath of Vigilance

James Wyatt

August 2011

Shadowbane

Erik Scott de Bie

September 2011

Find these novels at your favorite bookseller.
Also available as ebooks.

DungeonsandDragons.com